the truth about air & water

truth in lies series, book 2

katherine owen

The Writing Works Group

Seattle

COPYRIGHT

The Writing Works Group

DEDICATION

To my readers, Thanks for believing in the possibilities. *The Truth About Air & Water* is for all of you.

Katherine Owen

Author's Note: *The Truth About Air & Water* can be read as a stand-alone novel. *This Much Is True* is the first novel in the *Truth In Lies* series, which can also be read as a standalone. Many readers end up enjoying both reading one right after the other. It's your decision. Thank you for reading my work.

OTHER NOVELS BY

Katherine Owen

THIS MUCH IS TRUE

truth in lies series, book 1

WHEN I SEE YOU
SEEING JULIA
NOT TO US

the truth about air & water

PART 1

air

"She wasn't doing a thing that I could see, except standing there, leaning on the balcony railing, holding the universe together."

-J.D. Salinger

CHAPTER ONE

empire

TALLY

*"'Tis better to have loved and lost,
than never to have loved at all"* -Lord Alfred Tennyson

"Is it?" -Talia Landon

" THIRTY MILES. FORTY MINUTES. WITHOUT TRAFFIC." I list off the selling points of the church at Half Moon Bay. I really want this, and I have to hope Linc does too. We have six hours before he has to hit the field again for a late practice and it's a forty-minute drive one way. I have a rare day off from San Francisco Ballet, so here we are traveling out to Half Moon Bay to check out a place to hold our wedding and reception. I'm anxious. I want him to love the little church I've fallen in love with. I've already called Pastor Dan Reeve twice but he won't schedule a date or promise us one until he meets us. A strange enough request.

Linc and I finding time together takes quite a bit of maneuvering these days. "If we don't hit it off with this minister, we lose out on this place," I say.

Linc glances over at me. "I know you're excited about this one but, Tally, we're already booked at Hollins House for mid-October. It'll hold everybody. My dad sent over a more complete list a few days ago. I think he's just invited all the people who attended my mom's funeral years ago and there are a lot of names to add to the guest list."

"He's really nice. I think you'll like him. All he wants is to meet us first."

"That's pretty demanding though, right? He won't even give you the open dates the place has until he meets us? I don't like it. Hollins House is good to go and we really can't spend any more time on this, babe."

I let the babe comment slide. He knows I hate that endearment which is too similar to baby, which I really despise.

"I'm unclear as to why we have to invite four hundred and fifty people I do not know to our wedding. *That* limits our options." I bite my lip from saying more about that.

Linc's dad has become a major problem for us and every guest he adds skyrockets the cost and there's no offer from him to cover those. My parents are rightfully freaking out. Linc remains somewhat oblivious to it all because really it's the middle of baseball season, and that's the only thing on his mind these days. We don't really talk about money. We probably should.

I start again. "I mean, if we're going to do this thing…"

Linc shoots me a stern look. He doesn't like it when I refer to our wedding as a *thing*.

I start again. "If we're going to do this lovely, fantastic, blissful event, then I would really like it to be in this amazing church that overlooks the Pacific and Half Moon Bay. I'm sorry; I just don't want to get married at somebody's restored house on a golf course. That's not my idea of a wedding." Now, I'm coasting on thin ice because he likes the Hollins House a lot and has told me this at least a thousand times since he booked it. The one thing Linc did for this wedding while I have handled everything else.

Word of advice don't get engaged in the middle of summer and expect to be able to get married at an awesome venue three months later. Not going to happen. At least, not in San Francisco. Linc needs a place that will accommodate his four hundred plus guests from the must-be-invited list his father surreptitiously sent us three weeks ago. And now there are *more* names. I didn't expect Davis Presley to have so many demands, but then again, I have been wrong about a number of things when it comes to Linc's dad.

I sigh a little because I haven't told the groom-to-be the other part—what I consider to be the best part—about the little church in Half Moon Bay, it can only accommodate about a hundred people. Of course, there's the sanctuary nearby that can accommodate up to two hundred and fifty guests if you need that, but that's not what I want, and it still won't be enough for the four hundred plus people his dad has insisted we invite. So the guest list would have to be trimmed way down. I hesitate to tell Linc this part until after he's seen the place.

"I mean if we're going to do this, let's do it right," I say softly, feeling more anxious. "Look, we're almost there." I hold my breath as we get our first glimpse of Half Moon Bay.

"Right. Almost there." Linc sighs from the driver's seat. "Good 'cause I'm tired. Those flights back from Detroit are killer."

"I know you're tired, but it's the only time we could fit it in before you leave again. Just keep an open mind. That's all I ask."

"I will. I just don't understand why we have to come all the way out here to get married, but..." He stops talking when the church comes into view and looks uneasy. "There's no way over four hundred people are going to fit into that little church, Tally."

"Just wait until you've seen the inside. *Please?*"

Tension.

Yes, there's been some of that. An unexpected and enormous guest list. Linc's dad. Interference from all sides. Baseball. Ballet. Wedding plans that never seem to get done. A cake that still needs to be ordered along with the catered food. What about this? What about that? Try this. Eat that. Drink this. Color that. Dress in this or maybe that. His tuxedo has been ordered, but it still needs to be tailored—a fitting that the groom can never make. You've settled on the design of the invitations, but you can't print them until you find the place and set the date—a date that doesn't interfere with baseball or ballet's fall season. However, you have to find a place to get married first. That's my to-do list. Linc's to-do list is comprised of one thing, and one thing only, *baseball*.

Sure, the end of July and beginning of August were fun for us. We'd just gotten engaged but by the time September rolled around I've begun to understand more of what baseball season really means and my perspective has shifted. Linc is out of town three and four days at a time. His days off are rare and he's at practice when he's not playing, He's either dropping off dirty uniforms to be laundered or packing up his suitcase for the next series of games out of town. It's been infrequent hellos and too many rushed good-byes at the airport for us. Those two scenes seem to have become the most memorable ones for the past several weeks. Since I'm left to juggle little Cara's schedule as well as mine and hold the fort without him, there's been some tension between us. Yes, we've been engaged for a few months and that part is fun. But this part? Planning a wedding without him and trying to accommodate his dad? Not so much.

"It's great," he says with a notable lack of enthusiasm as he gets out and looks over the roof of the car at me. He smirks a little, then turns and looks out at the Pacific that you can just glimpse from the front of the church steps. I hear him sigh deep. "It's just great." I watch him breathe in the faint hint of salty air and gaze wistfully out at the ocean, but he's no longer smiling. "Great. Just great."

It doesn't sound *great* the way he's said it. And can we talk about the rhetorical use of the word *great* in describing everything in the past two minutes? "It's more than just great. What's wrong with you? Because this is about more than just being tired after a long plane ride."

I'm cut off from saying anything more to him because Pastor Dan Reeve stands at the top of the church steps waiting to meet us.

Great. We're fighting. That will go over big.

"Tally, you're finally here and this must be Linc. It's nice to meet you both." Pastor Dan shakes hands with Linc without even mentioning he's an avid fan of the Giants like he has to me every time we've talked on the phone.

"Come in. Come in. I just made some lemonade because Tally called saying you'd *both* be making the trip. How wonderful to finally meet you two." He lifts a quizzical brow at Linc. "I was beginning to wonder if you were a myth that Tally was just going on about, but here you are, Lincoln Presley, a living legend in person and everything."

"I'm just like everybody else, sir." Linc forces a smile and then attempts to catch my eye with some kind of subtle reprimand as if I *told* this man I was marrying a famous baseball player beforehand.

I smile sweetly at Linc and then turn to the minister. "We try to downplay the fame thing. Linc doesn't want to make me feel bad since he makes a hundred times more money than I do, and I work twice as hard."

I laugh and so does Pastor Dan. Linc makes an effort, but it's forced. And I know it. *We are off today, him and me.*

"Just call me Dan, everyone else does. You've got quite a girl here in Tally. I've enjoyed hearing about the two of you from her, but really want to hear from you as well. That's why I insist on meeting couples in person before we even begin to talk about wedding dates." Dan winks at me and I get a little red in the face thinking if he only knew what I've put Linc through in the past few years. Linc sighs a little, sounding tired and impatient, two things he actually never seems to be, normally. I kind of glare his way, telepathically telling him to keep an open mind about the church and this man who would be marrying us. "So, we should talk about your wedding plans and your future and the two of you."

Our future and the two of us.

Pastor Dan's words take me by surprise. I've been too focused on setting the wedding date and finding a place to get married to look beyond that. *Our future? The two of us? Wow. I'm about to marry Lincoln Presley.* That is surreal in so many ways and anyone who knows me would agree.

❧ ～ ～ ❧

"So how did you two meet?"

We don't even get to start with an easy question.

I hesitate so Linc answers for us. "I saved Tally from a car accident. Then, we met up at a party months later. It went from there."

Epic answer. Let's leave the rest out. I fidget with a thread showing on the edge of my blouse. I dressed up for the occasion forgoing my usual attire of black jeans and matching T-shirt in a concerted effort to impress the pastor and improve our chances at booking this place, but I already sense those odds slipping away.

"Is that how it went, Tally?" The pastor looks mildly curious.

"I was seventeen at the time. Linc was twenty-two. He'd just signed on with the Angels. Our age difference made it impossible to be together. You see I lied about my age. I was still in high school when we met so we broke it off. Linc went to LA to pitch for the Angels, and I moved to New York and attended the School of American Ballet."

"That's impressive. It's hard to get in, let alone make it, which you obviously have."

Linc's looking a little irritated probably because Pastor Dan just glossed over his entire baseball career essentially ignoring all of his hard-won accomplishments.

"A career in ballet is mostly made in New York. That's where you have to be," I say quietly. Yet, the hairs on the back of my neck rise up at the way Linc is looking at me. He looks surprised and uneasy at the same time. *He knows this, doesn't he?*

"Tally?" Linc asks under his breath. I wave him off because the pastor is talking.

"But you're with the San Francisco Ballet. Why the change?" The pastor asks.

I exhale slowly. *Here we go. Let confession begin.* "I moved from New York to San Fran to be near my family and try to work things out with Linc."

"And I felt the same way," Linc says impatiently. "Do we really need to go through all the whys and wherefores of our relationship, *father*?"

"*Dan.* Call me Dan; I'm not a priest."

He laughs and looks sympathetic for a moment, but then his features harden. "I always try to understand the dynamics of the couple's relationship that I'm planning to marry. Relationships aren't just ordered off the menu. There are *dynamics. Baggage.* Everybody has some. What are yours, Linc? You have this epic baseball career.

You have a lucrative contract. But that's just the public persona of you. What's the real Lincoln Presley like? What does he want out of his life? How many children do you want? I understand you have a daughter. Cara? Tally told me she's three. That's wonderful but starting out with a family is its own unique challenge. And what about Tally? She gave up an illustrious dance career to come back home and be with you. What are *you* giving up, *exactly*?"

"I…I don't know *exactly* what I'm giving up." Linc runs his hands through his hair and sighs. "She probably can't have any more kids, so I guess I'm giving up on the idea of ever having a son." Linc won't even look at me now after he's dealt this surprising blow. "I mean… we have Cara so it's all good, but I won't ever have a son. That's a bit of a sacrifice for me."

I look down at the ground, instead of at Linc, feeling essentially lanced by what he's just said. "We don't know that for sure. I'm seeing a specialist," I say to the pastor and then say in an aside to Linc. "I wasn't even sure you wanted more kids or that a son was so important to you."

"I've always wanted a big family," Linc says sounding uncertain. "I thought you knew that, but Tally, I want you more," he says, grabbing my left hand and putting it to his lips. I look at him intently, but still carry this wounded feeling. "I love you. You know that. That's the most important thing."

"Is it? You want a son, but I may not be able to give you one. *That* seems like a pretty important thing to discuss before we commit to each other and get married."

"We *are* committed. Stop it. I see where you're trying to take this. I love you. I'd give up anything for you, and maybe, I have. Yes, I want a son but I want to marry you more and be with you the rest of my life. We're already a family. We have Cara. Maybe, Dr. Eldon will be able to help us out, but it doesn't matter, not enough anyway."

Pastor Dan is nodding and seems perfectly at ease with the intense discussion taking place between Linc and me. He smiles wide looking pleased with himself. "See? This is what I'm trying to get at. Communication is so important. You won't always agree. You won't always want the same things. Marriage is a lifetime commitment, not these one-day affairs costing upwards to fifty grand where the world stops for a few hours, watches the two of you get photographed, and feed each other cake. Blissful, sure. Expensive, seems to be the norm these days. Epic. Maybe, on a grand proportion so out of scale, it becomes unseemly at times." He gets this serious face. "But that's not the true meaning of marriage. Not at all. It takes a half-hour to perform a wedding ceremony and actually only five people need to be in attendance to make a wedding work: me, the groom, the bride, and two witnesses. The rest is extraordinary but unnecessary. But after that? The marriage itself? That's just made up of the two of you. Even your daughter is a separate entity from you. You two are going to be tested in all kinds of ways. And you really need to ask yourselves if you're truly ready for all of that. A wedding takes place just one day in your life together, but it's the three hundred and sixty-four other days afterward of that first year and the ones that follow that make a marriage. And it's not easy."

He shakes his head. "May I be frank?"

"Well, I was hoping for that," Linc says while I just sort of nod because I'm already reeling from the way this whole conversation has been going so far.

"You two are on the fame track. Tally is already a recognizable figure in the dance world." The pastor turns to me. "I've read about you, Tally. You did well for yourself in New York already." Then he focuses in on Linc. "Let's face it; the Giants are looking good to make a real run this year and your stats are amazing." He smiles but then it fades. "But fame can be a destructive monster. You two lead very complicated lives on the world's stage already. Both of you will be tested in ways that a normal couple—sorry; I'm not sure how else to make my point—may never experience. I just feel it's important to get this all out in the open. Marriage is not an easy road for anybody. I find it even harder for the most famous ones. I don't want to discourage you, but I think you have some issues that need to be discussed. I'm not singling the two of you out by any means; I insist all the couples I marry be fully prepared, air things out before jumping into a lifetime commitment they aren't ready for."

He sweeps his arm around the room. "Yes, I spend an extraordinary amount of time upfront asking about a couple's relationship, and their wants and desires and expectations. If it makes you uncomfortable, I might not be the right one to marry you. That's why I insist on meeting couples together. I've got this fantastic venue. Every couple, famous or not, wants to commit to each other in this little church that looks out over the Pacific and say their vows to one another and start their lives together. Fulfilling those wishes are never the problem, but finding couples who are really ready for all that follows remains a challenge. I like to ensure the ones I take on are fully prepared for the marriage part, the day after the guests go home."

Pastor Dan laughs a little, but neither one of us do.

Then he looks intently at Linc, who looks seriously pissed off while I am the complete opposite—barely holding myself together. The last thing I want to do is break down in front of these two.

"I'm not easy to love," I say in an attempt to bridge the awkward silence and appeal to Linc's happy side, but now he looks even more unhappy with me. "Tally," he says.

"Why would you say that? Even think it?" Pastor Dan asks, incredulous at my simple confession.

"Because it's true." I turn to Linc. "I don't know why you love me. I'm not sure that you should. I've always wondered that. Why do you love me? Why? It runs through my head all the time. And you want a son and I may not be able to give you one."

"That's crazy talk, Tal. I love you because you're the most incredible person I've ever met."

"Okay, now we're getting somewhere," the pastor says. "Linc, why is she so extraordinary? Incredible as you've said."

Linc turns to Dan and audibly sighs. "We've shared the same exact fears—falling, failing, losing. We've had our fair share of bad luck in our relationship, with others. And still we persevere. Tally does. She has this amazing strength to overcome the biggest challenges and come out on top, flying high like she does in her performances. And I love that about her. And she's an extraordinary mom. The way she handles Cara is amazing. She gives infinite amounts of love and kindness to everyone she cares about and I want to be a part of that—Tally's brand of love. I can't imagine my life without her. I really can't, so I asked her to marry me and she said yes."

Linc looks at me for a long moment, grabs my hands, and kisses them. Tears fill my eyes. His assurance takes away some of the heartbreak from his revelation minutes earlier. He breaks our gaze and he looks over at Dan.

"I agree with you about probably needing to vet couples to ensure their eyes are wide open as to what marriage is all about, but Tally and I already know that and you should know that we've been tested more than most on that front. On fame and otherwise. We're ready to take the next step. So whether that's here in your church or someplace else I don't care, I just want to marry this girl. Make her my wife and ensure she's a part of my life because she is without a doubt the best part of me."

"I think you've just said your vows." Pastor Dan looks elated while Linc looks pretty much spent and I am still somewhat shaken by the enormity of Linc's words.

I withdraw my hand from Linc's and wipe at my eyes with the back of my hand. Linc affectionately tucks a stray hair strand back behind my ear and tiredly smiles at me.

And the world seems right again for about fifteen seconds.

"I have a cancellation in the middle of July next year. Let me see, yes, Saturday, July 19th, is open. Other than that we're booked solid through November of next year. Not as many requests in the winter months here after that other than at Christmastime. What works for you?" Dan asks easily. "I'd love to marry the two of you."

"Next July? That won't work for us," Linc says without hesitation shaking his head. "I'm going to marry Tally a lot sooner than that."

"It's less than a year away," Dan says. "Tally? You don't want to wait until next July?" The pastor asks, looking surprised.

"Noooooooo," I say. The disappointment at hearing Linc's automatic *no* and essentially answering for both of us without even asking me first stings. How far out the date itself is manages to whoosh through all of me too. *Damn.*

"I think we're done here, *Dan.* Thanks for the tour and the clarity." Linc gets up and shakes the guy's hand and starts for the door.

I slowly follow him in a daze.

What just happened? July of next year.
That's what just happened.

It's the middle of baseball season. July doesn't work, and Linc doesn't want to wait. *So why would I?*

I wistfully glance back at the church. Pastor Dan waves at us from the top of the stairs like before, but looks a little bewildered as to why we are leaving him so soon.

"Too small. Too long of a wait. Next July? Come on, Tally. *Please*. It'll be the middle of baseball season. That's not going to work at all. Let's go." Linc shakes his head side-to-side as he retrieves the car keys from his pocket. "It's a beautiful place, Tal. I'm glad we came, but it's not going to work for us."

"Yeah, it's beautiful." I look out the side mirror as we drive away from the epic view of the Pacific and Pastor Dan's beautiful little church at Half Moon Bay. I should be elated by most of what Linc just said back there, but all I feel is this extraordinary sense of loss at the overriding thought that he wants a son and I can't give him one. There's that.

It's just like they say. You've got your fingers in the dike preventing the dam from breaking, but it's only a matter of time before it does. That's how water works. That's the strength of water. You can't stop it.

"We could adopt." The words leave my mouth before I can stop them.

"We could." Rote words. He's said them but doesn't really mean them. The underlying anguish with his wish for a son is unmistakable, and he won't quite meet my gaze when I look over at him even when he says, "let's just see what Dr. Eldon says first; huh? Maybe it's a non-issue."

But it is an issue. I can tell by the way he's looking at me.

"Maybe." I turn away from him and look in the rearview mirror just in time to get the last glimpse of the amazing view of the Pacific just before it disappears.

Beautiful things are like that, extraordinary one minute, gone the next.

CHAPTER

TWO

where I stood

TALLY

Lincoln Davis Presley once told me how important it is to watch for the line drives. A line drive in baseball is a technical term—a pivotal moment in baseball when the batter drives the ball straight out toward the pitcher's mound with a thwack of his bat. When this happens, the crowd generally holds its collective breath and then ultimately sighs while finding itself somewhat morbidly fascinated yet somewhat appalled at the same time, in watching the pitcher simultaneously hit the ground just in time and avoid an outright collision with the ball that just zinged its way toward the player at ninety-some odd miles an hour in an valiant attempt to snuff out his life.

The line-driven baseball becomes as dangerous as a bullet, only in a different form. Most pitchers are lucky and incredibly fast. Elvis once told me that he's always been lucky and that he's incredibly fast, in baseball and so many things, as he likes to remind me. And oh how I love him for these two reasons—he's incredibly lucky and incredibly fast—and others, so many others.

A line drive in this case proves to be something entirely different. We're being interviewed by Candy Baxstrom, *Sports Illustrated's* up-and-coming special editions reporter. We're a breakthrough feature story worth covering because of Linc's incredible year in baseball this season and my own meteoric rise in San Francisco's ballet world. We're newsworthy, exemplifying the happy couple in both real life and the sports world. "Everyone wants to read about that," Candy assured us when we reluctantly agreed to the interview with Linc's publicist Kimberley Powers' begrudging approval.

"Avoid the hardball questions," Kimberley said. "*Lie*, if you have to. *Omit*, if you have to. Just get your photographs taken together and get the story down tight, the plausible one."

Kimberley was distracted, on her month-long honeymoon, calling us from some undisclosed location in the Caribbean. The cell service was questionable.

I ignored the tightness in my gut at her warnings.

I shouldn't have.

Line drives.

About those.

These come in all forms of life, besides baseball, but there's that one too.

"So how long have you two known each other?" Candy asks, slipping this one last question in just when she seems to be wrapping up.

We've answered all the easy ones. I should have known we'd get back to this one. I'm reminded of Pastor Dan from weeks before.

Tricky. This one.

Linc just smiles and nods. Then, he looks over at me raising his eyebrow in my direction that only I can see. His single glance says *you take this one. You lie better than me.* I smile back at him. *True.*

"A while," I finally say to Candy.

"How long?" Candy's sugary sweet persistence is pissing me off. I can feel myself caving to the pressure already.

"We met when I was still in high school. On Valentine's Day. The day my twin sister Holly was killed. Linc saved me from the burning wreckage of my car. After the accident." I pause telling myself to breathe. "After the accident. We met up again some time later."

My voice is no more than a whisper. It's been almost five years and I still can't think or talk about it without almost having a panic attack. Anger surges through an instant later for this blond viper in asking and at Linc for not answering like we practiced.

We met about five years ago. Both busy with our careers. Me on the west coast. Tally on the east coast. But we never stopped thinking about each other even though we had our own lives.

"I don't like to talk about it. The accident. How we first met. Is there anything else you need for your story? I think you have enough. On us."

"I just wanted to know how you two ended up together," she says with an innocent shrug. "It seems like a pretty straightforward question. You're getting married soon. You're both famous. I just wondered how it all came together and how you make it work."

Now, I'm the one without answers. I'm not sure how it works either. I can't quite believe it myself. I'm still trying to figure it all out and still waiting for the proverbial shoe to drop and watch it all fall apart.

Line drives.
These questions.
Our true story.
When does it all work out? Who does it work out for?
How long will it last? That's the real question. The one I need a guarantee for.

Linc squeezes my hand and brings me back to the present. He probably just heard my shuddering breath. I stare at the reporter somewhat unseeing. Tears threaten.

God damn it. Get it together, Tally.

And it's like she knows she's getting to me as I unconsciously slump further down in my chair. She smiles ever so slightly and I suddenly realize she has the dirt. *On me.* All of it. The full story.

Now, I'm really angry. "We've basically walked through fire to get here," I say in a low voice. "To this moment. To this time in our lives. We're amazingly happy. We can't wait to get married and commit to spending the rest of our lives together."

Oh God. Is that as sappy as it sounds?

I begin to fight the edges of a panic attack because I still get those and struggle for air. Linc strokes my hand in essence telling me everything is going to be okay. I glance over at him and attempt to keep the uncertainty from showing on my face with a shaky smile for him alone. "We've been tested by fate, fame, and lies," I say aloud for his benefit as well as mine. "Lies. Mine."

I dip my head in acknowledgment. "I'll own those. Others. All of it..."

Get it together. Breathe.

Get it together.

I do.

"I think we're done here." I quickly stand up and hold out my hand to shake hers.

She stares me down at first and then looks over at Linc imploringly him to keep talking. But eventually, she stands up too, probably accepting the interview is indeed over. She gets this bitch look—the snarl of a girl who hasn't gotten her way and isn't quite done trying. Her lips curl up a little and I know where she's going next, even as Linc moves in close and puts his arm around me pulling me closer subconsciously conveying that everything is okay.

No.

It's not.

Not this time.

"I haven't even asked about Moscow," Candy says testily.

"There's nothing to say about Moscow," Linc says a little more harshly then he probably intended. "This interview is over."

We don't talk about Moscow. Moscow was the proverbial test of us walking through fire together. Moscow almost destroyed us. Or, the lies did. Mine. His. Ours. Theirs.

Line drives. Moscow is one of those. We escaped, mostly unharmed, and eventually found our way back to each other, but we don't talk about Moscow. We never do.

Candy slips on her white jacket—some smart spring line thing that my best friend Marla would love—and lifts her silky blond locks from the back of her neck at the same time in a sexy, earnest reporter slash model kind of way.

Candy Baxstrom. Confident and sly. She's got her story. Her big break.

At what appears to be a last-ditch effort to get us to tell our side of the story, she gives us the stony, imploring reporter's look—the come-on-just-tell-me stare. "I just want the story to be complete—accurate, honest." She looks at me again with the coolness factor of a slight smile and starts to nod. Up and down, her lovely chin goes. "Honesty is always the best way. Isn't it, Tally?"

I try not to roll my eyes and I definitely don't answer her. She's going to write about us however she sees fit. She's got the story. *The whole story*. And she wants the fame. On some weird-ass level, I admire her for it. I know that feeling of wanting the fame so badly that you forsake all others to get it. I don't tell her it's fleeting and ultimately destructive. No. I'll let her figure that one out for herself. I'll let her experience her own line drive. Because she will. We all do.

"I have what I need."

In other words, she has other sources.

Candy nods slowly and shrugs her slim perfect shoulders in that blonde, helpless way she's got going. "Okay, let's go get some photographs to go with the copy. I want the money shot." She awards us with her best, winning smile.

A line drive.

This would just be one of them.

"She's got the story," I say to Linc hours later as we lie next to each other taking up only half of the king-sized bed because our bodies remain intertwined at an all but intimate level. The money shot photograph session took twice as long as the interview. After another three hours, we finally told Candy we had to go. I had to pick up Cara from preschool and Linc had a late practice.

We left Candy and her photographer while they were still packing up their gear. By this time, the reporter had given up on asking us any more questions. She had the money shot. She had the story.

We weren't going to like it. The unsettled feeling nagged at me, but Linc didn't seem to care. "She's got the story." Apparently, my fears need repeating.

"So?" He asks with a laugh. "Come here." He pulls me closer and trails his hands down between my legs knowing full well this is my ultimate weakness for him. I cannot not respond. His touch right there gets me to do just about anything for him. I moan. He laughs again as he starts to make his move.

We put Cara to bed fifteen minutes ago and left the bedroom door slightly ajar so we can hear her but closed enough so she doesn't hear us. Usually, we wait the agreed-upon half-hour before commencing with *doing the deed* as I still like to call it, but she was extra tired because I let her stay up late to watch *Entangled*. I'm not sure she understands the story line completely. I'm not sure I do either but she loves Rapunzel's long hair. We watched it together while we waited for Linc's return from practice. Cara played with my hair for most of the movie and kept running her little fingers through it over and over, while I filled out endless wedding invitations, imploring the ninety-five percent of strangers I do not know to come witness our nuptials in the middle of October.

"The article won't run for weeks. Don't worry about it. By the time it does, the season will probably be over. We'll be married. Settled. Nobody is going to care about how we met or what happened in Moscow. They'll be staring at your photograph, the *Dirty Dancing* one, and be thinking how did that guy get so lucky and get a girl like her? All those *Sports Illustrated* fans wishing they were me and holding you up in the air just like Baby."

"Even the girls?"

He laughs. "Even the girls. When are you going to start believing we're the two luckiest people in the world?" I turn into him then and stroke his face and search his eyes for solace and truth but I don't answer. "When are you going to let go and let this happen and believe in it? In me? In us?" Linc asks again.

I trace his lips and kiss him. Lightly. Just a trace.

In the next, he smothers my face with kisses of his own and eventually pulls me up beneath him. "Come on, Tally. Let it go. Let it all go. I'm here. I'm not going anywhere. Don't put a time clock on this.

Don't walk down the aisle toward me, less than a month from now, still not believing that this isn't real or this won't last because it will. I'm here. You're here. So. Believe it. In me. In us. Now." He pulls away from me and studies my face. Guilt arrives right on time. I wince along with it."What is it? What aren't you telling me? Because with that face? It is definitely something."

"Dr. Eldon scheduled an ultrasound. I just…she's optimistic and I just hope that we can find a way to have another child. I want to give you a son because you've given so much to me. And I want you to be happy. With me."

"I *am* happy with you. I love you because you're my life. You're my water. Don't forget that. I couldn't survive without you." He plays with a strand of my hair and lets it slip through his fingers. "And I'm your air." He sighs a little. "I love you just as you are whether we have more kids or not. That's why we're going to make it. But you have to stop believing that something bad is going to happen. You have to believe'in us as much as I do. We're going to have this great life together. We already *do*. I love you. You love me. And believe me; love is enough. *Our love* is enough."

I hold my breath and gaze at him for a long while. The commitment and compassion I see in the depths of his eyes begins to steady me. All the doubt, and even the guilt, begin to fade away. Like a protective shield, his love encircles me from all around.

Then when he pulls me into his arm and looks at me as if I'm the only one that counts, just before he kisses me, it is reassuring in the only way that matters.

Lincoln Presley, baseball star, is one of a kind.

And, he's mine.

It's a miracle really.

What an unbelievable stroke of luck at having him in my life and loving me back. I kiss him and let go of all my deep-rooted fears: falling, failing, even losing. I actually feel them disappear as if a strange wind has come by and blown them away.

I take in air—his air—that allows me to live and breathe.

"Okay," I eventually say.

Then, I grab his hand and lightly kiss the inside of his wrist, and then trail my lips along his broad chest. He leans back against the pillows with a knowing look pulling me along with him, but cedes all control to me. I start to smile, but then another errant thought crashes in on me and threatens to undo all of these joyous declarations.

Everything breaks.

CHAPTER
THREE

she is love

LINC

SHE'S BEYOND AGITATED, SLAMMING KITCHEN CUPBOARDS and doors. She insisted on making dinner for me because I told her I could make it, because I'm home, which hasn't been too often as of late. There are dark circles under her eyes which immediately tells me she's not getting enough sleep and she's rehearsing too much and most definitely not eating enough. I think this whole dinner scenario she's got going is to throw me off that last one. Food is Tally's nemesis. *One of them.*

I continue to watch her with keen interest and start to feel guilty because the Giants are doing awesome and one of the reasons I came over here early was to tell her we're probably going to have to postpone things. October seemed fine. But with the spectacular run the team has put together we've made it to the playoffs; the idea that the Giants might actually make it all the way to the World Series start to get real. And just like that, getting married in the middle of October like we planned may not work at all.

And I have to tell her tonight.

She gets this vexed look while she focuses all her outward efforts on *The Joy of Cooking* cookbook. The book was Marla's wedding shower gift a few weeks ago. It's a little dig at Tally. Marla knows perfectly well that her best friend doesn't do more than boil water— everybody's cliché for the non-cook, but, in Tally's case, it's absolutely true. I catch her eye and smile wide. She forces one my way.

The noise from the television and an old episode of Sesame Street filters into the room and to the two of us. Cara watches television in the adjoining room and claps her little hands every so often at the wondrous things Big Bird is saying.

It's the perfect domestic situation, except I should be cooking and Tally should be watching or resting or both. I continue my study of her in quiet amazement since she refuses to let me help with any of the food prep and reflect on how fortuitous my life has become in just the past few months with her and Cara. The crevice between Tally's brows deepens. She murmurs about the lack of clarity in the cookbook's instructions that is propped up against a full bottle of wine and sits precariously close to the edge of the granite counter. White flour streaks the left side of her face and travels upward into her dark hair. She's still beautiful even though she looks completely stressed out. *God, she's so hot.* My libido wants to skip dinner, put Cara to bed, and ravage her in a thousand different ways starting now.

"I missed you."

She looks up in surprise. I clear my throat trying not to appear so damn vulnerable and needy of her. I've been gone for the better part of a week traveling, playing baseball. It's good to be home—be with her—even if it's for just a day before everything ratchets even higher in baseball.

You start winning; everybody's expectations go up, exponentially.

"I missed you too."

She gets this tired smile, but avoids looking at me directly for some reason. She bites at her lower lip and then turns back to the pan on the stove. She's cooking some kind of marinara sauce. She pretends to be nonchalant, shrugging her slim shoulders, and yet her hands shake as she stirs the sauce. "You won, right? It's all good?"

Here's my opening. I'm going to have to take it.

"Too good," I say softly.

She looks at me closely, leaning in across the space that separates us. Me on one side of the counter-top, she out of reach on the other.

"If we sweep, we're in New York on Tuesday. And I pitch tomorrow." I raise an eyebrow and look at her more intently experiencing both joy and trepidation as I wait for her reaction. She recoils a little, and I know that's when she understands what I'm actually saying.

"So. We postpone." She stumbles over the last word and looks uncertain for a few seconds. "Because if you're pitching, you're winning and that means baseball through October. You're probably going all the way. That's...amazing." She pastes on this wide smile, but I see her disappointment just before she turns away.

"Looks that way. Yeah." I hang my head and then look at her with an unspoken apology. "I'm sorry. I really wanted to make this work out, timing-wise. I didn't think we'd get this far, but everybody's brought their 'A' game. There's really nothing to stop us from going all the way, just like you said, except maybe ourselves." I look at her intently. "I know you're pissed."

"No. I'm happy for you. I *am*." She frowns a little. "But I got a dress. Like you wanted. We set a date. Like you wanted. We booked the Hollins House for the 25th of October and invited four-hundred and fifty people. Like you wanted. And now, we have to cancel it all. See the pattern here? And all I wanted to do was to get married at that little church at Half Moon Bay."

"Yeah. Next July right in the middle of the baseball season," I say.

"I've had to handle everything while you've been playing baseball *all of the time*."

"Geez, Tally, I'm sorry we're doing so well. That baseball is such an inconvenience for you. It is my life, you know. It pays the bills around here, we kind of need me to play."

She blows out air with a heavy sigh. "First fight since we got back together. *Perfect.*"

"No, there have been others. Half Moon Bay, remember?" I say softly but suddenly try to reel back some of what I've just said to her.

"I remember…" She pauses for a long time, stirs the sauce, turns off the stove, and finally looks over at me. "Do you ever think that maybe we're just not meant to be together? Like God and the entire world is trying to tell us something? I mean, I don't know why we planned this wedding for October…" Her voice trails off and she just looks sad.

"Nothing was going on in October. Your mom could be here." I get up from the barstool and go around to her side. "Nobody died in October." They are stupid reasons to anyone else but the two of us. "You're not having any doubts about us, are you? Because I will fix that shit right now."

The clock ticks off time on the far kitchen wall and we both seem to hear it while we seemingly wait for the other to break the silence between us first.

"You have doubts." My voice is flat. My disappointment obvious. We've been through this enough already to fill a couple of romance novels. People would call them fantasies, but we actually lived through it all. There's been plenty of fucked-up shit that's gone down between the two of us preventing us from being together in the past. "Tally," I sigh in saying her name. "*Really?*"

"I don't want to talk about this," she says slowly. "Not now. You have a game tomorrow. Let's just let it…lie."

She get this weird introspective look—the I-think-I-can-lie-my-way-out-of-this-one look, but I sense her apprehension. I can practically see the thoughts racing through her mind as to how to handle this. I grow alarmed and desperate at the same time.

Yet, in the next moment, she delivers her lines so calm and perfect.

"We'll just cancel everything. And then, let's just wait and see where things are after the playoffs. After the World Series. Wow. How incredible is that?"

She smiles, but it's forced.

It's all an act.

She's got one of her cheerful smiles—the one she utilizes for public appearances when I know damn well she doesn't want to be there. I sigh. *This shit has to be stopped.* I move fast, taking a hold of her and set her up on the kitchen counter and then step between her legs and take full ownership of her and the situation. I grab the metal spoon from her outstretched hand, but not before accidentally splashing the two of us with red sauce. I slowly lick the stain from her T-shirt and make my way up to her neck and then her face. "Don't fuck with me, Tal. What is your problem?"

"I don't have one," she says irritably.

"Then, don't start making one up." I kiss her hard. Hard enough to clear away any doubts about my long-term intentions and my short ones too. "We're putting Cara to bed early."

"But you have a game."

I don't usually stay when I have a game. We have this weird-ass ritual worked out where I leave most of the time because we're still trying to figure out things with Cara. Maybe even between us too. The thing is I do need a decent night's sleep before a game which doesn't happen very often when we're together.

Compatible is not a word I would use to describe the two of us when we're together. Insatiable is probably better. Sometimes it seems as if we annihilate each other more than we love each other. Still, at other times, it seems as we resuscitate the very life back into the other person. Maybe we're undefinable. And with Cara, things get even more complicated. I can't ravage Tally any time I want because we have our amazing three-year-old little girl around us most of the time.

"Forget the game. I'll be fine," I say, pulling her close and trailing my hand between her thighs. My finger makes contact with her softness. She moves in closer to me. I feel her fight for breath. "I want to fuck you right now," I say low enough so our child in the next room won't hear us.

"Can't. Cara," she says with a moan and inches closer to my roving fingers. "I don't want to confuse Cara. Stop. Please. She'll hear us," Tally says even as her breath comes faster. "You have to stop doing this to me. I'm *cooking*. We have Cara. Geez, Linc. I said no!" She pulls away from me and pulls down her skirt.

"Is this about Cara? Or, is it about me staying? Or something else entirely? Because sometimes I wonder what you really want when you get all pissy and unsure like this," I say. She washes her hands at the sink. I move in to do the same. She glares at me. It sets me off. "Yes, I'm frustrated. I've got a game. I want to stay and fuck you properly. I want to own your soul and wake up next to you in the morning and pitch a baseball in the afternoon with you in the stands for once. Is that so much to ask? Am I so wrong in wanting all of that? Why does everything have to be so complicated between us? Why can't you tell me what's bothering you, instead of lying to me and telling me it's nothing when it is definitely something? You've been slamming things around since I got here. So tell me, Tally, just tell me what's really going on with you tonight? Why can't you be honest for once?"

I've unleashed fire, and I know this as soon as the last word leaves my mouth.

"For once?" She asks. "Oh, I don't know why I can't be *honest*. I really don't. Maybe it's because I'm seriously," she leans in close to me, "fucked up, and you knew this when you signed up for it. It's complicated. Us. We're complicated. We have a child who doesn't speak, who needs us—*me*, I guess—since you are *never here*. You want this gigantic wedding spun up on an epic scale with four hundred and fifty strangers that your father insisted we invite without a thought as to who is paying for it. My parents! Me! And yet! You are never around to plan a God damn thing for it. I wish Holly were here to help. I wish my mother could be of help. But my mother has been in rehab. *Rehab*, Linc. And I've been dealing with all the shit that comes along with that. Family sessions. Therapy sessions. How do-you-feel-about-your-mom's-addiction-Tally sessions? And all the how-you-can-help-the-alcoholic sessions, too. And I'm the one who has had to pick up all of the slack left by my mom's thirty-day absence in taking care of my dad and Tommy and Cara. And you. *When you're here.*"

She takes a deep breath and blows it out.

"And you?" She asks quietly. "You play the Yankees in New York on Tuesday, which means you'll leave on Sunday and need those uniforms washed on Saturday. Well, guess what? I'll still be here in

San Fran trying to keep my new boss Mikhail Rostov off my back and hold onto my job, continually hiding the chronic pain in my left foot from him, so he doesn't outright replace me before the season even starts, pick up Cara from preschool *on time* every day, hit the counseling sessions for my mother, help her cook something for my dad and my little brother; and oh, now I get to cancel all the Hollins House plans for the big wedding in October because the Giants may go all the way. Well great. Fucking fantastic. Bully for you. It's all good for you, but what and when exactly is it good for me? And now you want to fuck me? I am so sorry. But you know what? I'm just too fucking tired. Maybe the reason you don't know what's going on with me today is, *again,* because you're *hardly ever here.* You don't even remember what today was, do you? No. You don't. Okay then. Sorry to disappoint you but I don't want to fuck you right now. But at least I'm being *honest. For once.*"

She throws the metal spoon onto the kitchen floor and stalks out the door. "Make your own God damn dinner. I'm done."

"Tally! Come back here. Don't do this."

She doesn't answer.

Now, Cara stands in the kitchen doorway. A second later she picks up the castoff spoon and starts gleefully rapping it on the door-frame as if it what Tally did was a new kind of game. Now there's marinara sauce pretty much everywhere.

"Mommy's mad," I say softly to Cara.

No shit.

Cara looks at me and slowly nods. We both hear Tally as she stomps up the stairs.

"Don't worry, kiddo. Daddy will fix it."

CHAPTER

FOUR

perfect for me

LINC

MY MOM ONCE TOLD ME WHEN I was about fourteen never go to bed mad. Not at her or Dad or Elliott. "Someday you'll meet a girl, and if you marry her, the best advice I can give you is never go to bed mad," she said. I feed Cara the pasta, give her a quick bath, and cajole her to go to sleep. In fact, I cheat because I let her listen to an audio play of *Winnie The Pooh* because I know she likes that one and that she'll be out within minutes. Then I fix up a dinner plate of food for Tally because I remain determined to get her to eat something.

I run a bath for in the second bedroom down from the master and finally think to check Tally's iPhone calendar. *Dr. Eldon*.

This newest doctor served as our last ray of hope in determining if there was a chance that Tally could still get pregnant. With the promise of a new medical procedure, Dr. Eldon thought after studying Tally's films sent by her previous doctor in New York, it might be possible. An ultrasound was needed to confirm this which was scheduled for today. I forgot. *Shit.*

Tally's sleeping but her eyelids flutter open when I come into the room carrying her plate of food. "What did Dr. Eldon say?"

Silence.

"I'm sorry. I forgot. I'm a jerk. Hate me. What did Dr. Eldon say?" I ask again.

She sits up on her elbows and get this resigned look. She points towards the hallway. "The tub's overflowing."

Sure enough water is streaming down the hallway flooding the floor as it goes. "Fuck."

I set down her plate of food and go shut the faucet off and partially drain the bath water and just start throwing towels everywhere to sop up the mess. I look up and find Tally standing in the doorway with a satisfied smirk on her lovely face. I grin back at her shaking my head. "Hey between the marinara mess downstairs and the water mess up here, and the fact that I did get our child fed and to sleep early, I think I've made up for it, at least a little." She nods. "The bath is for you."

"I'm not ready to make up with you quite yet," she says softly. "Don't expect anything, Elvis."

"I know. So just take a bath. I'll watch."

She strips off her top and slips out of her skirt and shimmies out of her black thong with the red bow which she knows I like very much. I suck in air while she gets this smirk as she struts naked past me and then lowers herself into the tub sloshing water over the sides.

I throw yet another towel on the floor but like a good knave, I put one behind her neck while she leans back against the tub and closes her eyes. I proceed to lather up my hands with the lavender soap she likes then I start touching her beautiful body in all the right places. She has even more of a hint of a smile, so I know we're going to get past this. I'm reborn on that news alone.

"I'm sorry." I trail the water with my soapy hands near her breasts.

She opens her eyes and looks at me. "I'm sorry. I completely lost it. I was being a bitch and completely unfair to you. You have a game that you need to be ready for. I was out of line. So, I'm sorry."

"No need for you to be sorry."

"But you have a game," she says wearily.

"I'll be ready. Let's not talk about baseball tonight, okay? I want to talk about us. You, especially. I want to apologize. To you. You're right. I'm sorry I haven't been around and paying attention to things like I should. Your mom. Cara. Your family. Your job. The guest list. The wedding. I know you've had to handle it all. I'm sorry I haven't been listening very well or paying any attention to the pressure you must feel in trying to do it all basically on your own since I've been gone so much. But let's start with the last thing first." She gives me a questioning look. "What did Dr. Eldon say?"

Her face is wet but I see the single tear that trails down her face. "I'm sorry. I blew up at you. It's really not you or baseball. It's me. I screwed this up a long time ago and it is all coming back to haunt me now. I messed up and now I'm paying for it." Tally sighs big. "She is no longer optimistic. It is highly unlikely I can get pregnant."

I catch her tear. "Don't do this to yourself, Tal. Don't. I love you. If we can't have more kids so be it. It doesn't change how I feel about you. It *doesn't*. The most important thing is for us to be together. You and me. And Cara, of course. That's it. Everything else is a bonus. You are my life." I stand up and move to the door. "I'll be right back."

I take a long moment in the master bedroom. *Get it together.* I can't let Tally sense my disappointment at Dr. Eldon's news. After a few minutes of stalling, I retrieve the plate of food and take it to her setting it down on the wide edge of the bathtub. Then I strip off my shirt and undo my jeans.

"What are you doing?" She asks.

"I'm taking a bath. I've got marinara sauce in my hair. I'm going to feed you your dinner and make everything up to you." I step into the tub with the plate in one hand while water sloshes over the sides. We face each other. I twirl pasta around the fork and feed it to her.

"Mmm...good." She takes another four bites smiling wide after each one. Then she takes the plate and carefully sets it on the floor next to the tub. She moves into me, sloshing water as she goes and grabs the soap and wash cloth.

"What are you doing?"

"Washing the sauce out of your hair." Her fingers wrap around my dick in one swift move. "Well maybe later," she says lowering herself onto me in the next. "Water's a challenge. You've got to really get moving…like this. Just think we don't have to worry about birth control like ever again. No condoms. A silver lining I guess."

"Silver lining," I say forcing a smile.

"I'll make it up to you. I promise," she whispers pulling me closer so our faces practically touch. She looks at me intently. "I love you so much. Thanks for loving me back."

"You say that like you're a consolation prize."

She pulls back and looks at me. "Maybe I am."

"You're more than enough. Yes, I would have liked to have had more kids with you, but we have Cara. We're going to be okay. *We are*. But let's not talk anymore," I say nipping her neck with my teeth. "No more talking."

"Got it, No talking," she says.

I stay, breaking Tally's cardinal rule about that, especially considering it is the night before a playoff game, and essentially dismiss Cara's possible confusion, and tell her we should have stopped honoring this weird ass moral code of hers weeks ago because we are together, and Cara's knows it. Tally's not entirely convinced that me staying is such a great idea.

She stands there with her hands on her hips wearing nothing but one of my Giants orange and grey T-shirts. I get a glimpse of the filmy black material of her thong as she moves about the room. She knows I like that one too, and I am amused as to how she thought I was going to be able to walk out the door when she's dressed like this.

Uh. No. I'm not leaving tonight.

"You should go." She tries to sound convincing, but it doesn't quite work, which causes me to laugh in just hearing her wistful, sexy tone.

"No." I put my hands behind my head on the propped-up pillows and sink deeper into the bed with a contented sigh. I like it when she's like this. Conflicted is the only way to describe it. Being a sex goddess as well as a perfect mommy are these complete opposite roles. It makes her all the more charming that she doesn't even see it.

"What?" She asks upon seeing the bemused look on my face.

"Nothing."

"No, there's more I can tell. What is it?"

"I have a surprise for you. You have to wait for it though. For a little while anyway. Just trust me." I can't help but smile. "You're going to love it, but you have to wait a few more days before I can show it to you. It's big. It's a big surprise."

"Okay," she says looking wary now, "but you know I don't like surprises of any kind."

"I do. But this one? You're going to love this one. It's a good surprise." My smile gets wider because there's more to tell her. "So. I've been thinking about our situation, and I've got an idea of how to solve some things for you and me. Because let's face it, you and me are all that matters."

"Okay. I can agree with that much." She climbs up onto the bed and settles down on my lap.

I hold her face between my hands ensuring I have her attention. "Let's get married on Friday after my game tomorrow night. Let's just go to courthouse and get it done. Then, it won't matter when we get around to the big wedding for family and friends. We can do that whenever we want. Then, the pressure's off in trying to plan a big wedding while I'm trying to win the World Series."

She looks amazed for about five seconds and then the usual uncertainty flits across her features. "Are you sure? Elope now?"

"Marry me on Friday. Don't cancel the Hollins House stuff just yet. Let me cover the bases with my dad before we start to unravel everything right away. We can follow up with Pastor Dan at Half Moon Bay for next July or something. That's what we both really want, right? I'll call him and see if that date is still available. I'll take care of it. It'll be epic. Okay?"

She loves this idea. I can see the relief on her face.

"I thought we couldn't do next July because of baseball?"

"You love that little church. We'll keep it small so it's doable. Spare no expense for food and drink and family and a few friends. No more grand scale stuff. Just small scale and amazing. The Giants can work around it; they'll understand. It won't be a problem. We won't *make* it a problem. *I* won't make it a problem. We'll already be married by this Friday and you can have the sweet little wedding you really wanted looking out at the Pacific at Half Moon Bay. Say yes. Say yes to all of it." I study her closely as she wrestles with all these competing thoughts. "Your mom will be better by then," I say softly, trying not to upset her, but wanting her to face the reality of our situation.

The World Series and Tessa Landon's rehab are both unexpected events that we've had to contemplate and factor in to all of our plans. "Cara will be settled. *Talking.*"

"Let's hope." Tally doesn't say anything for a long time. I can see her going through the pros and cons. "Elope. We couldn't tell anybody. I'd need to break it to my mom gently, but only after a while. Dad would be okay, but Mom…" She hesitates. "Mom really wants to help me with a wedding. I don't want to deny her that."

"Okay. She'll love Half Moon Bay and that little church plus it will give you two more time to plan it all." She gets this little smile. "So we'll get married on Friday and we won't tell anybody," I say slowly, "not even Charlie or Marla. Or my dad. For a while."

"Not even Marla? That's a tough one. So it would be just us?"

"Just us. The judge, you, me, two witnesses. That's five just like Pastor Dan said."

"After your playoff game," Tally says slowly. "Just go to the courthouse on Friday and get married."

"You love this idea. It's all over your face. Marry me. On Friday. Say yes," I say softly. "Be my wife. Say yes, Mrs. Presley." I laugh at her shocked expression. "I can call you that because by Friday it'll be reality. You'll be Mrs. Lincoln Presley. Then, we can plan this amazing wedding at Half Moon Bay with Pastor Dan for your family, for your mom, and all of our close friends. But by this Friday, we'll already be married. Mrs. Presley. I like the sound of that. And you'll come running whenever I call you; right? Like a good wife should. Any time I call?"

She readjusts her hips even with mine and makes her intentions known as to what we're going to do next. I'm hard for her in a matter of seconds because she does that to me. Tally the goddess. Just watching her walk can turn me on but being inside of her is an experience like no other. It's like this crossing over to this completely different plane of existence—this true bliss that's so euphoric it's hard to come back down from. The only thing I can compare it to is a really good narcotic that gets you beatifically high. That's *Tally* to me. She grabs my face and my full attention at the same time and slides her silky way down my shaft in one lithe, practiced dancer's move. Her smile lights up her whole face. All is right with our world again. We both seem to share in this incredible feeling.

We've had plenty of sex. Slow languishing sessions and amazingly fast ones and lots of incredible ones in between where time and circumstance didn't matter. We do seem to be making up for lost time and satiating this unbearable hunger as we move in on each other. Physical need and pent-up emotion overtake us both all over again. *I do love this girl.*

I pay homage to God and experience this never-ending gratitude that we're together finally. The fear of losing her still exists at a soul level, but when she's like this—so sure of us—when we both really let go and allow each other to feel it, these rare moments prove to be our finest. Each one a perfect memory that I plan to hold onto for all of time. And yet, there is this real fear—the one buried deep in my soul—that still resonates and subtly reminds me that I could still lose her somehow. That it's only a matter of time. That time is finite after all.

Time and the fear of losing. Hate those two things.

All I want is to make it through to the next day and the day after that, to the next season and the one after that, to the next year and the one after that, through the next decade—two, three, four and five—with Tally. That's all I ask.

Whipped about this girl doesn't come close to explaining it.

"So what do you say? Want to get married on Friday?" I ask out of breath as we finish.

"Yes. I say yes to all of it." Tally laughs. Her miracle laugh. "You can start calling me Mrs. Presley right now if you want. And yes," she says, "I'll marry you on Friday, Lincoln Presley, just you, me, the judge, and two witnesses. It will be our secret until we're ready to tell the world. Deal."

"Deal. Any way you want it. You and Cara are all that matter to me. The World Series would be a big deal, but it's nothing compared to being with you. You know that, right?"

"I know." She traces my lips and I smile at first, but then it fades as the seriousness of the moment becomes all too real. "What is it?" She asks.

"Don't ever leave me, okay? I don't think I could take that."

"I won't," she whispers.

We drink and breathe within the same realm of each other.
Who knows what would happen if we were apart?

CHAPTER
FIVE

breathe (2am)

TALLY

BRIDE-TO-BE. ME. THE OWNER OF THIS exclusive shop is looking at me with dollar signs in her eyes. She tells me it's French silk tulle from London. Expensive. Fine. Luxurious. Did I mention expensive? Did I mention London? Linc said, "Spare no expense." Why not? He's major league; we can afford to be extravagant about this wedding, about our lives. Why not?

Silk satin. Gathered French silk tulle. London. Catherine Deane.
Who cares?
Not the bride.
To be.
Me.
Not today.

Marla gives me the look—the one that perfectly anoints her my best friend. She gives me the all-knowing, I-know-you're-feeling-fucking-crazy-Tally look.

She knows me well.

"I can't breathe," I whisper to the dressmaking doll assistant. She's a mousy woman. Pale skin. Dark witchy-looking hair. She has straight pins lined across her lips which she removes one by one and works into the delicate fabric at the hemline like she's working with a voodoo doll.

The owner rushes toward me. "Ms. Landon, are you all right?" Southern accent straight out of Georgia here in the upscale riches of San Francisco. I doubt she ever looks back. Her blond hair is swept high upon her head. She has the swankiest of bangs and will never look past thirty-five because of exceptional breeding and some expensive night creme she must use.

"I. Can't. Breathe. Can we take this thing off, please?"

The owner, Jenna, starts to argue with me but when I start to gasp she finally complies and orders her assistant to help with the *zippuh* in the back and all those pearl buttons that must be quickly undone.

"Can you give me a minute? Thank you."

Jenna gets this resentful look at my insistent tone but complies. The accusing swish of heavy expensive silk fabric clutched between them makes the only noise in the room besides my jagged breathing as she removes herself and the harried assistant from the dressing room. "We have what we need. Stella can make the final adjustments."

French silk.
Tulle.
London.
Expensive.
Who cares?

"Okay. Out with it. You're acting weirder than usual," Marla says from behind me after they've gone.

I stare at my beautiful blond best friend in the mirror. Her hands are on her hips in the all too familiar stance of get-a-fucking-grip-Tally. She breathes out in exasperation even as I still gasp for air.

I turn around and face her and just stand there feeling vulnerable and all but naked in the already bought and paid for lingerie purchased right after we first walked in. It's some new-fangled bustier number that the shop owner insisted I put on with the wedding gown. White French silk. Expensive. There's that word again. The dress and the lingerie equally expensive. The up-sale in this place proves to be fantastically obscene. We are already in the range of another five grand, and we have only been here for a little over an hour. I held my breath while the VISA went through the first time.

I am dangerously close to my limit by the addition of these three things—the dress, the bustier and the lingerie to match in addition to the deposit for Hollins House and the catered food, as well as hiring the band, and ordering all the decorations and flowers. All these things add up and appear to be without end.

I need to talk to Linc about all of it. He's been busy. Out of town so much of the time.

Distracted.

We both have been.

It's going to be fine.

It's all going to be fine.

He keeps saying this to me with every cell phone call or conversation we've had in the past twelve hours or so.

"Geez, Tally, you're scaring me."

"I can't do this."

"Which part?" Marla gets this vexed look.

She looks mighty fine in her matron of honor version of my dress. Swanky and lean in a hard to match periwinkle —a color so impossible to find—that I carry the Crayola crayon wherever we go, cajoling the florist to the cake decorator to the printer doing the invitations for the third time since the date has changed twice already that this is the color I want and to just make it happen.

Did I mention colors? Magenta and Periwinkle. That's what I want. Nobody has it. Everybody scrambles to find it, produce it, or replicate it because everyone wants a piece of the action for this once-in-a-lifetime event—The Lincoln Presley wedding.

Candy Baxstrom's article for *Sports Illustrated* hit the stands today. She said it best, although *People Magazine* piped in too.

It's not every day that a famous baseball pitcher, whose mother was Hollywood famous and whose father dominated Major League Baseball for so many years, marries an up-and-coming ballerina. Sure, they share a kid. Little Cara aged three and half. Sure, there's a mystery or two there about Ms. Landon. Her past and her present. Who is she to him? Who is she? Who was she? Where did she come from? Where has she been? There's the deal in Moscow that neither one is willing to talk about. There are so many questions. So many lies.

Presley met Landon when she was just seventeen. There is some speculation as to how old their daughter really is and where she's been all this time. Landon is the up-and-coming star for the San Francisco Ballet Company after having danced in New York City for a number of years. She toured with the European division of the New York City Ballet Company until she unexpectedly landed the lead role in Swan Lake for San Francisco Ballet Company. A source close to the couple stated that Landon originally gave the child up for adoption to the world-famous prima ballerina, Allaire Tremblay. Tremblay was killed in a car accident earlier this year, and the child was returned to Landon. Birth records do confirm Talia Landon is the little girl's biological mother and Lincoln Presley is the biological father, but it remains unclear as to how and when the couple actually reunited.

Presley and Landon announced their engagement in late July with plans to marry this fall after baseball season, but with the Giants run in the playoffs it's unclear when these two will marry and where. Just last year, Presley was engaged to Nika Vostrikova, who recently took a public relations position with Presley's current Major League Baseball team, the San Francisco Giants. Presley refused to comment on his relationship with Vostrikova other than to say, 'the two remain good friends,' But just what kind of friends are they? Ms. Landon won't comment, and if she did, what exactly could she say?

The two remain good friends.
   Let that sink on you a little bit. It did on me.
He said it. I asked him why, and he said, "because it was easier; you know how Candy is. Kimberley said not to worry about it so *don't* worry about it."
The two remain good friends. Five little words that invariably knifed their way somewhat permanently into my troubled soul.
   The two remain good friends.
And, we're back to *Sports Illustrated* article because if I'm ever asked to pinpoint the exact moment that doubt set in like a cancer

and took firm hold, I will lay it squarely upon Candy Baxstrom and her damn article and all the photographs and speculation that came with it. Somehow, they got a picture of me with Cara just outside her private preschool. Somehow, they got a picture of Nika and Linc shaking hands, and then leaning into each other like old friends do, right after one of his games in San Antonio, Texas. All Linc would say is that she travels with the team as part of her job because of her position. Is that in a prone position beneath my fiancé? You think I don't wonder? Do you know how life on the road works in professional baseball? With all sports teams? Do you know what goes on behind the scenes? Late at night when the fans go home? It's not the stuff you share with the friends or the family.

You like to think you're immune from it all, but then your arch nemesis, the Russian bitch from Moscow, takes a job that lands her back into your life and practically in the lap of her former lover, Lincoln Presley. There's that. Okay. Two things. Nika's arrival on my turf and the *Sports Illustrated* article show up on the same damn day.

Doubt sets in at a cellular level and travels straight through to mess with my DNA. It doesn't take much. I have trust issues. As anyone who knows me will attest to.

Somehow, they got a picture of me and Linc at the airport just before his last trip to Baltimore for the Orioles game. The last game of the season. Before the playoffs. I had rehearsals. I had Cara. I didn't go, but Nika did. Of course, I didn't know about that. But *Sports Illustrated* made note of that too. So did *People Magazine*.

Where were we?

French silk tulle from London. The elusive color periwinkle. Nika. People Magazine. Candy Baxstrom from Sports Illustrated.

The trust issues and the lack thereof.

Manipulation. Lies. Omissions.

These things make it all but impossible for me to trust and believe in us.

The two remain good friends.

It's an unimaginable situation all around for this supposed *bride. To be? Me?*

And our secret rendezvous at the courthouse is tomorrow and all I want to do is tell Marla. A part of me knows that getting married will alleviate this angst. *But am I ready? Does Linc really love me? Why does he love me?* Pastor Dan's tough questions come back to haunt me. At a deeply sane level, I know that getting married, secretly or not, will cause all of this outer turmoil to disappear. After tomorrow, most of it won't matter to me anymore.

But it's *today.*

Today it matters.

And I can't tell Marla because we agreed to keep it between the two of us for a while. Linc and me. No Marla. He was insistent upon that. He didn't want his dad to freak out, and I was worried about my parents finding out, especially my mom. She still wants to help plan everything. Thus, I'm spending a fortune I don't necessarily have on this dress. For the sake of my mom. Well, for me too and Marla and Holly watching from above. *Us girls love the dress.*

"I can't do this. I can't. I'm not ready." I get the last words out before sinking to the floor and hiding my face in my hands hoping it will be more difficult for Marla to guess how bad it really is. "No. I'm not ready. I can't do this."

"You *are* doing this. It's just weeks away. November. Plan B or C, right?"

If she only knew.

I look up at Marla ready to form my confession. *We're getting married tomorrow, not a month from now.*

Tell me I'm not crazy.

Silence.

I say nothing.

"It's just nerves." She scans my troubled face. "What aren't you *telling* me?"

The articles were bad. *People* and *Sports Illustrated* had a field day. ESPN wanted an interview now. Nika's arrival served as the tipping point and made things worse. The fallout has been almost catastrophic. *Me.* I'm the fallout. I don't attempt to hide my frustration.

"I can't deal with Nika Vostrikova, my permanent nemesis as well as two different articles trashing me from here to Moscow, and getting married all at the same time."

"It's just nerves." Marla glides in next to me and bumps my shoulder with hers.

"That's the thing." I glance at her sideways. "It's not just nerves. I can't do it. I thought I could. I really did, but I can't. I'm not exactly wife material *or* a very good mother. I can't even do toast properly."

My mind flashes to the episode with breakfast just this morning and I begin to tell Marla all about it. Burnt toast. Overcooked eggs. Linc pretended to eat them but finally gave up and made his own breakfast while Cara watched in her usual silent way. Still not talking. More than six months out from the car accident that killed Tremblay and essentially brought her back into my life, and she's still too traumatized by that event and the general upheaval in her life to trust either one of us yet.

"I think that Linc and Cara will survive your inability to toast bread."

I shake my head side-to-side at her. "The trust issues seem to multiply by the day for all of us. I don't know what I'm doing. As a mother. As a potential wife. As a ballerina. And my little three-year-old seems to have a better sense of this about me than Linc ever will. The bi-weekly visits to the counselor haven't done much. And my ability as a mom to take care of her is suspect. And it's all on me. Linc brushes my fears aside he just says, "We just deal." Easy for him. He's still on the road four days out of the week and I'm left to take care of Cara and battle these demons all on my own. I'm scared, Marla. I'm scared I can't do this. Any of it." I wave my arms around the dress shop.

Marla gets this determined look. "Get dressed. Let's get out of here. What you need is a margarita, some food, and a lecture. I'm here to serve." She grins.

"I don't know about the lecture, but the margarita and some food sounds good." She ignores my whine for the most part even when I add, "And, I need to talk to you. There's more."

Marla just vaguely nods and commands me to get dressed and tells the sales clerks to alter the dress by a good two inches all around and guarantees that I'll fit into it just fine. She grabs my purse and hands them the Visa card. "Just put the alterations charge on her card like everything else."

I hold my breath while the approval goes through.

It does.

But I'm close to the limit.
On so many fronts.

We stop in *The Promissory Note*, the restaurant bar near my house. I watch the movements of Sam the bartender with vague interest. I haven't been here in a long time, but he remembers me from before during the whole Moscow ordeal when Marla came to this very restaurant to pick me up that fateful day. *Sam was here. He's still here. Very dependable. This guy.*

He makes us the Bartender's Margarita Special and tells us that the drinks are on the house because we're his friends. *True.* Sam helped me out for a few hours during one of the most pivotal moments of my life, and I've never even thanked him for it.

"Thank you," I whisper to him now, holding his steady gaze with mine for a few long seconds.

He has blue eyes. Gold lashes. An easy smile. He is a blond knight in shining armor; I already know this by the deeds he's done for me already. He bows his head like a good knight does before his queen. I half-smile as an unexpected blush steals its way across my face.

I'm flirting with him out of some weird convoluted desperation.
Why?

"How's Cara?" Sam asks when he comes over and refills our drinks, unprompted, in fresh martini glasses rimmed with salt.

"She's good, still not herself exactly…since…Allaire…but she's doing all right. We go to family counseling sessions every week, and the therapist says it's just going to take some time for her to adjust. To trust us, really."

"Tally and Linc are getting *married*," Marla says with extra emphasis on the last word.

I turn and flip her off underneath the bar, unsure as to why the momma bear side of her has decided to come out.

Sam responds with a lazy smile when I quickly glance up at him to gauge his reaction. "Congratulations, Tally. That's great. I'm glad things have worked out for the two of you." There's this little hint of sadness that fleets across Sam's face, but then it's gone.

Maybe, it wasn't even there.

I know this feeling.

I know this pain.

I recognize this loss.

The magnitude is so great and I instantly realize that I may not survive it this time.

Here's the thing. We have this signal we worked out. A little lift of one finger on either hand will do.

We agreed.

Our signal.

Well, it's been Marla and my signal for years. I'd let Linc in on this little secret this past summer. We were lying in bed talking about our life and our future plans. Our fingers were laced together, and I remember telling him that since he's so far away from me so much of the time playing baseball if he could just signal to me every once in a while, just like the comedian Carol Burnett still does to her daughter every time she makes an appearance on television by tugging on her ear and giving her the faithful sign: I love you. I remember you. I'm thinking of you. Something corny like that. That's all I ask I told him. That way, I know you're okay, and then I'll be okay. Just that one little sign would indicate that everything was fine.

I wait for his signal.

I wait for some kind of sign, but he's not moving.

The network hurriedly switches to commercial, and I start to say, "no," over and over because we talked about line drives a long time ago.

"Just be fast," I'd said at the time with an uneasy laugh when Linc first told me about them.

"Faster than the ball," Linc had said grinning back at me. "Don't worry. I'll be fine. I'll signal to you that I'm fine."

Line drives.

You have to watch out for those.

They can change your life.

CHAPTER
SIX

wreck of the day

MARLA TAKES OVER. SHE MAKES THE calls on the way to the hospital where Linc's been taken by ambulance, while I talk to my dad on my cell. I beg him to go down to the ER and be with Linc and call me back when he finds out more. Meanwhile, Marla navigates the 101 like a Nascar driver and still manages to remember to call the preschool and let them know my mom will be picking up Cara. Then, she calls my mom again and relays the message. Within five minutes, my dad is calling me back, and I take a brief moment and close my eyes tight before I answer his call.

Soon enough, he's telling me not to worry, they're working on him right now, and Linc's awake.

Strangely, I'm cheered up at this weird piece of news, but still gasp for air all at once realizing on some level I've been holding my breath for quite a while now.

Breathe. I try not to think too much beyond that one act—taking in air. A strange rustling sound from the back seat captures my attention; I irritably glance back and discover the much-coveted bridal lingerie tote bag flapping in the wind that gusts through the half-open window.

I glare at the fancy scripted name, *Wedding Secrets,* stenciled across the front of it and dully think about French Silk Tulle and twenty-five pearl buttons and London and Catherine Deane's beautifully-designed dress. All the while, the mostly sinister part of me silently confronts the fact that I may never get to wear it. The very center of my psyche wordlessly succumbs to that singular idea.

I may never get to wear it. Any of it. He's not out of the woods yet. Not yet. These thoughts press ever downward upon my soul like an insistent bell tolls in a tower. The ringing is so loud inside my head that I glance at Marla to see if she can hear it too.

She misinterprets my glazed look.

"You okay?"

"He didn't move. He didn't lift his finger. The signal we worked out for the two of us. Like you and I used to do."

"I know, but your dad says he's awake, they're working on him. He's going to be fine. I just *know* it."

"How do you *know?*" My words grate across my lips like I've bitten down on a serrated knife and drawn blood. My mouth tastes like metal. Somewhere along the way I have actually bitten my lip and am just now noticing this. It stings and on some strange level I am consoled that I can even feel it.

Marla wisely chooses to ignore my obvious turmoil and I do my best to hide the fact that I'm beginning to fall apart. We exchange a singular look and seem to be transported back in time to when Holly died. The memory comes on just like that. Four and half years later and the recognizable pain returns in the same obliterating way as it did then and attempts to cut right through both of us like a chainsaw splits apart the base trunk of a tree. A classmate of ours from Paly died just last year and we experienced the same visceral response at hearing about Ben Donner's tragic car accident and looked at each other the same way at hearing the news. It's the same exact look we exchange now all over again.

Maybe it's the suddenness of it all. Maybe it's the profound understanding of loss and instantly knowing how it feels that rocks you all over again. Whatever it is, I wish it didn't hurt so damn much. I wish the experience didn't feel so achingly familiar. I wish the heartbreak didn't remind me so much of its permanence. Because the death of a loved one—that loss—is like a bacteria your body never really rids itself of. It's always there, just waiting to re-ignite and burn through you all over again.

Oh yes, death and loss like to stay acquainted, to revisit, if only to remind you that these two are ultimately in charge. Death. Loss. Grief. Guilt. They all take turns tormenting you. Invariably, one or all manage to infiltrate through any happiness, joy, or peace you find.

Sure, you naively convince your outer self you've moved on, that you've survived the death of a loved one, but you really haven't. You think you've outplayed them all, but these threats—death, grief, and guilt— will not be denied.

And yes, in moments like this one, you again realize that they just bide their time and pay a visit on a different day when you least expect. All four evoke irrevocable harm in new and different ways and extol pain in just enough notable measures in any way they can find. New or old. It's hard to tell. All you know is that the pain feels exactly the same no matter how much time has gone by. It's the exact same feeling. It makes me shudder.

"Get out of your head, Tally. *Breathe.* He's going to be okay." Marla looks at me intently for a moment and forces herself to smile. Then, she's whipping the SUV into the first open parking space she finds in the visitor's lot for long term.

I glance at her sideways. "*Long term* parking?"

"We don't know how long we'll be here." She gives me a reassuring look just as her cell phone buzzes and proceeds to read the text off of her phone. "Your mom just picked up Cara. She's meeting up with Gina and then she's coming here."

"This is going to set her back," I say with foreboding.

My mom is really close to Linc. That's happened over the last several months even before we got back together. I worry how she is going to do with all of this. Whatever *this* is.

"You don't know that. Don't even think that."

"Always thinking it," I murmur. "Thank God for Gina. And my mom too, I guess." I've run out of words and I'm out of air again. I sigh deep again in an attempt to keep it together, but my entire body convulses as if I'm feeling everything Linc is right now. Somehow, I slide down from the passenger seat of Marla's SUV even as my mind flails and begins to search for distractions.

I like Gina Masterson. I'm grateful she is taking care of Cara as well as Elliott. Cara loves being with Elliott. It's amazing to me how children can bridge an almost two-year age difference and find ways to relate and entertain themselves. Cara will be okay. My mom will be here soon.

These jumbled thoughts console me, enough so that I manage to transport myself all the way into the hospital's ER waiting area without really noticing, until I look up and discover the ordered chaos all around me. Copious amounts of angst and blood and a little gore greet me cocooned within the stark whiteness of the emergency room.

My ears hum. People are talking, but I can't really hear what's being said. I close my eyes to extinguish the scene.

I can do this. I have to do this.

I open them only to find the horror scene is still here. *It's real. And I'm here.* Here to suffer like all these others waiting for news, good or bad, or closure, or an ending, or a beginning. A woman in labor. A guy with a chainsaw sticking out from his upper thigh. A child with a nasty cut across his forehead swathed in a bathroom towel. "From a swing," his mother tells us even though we didn't ask. All the injured wait, while dire emergencies are handled behind half-closed curtains and the medical staff clothed in blue scrubs that race around like soldiers re-spawning in a video game. All of these victims experienced line drives in their own way. Line drives shatter-ing their lives or beginning them in an instant.

Life and death in the ER. Episodic or not. It's here.

I'm here. The last place I thought I'd ever be again.

I hate hospitals. My experience with them has been less than stellar, especially this one. I spent time here after the accident, after Holly died at the scene, and after being there and watching it happen. I tremble again as the memory rears itself upward to the foremost part of my mind and recognize the familiar excruciating pain as it tries to take over.

It's not the same. *It just feels the same.*

It can't happen again. *Can it?*

I can't lose anyone else. *I can't.*

Which is why you should never love them in the first place.

Marla hits my arm effectively bringing me back to the present. She saves me from drowning in the memories of the past and the ever fearful present. With purpose, she takes my hand and guides me along the hallway and right up to the outstretched arms of my dad.

Dr. Adam Landon. Daddy. His wide arms engulf me, and I allow myself to feel safe for a few seconds, but then reality crashes back in on me; and I pull away.

Dad looks a little disappointed by my actions. *What else is new?*

"He's awake," Dad says to me gently. He holds my gaze for a few seconds and exudes reassurance for me with his very presence. "He's asking for you, Tally."

I unconsciously gasp air realizing I've been holding it again since we raced through the hospital parking lot all the way to here.

"Daddy? Is he okay? I saw it on TV as well as the replay over and over." I swallow hard. "He was unconscious for a long time."

My dad pauses for a few seconds, choosing his words carefully, always at the ready as the doctor—*the famed cardiologist*—that he is. I can practically see him put on his bedside manner, like a winter coat, when he finally answers. "Babe, he's in the best place he can be. They're going to do a CAT Scan to see how he's doing. He may have a facial fracture to the right side of his face. They'll want to rule out other stuff with the scan."

"Other stuff?"

He doesn't answer for a long ten seconds and won't quite meet my eyes when he does.

"He got hit pretty hard, Tally." My dad sighs ever so slightly.

"Go talk to him. He's asking for you. I'll be right there." He turns to Marla. "Let me show you where the waiting room is. His pitching coach is there too. I'm sure the rest of the team will be along as soon as the game finishes."

"They're still *playing?*" I call out to my dad incredulous that they continued the game.

The two of them have started to walk away from me, but my dad turns back. "Yeah." His one word answer conveys his own frustration at this insanity.

God forbid the Giants would stop a game for their star pitcher's injury. I just nod at Marla and my dad, too helpless to form words and then slowly follow one of the nurses my doctor dad has assigned to take charge of me.

Ten minutes later, I've put on some blue paper gown and these ridiculous billowy covers for my shoes in the same nauseating shade of blue, and now I'm following 'Linda' the nurse into the trauma room, where no less than five people are working on Linc. I look around for a familiar face, but there are none. I can barely see Linc's with so many people surrounding him.

No Davis Presley. For some reason, this makes me uneasy that Linc's dad isn't here yet, and that feeling gets stronger when I finally get a look at Linc's face.

The left side is perfectly normal but the right side of his face is this dark, flaming red streaked with dried blood with the outer edges into his dark hairline turning a raging purple in color. His right eye is already swollen shut, while his open left one zeros in on me.

"Tally," he whispers, reaching for me. "This my fiancée," he says to the doctors and nurses crowding around. "Everyone, just back off, *please*, and give me a minute with her. We're getting married tomorrow."

Incongruent.

So incongruent with what I am seeing before me right now that I actually laugh and shake my head at him.

"Hi," I say shyly and with a bit of wonder at the medical team.

"I'm Tally Landon. Hi."

I smile at the sympathetic look of the doctors and nurses and catch their fleeting smiles. I turn to Linc again. "I thought we were going to keep that to ourselves?"

"No secrets anymore. Only the truth about us. In sickness and in health, remember? Soon enough anyway."

He tries to smile but I think it hurts him to move his face too much. "I love you, Tally Landon. Come here."

I forgo thinking about what he looks like, which is rather frightening on a level I can't even begin to comprehend yet, and rush straight into his open, waiting arms. We cling to each other for a few minutes not saying anything more, while I feel the presence of all the others in the room warily watching us.

I pull back and take a good look at him. Describing him as having been in a prized fist fight that he clearly didn't win doesn't begin to cover it. I reach for his left hand, where his wedding ring will soon be. My mind flashes that it's at home in my lingerie drawer. I bring his fingers to my lips and kiss them one at a time. Although this group of doctors look a little disconcerted by my arrival, my presence seems to calm Linc. One of them tells me they'll allow me to remain as long as I stay out of the way while they work on him.

"Deal," I say to the growing crowd of doctors and nurses.

"Careful now," one of them says to me as I hug Linc fiercely to me and stroke the back of his head, which appears to be the only uninjured part of him at the moment.

"A few more minutes," Linc cajoles one of the nurses who tries to lead me further away.

"You forgot the signal," I say softly to Linc.

"I did. I'm sorry. I don't know what happened. It all went black. All I remember is the ambulance ride, waking up and knowing all I wanted to do was get to you, to see you again." He tries to smile, but it doesn't quite work this time. Then, he winces in obvious pain.

I pull away and step back from him a few feet as the doctors start to move in on us. "I love you." He doesn't say anything in response and I stare at him hard trying to make sense as to what is going on with him. His breath goes shallow and he looks a little dazed now. "Yeah, well, you scared half the nation," I say slowly. "At least, all the San Francisco Giants' fans."

He frowns at first at what I've just said and appears to try and laugh but it comes out more this guttural groan. The doctors seem to be watching him as closely as I am now. I step forward and kiss him lightly, embarrassed by the unintended scrutiny by everyone here, but determined to show him that I'm here, and I love him.

"Are you his wife?" One of the nearby nurses asks. She gives me a sympathetic but hopeful look.

I glance over at her with a faint smile. "No. I'm his fiancée. We're getting married tomorrow. It's supposed to be a secret for a while, but I guess that cover is blown." My smile is erased by the sympathetic look that comes over her face. Tomorrow's planned courthouse nuptials fade just as fast. I draw an unsteady breath when she immediately turns to Linc and quickly points to the places he should sign his name.

After about thirty seconds, Linc has signed all the forms and I watch as the nurse races out the ER doors with them. Then, I keep my eyes on Linc, smile wide, and effectively ignore the tragic parts to this scene.

"You look like hell, big guy. Good thing we're getting married tomorrow, and that I love you so much because that baseball left a mark or two on your otherwise totally handsome face." I gently kiss him but then he's pulling back and looking at me funny. "Linc? Are you okay? Linc?" I ask again when he doesn't answer.

His good eye kind of glazes over. He's stares at me and doesn't say anything else.

Then I notice his lips are turning blue just as panic begins to grip me. I trace his lips checking his air. "He's…barely breathing. There's something wrong. There's something wrong!" I scream to anyone who will listen and frantically look around as the circle of doctors closes back in on us.

About that time, I hear one of the machines go off, and I'm unceremoniously pushed out of the way as more alarms begin to go off.

The nurse who spoke to me earlier about being his fiancée returns. She grabs my arm and half-pushes me out the swinging doors of the emergency room.

"You should wait out here, Ms. Landon. Right now, they are doing everything they can to help your fiancé."

She points towards the waiting room that I remember Marla being directed to earlier.

In a daze, I walk slowly, forcing myself to put one foot in front of the other, and make my way down the long hall toward Marla and my dad and some kind of reassurance. Someone grabs my arm at the halfway mark along this trek. *Mom.*

"Tally? What's wrong? Are you okay?" She asks after taking one look at my face.

"Something is wrong with Linc."

I glance back. Now, there are at least another half dozen doctors and nurses streaming in and out of the swinging doors to the ER where Linc is. My mind tries to tabulate the exact number, but I can't.

I can't even breathe.

I try to remember what I said to him last. What was it? But I can't remember.

"They're taking him to emergency surgery. They've brought in a neurologist. Tom Carter. He's good." My dad looks beyond stressed.

I concentrate on breathing in and out so I don't freak out right along with him.

"I thought Dr. Carter only did brain surgery," I say slowly, holding the cup of coffee in my hand and vaguely feeling the heat from the Styrofoam even as it begins to feel cold in my hands. *How is that possible? Cold and hot at the same time. Like me?* It's been sixty-five minutes since I last saw Linc, and I think I can measure it in days.

"He does. The CAT Scan showed some bleeding. They need to relieve the pressure." My dad is a man of few words but the ones he's chosen to use seem to cut into me as swiftly as a scalpel would.

I actually flinch as the familiar resounding edge of fear moves in and takes me over completely. The unbelievable pain comes on much more slowly. My dad holds my stunned gaze and starts to nod as if I've just figured out the scenario for all of us.

"It's really serious, Tally, but Tom Carter is the best."

"He could die." I've said this as if I'm reading from my first book in Kindergarten.

See Spot run.
See Spot run fast.
Does Spot die?
Does he get hit by a baseball and die?
Or die in a burning car?
Like Holly?
Cara will be five in a few years. I should be ready for this, for Kindergarten, with Cara. I should teach her to read now. I can't seem to get her to talk, but maybe I can teach her to read.
But if Linc dies, then so do I.
Then, where will Cara be?
These are the questions we have that we never give a voice to.
These are the thoughts we think but that we never actually say.

CHAPTER

SEVEN

no air

TALLY

MARLA'S HERE. SHE PUTS HER ARM around me. Her warmth seeps into me somehow after a few minutes. I look at her helplessly. "It's going to be okay."

Her words cause my lips to curve. *I can still smile. That's good news.* That's all the good news I have to go on right now.

I look at her even more intently. "I'm going to hold you to that." She nods. "Sorry about the have-to-keep-it-a-secret-we're-getting-married-tomorrow shtick. I really wanted to tell you. Today? We were trying to take in consideration my parents, my mom really; and protect Linc's dad from blowing a gasket, I suppose. So much for the secret. Or the surprise." I've said this like I'm reading off of a piece of paper at a eulogy. It feels like one.

I'm numb. I grow colder by the minute.

"Remember, I'm the expert when it comes to wedding plans. An elopement is really the only way to go. You'll just have to put it off for a few more weeks or keep to the schedule for late October? November?" She frowns, which makes me kind of smile because the logistics have just become a nightmare, and we both know it. She sighs. "You guys *love* each other. That's all that matters. All you need is love."

"What are you doing? Quoting the Beatles' song lyrics now?"

"Anything that will work for a distraction, baby."

"Thanks for being here. Don't call me baby."

"Nowhere I'd rather be, *baby*. Charlie's coming up after he does rounds. We're all here for you and Linc. You know that. Always."

"Always," I say in rote but I can't really breathe and I try to hide that fact from Marla. A distinct part of me worries I'll never be able to breathe properly again. I give voice to the overriding fear. "But what if something happens to him, Marla? What then?"

"It won't."

"How do you *know*?"

"I just *know*," Marla says squeezing my ice cold hands. "I just *know*, Tally."

Davis Presley arrives and essentially takes over. He makes no comment when my dad quietly takes him aside and tells him that Linc and I were planning on eloping tomorrow. He takes in the little bit of old news and in slow motion looks my way and finally rewards me with a polite nod. *And that is it.*

I decide he's scared. Scared for Linc. Maybe even scared for me and Cara. All of us. He says as much when he finally comes over. His hands shake as he absently drinks a cup of coffee. "Eloping. I guess congratulations would be in order, Tally." He takes my hand in his and weakly shakes it.

"If that were true. Yes," I say into his inexplicable silence.

And that is it. After that, we don't talk about Linc and me or the fact that we were eloping tomorrow after Linc's morning practice. That proverbial wish ship has sailed without us. He says nothing to me. That's it. That's all. No Tally-how-are-you-holding-up? Nothing.

Nada. Every once in a while he leaves to make various phone calls and returns with cryptic updates that can be summarized like this: "Kimberley. The Giants. ESPN."

The man has his priorities and they aren't me. There's no how-can-I-help-you, Tally? Where's-Cara? What-can-I-do? There are no words of comfort for me from Linc's dad. *There is nothing.*

One of Linc's doctor's come in and give us an update. "His surgery went well. He's critical but stable. And *no*, you can't see him just yet."

Four hours in, I conclude that Davis and I are on the same page. *We just want Linc to live. We just want what is best for Linc. We are in agreement.*

These thoughts continue to console me as I try to get some sleep sitting up in a chair in the family waiting room just off of the ICU as this horrible day draws to a close and another begins.

At three in the morning, I awaken in the semi-dark in a hospital that never really sleeps and discover Davis quietly watching me. Unveiled and way past the guise of serving as my future father-in-law, his brooding look is downright ominous. It serves as the first sign of the trouble that is to come, but I'm too tired to actually respond or stop him in any way.

By eight in the morning, some twelve hours have passed since the line drive, and we still occupy the same chairs in the waiting room. It now feels like a prison of sorts. We can't leave because we wait for news, for rounds, and for any and all updates about Linc. We live for the cryptic statuses.

"He's-critical-but-stable."

"We're-running-an-IV to get him some fluids and nutrition and avoid dehydration."

"He's-been-sedated-so-he-can-rest."

"His body's healing."

"You can see him later this morning, Mr. Presley." A curious side glance at me takes place. "We'll be limiting visitors to immediate family one at a time right now."

I don't think a fiancée is going to count as immediate family and a new kind of reality begins to dawn as I see Davis unconsciously nod in agreement at this rule.

Marla left with Charlie a few hours ago. My mom gave up at four in the morning and went into parent mode for her other kid to ensure Tommy gets off to school today. My dad is off doing rounds without having gotten any sleep and assures me he's fine because it's his day off.

None of it really reaches me or computes on any coherent level. I feel nothing. I just sit here and wait and wonder at the phenomena that I am able to breathe at all. Meanwhile, Linc's dad barely says anything to me and the silence from him is its own particular brand of heartbreak.

"He'll recover."

My dad.

He's taken another look at Linc's chart and tells me he likes what he sees. "His vitals are good. He's resting."

"More please," I say with a tight, improvised smile.

My dad pulled chief cardiologist rank, convincing them to let me in for a mere fifteen minutes to see Linc for myself, while Davis was off making one of his mysterious phone calls. We are in clandestine mode already without verbalizing why. Linc was sleeping. He looked peaceful but worn out at the same time. His head was mostly bandaged and I have no idea how much of his head they had to shave. There were tufts of black hair sticking out on the left side of his head. The only parts that weren't bandaged. He's still critical but stable. I still can't breathe and find myself still holding my breath at odd times when I finally gasp for air with the realization.

"More please," I say again to my dad now. "And thanks for earlier," I whisper.

He nods. "That's all I've got. You should go home. Change clothes. Get some rest. Cara's spending the day with Mom. You can check in with her, with both of them actually."

"What should I say? To Cara? About Linc?" I don't know what to say. I haven't known what to say for sixteen hours it seems.

"What if he doesn't remember me, Dad," I say in a low voice so that Davis doesn't overhear. I give voice to what I now know to be true about those last moments with Linc. The panic rises inside.

"At the last. Before he went for the second CAT Scan and emergency surgery. He didn't seem to know who I was." My breathing gets erratic, and I fight the onset of a panic attack. I can't afford to do this in front of my dad or Linc's. *Get it together.*

"It's probably temporary."

My dad grips my hands and holds them painfully tight, bringing me back, and forcing me to breathe. "Hang in there."

His stern voice centers me. I calm down in a matter of seconds as my dad holds my gaze and prevents me from falling apart. "His brain was swelling," he says in a low voice. "It affects different parts like that. Memory. Just know that the surgery went well. He's still critical, but he's stable. That's very good news. Got it?"

I slowly nod and attempt to take in what he's just told me, irrationally comparing it to what my dad didn't say.

Then, I glance over at Davis and attempt a watery smile for the man. He holds my gaze for a moment and rewards me with indifference and then resumes his post, looking out the blind-covered window toward at what must be a perfect view of the parking lot and says nothing, like always. The same attitude he's held since he arrived.

I look back at my dad. He gives me reassurance with a simple nod of his head. He and I share the same feelings about Davis Presley.

"He's intense," my dad said to me in late August once, after they had all returned from golfing together one sunny afternoon on one of Linc's rare days off.

"Understatement," I'd said back to him. "I'm a walk in the park compared to that guy," I'd whispered to my dad with a offbeat laugh. "No wonder Linc loves me."

"No wonder," my dad had said.

Now, Dad holds my hand and slides into the waiting room chair beside mine with a deep sigh. I appreciate his presence. His unwavering support. Linc's dad makes me feel unsure and uncertain. Two separate *un-feelings*. He makes me question myself, my feelings, my reactions to the situation. My obviously unwelcome status as Linc's future wife. Luckily, my dad makes me feel wanted and loved. I have to hold onto that.

"What do I tell Cara? She just got him back. We both did."

"Just tell her that her Daddy hurt his head, and he's resting. That's the truth. That's all we know."

"What are we afraid of though? What's the worst that can happen?" I give voice to more of the unspoken questions and allow fear to gain some additional harbor in the less than hopeful light spectrum of my psyche. I look into the warm eyes of my father that mirror mine and give life to the pure terror that has begun a slow crawl inside of me for the past sixteen hours in a bold attempt to take a firm and permanent hold of me.

It looks like it's been doing the same thing to my dad. It's hard to miss the empathy reflected in his eyes and the veiled softness in his tone when he finally speaks. "The brain is an amazing entity, but trauma to it is tricky and unpredictable. The good thing is they got him to surgery…so amazingly fast. I think they mitigated the damage from the swelling." He stops. It's fairly easy to discern the complete transformation from father to doctor within his single moment of hesitation. "They don't know his prognosis, and they won't know anything more until he wakes up, and they won't be allowing that to happen for a while. They'll keep him in a drug-induced coma to give him the necessary rest. And you need some too. They want to give his body and mind time to heal. So, you need to prepare for the long haul, Tally. Get some rest. Check in at work. See Mom. Talk to Cara. *Eat something.* He's in the best place he can be and there's nothing you can do right now except take care of yourself until he's awake. And then, we'll see where we're at."

They don't know. They won't know.

"Daddy?"

"They don't know." My dad is in clinical mode, divorcing himself from me as his daughter and beholden to the medical powers that be. *It scares me.*

He looks up and over at Davis, who watches the two of us from the far side of the room in absolute silence.

I don't know my future father-in-law well. He is a hard man to read. He is an older version of his son with a hint of grey at his dark hair line and the same startling grey-blue eyes as Linc. Davis is just as tall and tan and powerful, and he is most certainly all about baseball, just like Linc.

Linc's dad has been kind and receptive to me, for the most part, since we announced our engagement this past summer, although he tends to stare at me, at these odd moments when we meet up with him as if I am an enigma that he can't quite figure out. I get that he is less than thrilled to find out we were planning to elope and join his family even sooner than expected, but if the past hours have taught me anything I also sense he is actually more than a little puzzled as to why his son—his one and only prodigal son—has chosen me. It's the one thing we have in common I suppose. We both wonder why Linc loves me.

"Davis, you should go home and get some rest," my dad in doctor mode says. "I've told Tally this too. Visiting hours will be set for this afternoon. You both need to catch the doctors on their rounds and get an update. I'll be here in case anything changes, and you have my cell number."

"I'm staying. Tally should go. For a while." His gruff answer provides absolutely no leeway for any kind of argument, not even with my father.

I find myself standing still for a few seconds dissecting what he's just said and how he's said it and then I mindlessly start to follow my dad out into the hallway. I'm intent on exiting the room as quickly as possible because, in that singular moment, I realize that Davis Presley really doesn't like me. At all.

"I'll be back soon. A few hours at the most. With food and coffee," I say turning back and pasting on a ready smile for Linc's dad. Davis nods, but he barely glances our way and then turns his full attention back to the sports magazine in front of him just as the door swings closed between us.

He hates me.

My dad doesn't say anything about Davis' dismissive attitude.

I just get a sympathetic look from him. "He's under a lot of pressure. We all are," my dad eventually says with a little sigh.

"That's not it," I say with sudden understanding. "He's not exactly thrilled with the idea of me as his daughter-in-law."

"What makes you say that?"

"It's just something I know."

"Something he said?" My dad asks looking as if he's ready to defend my honor right this second with Linc's dad.

"More like what he doesn't say," I whisper back.

Our intense conversation is abruptly interrupted by the sudden activity taking place in the critical care unit. I'm trying to figure out what's going on while the speakers overhead announce *Code Blue*.

My mind somehow knows it's Linc. I stand motionless in the middle of the hallway as doctors and nurses rally for the sudden onslaught of trauma.

Line drives.
There are all kinds.
There are so many.

<hr>

Crisis averted.

Code blue with Linc remedied. The famous baseball player is pronounced stable once again forty-eight hours later.

On the third day, my dad drives me home to their new house in Saint Francis Wood which I've spent less than five hours in. I hang back, telling my dad, I need a minute alone. I lean back into the confines of the passenger seat and vaguely listen as the tick of the hot engine invariably begins to cool down. Then, I sullenly stare up at this newest Landon purchase and attempt to equate the idea of home with this house they've bought in San Francisco, which is so far away from our suburbia hometown of Atherton. Tommy will attend Lowell next year and create all new memories of high school that will be so different from the ones that transpired for Holly and me at Palo Alto High School. I haven't quite reconciled my family's move here, not in my mind or my heart.

We don't belong here. This isn't home. Home was Atherton. Home was my own room across the hall from Holly's. Home is now packed up in storage boxes in the basement of this small wonder of a house, half the size of the palatial homestead they had in Atherton.

"It's close to the hospital. It has a two-car garage. Grass. Some space." My dad points out these amenities in a quiet subdued tone each time I visit them here. "We're close to you, Tally. She likes that. She wants to be near you. You and Cara. And Linc. Your mom needs that."

Alamo Square.

Tremblay's house, which I inadvertently inherited via the estate she left to Cara, is twenty minutes away from this one by car and less than a half an hour by transit if all goes according to plan. I adhere to a schedule. Public transit remains my preference and mode of transportation when I can make it work. Yes, I am still terrified of cars, the 101 on rainy days, sunny ones too, I suppose, and black SUVs that are driven too fast.

I stare at the house some more searching for home. Home—the one I remember—is long gone. That's unfortunate because today I need home.

There's a small tap tap on the side of the car window. I sigh deep and alight from the car. Cara stands back from me right there on the perfectly cut green lawn in an introspective stance with her little arms behind her back.

She's not quite trusting. She's not quite sure. She is my daughter in every way. She reaches out one of her chubby little hands toward my face as I kneel down in front of her and lightly strokes my cheek. She fingers my hair and face. Her touch is the best remedy I've had so far in the past several days and exactly what I need the most. Welcome home.

"Hi, sweetie."

I gather up her little form in my arms and breathe in her baby shampoo scent and revel in her sweetness, wrapping myself all around her. For a few precious moments, I convince myself that everything will be okay.

Tears threaten and begin to sting my eyes and effectively slam me back into reality. I close them to avoid the fresh onslaught of pain and bury my face into Cara's little shoulder, take a deep breath, and hold it for seconds.

I need Cara today.

I needed her three days ago when a line drive from a baseball just about shattered our lives.

The weight of it all—the close calls and the unknowns and the ever-present fear—practically suffocate me, even as I take comfort in holding my precious three-year-old.

I truly need her today and always.

Eventually, I choke the words out. "Daddy hurt his head. He's sleeping at the hospital right now because all these great doctors are taking care of him. He's going to fine." I breathe these consoling words out to our little girl.

And I almost believe them.

CHAPTER

EIGHT

hold your head up

TALLY

LYING. I LIED WITH THE BEST of them. The worst of them. I could lie better than most anyone. My analyst—psychotherapist? Counselor? Whichever sounds cooler, said, "I use lying as a coping mechanism to better control the outcome."

"So it's destiny," I'd said back to her.

"Tally." She spoke my name in the same disappointing exasperated way my mother still employs. Even now.

Lying. I lied because I could. Well, I used to lie for that reason alone.

But now?

I finally resort to tell the truth and what does it get me?

Nothing.

I may not be able to breathe again.

The truth. Plain and simple.

With him. For him. Because of him. It doesn't matter.

I lied. It made the not too distant past bearable.

It became a necessary coping mechanism. For me.

That's what lying was for.

Lying appeared to be a way of life.

At least, for mine.

And, the truth?

Don't believe all that hype about it setting you free. It doesn't.

Instead, the truth will imprison you forever.

I cannot breathe.

All the air is gone from me. I just didn't know why quite yet.

"Who are you?" Linc asks me minutes after he first opens his eyes ten days after the accident. Then it is, "where am I?" Then back again to the burning question that already effectively skewers my heart all the way through to my soul. "Who are you?"

He's been in a deep, drug-induced coma for nine days after surviving the initial impact, after the swelling kicked in which ignited the need for emergency brain surgery, and after having stopped breathing and being coded back twice in the five days that followed. The surgery and the quickness of the medical team ultimately saved his life; and counting, *three times.*

We are so grateful he is still with us. It's a mantra. We say it all the time. *We're just glad he's alive.*

They moved him out of intensive care yesterday and began reducing the narcotics so he would start to wake up. I am finally allowed to be with him and have been with him in this hospital room for the past twenty-four hours since they officially and finally allowed me in. I haven't left the hospital for more than a few hours at a time in, well, ten days but I haven't left Linc's side in the past twenty-four. His dad has barely left his son's side either. Everyone else as immediate family, including his aunt and uncle, and Charlie and Marla, have been taking turns staying with him as the medical staff in the

ICU allowed it. And yet, Davis stayed vigilant in not leaving his son's side once he was allowed in and I joined him in that valiant effort when they finally officially allowed me in. *Davis and I.* We've been unable to leave the room or Linc for the past day. We've been here for the duration, and we let them know—the powers that be—that we wouldn't be leaving Linc's side again if we could help it.

We would stay. Davis and I.

We are a team of epic wonder.

Until now.

The thing is I wanted to be here when Linc finally woke up. As I believed he would. As I had actually prayed to God that he would. And yet, Linc's first words slice through me like a serrated knife surely would have. I feel severed even further by his quizzical look as he continues to warily watch me. Some part of me notes he looks like before—*before his surgery*—in those last few scary moments in the ER. *Confused. Undone. Indifferent.*

"Who are you? Where am I? Who are *you*?" Linc asks again and then he turns to his father. "Dad? Where am I? Who is she?" He looks back over at me in alarm.

Linc's dad gives me this surprising sympathetic look as he comes over and puts his arm around me and whispers, "why don't you go tell the doctors he's awake? And take a break? We don't want to upset him further."

I nod, rendered incapable of speech. I can't make any sense out of what I've just heard. A part of my brain ticks off all the positives. Linc is talking just fine. He looks fine. I watch in wonder as he maneuvers his bandaged-up head enough to look around. *Perfectly normal. Perfectly fine. He has movement. There's that. There's sound. He's talking. He's alive. We are so grateful.* And yet, another part of me continues to reel at what he's just said to me. "Who are you?" My mind tries to put it all together in this unnatural calm manner while the rising fear rips it away at about the same level.

All the various doctors warnings run through my head.

The side effects can be many.

There may be some memory loss.

There may be some confusion.

Some memory loss.

Some?

Memory loss may be temporary or it could be permanent. We just don't know yet. We'll have to wait and see.

Wait and see.

Memory loss. Temporary or Permanent.

We. Just. Don't. Know.

"Who are you?" Linc asks me for a third time. He looks more and more agitated, while his dad urges to me to just go. But I just stand here, somewhat immobilized by the dawning reality that he doesn't remember me at all.

"Find his doctors. Go get some help." His words reach me. I watch him as he distracts a now distraught Linc by urging him to take a sip of water. It's our first glimpse as to where Linc is coming from.

"I don't want any God damn water!" Linc waves his arm around and crashes the water pitcher his dad was holding out to him into the far wall. "Who is she? Why is she here?" Then, he looks over at me. "Who are you? And why are you staring at me like that?"

Davis' orders become sterner. "Go get his doctor. I've already pressed the 'call' button. Go!"

I start to leave, suddenly afraid of Linc's agitated state of mind, but attempt to hold on to the last remaining sane vestiges of mine.

He's back, but he's different.

He doesn't know me.

Which means what?

We won't be getting married in front of the family and friends any time soon.

I glance back at the two of them. Linc's dad cleans up the water mess wiping the floor and walls as best he can. Meanwhile, Linc still stares at me, open-mouthed, looking a little unhappy with himself for the sudden outburst. I start to smile, to reassure him. He traces his bandaged head with his free hand. He's probably wondering what's going on and trying to put this all together. Empathy kicks in.

"I'll find your doctor," I say to him softly.

However, his next words chase me out of his hospital room.

"Thank you, nurse."

There are no words for that one. No Tally Landon comeback for those lines once delivered. I am in the deep end of the Tally Landon pool of thought and all alone.

I make my way into the hall in search of his doctors to explain all of this. *To him. To me.*

To try and find some air.

CHAPTER NINE

west coast

TALLY

IT WAS A MEETING. AN INTERVENTION is what I refer to it as now, all this time later. Kimberley Powers flew in from New York. Davis Presley was there. Gina Masterson, Linc's aunt and Davis' sister, was there too, representing the psychiatry side of things but from a family perspective. I remember her looking squeamish, properly sickened as to what would eventually go down; I'll give her that. Uncle Chad was there too, in silent support of his wife. Charlie and Marla were there, siding with me. The only ones to side with me as it turned out.

It was a losing battle.
A setup.
I just didn't know it then.

"He thinks he's at Stanford still playing baseball for the Cardinal. He thinks he's still seeing Nika." I remember my audible gasp at this announcement, which only encouraged the man to go even further. Davis turned to me and said in that indifferent way of his I've come to know over the past two weeks, "He doesn't remember you at all, Tally."

Davis has adopted this official stance of disdain for me since Linc woke up two days ago and as everyone-in-need-to-know began to learn part of his memory was gone. Six years gone. Perhaps, permanently. No one knew for sure. There were no guarantees. We have been constantly reminded of that by all these doctors. Experts. Specialists. Every medical doctor involve with Linc's case at the hospital except for my dad has reminded us of this.

No guarantees. Got it. Now what?

I felt the full force of Davis Presley's hatred of me in this meeting. *I am a problem that needs to be solved. Pronto.*

Linc is to be released from the hospital some time tomorrow. This meeting, this intervention, becomes the subterfuge to that action, I just don't realize it at the time. The press has been hounding all of us. Every time we leave the hospital there is a request from a reporter for an update on Lincoln Presley. Linc remains national news from ESPN to ABC. Everyone wants to know about the baseball pitcher's condition. "Brain surgery can be serious; he may never be the same," one reporter has said.

I try not to watch the coverage because it sickened me and made it worse on all fronts.

News, good or bad, a breaking story is the goal for every reporter camped outside the front of the hospital. It isn't my job to help them out and yet I serve as the tastiest bait even if I don't want to be any part of it; the speculation about Linc and me has already started. Public records of our on-line application for a marriage license have been subsequently discovered and now the questions really begin.

"He was supposed to be getting married to his fiancée, Tally Landon, next month, but public records indicate the two were planning to get married at City Hall in downtown San Francisco the following day, just hours before his unfortunate accident put him in a coma twelve days ago. Ms. Landon refuses to comment on the marriage license application or the couple's future plans which seem to be in question at this point."

"Will the wedding with Lincoln Presley go forward as planned? Let's find out. Ms. Landon, over here, Jay Otter with Sports Network, is it true you two are going forward with your wedding in mid-November now? Can you tell us your plans?"

"Is he going to be all right? Is he talking?"

"Ms. Landon, can you comment?"

"Is it *true* he refuses to see you?" I whirl around at that one and look hard at the reporter who dares to ask me such a thing.

"Not true," I say fiercely but then the barrage of questions hurl from all directions like arrows from a thousand bows.

Holy shit.

I've stepped into hell.

Kimberley Powers comes to my rescue. "Ms. Landon will have no further comment. Yes, she and Lincoln Presley are still engaged and plan to marry when Linc is feeling better. Can you give the woman some space? She's had to put her whole life as well as her wedding plans on hold; back off. *Please*." Kimberley smiles sweetly at the reporters and ushers me through a side entrance to the hospital.

"That was bad," I say in the growing silence as we navigate our way to the ICU.

She gives me a hard look. "Don't talk to them, Tally. Ever. Like never. You'll never satisfy their curiosity. They're under a constant deadline, and they want the story any way they can get it. You think Candy Baxstrom was bad? She was a walk in the park compared to most of the reporters out there. Don't talk to them. Send all the inquiries to me. You've got my card. *Use it*." She smiles, but it doesn't reach her eyes.

"Okay."

"God what a flipping nightmare," she says more to herself.

Now, she won't meet my gaze and I'm left to wonder what we are really talking about here.

Yeah, it's bad.

Linc is a wreck.

So am I.

But we'll get through it.

I know she's upset about Linc; we all are. However, I sense there's more. I ask her as much, but she shakes her head at me and gets a tired smile and asks me if I've eaten.

My food intake is a constant quest for everybody around here. I just roll my eyes and refuse to answer.

Now, some part of me already knows my personal problems are about to get worse. I look over at Kimberley, silently soliciting her support. Her green eyes flash with anger and notable sympathy, but then she shrugs as if it's out of her hands and gives me with the familiar everything-is-going-to-be-fine smile. I know that smile. I use it all the time for every bad or uncomfortable situation I find myself in. Then, it dawns on me. *How gullible am I? How naive?* She works for Davis; she works for Linc as his publicist too. Money will sway and talk and carry the day even in this room. Future wife status be damned. I don't pay her, Linc does.

"Davis, let's not get ahead of ourselves." Kimberley's soothing tone in an obvious attempt to take over before things spin out of control completely. Her gold wedding band catches the light. It is the only sparkle in this cold room.

Minutes ago, Kimberley had walked in here just beaming as the giddy, newly-married bride of only a month or so, but then her smile slid from her lovely face at Davis Presley's opening salvo. "He doesn't remember you at all, Tally."

Actually, the smiles slid from all of our faces at his cruel choice of words.

But it wasn't a lie. It was the truth.

And sometimes, the truth hurts.

Linc doesn't remember me at all.

True.

Kimberley's sadness mirrors mine in every way. This is a nightmare of epic proportions, and I just want to wake up from it.

I met up with her in the restroom just before we were summoned by Davis to this very conference room. I don't know why I was so surprised to see her here in the first place. Of course, public relations would be involved. Linc's image centering around baseball was always at stake, at least from Davis' perspective and probably Kimberley's too. I thought we were past all of that. I should have known we would never be past all of that. Never.

Our small talk consisted of:

"How was Cara?"

"Fine."

"Congrats Again. You two eloping. That would have been nice."

"Thanks. There's been so much turmoil I haven't really even had a chance to think about that anymore."

"I know. So when *was* the big wedding planned?"

Was she said. An interesting choice of word. "We booked the Hollins House for November as plan B or C. After the World Series."

"How's Linc?" She asked in a guarded tone.

"Linc is a longer and very complicated answer," I said with a little sigh. "He doesn't know me. He doesn't remember the last six years of his life. None of it."

The light in her eyes dimmed at that moment. A crevice formed in the middle of her forehead. This brilliant woman was thinking. I didn't register it at the time because I was just happy to see her, to have an ally. She'd taken a step back from me and looked even more uncertain. Then, she seemed to recover, nodding slowly, and finally smiled. "Everything will be fine. I just know it."

Only Marla had been serving as cheerleader for me. The truth was I needed to hear it from someone else. I needed Linc to say it, but Kimberley Powers would have to do.

That was two hours ago, and now we are here.

I helplessly watch as Kimberley gets up from her chair and takes over the room, and motions over to Davis to sit down. Marla grabs for my hand from under the large conference table. Charlie squeezes my left one from the other side. I take these gestures as a good sign. I bow my head down for a few seconds and then glance up and over at Kimberley and just wait.

Somehow, I know this is going to be bad.

Will it be worse than the past two weeks?

That seems impossible.

But, is it?

"There's millions of dollars at risk. His contract. I've read through it. So has his agent. And, please remember Nika Vostrikova works for the Giants. She is *not* our friend, not Linc's anymore, not one of us. Capiche? And we really need to circle the wagons and ensure she doesn't get past security. The Giants don't need to know about his memory loss yet. And they're focused on baseball and the playoffs right now if they can pull those off without Linc."

This is the Kimberley Powers I know and admire. She is so incredibly smart. I am beholden to the idea that she will set all of us straight, so I do not see it coming.

She turns "The thing is…" She forces a smile and looks directly at me. "Tally, the most important thing right now—as Linc's dad has been saying—is that Linc fully concentrate on his recovery and baseball." She's nervous. But Kimberley Powers is never nervous or afraid or shaken, but now her hands tremble as she talks. "We don't know what his pitching is going to look like. We don't know what all he remembers. From what Gina has said we need to reassure him and keep him calm and protect him from unnecessary stress and—"

"From me," I say feeling queasy all at once.

"We need to keep him from unnecessary stress. *Yes.* Right, Gina?" Kimberley glances over at Linc's aunt. I don't miss the uneasy look they share.

"Yes." Gina Masterson levels a steady gaze my way. The chill runs through me at the sympathetic look Linc's aunt is giving me. "Tally, I just want you to know how sorry I am about all of this. I know how terrible this feels for you. I just think, speaking as his aunt, not his psychiatrist, it would be best not to overwhelm him right now. Let's just let him concentrate on his recovery and baseball. We need to keep him away from the press and let him get his balance back. Life balance, I mean."

She smiles. I attempt to return it even though I can feel parts of me actually shatter inside as I begin to comprehend what she's really saying.

You're out.

You're out, Tally.

You're out.

They don't want you here.

They don't want you around Linc confusing him or stressing him out. You're out.

"Mom, do you really think that's the best thing for Linc?" Charlie glances my way; his face is full of empathy. I return his gaze with a small smile of gratitude. "He and Tally are...*epic* in every way. What happens when he suddenly remembers who she is to him and you all have effectively shut her out of his life? What is he going to feel like then?"

"I would be ecstatic if that happened, Charlie. Truly, I would." Gina Masterson reaches out to me from across the table. I release Marla's hand and squeeze the older woman's, but feel uneasy as I do so. "Tally, *trust* us. We all want what is best for Linc. Right now? That's his recovery and baseball, concentrating on his career, and eventually getting his life back. We probably have, what, three months, Davis?"

"Three months. Then, spring practice begins and they'll be looking at him hard. I want to take him to Beau Wilson's camp in LA with private workouts and without the press. In a few months we can see where we are." Davis looks directly at me. "I think we can safely say a wedding of any kind is off. For now," he adds as an afterthought.

"You never liked me." Whoa, a brave salvo that I haven't quite thought through as I say this. Somehow, it seems like I need defending here.

"It's not that."

"Oh, I think it is. You think I'm just in it for Linc's money but you should know I *love* him very much. Ask anyone here." I glance around feeling confident at soliciting support from the others, but only Marla and Charlie actually meet my gaze. Feeling more uneasy, I turn back to Davis. "I *love* him. You can't change that regardless of what you do."

"I think I can," he says quietly. "There's the other matter of the six million dollar signing bonus Linc got from the Angels. We've checked all of his accounts." He glances at Chad Masterson who slowly nods and then both men are looking at me with suspicion, even Gina Masterson begins to look as grim as her husband. "We can't find it. Tell us about the money, Tally. The six million missing from Linc's account. Tell us about *that*."

The room goes deathly quiet.

Everyone looks at me, while the accusation behind the man's words wends its way toward me like a reprisal of the line drive that hit Linc. I actually start to duck before I get my act together and stammer an answer. "You think...I took his six million dollars from him? I don't have his money." I break from Davis Presley's accusatory gaze and look around the conference table noting the sudden distrust that appears on the faces of just about everyone here. "I gave Linc a cashier's check months ago." My words sound hollow even to me as the shock of being accused settles in. "Rob Thorn made it out to him. This was after Nika took Linc's bonus in the first place. *Unauthorized*, I might add. Why don't you accuse *her*?" I glare at him but he remains resolute. He's just standing there like he's already won. "Like I said," I say again. "I returned all six million of his signing bonus to him when I got first got here in San Fran at the end of July." I shrug attempting to appear nonchalant, but my shoulders shake as the fear deep inside begins to reverberate with me. *They don't believe me.* "I assume Linc cashed the check after I gave it back to him. We didn't talk about the money after that. We didn't—"

"You've been known to lie." Davis' eyes narrow as he attempt to stare me down.

True.

I swallow hard and look only at him while I can feel everyone else staring at me. There have been a number of times I lied in the past. To Linc. To everyone.

So this is what payback feels like.

I take a shallow breath, willing myself to keep it together and try to defend myself. *He hates me. He really hates me.* The realization makes me shudder and I struggle to control it.

"I don't have his money," I say looking only at Davis. He raises an eyebrow and then looks around the room at everyone else soliciting their support. Suddenly, I'm very tired. I think the stress of all of this has finally caught up to me. That and the fact that life, as I know it, is being dismantled right in front of me by Linc's father.

"We haven't co-mingled our funds or our stuff," I say with disquiet. "He's been mostly living at the guest house. We were trying to keep things fairly normal for Cara until we got married."

"Which isn't happening *now* or any time soon."

The vehemence with which Davis has said this is both devastating and alarming all over again. I can't quite hide the sudden onset of panic. I start to shake. My heart beats wildly out of control. *No panic attack now. Not in front of all these people. That will just make me look even more guilty.*

Keep it together. Keep it together.

"We need to find the money," Kimberley says to me gently from my far left.

I slowly nod, shamed into silence however innocent I might be. My mind races. *What did Linc do with the money?*

This is a nightmare. It just got worse for me. His father thinks I've stolen Linc's money. Linc's family looks at me with a renewed sense of distrust except for Charlie and Marla.

Even Kimberley looks unsure of herself. She bites at her lip and stares at me, as if by doing so long enough, I will come up with a different answer they can all live with. Then she shrugs, helpless all at once. "We need to find the money, Tally," she says again.

"Yes, we do," I say as the accusation begins to resonate with the entire room made up mostly of Linc's family, and I begin to feel more uneasy.

"Come on. This is ridiculous!" Marla glares over at Davis, but looks less certain as she takes in the grim expressions all around the table.

Where is the money? I can see them all thinking it as they take turns looking at me as if I'll suddenly have a different answer from *I don't know.* We never talked about the money. I handed Linc the check for six million dollars and we moved on. Obviously, this crowd doesn't believe that particular scenario. The silence around the room gets deafening. I focus on breathing while my head swirls with endless possibilities as to what Linc actually did with the money. "I didn't take it," I finally whisper to Marla when the silence becomes almost unbearable.

"I know," she says grabbing one of my hands.

Charlie loosely puts his arm around my shoulders. "We'll find the money, Tally."

"Sure. I know." I give them both a weak smile.

But then, Davis decides to have the last word as he slowly makes his way to the conference room door. When he passes me, he gets this triumphant, little smile that only I must see that clearly conveys he got what he wanted—I'm out of Linc's life and nobody believes me. "Kimberley will keep you informed. Right now, I think it's best for you to stay out of Linc's life until we get a few of our questions answered."

My supposed future father-in-law's last hateful glance and dismissive words lance right through me. His open hostility for me begins to weigh me down. It feels as if I've been shot. In some ways, I think I have. The shock and disbelief of the situation begin to take me over. I stare with an open mouth at the closed door after he leaves and attempt to find air.

A part of me can't believe this is happening. I lied in the past. To myself. To Linc. To everyone. But this? This is unbelievable. I stand accused and no one believes me when I say I don't know what happened to the money. I can feel their questioning glances as they each take turns looking my way. Still, I attempt to keep it together and ready my performance for the ones who remain. I paste on my best smile and grace them all with it while gathering up my things and preparing to leave. Marla hugs me, but then I pull away from her in an effort to keep it together in front of all of them.

"No, it's okay. I'm all right. I need to make a phone call or two. Find Linc's money, I guess." I give her a tight smile. "I promise; I'll call you later."

I practically run from the conference room and race down the hallway, intent on escape in any way I can find it. There's a hospital staff restroom marked in familiar blue type. S-T-A-F-F. It's unlocked. I gratefully slip inside. The walls close in as I slowly sink to the floor. I am beholden to the darkness and the absolute of silence. I close my eyes. *I can't breathe. Get used to it.*

CHAPTER
TEN

blurry

LINC

I HOLD OUT THE PHOTOGRAPH FOR MY dad to see, intent on getting answers because of the evasive way everyone treats me now from the doctors to my dad to my aunt Gina, even Kimberley, and it's pissing me off. Their combined protective attitude is driving me crazy. *Crazier.* My head pounds, and it appears; I will have to get used to that too. "Tell me who she is to me. I found this in my wallet today when you went out for some coffee. This girl. Who is she? She looks like the nurse who was here when I first woke up, but then in this photograph she looks younger. Do I know her? Who is she? What's her name? Who is she to me?"

My dad looks uneasy and seems to search around the room for

reinforcements, but Kimberley left about an hour ago to go check into her hotel at about the same time Aunt Gina and Uncle Chad took off. Other than in an aside with Kimberley without my dad hearing where she told me that Nika was no longer in the picture with me and was definitely off-limits and under no circumstances was it okay for me to contact her. Kimberley actually deleted Nika Vostrikova's number from my cell phone 'for my own good,' as Kimmy put it. Then, she'd rushed off without answering any more of my other questions.

So now, it really is just me and my dad. It's *always* been me and Dad. For a long enough while anyway, after Mom died along with my older brother Elliott in that car accident. Dad is all I've got, which can be both alarming and consoling at the exact same time. *Like now.*

"I'm not sure who she is anymore." Resigned, my dad takes a deep breath then looks at me intently, prepared to give the big speech—the one I've heard a hundred times before. I brace myself for the guilt that tends to swallow me whole when he delivers this particular rendition.

"I just want what's best for you. You know that, right?"
Here we go.
I nod like I always do.

"She's a distraction, this girl. From baseball. The thing you've put your life's work into. And there's the discrepancy of the money—your six million dollar bonus. The money isn't there. And as I said, I'm not sure who she is anymore." He gets this grim look that seems to center around the corners of his mouth.

"You think this girl took my money? My signing bonus?"

"Your account registers a little over a hundred grand. The rest is gone. She says she doesn't know where it is or what you've done with it. And you—"

"I can't remember." I sigh and try not to move my head because the pain rages and all I want to really do is yell or something. I held out on the drugs they give me for pain because I don't want to get dependent on pills to solve this particular problem. Headaches. Memory loss. My new nemeses. The painkillers make me drowsy. I'm hoping by not taking them I can solve the memory thing, get back to my life, and pitch a baseball as well as I was able to a few weeks ago. Now, I'm regretting that decision of not taking the meds. I look at my father more closely because it seems like he's holding something back from me. "Who is she? And does she seem like the type of girl that would lie about something like that?"

He sighs and then shakes his head. "She can't be trusted. She's lied to you before."

"About *what*?"

"Pretty much everything. She's trouble, Linc. For you. For all of us. She can't tell us where the money is. Maybe, she had it planned all along." My dad gets this troubled look as if he can't quite believe it himself—what he's essentially saying. "She's trouble. Always has been. Since day one. Ask Kimberley if you don't believe me."

"I believe you." I cringe feeling uneasy all at once for saying this. *Why? I don't know.* But as soon as I say this to my dad the air rushes from my lungs. I cough, feeling uneasy all at once. "Can you get me some water? God, I'm so thirsty all the time now."

"It's probably the medication they have you on." My dad reaches for a plastic cup, fills it, and hands it to me. I drink it down and he fills it up again. I drink that one down too.

I pick up the photograph and stare at it some more, wracking my brain trying to remember. *But there is nothing familiar about this girl in the photograph. Nothing.*

"Who is she to me?" I finally ask again.

"I already *told* you. She's nobody. And she's trouble. Don't worry about it or *her*. I'll handle things."

My father gets up and goes and stares out the window. A clear sign that he is done with this particular conversation.

"Dad," I say with growing irritation, "does she seem like the type of girl who would lie about things? Or worse, take my money?"

"I've lied before, but I don't lie anymore. To you. Not to anyone anymore, actually." A woman's voice reaches us from the now open doorway. We both look up.

And, there she is—the girl from the photograph—the same girl I woke up to seeing, just days ago. The one I can't quite get out of my mind, although, at times, I would like to because she eerily resonates with the persistent timed arrival of my headaches.

She stands there—framed by the doorway like a portrait—looking defiant. Her green eyes gleam like flawless emeralds. It does not take a rocket scientist to figure out that she is royally pissed. Her entire stature exudes a certain fury.

"You want answers. I'm here to provide them. You accuse me of taking his money without so much as a paper trail to back up your claims. Oh no, Davis Presley, world famous baseball player, doesn't need facts or the *truth*. No, all you do is wield an unfounded accusation around like a sword among your family and my friends in an attempt to crucify me, Davis."

She's said my father's name with such loathing I begin to sweat.
Nobody challenges my father.
Nobody. Not even me.

And yet, I find her incredibly fascinating and brave. I can't help but watch her as she stalks into the hospital room. Her fury protects her like an invisible shield even though her hands shake as she holds up a sheaf of papers toward my dad.

"He bought a house in Sea Cliff. Five bedrooms. Two masters. Seven Bathrooms. Four-car garage. Grass. Trees. Bay view. All cash. It closes in a few months. Here's the real estate agent's number; you can call her and *verify* what I've just told you."

Profound sadness crosses her face and she absently wipes at her eyes and then brushes back her long dark hair and stares hard at my dad.

"I think it was supposed to be a surprise." She gets this tired little smile and then she looks over at me and it disappears. "Anyway. Problem solved. Call off your dogs," she says, looking back at my dad who just stares at her with his mouth open.

She turns from him and purposefully walks over to me and hands me the papers. "Here's what you did with the six million. Sorry," she says, shyly dipping her head at me. "You paid five million, nine hundred thousand dollars and change and bought a house, Elvis."

I hold my breath in an attempt to make sense out of what all she's just said.
She is captivating and I am…captivated by her.
Finally I say, "why did you just call me that? *Elvis*."
She shrugs. "I always call you that."

"Why?" I lean in close to her face. *Cloves. Vanilla.* Her scent is amazing. I start to smile.

She bites at her lip and looks uncertain and glances over at my dad with this recognizable hostility.

What did he do to you?

"You shouldn't be in here," my dad says. "It's *immediate family only* as I instructed."

"Have me arrested then," she says softly glancing back at me with this wicked half-smile. "My *dad* arranged it. It's fine. Go…" She waves a dismissive hand back toward my dad but leaves the rest unsaid, apparently realizing she's probably taken the hostility with *the famous Davis Presley* a little too far.

"Dad, give us a minute," I say sharply in an attempt to help her out. The thing is I rarely go up against my dad, but for some reason I feel compelled to do so with this girl here now. *She gives me some extraordinary power, this girl. Or permission to be defiant. Or some kind of courage. One of those. Or, all of them.*

My father looks increasingly offended by this turn of events—this girl's sudden arrival on scene and my unusual defiance. I think he's about to argue the point of me actually *telling* him to leave instead of asking, but then she turns to him and says in a low voice that I somehow deem incredibly sexy, "I've got this, Davis. I won't say anything to upset him. *I get it.* It's all about *baseball*."

She's said the word *baseball* like it's a swear word. I imagine she uses those quite well too.

She turns back to me and rolls her eyes and then rewards me with this little angelic smile that my father can't see. The gleam is back in her eyes, and she raises her chin defiantly and just looks at me, silently imploring me to make him go.

"Dad. A minute." *Holy shit. It is liberating to go against my dad.* "And you don't like baseball," I say softly smiling at her again.

"I'm not a fan."

My dad snorts at her honest answer, but then he surprisingly leaves the room and the two of us alone.

A long silence ensues. It appears that since it is now just the two of us we've both run out of things to say to each other.

Wary.

We are wary of each other as if it is our first date and we are filled with complete awkwardness.

"How are you?" She finally asks drawing in her breath so slowly it's as if doing so requires her sole concentration.

"I have a raging headache. Probably should have taken the pain-killers they offered up a few hours ago."

She snatches up the call receiver that dangles at the side of my hospital bed and presses the button. When a nurse answers and talks through the speaker at us, she says, "Mr. Presley is in a lot of pain. His head hurts. Can we give him something?"

She gives me a conspiratorial smile at the word *we* and then proceeds to catch me watching her face and the way her lips part. She gestures with her small hands and tilts her head to one side as she hangs up the call button.

I've seen her do this before. Tilt her head like that.

I ignore the throbbing headache and dazedly sit up in bed a little straighter in a vague attempt to concentrate more fully upon her. Meanwhile, her scent intoxicates me as she shifts around the edge of the bed and stirs the air with her very presence.

She clasps her arms around her knees in an effort to get comfortable or to just keep moving I'm not really sure which. She's wearing black jeans and a matching T-shirt. I decide this must be her signature style.

Awkward. She's caught me examining her fashion choices and now subconsciously pulls at the neckline of her T-shirt.

"So, you're a nurse," I say in an attempt to say something meaningful and cover up the fact that I was checking her out so closely.

"Not a nurse." She looks amused and gets this ghost of a smile, unable to stop herself.

We share this weird moment and just stare at each other some more.

The thing is if she could read my mind, she might actually freak out because I want to feel her lips on mine. I really want to kiss her however inappropriate that might be. *She's attractive. Seriously attractive.*

It must be pheromones or something, or the remnants of all the drugs in my system from the past couple of weeks, I'm not sure.

She is causing all kinds of strange sensations for me. And so, yes, if watching her facial expressions change, or watching her body gracefully move through time, or seeing her lips part whenever she speaks over the next hour of time, is part of the plan, I am all for it.

She's talking, but I can't hear a word she's saying because my heart beats so damn loud and fast. I just nod instead.

The hospital door swings open. It takes us both by surprise. Our mouths partially drop open as if synchronized. We exchange this conspiring look rimmed with panic as if it might be my father returning all too soon.

But it's just Elissa, the night nurse, who hands me a paper cup of pills and a fresh glass of water and watches me as I take the medication. Then, she makes a note on her hand-held chart, refills my water pitcher, and continues to chatter away to both of us.

Meanwhile, this girl and I share a look that seems to connect us almost physically. *We are bound, somehow, her and I.*

I start to smile and she slowly returns it.

Elissa must see our heady exchange because she sighs to herself and exits the room within next ten seconds. We both take a breath at the exact same moment as the door closes behind her.

"Not a nurse," I say softly again in an attempt to restart the conversation with this beautiful girl.

She slides off the bed and away from me with a little laugh. "Not a nurse. I'm a dancer."

She shakes her head side-to-side and starts to laugh. "Not that *kind*, Elvis." Then she looks troubled by what she's just said and looks unsure as to what she should say next. After a minute or so, she says, "I dance for the San Francisco Ballet Company. Lead role in *Giselle*, actually. *Hopefully.* My boss? Mikhail Rostov? He's not too happy with me right now. C'est la vie. Right?"

She does this little pirouette. That's when I notice the ballet slipper-like shoes on her feet. I grin at her.

"Can you do the toe thing with the shoes?"

Her smile falters as if she's remembered something that can only make her sad. She kind of gasps at the air before saying, "I can, but not today. I've spent the last few weeks away from rehearsals so I'm not in my finest form today." She gets this haunted look, similar to my father's. It's always how I know he's missing my mom. It's uncanny. The look on her face is exactly the same as my dad's.

"Can I see you dance sometime?"

"Sure. That would be great." She looks even more uneasy and bites at her lip again. "There's more to say. Just not today. I think your father's right about that. You need to concentrate on your recovery right now. I talked to Kimberley after the big meeting, and she said—"

"What big meeting?" I ask, confused and irritated with her all at once. The drugs aren't working yet. My head starts to really pound, and this girl suddenly isn't making sense anymore. "You've got to tell me what's going on. No one else will."

"There was a big meeting. What one might call an *intervention*." She smirks at saying the last word, but then her features harden. She's angry again. It's written all over her face.

I go for a change of topic. "I leave for LA for Beau Wilson's camp tomorrow as soon as they let me out of this place."

"It's always about baseball. Isn't it, Linc? It always has been. No matter that you almost get yourself killed with that line drive. Baseball is all that matters."

"Well, yeah, that's all there is."

She takes another step back. "Well, when you finally figure out what's more important than baseball, you give me a call."

"Baby, I don't even know your name, let alone have your number, but I'd love to call you sometime, if you—"

"You're trying to pick me up with that line?" She shakes her head in disgust. "Word of advice here. Don't call me *baby* like ever. I hate that term of endearment. I really do." She rolls her eyes, sighs big, and then digs her iPhone out of her bag and checks the time. "Look, I've got to go. I've got a late rehearsal, and Mikhail said he'd replace me if I didn't show tonight."

Now she looks as if I've disappointed her in every possible way.

"Don't go yet. *Stay*."

My word choice seems to make it even worse. She looks even more unhappy.

"No. I really need to go. I've said too much already and we certainly don't want you even more *confused* than you already are."

She's not exactly sounding sympathetic and for some reason her jeering attitude seriously pisses me off.

"I've got a head injury, *baby*...cut me some slack."

"No slack, *baby*." She starts for the door without a backward glance.

"Hey, *come on*, wait a minute. I don't even know your name. How will I find you? When will I see you again?"

I'm desperate now and fear an ending because I've mangled up the last five minutes with her. She's pissed and disappointed in me for calling her *baby* again and who knows what all else. I can see it in the way her hands shakes and the way she stalks toward the door. I know what that kind of fury feels like. Then my own anger comes out of nowhere because this supposed truth-telling session has been little more than a dangerous sexy taunt and a waste of my damn time.

"You're supposed to be giving me the answers here. You're supposed to tell me the truth and not keep me in the dark. You're not supposed to *lie*!" My voice gets louder with each word.

She turns back looking stunned as if I've never yelled at her before. *Maybe, I haven't.* I attempt to clamp down on my rising anger and take in some air hoping it will lead me straight back to calm like the counselors here keep telling me it will.

"I'm *not* lying to you," she says quietly. "And we don't *fight. Hardly ever*." She takes an unsteady step toward me. "We don't fight. We don't...fight." She brushes at her face and then looks away from me. When she turns back I can clearly see the grief that swells her features and the tears that rim her eyes. "I don't even know who you are anymore," she whispers in defeat, lifting her arms, looking helpless. "Who are you?"

"Who. Are. *You*?" I shout the words back at her, but get uneasy when she actually flinches as if I've just slapped her.

Now, she stares at me, transfixed, for a full minute as if she can't quite believe what she's just heard me say. Then, she gasps for air as if all the oxygen has somehow been sucked out of the room. "I'm no one. Just a girl you hooked up with one-night."

She winces and then smiles ever so slightly. "I'm just one of those mistakes you wished you'd never made and most likely the one person you never should have laid eyes upon. That's me," she says with disquiet and takes an unsteady breath but looks determined to finish what she has to say. "The thing is…the thing is, it will always come back to baseball, won't it; Elvis?"

She nods while a single tear starts to make its way down on her face. She impatiently wipes at it with the back of her hand and forms this tight smile with her lips and then suddenly laughs. But it's a bitter sound, not joyous.

"I was the best one-night stand you'll ever have, but that was a long time ago—a time you don't even remember. So, let's just forget the whole thing. Just say our goodbyes and move on, shall we? And I didn't take your money and now that that's all straightened out, just get your dad to stop accusing me of things like that. *Enough* already. *I get it.* And just know that I wouldn't lie to you. I actually never really did."

"*Never really did?*" She is seriously pissing me off right now for some inexplicable reason and my head hurts and the meds Elissa gave me haven't kicked in yet.

"Forget it. When you're feeling up to it, give my lawyer a call, and we can arrange things through him."

"What lawyer? Why would I need a *lawyer* to talk to you?" *Wrong question.* I see it in the withering look she throws my way. Her beautiful green eyes narrow further as she studies me and my response to this news that she was a one-night stand at some point in my forgotten life. *I'm going to fuck this up. I just know it.*

"The thing is I can't be the only one who remembers." And then she just stops talking for a moment as if taking in the full measure of her own words and starts to nod as if she's suddenly figured out an answer to a really hard question she already knew. "I'm sorry. I just can't do this. I wish…I wish I could be that strong for both of us. I really do but I have to think of... And I can't do this." She waves her arm wides around the room and gets this dazed look as she absently wipes away her tears. "It is truly hard to compete with America's favorite pastime, and you have to really love it." Her smile disappears completely. "And I just don't."

And then she leaves.

She leaves without a backward glance at me.

And I let her go because, somehow, I know this is the way we've said good-bye before.

My hands shake.

Despite the tremors, I pour myself another glass of water and drink it down.

Then, I drink another.

And another.

But no matter how many times I try to quench this thirst that rages up deep inside of me, I can't find enough water.

Anywhere.

CHAPTER

ELEVEN

realize

TALLY

I SIT IN THE MIDDLE OF A metal bench cloistered at the front entrance of the hospital between two Magnolia trees and keep my face hidden from the two sports reporters I recognize from Chronicle. The last thing I want is to be asked about Lincoln Presley. I pull Linc's Giants baseball cap that I found earlier in my bag lower over my face and avoid eye contact with them altogether.

A cool breeze messes with my hair. The chill in the air eventually makes its way through my clothes.

And yet I feel almost nothing.

Fall is almost here. I refuse to examine what that means.

Time has stopped in my world.

I am dead inside.
Who cares what time it is?
Or what day?
Or month.
Or year.
It's all gone.

There is just this incredible amount of emptiness but it is surprisingly so heavy; it weighs me down.

There is nothing left. Nothing to look forward to.
Nothing left.

Well, there's Cara. Mom. Dad. Tommy. I'm not completely alone. It just feels like it.

I take an unsteady breath and breathe out.

My lips still work.

I stare at my phone for a few minutes and then send the inevitable text to my mother.

"Hey, I've got to go by the studio for a few hours. You good? Cara good?"

Johnny-on-it replies within thirty seconds. "We're fine. You okay?"

Am I okay?
Am I okay?
Will I ever be okay?
Probably not.

I text back: "I'm fine. Good. Linc's good too."

I add this little tidbit because I don't want to get into it all quite yet about Linc and me. *Not yet.* I'll deal with my parents later when I pick up Cara. Hours from now, when I trudge the two miles from the studio to Mom and Dad's, and pick up Cara, and just before the two of us take the Metro home, right then I'll tell my parents what I know to be true; that we're over.

I practice these words out-loud. "We're over." I say them at least ten times until just the idea of us being over begins to resonate. Yes, I'll tell them when the weight of the world and this confounding emptiness doesn't crush me quite so much.

Then, I'll tell them.

That's when I will tell myself too; and I'll believe it, but only then.

My mind races through the scene with Linc this last half hour. Fragments, like glass, cut at me. *Where did it all go wrong?* I had this naive idea that producing the papers for the house in Sea Cliff would somehow change everything, but nothing changed.

He doesn't remember me.

And I need to forget him.

I need to move on. Let go.

A tear trails down my face. I angrily wipe it away.

I go over the unexpected father and son scene from a half hour in my mind that I was able to witness from my unique vantage point just outside of Linc's hospital room. Unfortunately, I got to hear the hatchet job done on my character by Linc's father. His venomous words are still fresh in my memory. The absolute fury for Linc's dad resides there too. And this little modicum of disgust—this seed of hatred that has been consciously planted, however subconscious— begins to take root for Linc there too. It takes root inside my heart and seemingly attempts to destroy it.

I can never believe in love again. This much I know about myself.

Of course, Davis Presley is to blame for all of this, but Linc's utter and absolute acquiescence in believing the worst about me and choosing baseball once again is a fresh assault on my psyche. I can't quite shake the fury I have for him now. The loathing. The disgust. The acrimony. My rage at Lincoln Presley is incalculable. My love for him begins to die beneath the weight of all these hostile feelings that have burst forth and all but taken over.

Sure, I know he's a victim in all of this. He's the one that got hit in the head with a baseball, but does he have to be so oblivious about the two of us and easily accept every lie his father has told him about me? I think I hate him now. I really think I do. Maybe I never really loved him that I'm able to give up on us so easily.

Empty. I feel empty.

I have to hope that feeling absolutely nothing is enough to get through the next part of all of this.

Please God, let it be enough.

Marla stands before me.

How long has she been here?

It's hard to tell.

I stare up into her face. Mine unreadable. I try to hold onto nice words and simple gestures. The depth of my anger starts to drown me but I claw my way to the surface of sanity and conjure up a smile for her.

Meanwhile her face twists up reflecting a mixture of sympathy and guilt.

Nobody wants to be Tally Landon like ever.

"Hey, you okay?" She asks gently.

Such simple words but such a loaded question.

"I'm fine."

She starts to laugh at my easy answer but then stops. "You're sure you're okay? I thought you were going to go talk to Linc about the mortgage papers you found, but you're out here..." Her words trail off. She must get a glimpse of the fury. I'm sure my eyes glow Incredible Hulk green. I look away but the Hulk thought causes me to emit this weird laugh and when I glance up now she really looks worried.

Because I am crazy and she knows it.

"I *did* talk to him. It's all straightened out. The mystery of the missing six million is solved. He bought a house. It's all good." I practically purr the words like a cat would. "But I do need to get to the studio. I could use a ride, so I get there on time because if I'm late it will further fuel Mikhail's crusade in firing my awesome ass and then he'll finally have the valid reason he's been seeking." I smile wide.

Marla looks confused by the Cheshire Cat smile, but she slowly nods as she seems to go over my answers in her head, one by one. "Okay. Okay. Charlie will be right down. We can drop you off. I don't want you taking the metro this late at night. And anyway it will give us a chance to talk."

"Sure."

Talk. *Great.*

Breathe. Just breathe.

Smile and curtsy if necessary.

Get up from the bench and make your way over to her car.

Smile at her again.

Nod at what she says even though you can't understand or hear a word she says.

"I *said*, when are you going to talk to Linc again?" Marla rolls her eyes at my lack of response.

"Tomorrow."

That's the nice thing about best friends; they believe you when the world doesn't, even when what you say isn't true. She nods and her lips curve into this sweet smile. *Marla, my life saver, rescues me once again.*

I climb into the back of her SUV and close the door. I try not to think about the almost three months before when Linc proposed to me in this very beast of a car. That's another lifetime. One that is clearly now gone. I look out the dark window while Marla goes on about Elliott and Cara until Charlie arrives a few minutes later. He gives me a sympathetic look while Marla fills him in about my plans to talk to Linc again tomorrow and the mortgage stuff I found for the house Linc bought in Sea Cliff. All is right with the world again from everyone's point of view, except mine. Yay! I'm no longer accused of a being a thief. Although Davis never really apologized to me for that.

I look out the window as we move through the parking lot and attempt to concentrate on moving air in and out of my lungs as we leave.

"Tomorrow," Charlie says, looking at me in the rearview mirror.

"Tomorrow. Because tomorrow is another day," I say from the backseat. The two exchange a peculiar look at my silly answer.

That's right I don't make any sense, but no one cares. No one notices, not for long anyway.

A half-hour later, I say good-bye to Charlie and Marla, thank them for the ride, and promise I'll talk to Linc again tomorrow. They miss my sarcasm when I once again say, "After all, tomorrow is another day." Personifying Scarlet O'Hara only makes sense to me. I laugh and manage to wave at them at the same time and soon their SUV is out of sight. They are forty miles from home. They have been going back and forth for days now. For Linc. For me. I love them, but a part of me is relieved to see them go so I can be alone.

Alone.

I stand there outside the dance studio for another five minutes acknowledging the time while it silently ticks off. There's a buzzing sound in my ears. It takes a few seconds to make the connection that I've been holding my breath and could in fact pass out from the lack of oxygen to my brain.

This is going to be a problem. Not being able to breathe. I just know it.

I'm alone.

Insert the key to the back door side entrance. Take the long way to the dressing room. Put on rehearsal clothes. Pin up your hair. Stretch before you break something or break into two. One of those.

Slowly, I make my way to the stage only seven minutes late to night rehearsal. I've missed more than two weeks of them.

There will be a heavy price to pay.

This I know.

I smile at the crowd of dancers as they step back and make way for me. I go to the center of the stage.

Mikhail Rostov is yelling. He is always yelling. Right now, the pianist is his target, but I prepare for it to be me. I'll be next.

My smile widens. I pose in first position knowing full well he will make me wait. I will stand this way for ten minutes if I have to. I will wait and face Mikhail Rostov with a smile. My best one because, as if today hasn't been hard enough already, now I have to dance like I care to save my job.

And even though I can't really breathe. Even though I feel as if I'm suffocating every time I try to take a breath because there just isn't any more air left in the world for me. Even then. I will dance because ballet and Cara are all I have left.

And breathing? Actually, not being able to breathe?

I'll just have to get used to it.

PART 2

water

CHAPTER TWELVE

heartbreak hotel

LINC

Two months in LA does nothing in resolving my headaches. They just keep getting worse. I give up on the idea of forgoing medication—going it alone—and start popping pills more frequently in a fervent search at experiencing some kind of relief from the painful pressure that continuously swirls through my head. Plus, no matter how much water I drink down, the raging thirst still plagues me.

Beau Wilson's baseball camp only confirms everyone's worst fear—I've lost my edge.

Now, we're all intent on me getting it back.

It is our only focus.

Kimberley's familiar stilettos can be heard along the linoleum floor as she stalks down the hallway toward my room. She never walks. Not that one. I knew she'd be flying in sometime today. I shouldn't be surprised she got to Beau Wilson's camp so fast after her phone call to one of my coaches as soon as she landed at LAX.

Her dolled-up self appears in the my doorway within seconds.

I was supposed to be resting and then expected to go at it again in a couple of hours, but all I've done is lay here and contemplate how fucked-up everything is. So Kimberley Powers is a welcome sight because the past eight weeks have been hell. Maybe she can figure all of this out for me.

After all, that's what friends are for.

"I saw the tail end of your session. Your fastball isn't fast and your slider is M-I-A." She gets this vexed look as her lips clamp down in a thin line and she is definitely not happy

She's worried.

Everyone's worried.

Welcome to the fucking club.

"But the food's great here. Thanks for the recap. Anything else?"

I don't attempt to be charming. Right now, I save every ounce of enthusiasm I can find for appearing positive and completely open to the constant flow of suggestions and just super fantastic advice that everyone else who has been here with me for the past two months has thrown my way.

Kimberley just got here. Some part of me resents her for the late arrival. Where the hell has she been all these weeks while I've suffered with overly helpful coaching from just about everyone but the maid around here? It's not fair that I resent her for having a life outside of the dark abyss I find myself in. But I can't throw a baseball. So who cares how she feels?

I can't throw a baseball.

Where the hell does that leave me?

Nowhere.

The futility tears me up inside where no one can see it. *Failing.* One of my biggest fears seems intent on staying around a long time.

I can't throw a baseball.

Now what?

The contents from my stomach starts to rear up in my throat as the fear gets unleashed. *Holy shit. I can't throw a baseball.* I sit up quickly to stave off the nausea swinging my feet to the floor. *Steady.* Nap time is clearly over in this little league baseball of a place. No matter that the rest did absolutely nothing for me.

My head still pounds. The pain never rests, not for one second. It's just this dull ache designated to follow me around wherever I go.

Frustrated, I grab the nearest glass of water, brush the little white pills I set up earlier into my hand, and pop them directly into my mouth before Kimberley has a chance to say something about it.

"Shouldn't you take it easy on those?" She gets the concerned sisterly look I know too well. Her mouth draws in further at the corners as she eyes the half-empty pill bottle and seems to do an automatic count on how many I've taken. Her ever watchful green eyes narrow in on my face and begin to judge me like everyone else does around here.

I glare back at her, hold up my finger and gulp more water to avoid a word exchange for another minute or two. "Back off, Kimmy," I finally say wiping my mouth with the back of my hand. She doesn't like to be called Kimmy by anyone other than a select few of her closest friends, but I ignore her warning glance and go on. "Besides, they just take the edge off. Nothing to worry about."

"Yeah. Tell that to the subculture of addicts across America who are addicted to painkillers. You need to be *careful.*"

I sigh big. "Please don't tell me what to do. My dad is already way over the line with that shit as it is. Oh and as is the *famous Beau Wilson.*" I affect the nasally, southern accent of this place's owner like a natural.

Kimberley actually laughs and then nods with approval of my impersonation. On my dad and Beau Wilson, we apparently agree. On the pills, probably not so much.

"Obviously, this isn't working. I think what you need is a break from it all. The experts in baseball and even your prized medical team don't seem to have all the answers, so I'm here to break you out of this place for the afternoon," she says in a low voice as if we're being watched.

Maybe we are.

"We're going somewhere?" I whisper sounding hopeful like I'm ten or something. "You'd think I would have thought up that idea on my own."

"Clearly you're not thinking *clearly*." She gets this wicked smile at her own redundant turn of phrase and then manages to look amazingly apologetic. "I'm sorry it took so long to get back here. It's been crazy the past several weeks, and I was really hoping things would come together for you here. I should have known it wouldn't be that easy. I have a direct flight to Miami tonight to meet up with Brad. We're headed to the Caribbean through Christmas. Can you handle another couple of weeks or so before I get back to LA again? Maybe things will come together and finally get easier."

"Nothing is coming easy. My balance is way off. I can't even find the strike zone with my eyes open, or a flashlight." I laugh a little. "We tried that. One night Beau had me pitching in the dark with some glow-in-the-dark baseball. Jesus Christ, Kimberley, *in the dark*. What's that all about? It's been a fucking nightmare."

I shake my head side-to-side. "They get these expectant looks like kids pressed up against the window of a candy store, and I wipe it from their faces with every pitch I throw." I groan and shake my head. "I really don't know what to do anymore. It's all fucked up."

"Where's your cell phone by the way?" Kimberley asks rolling her eyes at my obvious feel-sorry-for-me speech.

"On the charger. Over there." I point to the far wall. "My battery ran out. My voicemail is full; I haven't checked it…in weeks."

I haven't checked it since my life went to shit.

I don't share this with Kimberley.

I don't fucking care.

"Which explains why you haven't answered *any* of my calls. No wonder I had to call the field coach." She shoots me another dirty look.

"You're resourceful. You figured it out. Look, I've been too busy trying to remember how to pitch a baseball and resuscitate my dying career. The hand-wringing around here is mind boggling, and it gets worse with every workout. If I could remember anything, maybe everything would come together for me again, but my brain hurts from trying to remember any of it."

Kimberley looks sympathetic for about all of ten seconds then she shakes her finger at me. "You're kind of whining, Linc. It's really *not* attractive. Maybe what you actually need to do is stop trying so hard and focus on something else besides baseball."

I glance up. "What, did you just say?"

"I said stop trying so hard and focus on something else besides baseball."

"Kimmy, I say this with as much love as I can muster, fuck off. I've got this. On my own. I don't need you here giving me advice about how many pills I take or when I take them or how to throw a baseball. Back off!"

My headache worsens. I get up and start pacing hoping the movement will cause a different outcome.

Maybe I do need to focus on something else besides baseball. But why would I do that? What else is there?

That girl at the hospital the last night I was there said this too, but why? Why did she say it? And where did she go? *Miss Vanilla and Cloves* disappeared.

Then I checked out.

The headaches continue to rage. Baseball seems to have deserted me. And drugs are good. The summation of my life's existence right now.

"You okay?" Kimberley's frowning at me.

My little speech has pissed her off. The weird thing is I do not care. I do not fucking care.

"Never better." I stop pacing trying to recall that girl's face but it fades away from me. The drug starts to kick in. It feels like I've drunk about five beers in quick succession. Something I normally would never do, but when the drug kicks in like this, the pain goes away for a little while. I nod at Kimberley even though she hasn't said anything.

"You sure you're okay?" Kimberley asks for the what must be the fifth time.

I fill up my glass with more water and drink it down. "Never better." My problems with baseball float away from me. Well, everything floats way from me. I beg off from going with Kimberley and tell her I'm too tired to go out. She looks disappointed but then I sense her relief. She has a flight to catch to the Caribbean with Brad. *She has a life.* She has a career and a free-flowing, positive cash flow.

Right now, I have none of those things. I bought a house for some unknowable reason that has tied up all my available cash. I have a life I don't remember, and I can't throw a baseball even if it would save my life or at the very least my career. *I have nothing. I can't remember my past. I can't fucking see my future.*

The anger comes on and I wield it like a lightsaber her way. "Hey, I need to get some rest. I've got another practice this afternoon. Rain check. Go catch your flight. I'll see you at the end of the month. Maybe we can do New Year's together or something."

"Are you sure?" She stands in the doorway looking more uncertain and not used to being dismissed like this and definitely not by me from what I *remember.*

"Never better. Stop worrying so fucking much, Kimmy. Just go. I've got this."

"Call me later," she says while her jaw works double-time.

I know she's pissed at me for treating her this way. I don't care.

"Just go," I say. "I've got another session this afternoon. I've got this. Quit with the hand-wringing." I force myself to smile and keep my temper in check. "I'll figure it out on my own. Just enjoy the beach and Brad. You got that, Ms. Powers? I mean, *Mrs. Stevenson.* I've got to remember you're married these days. Look, just handle my publicity stuff when it comes up. No interviews for a while. Just let me concentrate on baseball and getting it all back together."

"I'll talk to Brad."

"Yeah, *do* that. Talk to Brad. I'm sure he has *all* the answers."

"He probably does," she says knowingly. "Okay, I'll go. I'll call you as soon as we land in Miami."

"No. I got this. Enjoy yourself. Call me a in a few weeks or so. I'll be fine." If she's listening closely enough, *I'll-be-fine* just became a three-syllable word for Webster's. *Drugs are good. Drugs alter everything. And everything is good. It is all good.*

CHAPTER THIRTEEN

paralyzer

LINC

AMY RANSOM SEEMED LIKE A GOOD idea for the first part of the evening. I'd borrowed the keys to my dad's Range Rover after another disappointing pitching session and decided I'd had enough of Beau Wilson's brand of baseball and my dad. I lied and told them all I had a physical therapy appointment. I was actually supposed to meet with my speech therapist, the LA one, who seemed to have the only good ideas on how to get my life back on track as it relates to memory strategies, but I blew her off too.

So. Amy Ransom sat on the bar stool next to mine at some out-of-the-way place in LA, and she seemed to understand my issues.

How could I have known she worked for the LA Times? *I didn't.*

How was I supposed to know that she was looking to make a big name for herself with my story? *I didn't.*

Amy Ransom and I had a brief conversation, but I stopped paying attention to her after the first couple of drinks. And yes, I started talking even more to the blonde sitting next to me on my right, whose name I did not even bother to ask while Amy just listened in.

I was on a mission for recreational entertainment. I just didn't know my actions would torpedo my good-guy reputation so thoroughly and in such a big way.

No. Five drinks in, and I let the blonde drive me home, or rather to her house—some small bungalow on the edge of town. I didn't pay much attention even as the camera flashes went off when I emerged from her car after we arrived. No, I just followed that sweet piece of ass up the front steps and inside because I wanted to be with somebody, not knowing that suddenly I had become somebody else in everyone's eyes with that particular bad-boy move.

And it happens just like that.

It's just that easy.

To fuck up your life.

The incessant ringing of a cell phone wakes me up. *Who's calling me? Hell.*

I roll over in an unfamiliar bed and vaguely recognize the blonde from the bar the night before sleeping right next to me.

Holy shit.

I'm fucked or I fucked up.

Holy shit.

My cell phone resumes ringing all over again. The shrill sound skewers all the way to the very center of my brain. *Kimberley Powers* comes up on the screen.

"Where. Are. You?" Kimberley screams so loud I hold the phone away from me as I answer.

"I don't know."

"Get up. Get dressed. Find her mail and get me the God damn address right the fuck now!"

"Where are you? I thought you were still in the Caribbean?"

"I'm at LAX. Brad and I just flew in on a red eye from Miami. Have you *seen* the Times? Of course, you haven't." She sighs big.

"Find the address. God dammit, Linc. God dammit. You've just committed brand suicide; and yet, here I am still ready and willing to help you get out of the shit hole you've just climbed into. I tried to contain the story, but it hit the wires a few hours ago. I'm sure she's already read it. This is what I get for thinking I could find peace and quiet in the Caribbean for a few weeks and that you could manage without me for a while. Jesus Christ! Why do I even *try?*"

"*Who?* Read what?"

"Never mind. Amy Ransom got her byline. We'll talk about all of it later. Get me an address so I can come and rescue your sorry ass."

"Who's Amy Ransom?"

How much did I drink? How many pills did I take?

"Amy Ransom is the LA Times sports reporter who broke your story. About your memory loss. About your new hook-up. Is there *anything* you didn't tell her? Why do I even try to save you?" Kimberley asks.

"Oh shit," I groan as the reality begins to sink in. *I have seriously fucked up.* I stumble through the bedroom, grope the walls on each side of hallway, and then proceed to go through this woman's mail like I have a clue as to what I'm doing as if I'm Jason Bourne or something. I rattle off the address to Kimberley in my somewhat still drunken state and can hear her tapping on her iPad, which is never more than a few feet away from her at any given time.

"Trinna Danner. White. Female. Works at The Lantern part-time as a waitress. Wants to be an actress. *Wonderful.* So far, her commercial work consists of toothpaste ads and shampoo. Nice. Blond. Blue-eyed. Twenty-five." Kimberley sighs big into the phone. "Get dressed, Linc, and get ready to be picked up. Looks like we can be there…in twenty minutes. The lady lives near the airport. Does that give you enough inside intel to put together as to *what you've done* and *who* with? And go gather up your used condoms."

"What the *fuck?* Why would I do that?" I shake my head because now Kimberley's really over the line.

"You want some clever fan-girl you do not know handling the DNA you've left behind? Do you know what you're worth, buddy?

Do you think she doesn't? She wants your babies. She wants your alimony. She wants your entire fucking contract. Are you seriously fucking with me? We've *had* this discussion. Okay, maybe you don't remember it. Jesus! Go get them. *Now!*"

I slink back to the girl's bedroom. She's still asleep. I quietly gather up my discarded clothes and find the two used condoms near the bedside. "Got 'em."

"How many?" Kimberley asks.

"Two."

"Look around for one or two more. *Check* her freezer!"

"Are you *insane?*"

"I've seen it all," Kimberley says. "Go check. Do it now, before she wakes up and catches you."

There are two condoms in the freezer. My brand.

I start to shake. I think it's a combination of drugs, alcohol, and a glimpse of my future being involved with this blonde on any level because I have seriously fucked-up in a big way. This happens to every other guy, not to me. I don't do this kind of shit. "I messed up," I say into the phone.

"You have *royally* fucked-up. How many in the freezer?"

"Two."

"Holy shit. She's a professional fan-girl looking for her big-time break. Get the hell out of there. Get dressed. Take all the condoms with you. Find a plastic bag and put them in your pants pocket. Wash your hands. Find some alcohol wipes and just wipe down anything you may have touched."

"What are you? With CSI?"

"Funny. I see we're going to have to have the sex talk all over again. I gave you all of this years ago, but you obviously don't fucking remember. Oh my God. I really can't believe this is happening. I can feel a migraine coming on." Kimberley says to me. "Do you know who she is? Do you remember *anything* about last night with her."

"No. I don't remember much of anything," I say, properly shamed. "Shit, Kimmy, what have I done? Is my dad looking for me?"

"He *was.* I told him I was on my way and I'd take care of it. And now I have to make *that* phone call." She sighs big.

"I'm sorry. Just come and get me, okay?"

Kimberley starts in on one of her lectures and I keep her on the phone for both of our sakes. She needs to say it and I suppose I need to hear it.

In the mean time, I put the four condoms in a Ziploc bag and then stuff it all into my jeans. *Mad scientist stuff. Me.*

I start wiping things down as I look around the apartment trying to assess last night's activities. There are at least three empty wine bottles scattered about. And it looks like the party consisted of just the two of us.

I look up then and discover the blonde watching me with this bemused look on her face from the doorway. She's pretty in that waitress wanting to be discovered by Hollywood kind of way. And if it wasn't for my used condoms I found in her freezer, I'd say she was harmless enough.

"Gotta go," I say to Kimberley. "Call me when you get here."

"Go out the back. I'll figure out how to get you to the car. The press will be there so don't even think about *leaving*, especially through the front door, until I call you back when we're there."

"Got it." I hang up the cell and look at the girl. She has big blue eyes, long blond hair, and an endless pair of legs. She's wearing my white dress shirt like a dress and a little shy smile. *Liar.*

"Hi," I say, sounding uneasy. I clear my throat. *This is bad.*

"Hello," she says. "Sounds like you're leaving."

"Yeah. Probably need to go. Can I…can I get my shirt back?"

She nods and slowly smiles as she takes off my shirt and hands it to me. Now, she's naked and doesn't attempt to hide herself. The reality that this whole scene has become probably the worst experience from start to finish begins to resonate with me while she eyes me looking perfectly calm.

Holy shit. What have I done?

And who is this girl?

"Thanks for the…time." I botch up the placating line. She just nods still looking at me expectantly. I swallow hard. "Did we? Did we…have a good time?"

"One of us did." She laughs a little and tucks a strand of blond hair behind one ear.

"Look, you probably took one too many of those little white pills you have with you. Don't worry about it. Maybe we'll see each other again sometime, and you can make up for...your lack of participation?"

Does that mean the drugs kicked in, and I couldn't get it up? But then, how to explain those used condoms in my pocket?

She's lying. I don't like it.

Holy shit.

For once, I'm hoping that's the case, although it's of little consolation because I already *know* that Kimberley will be reading me the riot act for just about everything else to do with this scene. She's only drilled it into me for years. Okay, more than six of those years I can't remember, but still. She's been saying this for some time now, since we first knew each other, when I was getting good at baseball. "Don't hook up with girls at bars, after games, at parties, in LA, in San Fran, in New York, or on vacation, which pretty much eliminates most encounters." *This*, from the most promiscuous girl I know, but on this point, she's always been right. *No groupies. No girls at bars. No one-night stands. Ever.*

My mind flashes to the green-eyed girl in my hospital room from a few months ago. I really need to do some research, pull up Google, and research that girl and our history. *But how? Maybe, I just Google myself and she'll come up in another photograph or something.*

I seriously need to start paying attention and doing things for myself. *I digress.* Meanwhile, this girl watches me intently now and gets this secret smile.

Yeah, babe, I'm on to you. My DNA is coming with me.

I put on my shirt pulling it down quickly. I'm sure she's a nice girl, just like I'm a nice guy. I go for politeness—*chivalry, what's left of it*—in some form.

"So I'm sorry..." I force a smile. My best one. "What's your name?"

"Trinna."

"Trinna." I nod like hers is best name in the world I've ever heard. "Thanks for the...hospitality. It would really help me out if you didn't mention this little visit to anyone. I'm still recovering from an injury."

"I know. You mentioned that several times. You really can't remember anything?"

"Not much." I grin and try to control my breathing.

Now, I've broken yet another rule of Kimberley's.

Don't tell anyone that you can't remember anything.

That's career suicide.

"The thing is my memory is slowly coming back, so it's going to be okay." I nod as I tell her this lie. "Anyway, my ride is almost here and I would really appreciate it if we could just keep this between us."

"I won't say anything. It'll be our secret." She smiles. "You seem like a nice guy. You paid for the drinks…and everything. Are you sure you have to go?" Now she looks slightly disappointed with this particular outcome.

I sense things could get complicated and ugly really fast. "Maybe, I'll see you again some time. Can I get your number?"

She gives it to me, and I input it into my cell even as my fingers shake while tapping out each number.

Too much alcohol and too many pills form a bad combination. My ego is wounded and obviously, my moral code is missing, and this inexplicable guilt swirls around me for no reason at all.

I try to remain impassive under Trinna's watchful gaze, knowing this encounter will probably cost me a great deal in lots of ways from money to pride as well as Kimberley's outright wrath, which will inevitably be the worst part of all. I have no intention of calling this girl, but Kimberley will want Trinna's number.

It's the one way to placate Kimberley what with all the other stuff she's bound to call me out on.

Kimberley is a collector of facts. She always has been. It pays off in her line of work. So she'll want the girl's number for reference at least because that's how Kimberley works. She's thorough, and she teaches her clients to be that way too, even when they make the stupidest of mistakes like this one today.

"Do you want some breakfast?" Trinna stoops and picks up a robe off the floor and puts it on.

I breathe a sigh of relief that she's half-dressed now. "No, I'm fine. Thanks."

She lights up a cigarette and swings away at the smoke and gets this wry smile. Apparently, it's her way of apologizing for the smoke. "So a baseball player, huh? That must pay big."

Shit.

"It has its moments. Depends on the contract, who you play for." I'm wary by her sudden interest in my paycheck.

"So, who do you play for, Elvis?" She looks completely sincere as if she believes my name is Elvis.

Why would I give her that name?

A memory stirs but then it's gone.

I wave the smoke away from my face with a backhand move. "I play in the minors. The Eagles? Know them?"

She shakes her head at my lie while I attempt to breathe.

Tread carefully here.

Where is Kimberley? I need her right the fuck now.

As if on cue, my cell rings again. I shoot Trinna an apologetic look for the interruption. "Ready?" I say into the phone.

"Okay, we're out in the alley about fifty feet from the back door. Black limo. Hard to miss. Let's go, lover-boy. Tell her good-bye, kiss her warmly, and get the hell out of there."

I don't need to be told twice.

"Yes. On my way."

I sweep my lips across Trinna's willing mouth, promise to call her, and take a few precious seconds to look around and make sure I have all the things I came with—wallet, ID, meds, clothes, shoes, shirt, condoms. I give her one last shy smile and head out the back door of this girl's house that I plan on never seeing again.

Breathe.

Thirst rages up my throat and this overwhelming guilt for what just happened comes out of nowhere again. The guilt I cannot explain. I take another deep breath and start to envision Kimberley's angry face even before I see it. I actually sprint towards the limo and manage to get inside and slam the door before the paparazzi get wind of us parked in the alley and immediately rush our way. The limo speeds off as the first reporters and their cameramen reach the alley.

I've done this before. My ears hum. Kimberley's talking, but I can't hear a word she's saying nor do I attempt openly acknowledge the blond guy sitting next to her.

"I *said* this is Dr. Bradly Stevenson, my husband. *Brad.*" Kimberley is surprisingly all smiles and I, for one, am glad for the presence of Dr. Bradly Stevenson because otherwise Kimberley would most likely be tearing my face off with her sharpest fingernails right about now. They twitch on her lap as it is.

After Kimberley provides the driver with an address, he tells us it will be about an hour drive and then he rolls up the window between us and him.

Silence follows.

A reprieve of two minutes is unceremoniously granted. I take a tiny breath.

"Now, *that* was a major fuck-up. How do I know this?" Kimberley asks. "Well, the papers are running this on just about every sports page in the nation this morning. Nicely done. I mean if you want to fuck things up royally with Tally this is certainly one of the ways to do that."

"Who's Tally?" I venture to ask when there's a lull in Kimberley's tirade.

"What? *Who's Tally?* Are you *serious?* Are you *fucking* with me again already, Linc? *Really?*"

"No. I don't know who you're talking about. *Really.*"

"Holy shit. I might actually kill your father for this. I swear!"

Brad decides to chime in. "Kimmy, he doesn't *know*. Ease up. Let's just head to Malibu and sort this all out. But call his dad and tell him to lie low too. And you'd better call Tally too."

I've never seen Kimberley actually follow someone's orders on command, but she does. "Fine," she says through her teeth. "I've already left two messages for Tally. I guess I'll call Davis." She frowns and bites at her lower lip and just sits there. Brad kisses the inside of her wrist and tells her everything is going to be all right.

I watch the two of them interact somewhat fascinated but then begin to feel this unexpected envy and raging guilt all over again. *What is this?*

"Linc," Kimberley says sadly. "This is a nightmare. Truly."

She sighs. "All right. Let me make some phone calls and see if we can get ahead of this on any level."

She moves to the other side of the limousine away from me and Brad and starts dialing.

Her husband grants me with another sympathetic but curious look. I give Dr. Bradley Stevenson an obliging handshake and finally introduce myself properly because he appears to be on my side, on our side.

"Sorry about interrupting your vacation," I say slowly. "I understand I interrupted your honeymoon with my accident in October too. Sorry."

"No worries. It was time to return to the States. She can't be gone too long." He shakes his head in wonder and smiles. "I was lucky to talk her into a few weeks away as it is. Anyway, there's the place in Malibu. Her best friend is letting us use it. That's where we're going now. It's big enough. We can all stay there. That's my doctoral advice to you anyway."

"A *doctor*. Right."

"A psychiatrist, actually."

"Ah…so that's why she brought you. You treat my special brand of crazy, Doc?"

"I treat all special kinds of mental health issues. We don't like the word *crazy*."

"I bet not."

"Kimberley briefly gave me some of your background. I'm here as a *friend* just like Kimberley is to you. I actually practice psychiatry in the state of New York, although I should get my license for California too," Brad says more to himself. "I've helped a number of Kimberley's friends."

"*Really?* Free of charge and everything?" I say sarcastically.

"I know you're pissed. It's a rough deal having your life fall apart, losing some of your past, and yet having everybody expecting you to remember it. But I can help you. My specialty is neuropsychology, and I've put it to good use in my practice." He eyes me directly. "I'm pretty good."

"I bet you say that to all Kimmy's closest friends."

He laughs at my insolence. Eventually, I do too. I like this guy.

And after more than two months in LA at Beau Wilson's camp where nothing has helped with my pitching, I'm a little desperate.

I look at him intently before saying, "I still can't throw a baseball, Doc. Can you help with that?"

"I think I can, yes." Brad nods with an air of confidence I haven't felt in months.

Kimberley stops herself from dialing and looks over at me intently from the other side of the limo in response to what I've just said. "Still no fast ball?" She asks looking worried.

I shake my head side-to-side. Just admitting to the failure seems to lift a phantom weight from my shoulders. The publicist and the psychiatrist both watch me closely now. I fold my arms across my head to try and ease the pain, but the headache just gets a little worse. "Can't throw a baseball, and have now landed on the front pages of every sports page in America," I say with a groan throwing my arms up in the air, "what else could possibly go wrong?"

Kimberley looks like she already knows, but she won't tell me anything more even when I ask.

CHAPTER
FOURTEEN

you belong with me

TALLY

"S O HE FINALLY CLOSED ON THE house—a nice one in Sea Cliff of all places. He's like five blocks away from Rob Thorn's parents. Tally, are you *listening* to me?"

"Yes. So he closed on the house. He's a busy guy but what does that have to do with me?" I shrug for emphasis indicating I don't care, but my shoulders shake betraying me.

It's been more than two months almost three since the line drive and the accusations from Linc's dad about me that followed. October, November came and went. It's almost Christmas. Life goes on. It's incredibly slow and painful, but it goes on, just like all the Zen people say it does.

Lo and behold, some real estate agent confirms my story about the big wonderful house sale to her secret client—the infamous baseball player—and it turns out to be an all-cash deal just like I told them. The missing six million dollar mystery is no more.

And life goes on. Did I mention that?

"All cash deals are normally rushed through," Marla is saying. She's the expert on real estate agents now. Apparently, this is a future career path. I say nothing. "But I guess he had some work done on it. Interior painting, a few remodels including the addition of a dance studio…"

Marla's last words slam into me. *Chink goes the armor. Clink goes the heart. Swish goes the breath.*

Her mouth closes and forms a thin straight line as does mine.

"A dance studio how nice. That'll come in handy for him," I finally say rewarding her with a withering look that says-let's-not-talk-about-this-anymore, but she keeps babbling. I move away from her on the off chance I'll be able to tune her out.

The Linc of old loved me. The new one? That one? He doesn't know to care, apparently. I haven't heard one word from him. Not one. My ability to care and even love him is on life support at this point. I'm breathing one day at a time. It's been more than two months since I saw him last. No calls from him. No emails. No texts. No voicemails.

Whatever.

It's been seventy-one days without communication.

But who's counting?

I've had plenty of time to think. My thoughts are mostly centered around coming up with cruel and unusual punishments to wield upon both Lincoln Presley and his father. I don't share this vengeful part of myself with Marla. Instead, I just stare at her, waiting, until she finally stops talking after finally realizing I haven't heard a word she's said.

"Like I said," I say slowly, "what does any of this have to do with me?"

"Linc's dad accused you of a horrible thing, but the mystery of the missing six million was easily solved by you."

"By *me*. *Months ago*, I might add. So what now?"

"At the very least, Linc owes you an apology, even if his dad won't give you one, about all of that…at least. I told him as much when he called to talk to Charlie the other day and again when he called this morning."

"You *talked* to him?"

"Yeah, he called early this morning, a few hours ago, before Charlie left for rounds." She looks away and starts to fidget.

"He called Charlie and his dad the other day to review the real estate papers with them over the phone…, but I answered the phone today." She takes a sudden interest in Cara's swing set in the backyard and stares out the kitchen window. She turns back to me and looks uneasy. "He's…different now."

She doesn't say anything else, just begins to pick at an invisible thread on her designer jeans. She looks up and catches me scrutinizing her. She gets this guilty look then rewards me with one of her most winning smiles, but it's forced. *And I know it.*

She's holding something back from me. The thing is she went out of her way to meet up with me today, practically invited herself over when she called early this morning, and insisted again even when I told her today wasn't good. I have a run-through later this afternoon. I need to drop off Cara at Mom and Dad's before that. Even so, she still insisted on coming by, driving the forty odd miles from Palo Alto to meet up with me.

Why?

We've been sporadic with seeing one another over the past couple of months. I intentionally isolate myself from her because experiencing firsthand her fabulous life with Charlie is more than my present state of mind—*a special brand of crazy*—can handle.

But it's almost Christmas. Three more nights of *The Nutcracker* and I have three weeks off before winter rehearsals begin in mid-January for the next production this spring. I practically panic at the idea of having free time. I've tried to keep busy. It's work or Cara or time spent at my parents. I've learned to cook a little more and clean a lot. I willingly take on anything that will keep me moving because thinking is the last thing I want to be doing.

My strategy mostly works.
Until now.

Until Marla starts looking at me with recognizable sympathy. It's the bad news look—the how-can-I-possibly-keep-Tally-from-falling apart? look. We know each other so well. She's been here for every bad thing that's happened to me. The good ones too, but the bad ones are more prominent.

Bad news.

Right.

"Tell me," I say softly, "*how* is he different?"

"He's not himself. He's acting so *different*. He's—"

"He's *sleeping around* or *seeing someone*," I say finishing her little speech for her.

Marla's face twists up. She's uncomfortable in delivering this ugly news. "Possibly both," she says hanging her head, she won't even look at me.

"Fuck me."

"*Language.*" Marla frantically gestures towards Elliott and Cara who play side-by-side on the living room floor not far from us. Wood building blocks painted red and blue and yellow are scattered about the floor. Elliott dutifully goes around and picks them all up and hands them back to Cara, who then works deftly in silence building the tallest tower possible. Elliott claps and gleefully laughs every time the two of them work together knocking it all down for the umpteenth time. It's been fun to watch.

The idea of knocking something down begins to sound pretty good about now.

Simple joy.

Catch me some, and let me drink it down right the fuck now.

I attempt to smile over at Marla, but my lips are frozen. My mind is stuck on her words, *possibly both.*

I hate being right. I hate being clairvoyant. I am a little bit of both and most often at the same time. *Like now.*

Marla grabs my hand from where it rests on the table between us. "Got any wine?"

"I have a run-through in a couple of hours. I can't. Mikhail would have my head. There are only three more performances. I need the money. Daycare is expensive."

"You need a nanny or an Au pair."

"Yep, but that stuff doesn't come cheap, now does it?" I wince and feel the edges of a raging headache coming on fast. "I'm some thirty thousand dollars in debt for a wedding that didn't happen, and my former fiancé is sleeping around. It doesn't get much worse than that."

I take an unsteady breath and blow it out. "*Sorry*, it's not your fault, he's W-H-O-R-I-N-G around."

"Right." Marla laughs a little and finally so do I.

I mean what am I going to do? Cry? No way.

"Her name is Trinna," she says helpfully. "It was on the sports page of the Chronicle and the LA Times, just about everywhere this morning. ESPN." Her voice trembles as she delivers the news.

"He made national news?" She nods looking as miserable as I suddenly feel. "Trinna," I say the name as if it is somehow foreign and sounding it out will make it all better.

"She's pretty enough. Blond. The papers say she wants to be an actress. That she met him in a bar. That kind of thing..." Marla bites at her lower lip and looks miserable.

"Right." My one word answer gushes with all kinds of sarcasm.

"Didn't know that. *Don't* want to know that. *Don't* tell me anything more. *Don't* want to hear it."

I put my hands over my ears like Cara sometimes does. She might not talk but she still knows how to throw a tantrum when she wants to.

"How many *don'ts* is that?" I ask lowering my head to the table unable to look at my best friend.

"Quite a few," Marla says on a sigh. "I don't blame you for being pissed. I don't. But I just think you should talk to him and maybe you two could try and work things out."

I look up at her and toss my hair back over my shoulder because her sudden empathy for Linc sets me off. "Work *what* out? He *doesn't* remember me. He's obviously moved on. Exactly what would we be working out?"

"I don't know. I just think you shouldn't give up so easily."

"You think it's been *easy* to give up? Try living my life for just one day, Marla. One fucking hour in fact," I whisper. "Think what it would be like if Charlie didn't remember you at all, that when he woke up from a coma and looked at you and he saw *nothing*. He saw through you or just looked right past you. And then asked who you were? Demanded to know who you were and why you were there? Please don't sit there and tell me how to feel or what to do because you just don't know what it's like to lose somebody who used to love you. You don't know. Please, don't do that. I've managed to fu... *screw* up a number of times in my life, but this isn't one of them. *Okay?*"

"Okay. I'm sorry. I just don't want to see you unhappy like this."

"I'm not *unhappy*." I choke on the word but force myself to smile. "See? I'm *happy*." My voice trembles and Marla waves a finger at me. "Not completely unhappy. I have Cara. A roof over my head. A job. *For now*. My parents. Tommy. You. Charlie. Elliott. A semblance of a life. I just don't have...*everything* anymore. I just don't have *him* anymore."

"I'm so sorry."

"I know."

"So no wine?" She sighs again looking even more unhappy.

Her mysterious obsession with the wine request pisses me off but it gets me moving up and out of the chair. I start rummaging through the kitchen cupboards and slamming doors. Two minutes later, I hold up a bottle of scotch in victory.

"That's all you've got?" Marla asks looking at the amber-colored bottle in disgust.

Linc's favorite scotch. Glenfiddich.

The one unopened bottle he was saving for a special occasion.

I should have poured it down the fucking drain.

"This is it." I hold up the fancy bottle and grin wide. "Take it or leave it."

"I'll leave it. I'm supposed to drive back to Palo Alto anyway. And, I have a kid."

"Such a responsible soul."

I work at the fancy cork by tearing off the foil with my teeth.

"Something like that." Her face twists up as she watches me. "I'm sorry about everything."

"A loaded statement if there ever was one."

"You should start seeing someone, to even the score."

"There is no keeping score. I'll move on when I am good and ready. And I'm not ready. And you know what? I may never be ready. Fuck love, fuck marriage, fuck Tally and the baby carriage," I chant while pouring a healthy shot of scotch into an over-sized water glass.

Marla's mouth drops open and her eyes go wide. "Are you *seriously* going to drink all that, Tal? Did you even *eat* today?"

"Yes. And no."

I smile feeling completely wicked as I hold the expensive glass of scotch up to the light as if it's under some kind of inspection.

"Will you drop me off at the studio after we take Cara to my parents?"

"Sure," she says softly.

I think she's sorry she suggested drinking. I'm not sorry. I'm relieved. So fucking relieved.

"Thanks for telling me I guess and for being here."

I drink down the whole glass of scotch in one long swallow and then wipe the corners of my mouth with the back of my hand. The liquor burns my throat all the way down. The alcohol rushes my veins like a narcotic would.

I begin to feel a little dizzy even as I push a stick of gum into my mouth to keep Mikhail off the trail. The man looks for any reason he can, threatening to demote me or fire me at least every other day. I haven't figured out what his problem with me is quite yet.

Does it matter?

No, not at all.

As long as I stay two steps ahead of him, I'll be fine.

And keep busy. And keep myself from thinking. I'll be fine.

Possibly both. Marla's words burns all the way to my soul.

CHAPTER

FIFTEEN

you oughta know

TALLY

"SO YOU SAW HER PICTURE IN the paper?" I ask, deciding to dive right in and open all these slightly healed-over wounds of heartache and jealousy about Lincoln Presley all over again.

"Yeah." Marla looks down avoiding my gaze like before. "It was one of those bad PR moves on his part. In other words, it looked bad, but he says nothing *bad* really happened. That's what he told Charlie anyway when he called earlier today. Charlie told him he should apologize to you for it though."

"He doesn't know about me to apologize. He doesn't even know my name or know about Cara. *Remember?*"

"I know. I was hoping since a few months had gone by that he somehow…remembered or something. I guess it's not surprising then that he told Charlie he had no intention of apologizing for something he didn't do to someone he doesn't even know."

"That hurts." I swallow hard on the lump forming in my throat. "You know; I went along with his dad's whole program about staying out of his life for a while, so he wouldn't be confused or stressed out, but I thought eventually he would call me. How stupid have I been?"

Now it's my turn to stare out the window. I give it a few minutes and take in the view—the consolation prize of a backyard and Cara's swing set—and then casually wipe at my eyes before turning back to Marla's scrutiny.

"I've been holding onto this silly thread of hope that he'd remember everything. And now I find out he's slinking around with somebody else." I fist pump the air. "How am I supposed to explain all of that to Cara. Imagine what it would do to her? How confused she would be. I have to do something about this. I really do. I have to do something about this."

I start pacing. "I've got to think about this. Think this whole thing through. And *do* something."

"I *think* you should talk to him."

I stop pacing and study Marla's face intently. "*Whose side* are you on, babe? Because you have to pick one, Mrs. Masterson. If it isn't my side, then I need to know that. I know you're somewhat caught in the middle because of the family connections—what with the first cousin ties and all. *I get it*, I do. But you need to understand that I have to protect myself *and* Cara. It's becoming a little hard to explain to her why her daddy doesn't come home. Imagine trying to explain that Daddy doesn't remember her at all on any level whatsoever and he has a girlfriend? She's dealing with enough as it is right now. I don't want her confused or hurt any further by any of this. I should have done something about this a long time ago," I say quietly enough that Cara won't hear me from the open doorway.

Suddenly decisive, I pick up my cell phone. It's been on silent since last night. There are ten missed calls from unknown callers—reporters, no doubt—and two missed calls from Kimberley Powers from over an hour ago.

I stare at the screen. Two missed calls from *PR Nightmare* aka Kimberley Powers. Her moniker was changed two and half months ago.

I would have deleted it but there was a small part of me that knew having her cell number might come in handy at some point. "Kimberley Powers called me."

"What does *she* want?" Marla asks looking even more wary than me.

"I'm sure she wants to disarm the bomb that is me right now. Can't have the ex-fiancée talking to the press, now can we?" I pound the counter-top hard. "Maybe I don't need my lawyer. Maybe I can handle this on my own."

"Maybe, Kimberley wants to ask if she can give him your number, so he can call you and apologize." Marla sounds wistful and more uncertain than ever. She starts twisting her wedding band.

"Would this be *after* he told Charlie that he wasn't going to apologize for something he didn't do to someone he *doesn't know*?" I kind of laugh—one of those crazy laughs Anne Hathaway would surely make while portraying Catwoman.

I jerk my hands back through my hair pulling out loose strands as I go. Enchanted for a few seconds, I watch them float in the air and silently land in the kitchen sink.

Fascinating.

I'm losing it.

I glare at Marla and start to scold her for withholding the information about Linc so far into our conversation and for the shameless suggestion that I talk to him. I flip her off for good measure and grab my iPad from the charger and tap *Google*, then tap *news*, and finally *sports*. And there is Lincoln Presley doing little to hide his face from the cameras as he follows some shadowy blonde with long wavy hair up the stairs toward the front door of some house.

"It's true. And it doesn't matter," I say slowly. My eyes blur for a few seconds looking at his photograph after all this time. "If he is going to behave this way, I don't want him around…*Cara*."

I swallow hard. It's painful seeing his photograph to say nothing of the blonde he's with. I skip the headline and start reading the story.

"Lincoln Presley, star pitcher for the San Francisco Giants was spotted in LA last night with an unidentified blonde leaving The Lantern Bar & Grill. The two were later seen going into what was later confirmed to be the woman's Los Angeles residence. The woman, later identified as Trinna Danner, could not be reached for comment. Little has been seen of Presley since he suffered a life-threatening injury from a line drive during the first round playoffs in the Giants' second series game just over two months ago. In September, the couple confirmed in a Sports Illustrated article that Presley and his fiancée Talia Landon, San Francisco Ballet's star ballerina, planned to marry this past fall after baseball season ended. The couple's wedding plans were soon canceled due to Presley's subsequent injury and expected long rehabilitation.

Since the accident, Ms. Landon has refused comment on the status of her relationship with Lincoln Presley, but the two have not been seen together since before the accident. Public records indicate the couple applied for a marriage license in early October right before Presley's accident but the two did not marry. At one point during the exclusive interview with the ball player, Presley admitted to suffering memory loss and stated "I don't know who you're talking about," in relation to direct questions about Landon. It was confirmed that Presley left the bar with Trinna Danner. Unnamed sources state that Presley spent the night at Ms. Danner's home."

I look up from the screen at Marla. "That's probably enough of that." I glance back down at the article, slide my finger along the screen and scan the rest. There's a photograph of the two of us further down from the *Sports Illustrated* photo shoot. "But there's Candy Baxstrom, of course, always willing to make a buck or two on my life for her part of the precious story." I hold out the iPad for Marla to see.

"The *Dirty Dancing* photograph. I love that one." I glare at her. "*Sorry.* I read the whole thing four times before I even got here," she says sounding more miserable than me.

"Marla, are there photographers outside? Did you see any when you got here?" For several weeks, they camped out on my lawn, but as my sensational side of the story died down they finally moved on.

Marla wordlessly slips off the chair and stands to one side of the window in the living room and looks out. She gasps which is all I need for confirmation.

"They're here," she says sounding a little scared.

"We're in *Poltergeist*. Great. Just great." Cara comes over to me and grabs my leg and looks up at me with this worried expression. "It's okay, baby. We're okay. Marla is just going close the curtains and we're going to play a game or something in a few minutes. Okay, sweetie? Elliott, you want to play a game with your mommy and me?" I turn to Marla. "I'm going go upstairs to close all the shades and curtains, and try to figure out how many there are. Can you make sure all the doors are locked down here? I usually lock things up during the day, but let's not take any chances. It depends on who they are. Sports reporters no problem. But paparazzi? That's a problem."

Cara and Elliott watch us closely. It's amazing to me what kids pick up on. I glance at Marla. "Just distract them, okay? Get a movie going for them."

Marla, normally the talkative one between us, looks a little unnerved by it all. I am too, but I try to hide it from her and the kids. Instead, I smile at them all and assure them everything is fine as I grab my cell phone along with my iPad and climb the stairs taking two at a time.

You never know how many windows you have in a place until you can practically feel a camera lens trying to look at you through one. With growing anxiety, I press the link for Kimberley's number, while closing shades and curtains with the other.

"Powers," she says after the first ring.

"Why do his fuck-ups have to become my problem?"

She sighs big. "It's not quite like that, Tally."

"I just counted five teams of reporters outside my house, Kimberley. Tell me, what it's like on your end?"

"I know it looks bad. It is terrible from your perspective, but he says nothing happened. It didn't happen the way the papers portrayed—"

"You're lying. How many condoms did he pick up or take out of the freezer?"

Silence.

"Tally, I know it looks bad and feels worse…"

"Fuck off, Kimberley. I know how it works. *Does he?* You better give him that speech again. Whatever. It. Doesn't. Matter. He is no longer my problem, and yet I am here dealing with the fallout for his bad-boy behavior. And *my kid* is downstairs wondering why her mommy is pulling down the shades and closing the curtains in the middle of the day! And I have to go to work or Mikhail will surely fire my sorry ass since he's always looking for any excuse he can find to do so. And let's be honest; I don't *deserve* any of this. Not really. And *you* seriously *owe* me."

"All true," she says soothingly. "I'll take care of Mikhail. Is it a performance tonight?"

"No, a run-through. I perform the next three nights though. And let me guess you're good friends with Mikhail Rostov."

"Something like that." She laughs a little.

"I really wish you were on my side," I say with a little hostility.

"I *am* on your side. Look, Tally. It looks bad. We'll mitigate it though. He used poor judgment in a highly questionable situation, but *nothing happened* and—"

"Why do you always give him the benefit of the doubt? Why doesn't anybody ever believe me, just once? What did I ever do to you? I mean *really*, Kimberley. God!"

I take in air and start pacing the floor. "Look, I've got to think of Cara. She's all that matters to me. I will not have her exposed to Paparazzi every time her daddy decides to pick up some whore in a bar only to have it splashed all over the news for her to accidentally see. You tell him to *zip it up*— good and tight—or I will get a restraining order for that unpredictable rage he's got going on now in order to protect my child—her well-being—as well as her general safety. You *got* that? Yeah, Tell him that. And tell him I am truly disappointed in him. Something I thought I would never be. Tell him there are no words to describe how he has made me feel. Tell him all of that. And, Kimberley? My next call is to my lawyer. And you should know that. Tell him that too."

"Okay. Okay, I can see where this is going and I believe you. Don't get a restraining order, Tally. That's not necessary. He'll respect your privacy from here on out. I promise. I will ensure that happens. I was out of the country. He's been struggling—"

"Don't talk about him! I don't want to hear about his problems, and it looks like he was having a pretty good time last night with that blonde. So don't tell me how bad it is for him. *Don't.* Just tell me you've got this under control, or you will soon have *him* under control. You asked me not to comment about him and I haven't; right now he's doing enough damage for himself all on his own. But if I have to defend myself from any more defamatory remarks from his father or the press about me or my kid, I *will*. You got that, *Kimmy*?"

"Yes. I got that. Yes, I know, and I don't blame you…for any of this. Linc's dad was horribly wrong to accuse you about the money and Linc…he just isn't himself right now. Just know that I've got this. I'll handle it." She pauses and I hear her as she takes a slow, deep breath. "Tally, just let me make some calls. One of them will be to Mikhail. I know he can be a real bastard to work for and with Sasha in Moscow I'm sure it's been doubly hard for you. Let me fix it, okay? I promise I will. At the very least, I'll call Mikhail and get you out of the run-through tonight. Can you stay put for the night at the house? Or go somewhere else where they won't think to look for you or be able to find you?"

"I'm going to Marla's if you get it worked out with Mikhail."

"Okay. Okay, that's good. That's good."

She sighs and sounds a little uncertain while I feel all powerful, shaken up, but strangely alive all at the same time. Remorse filters in for my tirade. "*Elvis* would never do this to me."

Breathe. Just breathe.

"I *know*." She sounds like she's about to cry which seems to unlock the floodgates for me too. "Just give me a couple of hours; okay? I'll make the calls and then I'll call you back. Just stay there until you hear from me, okay? And, Tally? I *am* on your side. More than you know. Trust me."

"A few hours then. Two max. That's it, Kimberley, then call me back."

"I will. I promise." She sounds properly mollified.

The threat of a lawyer and a restraining order on Linc do their thing. They take the publicist extraordinaire a little off her game as intended and put me on some weird-ass level I've never been to before.

"Fine. Make it happen." I end the call and take a shallow breath. And another.

I want to hate Kimberley Powers so bad. She's messed in the affairs with me and Linc before, but there's a part of me that likes her, even admires her. She is normally a force to be reckoned with. If anyone can handle things and change things by waving a magical wand and induce a change in perception construed as reality, it's Kimberley Powers.

And the truth is I have to put my trust into someone at some point, but I'm not so sure it should be Kimberley Powers.

Marla turns on the light as she sweeps into the master bedroom. She instantly scowls at the unmade bed and the crumpled sheets scene which has been going on for the past ten days that I can remember.

"Do you do laundry, like ever?"

"Only sometimes." I run the back of my hand across my face and turn to adjust the drapes that don't need adjusting because they're closed.

"I heard you yelling. The kids are watching *Frozen*."

I tilt my head to one side and listen. I can vaguely hear little Elliott singing the words to one of the songs. "I was talking to Kimberley. I told her I'd get a restraining order for his temper to protect Cara if I had to." It doesn't sound like such a proud moment when I tell this to Marla. My eyes sting. I try again. "Like he remembers who Cara is. Like he *knows* who I am. And this is my life. What a fucking mess."

She nods and doesn't even bother to correct my language.

Instead, she laughs ever so faintly and shakes her head. "It is a *fucking* mess," she says with a sad smile.

"Yeah. So. How much did you *hear*?"

"All of it. I especially like the "you tell him to zip it up good and tight" part. Nicely done. And you did that entire speech without swearing at her too much. Impressive."

"*More* swearing might have helped."

"Nah, I think she got your message loud and clear. It *was* good," Marla pronounces as she starts to strip the bed while I look at her in new wonder. "What? It looks like we're here for the duration. At least a few hours, right? So let's do some laundry. Get you caught up to the real world. Then, we'll pack your things so you two can stay with us for a few days, at least through Christmas. Don't worry, I'll drive you to the studio when you need to be there. And by the time the laundry is done, Kimberley will have worked out some kind of mysterious deal with your boss and probably the press too."

"But it doesn't matter, does it? If it's true or not. Whether something happened with that girl or not. Actions speak louder than words, Marla. A part of him wanted something to happen with that blonde. The circumstances don't really change anything. And I have to protect Cara."

"So what are you going to do?"

"Call my lawyer. Let's face it; I've been waiting around for... *him*...to make the first move. It's never going to happen. He doesn't remember me. He's never going to remember me. I mean maybe someday someone will give him the details about Cara, and he may have some legal rights to her then. But right now? I have to protect her. My lawyer can deal with all of that. Leave the laundry. Help me pack some things for Cara, will you?"

"Maybe you just need to start over with him."

"No starting over. Obviously he doesn't want to or doesn't know to want to." I grab my cell phone searching for Everett Madsen's number. "Everett will help me. He has before. Just let me make a phone call or two. Can you check on the kids?"

She nods but looks on with disapproval. "Okay. But are you sure you want to do it this way?"

I look at Marla intently. "Yes, I've waited long enough. I've kept silent long enough while my name and reputation have been dragged through the proverbial mud along with his. I didn't do any of this. He has Kimberley on his side and his dad and the Giants. Who do I have? You. Charlie. Not very formidable odds for us. I have to do this. I should have contacted Everett Madsen about all of this a long time ago. We need to have to have some ground rules in place. My lawyer can help me figure out what those should be. I can't keep having Kimberley Powers and Lincoln Presley determine the outcome of my life or Cara's. I need to take charge of it for our sake, for us."

I turn away from Marla who sighs behind me.

I only take in air when I finally hear her leave as her footsteps retreat down the hallway away from me. Then, I consciously wipe at the tears streaming down my face. It takes another five minutes before I get it together enough to make the call.

"Everett, it's Tally Landon. I need your help." The power returns to me in just admitting this to my lawyer.

But I still can't seem to breathe.

I don't stop to wonder why that is.

CHAPTER
SIXTEEN

who's that girl

LINC

I STAND BACK FROM THE STEEL RAILING on the second floor of the Malibu house and listen in on the discussion going on about me in the glass-walled living room below. The views of the Pacific even from the vantage of the second floor are pretty spectacular but neither Brad nor Kimberley Stevenson is appreciating these right now.

"He has a right to know! She is royally *pissed*. I don't necessarily blame her at all."

"Yes, of course, he needs to be told, but one thing at a time. One crisis at a time. Let the story die down, then we'll move on to the next one."

"How long?" Kimberley asks, sounding impatient.

"A month. Maybe two. I've already called the office and delayed my return by at least three weeks. He needs our help. You heard what he said. He's been attempting to throw a baseball for the past two months. He has all kinds of pressure on him to perform. I imagine even his escapade last night was a way of coping with all the pressure he feels. He's *lost*. His course of treatment appears sporadic. It sounds like they've been solely focused on the physical aspect and largely ignoring the mental part. He needs some strategies that will help him learn how to deal with his memory loss in order to better navigate and figure things out and determine where he needs to go from here. Doling out a bunch of heavy narcotics is *not* a strategy, and that seems to be what his stellar medical team has been doing. I've seen it often enough," Brad says.

"So you're taking over?" She asks, incredulous.

"That's what you want; isn't it? He's like a brother to you. You want him to get better, right?"

"Yes. Of course, I do. I love Linc. He's the best. *Usually*."

I wince at hearing Kimberley's obvious disappointment. *I've really fucked this up good.*

"So cut him some slack," Brad says easily. "He needs to rest in order to regain his equilibrium. Give it some time, Kimmy. And let me talk to him alone so I can figure out the best way to help him."

"What do I tell Tally?"

"Be honest and tell her how it is. She's reacting to the perception—the innuendos—of what took place with Linc, not the reality. Reassure her too as much as you have Linc. His accident has been just as devastating for her. Let's see how things go for the next couple of weeks with Linc after I've had a chance to work with him. Maybe they can start to work some things out. It sounds like his dad has cut Tally off completely from Linc's life. I wouldn't have prescribed that. No wonder she's upset. So yes, call her and reassure her that things are under control, and we'll know more in the next few weeks about his progress in remembering anything. I need to talk to him first. So don't make any promises, just reassure her that you're handling this for him, and that he says nothing happened."

"I don't know if I'm going to be able to convince her of much, especially after what just transpired here in LA last night. She was pissed off enough already with the stuff Davis pulled and now this? I don't know if I'd believe me either. She asked how many condoms he found. She *knows* about that stuff already. She knows how it works. She knows what a fan-girl can be like. She's not a fool. She deals with fame herself. Right now, she's finishing up the holiday season with SF Ballet. She'll have some time off after that but whether she's willing to spend it in LA to try and work things out with Linc is questionable. Romeo, upstairs, really fucked things up, and I should have seen this coming a lot sooner. He wasn't himself when I saw him a few weeks ago."

"You can't control everything, Kimmy. Nobody can," Brad says.

I walk down the stairs and the conversation between them stops as soon as they see me.

"Hey, Linc. How'd you sleep?" Kimberley is all smiles as if the serious conversation about me they've been having never happened.

"Fine. Nice place."

Right after we arrived, I was ushered by these two to the upstairs guest room and after a lousy night's sleep at Trinna somebody's, not surprisingly, I fell asleep within minutes. This is my first opportunity to look around. "Wow," I say in getting a better glimpse of the Pacific. The sun is halfway down the horizon. "How long was I asleep?"

"Three hours, my sleep-deprived friend." Kimberley says. "This is my best friend Julia's place. Remember her? I think you met her years ago. She lets us use it when we're in LA—"

"Cleaning up my messes."

"Then too. And those are not too often." Kimberley looks over at Brad and then smiles at me. "It'll be okay. It'll work out."

"I think I used to say that, didn't I?" I look hard at Kimberley and she answers with a slight nod.

"All the time. You remember?" She sounds wistful.

"No. I don't remember anything. I *try* to, believe me."

"Maybe you try too hard," Brad says. "That's what we'll start working on, if you're okay with that."

It's not really a question. He makes it sound like more of a challenge that I should be willing to take.

"Well, what we've been doing isn't really working," I say with a touch of sarcasm. "So yeah, I'll try whatever you me want to try."

I look at Brad and then over at Kimberley. "So, who's this Tally? Let's start there," I say softly. "So she's pissed? At me? Why, exactly?"

"I say we talk more about all of that later. Let's go for a walk if you're up to it," Brad says to me. Then, he's talking to Kimberley. "Let me talk to him. You make some of those phone calls. Start with Tally. She's expecting your call back, right?"

"Yes. I've got about ten more minutes." Kimberley grumbles about missing a walk because she has so much work to do, but manages to lecture me about going incognito and tosses me a baseball cap as well as my Ray-Ban's at the same time. "No more opportunistic photo ops," she says with a sniff looking a little put out all over again. "The paparazzi will be all around, after all this is Malibu, but they won't expect to find you here. So just follow Brad's lead, lie low, and let me do my job by smoothing things over with a few necessary phone calls. Okay, Linc?"

"You do one hell of a job, babe," Brad says to her as he grabs her around the waist and kisses her.

Then I follow out behind Brad toward the endless stretch of sand and the Pacific just up ahead of us while Kimberley waves at us from the deck. We wave back.

"She's intense," I say knowingly.

"Yeah, but she's worth it."

Brad keeps to such a fast pace that I have to run to catch up to him, which, after a while, I decide was his intention all along. Somewhere along the way we seem to call a truce and settle into an easy enough jog.

My headache becomes a dull throb, and I start to wonder when was the last time I went running on a beach like this. *Of course, I can't remember.*

"So. What do you like to do?" Brad asks looking over at me.

"I thought you were going to ask me what I *remember*, like everybody else does."

"What's the point of that? Asked and answered several times already, I imagine."

It makes me like him even more. I relax a little and take in the fresh ocean air and appreciate the simple act of running on a beach in Malibu.

After a few minutes of running in silence, I say, "I like to cook. I love baseball. I love seasons. Spring. Summer. Fall. Winter. All of them for different reasons. I love sun. Baseball. Wait, I already said that. Wine. A good scotch. Field dust. The smell of rain, and recently the incredible combination scent of cloves and vanilla." I laugh. "I like fast cars, and I think I've had my share of fast women, but I'm not sure why I know that because I don't remember it. *Them.*"

I slow down. Brad follows suit.

"I think I've loved someone so greatly that I experience this unquenchable thirst all the time now in trying to remember her. I don't know what it all means. I just know I feel it. What do you think that means?"

"I think it means your mind remembers more than you or I or anybody else thinks it does. We just have to find the right mechanism to unlock it. Sometimes it involves talking it through. Sometimes it means working with all the senses—sight, sound, touch, taste, and smell. It's good that you have favorite smells like rain and cloves and vanilla. We just have to figure out what or who you associate that with now."

I slow down and look over at him and slowly smile. "There was this girl at the hospital. She smelled like cloves and vanilla. I can't get her scent out of my head half the time. It's weird. I'm not a stalker, I promise." My smile disappears. "My dad wouldn't tell me who she was. And she never told me her name. I called her baby and she didn't like that, and I didn't remember her and my dad warned me she was trouble. I have a photograph of her I found in my wallet but I forgot to ask Kimberley about her. Maybe she knows her…the thing is my recovery has been all about baseball. I haven't ventured too far into looking at my past. These headaches I get make it hard to concentrate on anything other than baseball. Sometimes, even baseball proves to be too much to think about."

"You've had a lot on your plate. Just recovering takes time and a lot of energy. What kind of medication do they have you on? And is it working? I mean, if you're still getting the headaches, maybe you need to try something else."

"Sometimes," I say slowly. "The pills dope me up. I try not to take them before I do a pitch session. I've slowed down enough as it is.

But they dull the pain and some days I couldn't function without them. I guess you could say they serve as my biggest crutch on those days. And they don't prevent the headaches. I still have those all the time."

"Could you be sensitive to light?"

"I don't know. Maybe. But I'm in the sun all time and that isn't going to change. Baseball is all I've got. Failure isn't an option. We should probably start there."

"Okay. That's good to know. No giving up on baseball; got it," he says.

My admission and his acceptance eases the tension. I'm not here to sacrifice my career and I'm relieved I've told him this. Time will tell if he supports my decision or not.

We jog for a while at a slower pace, staying clear of the waves and the various people scattered along the shoreline.

"We'll just go through things one at a time. We can make of a list of your medications and determine one by one how they make you feel. Perhaps, adjust the dosage. We need to document how much sleep you get and how well you're eating. All of that contributes to your stress levels and your general state of mind. Then we can make some initial assessments and go from there."

"Nobody has really paid attention to any of that stuff," I say slowly. "My sleep is sporadic because of the headaches. I can't remember the last time I had a decent night's sleep. The headaches wake me up at night. I've become a light sleeper since the line drive."

"Right. Sleep deprivation is not good. I don't like that. Part of our goal here should be to just get you powered down. They have you all worked up about your form. There's been this singular focus on you coming back to baseball. I think we need to step back and assess what all is going on with you. For example, do you have flashbacks? Unrelated episodes. You're doing something or thinking about something, and you flash back to a completely different time? And are you losing time? Do you find yourself staring off into space?"

"Sometimes," I say warily. "I thought it was the drugs."

"Could be. Or, it's related to how your brain is working to put things back together for you. I'm not saying you're ever going to remember everything, Linc. I want to state that up-front. I can't promise you that kind of progress. But if we get you to a calm state and give your mind and body the much-needed rest, we might be able to bring some of it back. I've seen it before. It's a reasonable goal. It could be as simple as looking at photographs and listening to sounds, even music. These strategies might be enough of a trigger to help you make connections with your memory. This is simplistic I know but think of a child's coloring book. The dotted black lines are there but need to be drawn in and then be colored in to properly fill out what the picture is supposed to represent. The latest research in neuropsychology shows us that the mind can work like that too."

"How would it work exactly?" I ask.

"We help your mind fill in the dotted black lines and missing colors using things like photographs of people you used to know that you no longer remember. Kimberley can help us with some of that since she's known you for so long by helping us identify dates, times, important events and when they happened. She's prepared profiles like that for her other clients for completely different reasons, but her team can help us with the research of all of that. All of these things will help you, and your mind will probably start to make the connections, and your memory may begin to come back. Maybe not fully, but enough so that you can function in life a little more effectively. It's worth a try in any case." He looks at me. "If you want to try, of course."

We turn and head back toward the beach house at about the same time.

"I want to try," I say slowly. "Thanks for being so willing to help me. I appreciate your time." I start to smile. "But I'm not sure what to call you."

"Just call me Brad. I'm just here to help you out. Ask me anything. Tell me anything. It stays between us unless you want others to know. That includes Kimberley."

"Okay."

He stops running all together. "You don't have to remember anything if you don't want to. We can eliminate the pressure altogether if you just want to move forward instead of confronting your past. I wouldn't recommend it, but it's not up to me. It's up to you and you alone."

"I have a life I can't remember but on some deep level I can't quite get to, I know it's important to try. I don't know how I know that, especially given my questionable behavior in the past twenty-four hours, but maybe just approaching things differently will help me out in some new way."

"That's good. That's what we want. A different approach. That's all I can promise, but I'm fairly certain we can make your memory work better."

"Then, let's do this thing," I say.

CHAPTER SEVENTEEN

never say never

LINC

TEN MINUTES LATER, WE'RE CLIMBING BACK up the steps that lead to the house from the beach. Kimberley's on her laptop typing away furiously. She stops when she sees us and looks solely at Brad for some kind of reassurance. He smiles at her. She doesn't smile back.

"She didn't wait for my return call," she says. "Instead, she contacted her lawyer and he's already responded for her."

"Who didn't wait for your call?" I ask feeling uneasy by the anxious look on Kimberley's face. Brad gives Kimberley a warning look, but she starts to wave him off.

"He should know, Brad. He needs to know."

"I agree but it's complicated and maybe today isn't the best day to tell him all of that."

"Tell me what? Can you two please stop talking about me like I'm not in the God damn room? I really hate that." I turn to Kimberley. "Who didn't wait for your call?"

"Tally," she says flatly. "It's bad, Linc. Things can get a whole lot worse for you."

"*Tally*. You keep talking about Tally. Do I know her?"

I stalk off to the house and return with my wallet. "Is this her? My dad wouldn't tell me."

"That's her. A long time ago. Yes."

"Jesus Christ! This is the girl from the hospital I talked to that last night. *This* is *Miss Cloves and Vanilla*," I say to Brad as I hand him the photograph. "I've really fucked this up with her, haven't I?"

"Okay. Wow. Okay. Let's take a minute or two here. Sit down, Linc."

Brad pushes me into one of the deck chairs and moves over to his wife.

"*Trust me*. Now is not the time. If we want this to work, you need to listen to me. First, let me see what the email says." Brad leans over Kimberley's shoulder and scans the message. "Not today. No way." He looks intently at Kimberley. "Just respond saying he'll comply. We'll deal with the rest of this later. He needs to know everything, but let's not dump it all on him at once, okay? He doesn't remember. He's trying to put his life back together. Not much of this is his fault. He got hit by a line drive going ninety miles an hour in a baseball game. Let's give it a rest for a second, shall we?" Brad says with growing irritation.

"Having the world know that he's lost some of his memory is not the worst thing that could have happened to him. He could have *died*. That didn't happen. I know she's hurting, and I get why she's doing what she's doing, but Linc needs someone on his side too. And I thought that was *us*, working together as a team to help him. I thought that was what you wanted, Kimmy. All I'm asking for is a little time here, until I can assess what all is going on with him. Let's stop the crazy train, shall we?"

"I thought you didn't use the word *crazy*, Doc?" I say.

We all laugh, which breaks up the tension that's begun to circulate among the three of us.

"You're absolutely right, Dr. Stevenson," Kimberley says with a hint of a smile. "You're right. ESPN and the LA Times are not the worst things to happen to him. You're right." She turns and looks at me. "I've got this. You don't have to worry about any of this; I'll handle it."

Brad clears his throat and hangs his head a little before looking at me as well. "I'm sorry too, Linc. I don't usually lose my temper quite like this in front of a friend or a patient or with my wife, for that matter. I just think we need to take some time with all of this and not react too quickly or to everything that transpires. We need to be patient and think things through."

"I know you're right, but you're messing with my *mojo*, mister," Kimberley says with a tired smile.

"Only when I have to," Brad says back to her easily.

"Okay. We'll think things through but I still need to call Mikhail Rostov. Tally's boss," she says looking at me, "and try to help her out." She slides out of her deck chair where she's been working and goes to stand at the deck's edge staring out at the magnificent Pacific. Brad follows her. It's a surreal five minutes while Kimberley seems to quietly count the ocean waves that hit the shore and Brad methodically strokes her back and whispers words I cannot hear.

I hang back from the two of them feeling ashamed of my escapades from last night with a woman named Trinna whose face I can't even recall now. In vain, I search for a silver lining in all of this, but I can't seem to find one.

Kimberley comes back to the table and grabs her cell phone and immediately transforms into the publicist extraordinaire we all know with a single smile.

She moves away from us as she dials.

"Mikhail, it's Kimberley Powers. God, it's been a while I know. I miss you. Yes, we should totally work together again. I may be in San Fran in the next week or two. Let's meet up." She pauses. "Yes, that's why I'm calling actually. Tally Landon is amazing. It's been a bit crazy for her the past few months, and it's gotten a little worse today. Look, she's one of my best clients just like Lincoln Presley is, so I was wondering if you could spare her for the next couple of nights?" She stops again.

"After all, tonight's just a run-through, right? That would be great. I don't want there to be any repercussions if she misses it, you know? I told her I'd ask you personally. You've always been so good to your dancers, Mikhail. You're the best." Kimberley vaguely smiles and then winks at Brad and me. "Yes, I still work with them. It's a three-year contract with the NYC Ballet. Yes, they'd take her back in a heartbeat; that's a fact, actually. But you've been good to Tally, right? I'm sure I'd know if one of my best clients was unhappy on any level with you or SFB. We go back pretty far. Tally and I." There's a long pause and finally a victorious laugh from Kimberley. "Thanks, Mikhail. I knew I could count on you. I'll let her know. Thanks."

She ends the call and looks over at Brad. "Alrighty then," she says with a ghost of a smile.

"*See?* You threatened to take his best talent straight back to New York, and he fell right in line," Brad says.

"Hopefully, Tally will see it that way," Kimberley says looking anxious all at once. "She is really upset and I need to call her back within the next fifteen minutes like I said would. I mean who knows what she'll do next."

"Babe, she's just hurting, probably as much or more than Linc but in a different way. Let me call her. I'll tell her you wanted to ensure you got back to her within the agreed-upon time frame, but you're stuck on another conference call. Let me try to smooth some things out with her."

Kimberley hands Brad her cell. "Call her. If anyone can talk her down from the ledge, it's the great Dr. Bradley Stevenson."

Unassuming and confident enough for all three of us, Brad dials Tally's number while Kimberley and I stand together leaning up against the railing and watch Brad the psychiatric maestro at work.

"Tally, it's Dr. Bradley Stevenson. Yes, I'm Kimberley's husband."

He smiles and I actually feel myself relax just watching him. "Thank you. It's been a few months but I love being married to Kimberley. Married life is good. We're worried about you. She's on another phone call and didn't want to miss the time window she promised in getting back to you. She's got everything worked out with your director. He called? That's good." He pauses.

"So. How are you holding up?" There's a long silence.

Brad winces and looks away from us. "That's awful. I wish we were all there to help you. Can you make it safely to your friend's car? Why don't you keep me on the line until you do? Sure. I'm right here." He sits down in one of the deck chairs and waits. "And just remember about the worst thing that can happen is they take a picture of you. And so what, right? *Exactly*. They'll caption it however they want. I know it's frustrating. Good. She sounds like a great friend. I'd love to meet her sometime."

There's another long silence. Then, Brad looks over at me.

"I'm here with him actually. We're going to do some work together about all of that. I specialize in neuropsychology and have a practice in Manhattan. You did? Where? I know that area. Yes, of course; they serve the best burgers that side of town. You do? My favorite thing, too. Yeah, Kimmy's always after me about that," he laughs a little, "but I love them too much to give them up."

"We are no longer here," Kimberley says looking enchanted with Brad.

I glance sideways at Kimberley. "He's pretty great, by the way."

"I know."

For his part, Brad looks our way again and gives us an all thumbs up. "That's understandable and no, I won't make any promises about that. I can only imagine how hard this has been on you. I know. I'm sorry too. If it makes you feel any better, he says nothing happened."

Brad looks over at me, and I slowly nod but feel guilty and foolish at the same time because I cannot explain those used condoms.

"Either way. It looks bad. And it made you feel worse. Just know that I think you and he share the same interest in safe-guarding Cara's well-being right now. Yes, I agree. Let's give it some time. *More time*. That's probably best. Okay, so you're on the way to your friend's house. Great. Why don't you call Kimberley when you reach Marla's? That would make us all feel better. It's nice talking with you too even virtually like this. You're welcome. I will. Thanks, Tally."

"See how he does that? He could charm feathers off of a bird," Kimberley says softly with a little smile before pushing away from the railing and launching herself directly into Brad's arms. "Thank you, husband."

"You're welcome, wife." Brad kisses Kimberley but then steps back from her and looks over at me. "We've got a lot of work to do. I know you want to know everything, Linc, but I don't want you be overwhelmed by it all and have it set you back any further. Kimberley, you need to do up those profiles, so we can go over those with Linc. I need photographs, time lines that call out important events in his life he may not remember. That's how we should start out anyway."

He puts his arm around her and whispers something to her as the two of them head inside and pulls her along inside.

"So when do we start? When are you two going to tell me about Tally and how I used to know her?"

"Soon," Kimberley says looking somewhat guarded now by whatever Brad has just said to her.

I watch the two of them interact from my vantage point on the deck and appropriately feel like a third wheel. Sighing with frustration, I turn and lean on the railing and watch the Pacific. The sound of the waves and the promise of a spectacular sunset offer me a reprieve, but I have to wonder if I'm going to get one. Or, if it's already too late for that.

CHAPTER
EIGHTEEN

wanna get to know you

S AM WILDE STOPS WHAT HE'S DOING and stares at me for a
few seconds, then he nods slowly. Eventually, a little smile
flits across his face as if he's just learned an important secret. A little
undone by the intensity I detect in his gaze, I shimmy up to the
edge of the bar and sweetly order a Diet Pepsi and a hamburger with
everything but tomato from him. He raises an eyebrow at my special
request and my somewhat failing flirtatious efforts, but promises to
have it ready for me *very soon*. I return his winning smile with one of
my own, the one I reserve for special occasions. It's been a while. My
facial muscles ache with the unusual effort.

He starts to leave, but then he turns back, pauses in that

unnerving, sexy way of his I remember. My heart beats erratically. I go for nonchalance with a slight shrug of one shoulder. His sudden attention for me alone does not go unnoticed by the other female patrons still languishing late at the bar who undoubtedly vie for some of his time.

"To go?" He conveys nothing but innocence in the way he asks this. "*Or*, are you staying here? You could…wait for me while I close up." There's this long moment where we stare at each other, suddenly very much aware that my answer will have an effect upon us both. The rest of the bar goes silent fully cognizant of our noteworthy exchange. "And then, I could walk you home."

Now he shrugs and gets this little smile. Meanwhile, all these open sighs of disappointment and a few hisses from the ladies in waiting to my right at his bold suggestion are audible all around.

A loaded question for sure.

Yet, he just stands there waiting patiently for my answer. He gives me this I-dare-you-to-say-yes-with-this-crowd look.

Despite the growing ruckus of protest surrounding us, he makes me laugh. I am grateful for this little respite even if it's just for a few minutes from the dark turn my life has taken.

"I'm staying." I catch my lip and attempt to hide a sheepish smile. Then, dip my head, a little embarrassed at his brazen suggestion and my unexpected answer, especially since I'm obviously situated among his most avid female fans, and may even be risking bodily harm for accepting his invitation.

I'll let him walk me home.

We can play house.

Or, something else.

I've toyed with this idea long enough and I'm here to make good on it. The look I reward him with tells him this. He slowly nods as if he's already figured out the plan for both of us.

His blatant self-confidence in our little exchange has me laughing again. He looks surprised by this, shakes his head, and begins to laugh too.

It's ten o'clock at night. I'm at loose ends with absolutely nothing to do. Rehearsal for the part of Cinderella doesn't start for three weeks. The part of Cinderella is mine, *if I don't screw it up.*

These were Mikhail's last threatening words to me after the final night's performance of *The Nutcracker* on Christmas night. Two days ago.

Cara is spending the night with my parents as agreed to earlier in the week when we were there for Christmas. I am supposed to be resting up, having fun of some kind—like sleeping in and enjoying my time off. My parents have not yet learned the sordid details about Linc's escapades in LA just four nights ago. Not really tabloid people my parents, although I suspect my dad has heard a few things. He does follow the sports pages. In any case, neither of them have brought it up to me.

We're all going for normal, coping in any way we can find. Thus, I am here because it was a half-hour ride back on the Metro, after I dropped Cara off at Mom and Dad's, and in lieu of going home to a dark house by myself, stopping by *The Promissory Note* seemed like a good idea. It has seemed like a good idea for some time now. One I have had several times over the past fours days or so since Linc Presley's whoring around episode in LA began. The rage over all of that still burns through me.

Distrust lingers and actually grows. I've been put through too much. I have nothing left to lose. Even so, I've never been brave long enough to actually walk the two blocks from Tremblay's place to this one, keeping the idea alive and finally following through on the-girl's-got-to-move-on mission in seeing Sam Wilde again.

Until now.

Two months, twenty-three days, twenty-one hours, and eighteen minutes since that line drive obliterated my life.

Who's still counting?

I sip my diet soda and contemplate things.

I revel—*or is that wrestle?*—with the idea of moving on.

My body still trembles at the idea of coming here to see Sam and battles these gigantic doses of knowable fear which zing me from all sides like endless shock waves.

All my fears—falling, losing, and failing—come calling. Granted, these fears visit my psyche quite often, just not usually all at the same time like now.

Breathe, Tally.

Marla has continued to champion her cause—*me*. Her chant every time we talk now begins with her best you-should-just-move-on-Tally speech. It gets more frequent and louder.

The LA debacle just a few days ago still follows him around and inadvertently me. Yet, I hate reading or hearing about it because the pain is too far reaching. Any more news of Lincoln Presley and his escapades and I fear I may not survive it.

I am broken by it all.

Why doesn't everyone see that?

The truth is I have my answers regarding Lincoln Presley. He's met someone. Or, he's considered a player. And maybe he is now. The papers and ESPN all still say so. No retraction was ever printed although Kimberley Powers has been quoted as saying her client denies all involvement with Trinna Danner.

But does it even matter?

No one has heard from Linc for the past few days. Beyond the he'll comply with my lawyer's request, I haven't heard anything more from Kimberley Powers. And why would I?

Six months of no-contact from Linc is what I requested. Six months of no-contact from Linc is what I'm getting. So why do I feel so empty with this supposed victory in what has become a battle between us? *I got what I wanted. I wanted this; didn't I?*

Just this morning, Marla suggested a visit to *The Promissory Note* was in order because reaching out to Sam is most definitely a good idea according to the bestie. She said, "You should go see Sam," at least six different times during our conversation today. "It would do you good. *He* would do you good. And hey, there's this doctor that Charlie knows."

And, so it goes.

While Marla launched into her best, let's-fix-up-Tally-with-someone mode most likely to assuage her own guilt over having the perfect life, in comparison to mine, which is so clearly fucked up, I withdrew from her completely. By the time our phone conversation was over, I agreed to see *somebody*—a counselor, a therapist, and or date the entire Lowell High School football team even if jail bait as they most certainly would be—just to get her off of my back and off the phone.

And yet, I've been thinking.

I've been contemplating things ever since the news stories began to circulate.

So.

This is what moving on feels like.

Sam returns with my hamburger and places the plate in front of me with a French waiter flourish. Then, he proceeds to lean directly across from me with his arms folded across his wide chest and judiciously watch me as I perform my unique ritual surgery upon my meal. Under his guise of continual fascination and open disgust, I proceed to destroy the masterpiece that he's so carefully put together by adroitly removing the top bun, tossing it aside, and then slicing the burger into eight equal parts with the steak knife he's provided, just like a surgeon's daughter surely has been taught.

I glance up at him after savoring the first lovely bite, and note he is properly captivated.

And I can admit to liking it.

This is what moving on looks and feels like.

I attempt to smile, but that proves to be too much.

I'm still too close to the edge of despair.

I might actually cry instead.

And that, I absolutely cannot afford to do here.

I wait for Sam and decide we will have the Lincoln Presley discussion on the walk home. I silently congratulate myself for inadvertently planning ahead by invoking the aid of darkness. Yes, I can take much-needed protection in the dark, which will hide any unexpected tears because I might cry. It happens. Sam just won't see it or know it, although I have recently concluded that I am all cried out. There appears to be no tears left for the baseball player.

Thus, my unexpected debut at *The Promissory Note*. It's another ninety minutes before the last of the bar patrons clear out after having been served last call. Sam's clearing all the remaining empty glasses they left behind as the last one files out. Finally, we exit the restaurant's front doors. I patiently wait for him as he locks up while attempting to breathe and appearing normal.

What am I doing?

Why am I here?

Sam looks calm, cool, and collected as if girls come by the restaurant every night to ask him for a walk home. *Maybe, they do.* He gets this lazy smile as he comes toward me. Still, I'm taken aback when he deftly takes a hold of my left hand as soon as we step out onto the sidewalk together.

In the next moment, he brings it to his mouth, brushes his lips across the top of my hand, and then plants an actual kiss on the inside of my wrist. I avoid crying out but just barely because his simple, sensuous gesture has just about unraveled me already.

I'm being outplayed on the seduction front.

This, I am not prepared for.

He slides his arm through mine and matches my gait within seconds. I try not to think of Linc and the way he would do this too. I try not to think of *him* at all, but of course I do.

"Merry Christmas, belated," he says.

"Merry Christmas, belated. And Happy New Year."

"Happy New Year. So, how's the baseball player?" Sam says with a sign of clairvoyance. "What I mean to say is how is he doing? I mean you're here, and he's not."

Hidden by darkness, I take perverse delight in hearing the trembling in his voice and note the quick succession of false-start statements. Still, I say nothing. Instead, I just shrug my shoulders and keep on walking. I revel in my penchant for silence.

"I tried to follow the stories for a while," Sam says after a few minutes. "But then, they seemed to stop with the ending of baseball season until the thing four days ago."

"The *thing* four days ago. That's a nice way of putting it," I say with a hint of sarcasm.

"So how is he?"

"He's fine? I guess. I don't know," I manage to say in a low, husky voice. "We're not together. He's concentrating on baseball among other things, *obviously*." The bitterness left behind by the salacious news story in LA is still fresh. "I'm concentrating on ballet. There's a no-contact agreement in place for the next six months because… it's complicated."

I shrug my shoulders and have to hope he'll take the hint and drop it. He doesn't say anything more. I keep my eyes focused on the sidewalk because suddenly this act of putting one foot in front of the other has become complicated. Sam is right beside me, gripping my arm ever tighter, which proves lucky when I almost trip over a raised edge in the sidewalk.

"Careful, now," he says softly. "I'm sorry. You don't want to talk about it, do you?"

"No." I gaze up in silent wonder at Tremblay's house.

How did we get here so fast?

Tremblay's house. I still call it that because I am incapable of thinking of it as home actually. Carelessly, I admit this to Sam and then wince because he's probably been here hundreds of times with Tremblay. They dated for something like two years.

"I shouldn't have brought Allaire up. I'm sorry."

"It's okay. It's been a while. Almost a year since she…really a year and half since we were…you know *together*."

I nod in the darkness. I'm not sure he sees it.

And, I cannot care.

"Right. A year. Almost. Many months. Years. But time just… marches on, doesn't it? Just like they say. You think we're the only ones that count it so maniacally?"

"I don't know," he says sounding hollowed out all at once.

"See, Sam?" I say softly. "That's what I do I destroy your most pleasant thoughts and memories of someone with all these taint- ed fucked-up ones about the passage of time and death. And now, I'll apologize for a second time. Keep track. There will be more of those." I raise my arms and offer it up as a prayer or penance, one of those, to the dark cloudy sky above us.

Sam doesn't say anything of course.

What could he say? I am a piece of work and he best find that out right the fuck now.

The moon decides to go behind the clouds starting to form. We're apparently lost in all these separate but tortured thoughts of our own making because the sudden darkness envelops us into this long protracted silence. Together, we study the clouds and search in vain for the lost moon and our missing breaths.

"Missing persons," I whisper. "That's what we are."

"Maybe," he says on a sigh and then clears his throat and reaches for my hand. He smooths it over and over with his long tapered fingers, and I inadvertently smile. "So, Tally, what—"

"*Why* did you want to walk me home?" I interrupt his speech and forcefully pull my hand back from his. I seek out his face in the confounding darkness, suddenly disturbed by his touch and my automatic aching for it as well as my inability to clearly see his face.

"Because I *know* you want to talk about it."

"No. I really don't. There's been enough *talking* about it. In fact, *everybody's talking* about it." My smile disappears altogether. "Thanks for walking me home. You should go now. I mean it. Run like hell. I am a very bad idea, Sam Wilde. *Trust me on this.*"

"Thanks for the warning." He smiles in the dark at me. I gasp when he suddenly pulls me along toward the house.

Fascinated in some way by him, I watch as he stoops down and retrieves a key from the flower box where Allaire must have hidden it years before. He raises it in triumph while I watch in stunned silence as he unlocks the door, turns on the porch light and then all the living room ones inside as well as if he owns the place. *Maybe he did at one time.*

He guides me through the doorway touching the base of my spine, gently pushes me down onto the sofa, and disappears in the direction of my unused gourmet kitchen. I'm too surprised to even respond.

This is what knights do, apparently. They take over.

A part of me can admit to liking that about him.

I take respite in counting the minutes since he left me in the living room.

Ten.

I can plainly hear him working away in my kitchen. Good luck with that since my food offerings consist of Cheerios, milk for Cara, and plain yogurt for me. Perhaps, he's a magic chef and can conjure up real food too. I grin at the prospect. I'm still smiling when he finally appears bearing two steaming cups of hot chocolate on a fancy silver tray. *A wedding gift. One of those early ones someone sent before it all went to hell.*

All should be warned; I remain in rare form. I returned nothing. I let them all figure it out when the date came and went and no wedding ensued and no thank you card was ever sent. I blame my bad form in the etiquette department all on Lincoln Presley or Davis Presley. One of those Presley men is surely to blame for all of this—the fucked-up turn my life has taken, including the faux pas in not sending thank you notes to anyone for the early wedding gifts.

My anger for all of it, especially after the LA incident grows exponentially—upwards, and downwards, and sideways—like a bad weed, or better yet, raging bacteria that the greatest antibiotic is unable to kill off.

I must hate him now. I love him and hate him at the same time. I wield this newfound rage deep inside, so deep that no one sees it, but it's there growing and changing and getting stronger with every passing day.

It's true that my heart first broke in October when he didn't remember me, but the pain keeps going and breaks up the rest of me from the inside out like the spreading of shattered glass, one irreparable crack at a time.

Yet, I feel nothing but the pain.

I must warn Sam, at some point, but not tonight. Tonight, I will live and breathe and be with a man who wants to be with me, obviously.

I will not feel the pain.

I will take a respite from the pain.

This I will do. For me.

I will take and not give back, and I will enjoy it.

Somehow.

I look over at Sam. And some minuscule part of me finds the strength to smile at him.

Shit.

Do not care.

You cannot afford to care.

CHAPTER NINETEEN

TALLY

M Y SILENT SOLILOQUY LEAVES ME ON edge when Sam hands me the mug of hot chocolate with a jaunty waiter flourish just like before at the restaurant. I attempt to appear at ease and gracious, and try not to count the calories but I do anyway. The melting marshmallows on top are throwing me off. I frown and start over.

"Let it go," Sam says as if he knows I'm counting.

He probably does. He dated Tremblay. He probably lived here at some point.

Surely, he knows how the dance world works. It's either splurge and purge or starve and live small. *The Boxer's Diet.*

It's my religion and basically the only one I follow these days.

Religion. My mind flashes to Pastor Dan and the gorgeous church overlooking the Pacific and briefly strays to thoughts as to what could have been my life by now. I get lost for a little while.

Sam's pushing at my hand. I almost spill the hot chocolate.

"Sorry." He smiles. "Stop it. Just drink it. Let it go."

I sip at it tentatively at first, then taste the peppermint Schnapps and the hint of Kahlua and look at him somewhat quizzically.

"It's almost midnight," Sam says with guy authority. "I need a drink, don't you?"

"I don't know what I need."

"I do." He gets this smug look and then drinks his own hot chocolate concoction. "First, I feed you. Then, you sit for a while *thinking.*" He smiles wide. "And then, you talk. And *then*, we'll see where it goes from *there.*"

"I'm ready for *there.*"

"No. You think you're ready for *there*, but you're so far from *there* that it's as if we're coming at each other from separate universes."

"How cosmic," I say irritably.

He raises an eyebrow and begins to study my face rather intently for signs.

Of what? Wreckage? Brokenness.

A special brand of craziness?

That we will need to discuss. *Later.*

I catch my lip between my teeth to stop it from trembling. I'm nervous all at once because this seduction isn't going at all the way I imagined it would go which stirs up equal parts of madness and fury. I force a smile. "The thing is I just want to get lost for a while. I don't want to talk about *it*. What's the point? It doesn't help. Nothing does. *I know this.*"

"See just *talk*, Tally," he says quietly. "That's all. Just talk it all out."

Now, I sit silent.

I am not a talker.

He may as well learn that right now.

"Okay. I'll start." He sets down the mug and steeples his fingers together as if he's praying or contemplating deep thought. "Allaire and I. We were never right for each other. She was incapable of deep feelings and always vying for control. At first, I thought it was because she was older than me. Four years," he says and then hesitates. "I'm thirty-one by the way. You?"

"Twenty-two but way past forty." He nods and then gets this faint bemused smile. I decide it's because he's gotten me to answer. "Clever," I say drawing the number one in the air indicating he's scored a point.

He gets this little smile but it disappears as he continues. "So with Allaire, after a while, I began to realize it was just the way she was. She wasn't going to change and our relationship would always be this kind of twisted cat and mouse game. One of us had the power, the other didn't, but that was always changing."

He shrugs with nonchalance.

"I guess it worked. We each got what we wanted out of it to a certain degree."

"Which *was?*" I shouldn't care, but I am way past curious. Here's this knight in shining armor with this older woman, and she ruled him. I don't pretend to understand the dynamics of their relationship, but for some inexplicable reason I want to.

"It was easier." The way he answers seems like it costs him a great deal as if he's had to exchange a brief encounter with pain for this admission alone. He gets this funny grimace and sighs big running his hands through his hair. For a few seconds, he seems to lose his train of thought and gets this dazed expression. The sadness taints his features for a time and then disappears again.

Empathy for him bursts forth.

Unexpected.

"It was easier," I say softly. "You see I completely get that. Not with Linc, but with others…we don't have to talk about any of this," I say airily sweeping my hand through air while he watches me do it.

"No, we don't, but we should. Guns on the table, right?" He settles further back in his chair directly across from me. "She had an older sister. Lise was her name. She came to visit Allaire a few times, especially after Cara was here, more after that, and I foolishly thought maybe…just maybe, we could take it all to a different level because she had a family she obviously cared about." He pauses for a long moment. "So I asked her. *I proposed.* I thought that was what she wanted. I thought somewhere in that dark soul of hers, she wanted the same things I did." He frowns and then tries to laugh but it comes out sounding hollow and soulful at the same time. "She threw the ring in my face *literally*, and moved out ten days later to God knows where, without really saying good-bye. She gave me those envelopes for you, a few instructions, and basically left me, knowing I'd figure it all out one day."

His words and complete openness about Allaire Tremblay and their complex relationship surprise me. I'm not sure what to say to all he's revealed so I start with the last thing.

"Why would she do something like that? Leave you and hide Cara away from me intentionally like that?" I pull up my knees and tuck my head into them without meeting his eyes.

"I scared her because I wanted more. You scared her because you wanted more. I missed all the signs. She talked about your visit for weeks after. She was uneasy. She saw how good you would be with Cara and it scared the hell out of her that she might lose that little girl to you one day. So she gave up everything, including me, for a secret life with Cara away from all of us."

"What if I'm just like her? All hell bent on a career that makes you commit at a soul level? What if I have a dark soul like that too?"

"You don't. You're not like her." He stops talking and then looks back at me intently. "She wasn't a bad person, Tally. She just couldn't let go. You know what I mean," he says sounding somewhat unsure as to how explain it all. "She was happy. We were happy. Allaire just had a tendency to protect whatever she felt was hers, rightfully or not. I asked her about you once—about the adoption of Cara. She told me she manipulated you far too much in gaining the rights to Cara. You were young and scared, she wanted a child, and you needed a way out at the time. Geez, you were *eighteen*. She took advantage of you. She felt bad about it—the way it went down. I don't think she meant to be evil or even behave so badly in the end. She was just being Allaire; and, in the end, that proved to be too much even for her."

"She left you."

"Yes. I scared the hell out of her about getting married." He gets this twisted smile.

"Scared you too, I bet."

He dips his head and won't look at me. "She definitely caused me to want things I've never wanted before. Monogamy. Commitment. Marriage."

"You loved her."

"Yes. Like you love Lincoln Presley. She was my water."

Water.

It's as if he's pointed a gun at my heart and fired. I get up in one swift motion and move to the furthest part of the room away from him while my breath whips away from me like an unexpected wind gust.

I hear the rasping and it takes a few seconds to realize it's coming from me.

Sam is here. He strokes each side of my face, smooths back strands of my hair, and tells me to breathe. "Tally, take in some air. Just breathe. Focus on me. Look at me, Tally. Open your eyes. That's right. See? You're okay. Just concentrate on breathing in and out. See? Okay. Again. Breathe in again, just like that."

I recover.

His coaching helps.

Eventually, I become aware of his arms draped across my shoulders in this platonic embrace. His discernible strength seeps into me.

I look up at him then and concentrate on the faint lines in his fine face that sun and nature have extolled upon him now visible when I am up close like this. His eyes are this amazing glacial blue with flecks of gold. His eyes. You could look into them every day and experience this glimpse of true wonder. His golden hair is a little long and in need of a scissors. He has this faint white scar across one brow and another on the left side of his face as if someone has taken a thin white pencil and drawn on him. *How lucky were they?*

He is a gold rush.

A mountain stream, cool and fresh and colorful.

He is ice and snow.

He is sun and rain.

He's got the look of Thor going on and it takes every bit of my willpower to avoid tracing his lips with my own because he is a god.

And I am attracted to those.

Shit.

"You okay?" Sam drops his arms to his sides and steps back from me. The warmth disappears with him. I shiver. He takes my hand and leads me back to the sofa. "How many of those have you had?"

I miss the clinical part of him in asking me this. "A couple times a month. Twice on Sunday."

"How many for *real*?"

"A couple of times a month. Sometimes more when I'm stressed out. I've had them for years. Since Holly…" I bite my lip because I've said too much, and now he's looking at me like I'm a rare bacteria strain he's discovered under a microscope.

"Holly?"

"She was my twin. We were seventeen. She died in a car accident on Valentine's Day. It'll be five years in February. So yes, *years*, I've had them for years at least five, maybe more." I become notably defiant.

I have this down.

Defiance and defensiveness. I'm an expert at wielding these two things for just about any situation.

Bring it.

"Who knows about these attacks?"

Now, I'm getting uncomfortable but feel compelled to answer for some unknowable reason. "*He* used to know. Marla. That's it. No one else knows."

"Are you being treated?"

"Like with a psychiatrist or something? No. Why? You think… I'm crazy?" My question is laced with disappointment as to where he's taking this.

"No one is crazy just because they suffer with panic attacks from trauma. But you can't handle them on your own forever. So what else? Tell me. You have triggers, obviously. What else triggers you? Sets you off, so you can't breathe where you begin to panic, like what just happened?"

"You want the list?" I stall, and he's looking at me more intently now. There is no way he's going to let me off the hook on this. I run my tongue along my lips thinking about how to answer while he openly watches me. *But why should I? Why does he need to know?*

So I ask him. "Why do you need to know all of this? What do you care?"

He nods with understanding like a doctor would and then slips my hand into his. It takes another full minute to realize he's taking my pulse. "I used to be a medic in Special Forces. Covert ops. Saw it all the time. There are triggers. You have some. Tell me what they are."

"Special Forces. Like hot-shot soldier stuff?" I smile, intrigued.

He gives me this stern look. "You can make this as hard or easy as you like. You choose. I'll listen. Tell me what your triggers are."

I start out slow. "I've always had fears—losing, failing, falling. I'm a dancer. Falling was the worst for a long time. Next up came failing. The part. The show. The director. I got serious about ballet when I was eight. *Eight years old.* I didn't like losing parts, missing steps, falling, or failing. Those were my fears and they just got bigger over the years. Harder to overcome. And then, Holly died. We were seventeen. And the big three seemed to metamorphose into this never-ending, ever present fear of loss. So yes, there's this big gaping hole inside of me that I try to avoid feeling at all costs, but sometimes it engulfs all of me no matter what I do."

I take an unsteady breath and look over at him. He waits patiently with a gaze that implores me to finish.

"I was driving. I suppose I live with that guilt too." I nod slowly and start over. "I was driving. It was raining. A black SUV clipped my car on the 101 on Valentine's Day. Almost five years ago. I barely got out of the car in time. Somehow I did, but Holly didn't. There was a fire, and then an explosion on the freeway in the middle of the 101 on Valentine's Day, and I was driving. My identical twin sister died. You do the math." I wince in admitting to it all.

My breath gets shallow all over again. I start to wheeze while Sam still holds onto my wrist and must feel my rapidly rising pulse for a second time.

"Breathe. Just breathe. Keep your eyes open. Look at me, Tally. Just concentrate on taking in air, in and out. You can do this."

It takes a few minutes, but I recover again just like before. I'm less afraid and simply amazed by what he's taught me to do in the last fifteen minutes when an attack comes on.

"Tell me the rest," he says gently.

"Linc was there. At the accident. I didn't know or remember that until much later." I look intently at Sam, who nods encouraging me. "And he was my air, and he used to tell me…I was his water. So my triggers would seem to be the rain, the 101, Valentine's Day, black SUVs, sometimes just riding in a car, let alone driving one, the mention of Holly, air, or water and just this overwhelming guilt that I lived and she didn't. The good twin dies; the bad one lives. How is that fair to any of us?"

He reaches for my hand again and just holds it in his. It reminds me so much of Lincoln Presley that I catch and hold my breath and begin to shake my head at him.

"Don't," I finally say.

"It's going to be okay."

A single tear betrays me and slides down my cheek. "That's the thing. It's *not* okay."

"It *is*. You're alive." He traces the tear trail. "You need to stop apologizing for that."

"What makes you so sure?"

He looks confused and then he slowly nods. "That you're *alive?*" I nod. He touches my breasts with his hand. "Your heart beats. You're an amazing dancer in one of the most demanding jobs, physically and mentally, that one can do in the world. And you are a star at it, besides. You've experienced as much tragedy as some of the men I've served with, and yet you deal with the terror and the aftermath all on your own. It's incredible, really, that you've been able to do that, function, rise above it all, let alone keep it all going. You survived, Tally. You're here and—"

"Broken. I'm broken and you should know that," I say interrupting his poignant speech. "I should come with a warning label like dynamite does. I'm broken, Sam."

I pull away from his touch.

"Let me fix you," he says after a time.

"No."

"Yes," he says nodding at me slowly.

Then, he pulls me forward turning me in his arms so I face away from him and closes his arms around me tight. After a long while, his heart beat synchronizes with mine. I close my eyes and just listen to his living sound.

"Okay. Then," he whispers to me. His simple words reach for me and my heart tumbles as if it is a key has just been inserted into the right lock. Miraculously, everything clicks.

I open my eyes and turn to look at him. Then, I genuinely smile for the first time in what feels like forever.

"Okay. Then," I finally say.

CHAPTER TWENTY

I'm gonna find another you

TALLY

It's three in the morning. Sam and I are still talking. Over the last four hours, we've rehashed the same topics—Linc, Tremblay, Cara, San Francisco Ballet, *The Promissory Note*—and invented new ones—relationships with or without benefits, what is love *really*, the merits of *Silver Linings Playbook* versus *The Lone Survivor* versus *The Hunger Games*. We found common ground in just about everything and agree we are eclectic and broken; and it remains fascinating to the two of us.

For the past twenty minutes, we've shared this companionable silence. I thought maybe he'd fallen asleep so I finally give life to another confession of mine.

"There isn't a day that goes by that I don't regret giving up Cara." I've never given voice to this admission before, and I tremble with the guilt but at least make an attempt to hold myself together. I turn to gauge Sam's reaction.

He's awake. I bite my lip regretting saying this aloud.

"Cara doesn't remember any of that," he says softly. "She just knows you're here now. That's what counts." He stops, sits up, and takes a long pull of his drink which has now gone cold. "You know, Allaire even said to me once, 'you'd like Tally.'" He looks over at me with undeniable interest. "And, I do *like you.*"

"Why would she have said such a thing?"

"You take risks and live to tell about it. I find that *very attractive.* Somehow, she knew I would...*like* you."

I ignore the gist of what he's just said and concentrate on the chocolaty film that's formed on the top of my own doctored drink. "Why would you like me?"

"I don't know. I just do."

"I'm broken and selfish and a head case. I destroy every relationship I've ever had, or it destroys me. One of those two things always happens. I'm broken." I look up at him. "Don't *like* me, Sam."

"Can't help it." He gets this intense look.

I shake my head at him. "This is a bad idea. You know that, right?"

"Probably." He looks intrigued.

We sip our now-cold chocolate concoction in companionable silence about a foot away from each other. Then he eyes me curiously. "So Cara...I imagine she's a little confused about Linc, at this point. Does she talk about him at all?"

"After the accident...it was hours before they found her at the scene with Allaire still in the car with her. To this day, I don't know what all she saw, but she still isn't talking, hardly at all. She'll say '*Momma*' occasionally, but that's about it. We don't talk about Linc anymore." I say softly. "She has trust issues, bonding issues. We've been seeing a counselor every two weeks for almost the past year. She can't figure out why Cara isn't talking by now either, but then again, with what's happened to Linc...we're just doing the best we can."

"What did you tell her about him?"

"At first, I told her that Daddy hurt his head, and he'd be gone for a while. Of course, that reason doesn't really work anymore."

He frowns and then gets this dazed half-smile but continues. "I'm sorry. I was going to let you bring him up first, and here I am jumping ahead to the *real* topic at hand."

"The *real* topic at hand. I'm not good with that one." I force myself to smile.

"Well, what happened that the two of you didn't stay together? He gets hit by a line drive. It's all over the news. It sounds like it was touch and go for a while. Next thing I know, they're talking about what went down in LA and then most recently it has been all about the possibility of sending him down to the minor leagues. The Giants are all hush hush about his contract, but they obviously aren't happy. And yet, you're here and not that I'm complaining—"

"You think they'll send him down?"

"The Giants have a pretty full roster. They need him pitching. If he doesn't have it? Yeah. I'm sure they want to give him time to get his pitching back. That's the rumor anyway. Sometimes, teams do that before they bring them all the way back up to the majors. He'll probably play in the minor leagues for part of the season at least, and then they'll likely bring him back up. If it happens, he'll be working out with the Fresno Grizzlies by late February probably before then."

"Fresno. Mars. No difference," I say in a wooden tone. "Maybe that's easier." I don't say anything more.

There's a possibility he'll be sent down. That can't be good. A part of me is sad for him. Let's face it; I haven't exactly focused on Linc's problems in all of this, although there isn't a big enough excuse in the world that will explain what happened with him in LA, and I've been nursing my own heartbreak over that since then. I didn't take the time to feel sorry for him on any level until now. But being sent down would be a huge blow to his ego. At least, I think it will. Maybe, he'd be secretly relieved because he wouldn't be pressured to remember everyone's name. The Giants would expect him to know them, just like I did. Remorse swirls because I never really looked at the world from Linc's perspective before.

Selfish, Tally. You're selfish and self-involved.

Sam watches me closely. I am definitely not portraying the girl who wanted nothing more than to get laid tonight.

"See? You do need to talk about him. I take it you haven't been tracking all the news about him."

"No," I say with a sigh. "LA pretty much did me in."

"News about him being sent down started a few days ago. Right after the LA thing. He's on the IR list, and sending him down to the Fresno Grizzlies might be to prove a point to him as to who's in charge. It sounds like he refused to attend all press conferences based on the news reports. *That* must have pissed off enough of the Giants' brass. Maybe that's why there's more talk about sending him down. I thought you knew. That's why…I was surprised to see you. I thought maybe you'd be going with him."

"No. I'm not *with* him. Definitely not going to be with him. Definitely not with him."

News of Linc's troubles travels through me like a fuse that's been lit. *Why do I care?* After LA, I shouldn't care. And yet, for the first time, I actually confront reality that he is really never coming back. He doesn't remember me, and he isn't ever going to remember me. I try to hide this feeling of complete devastation from Sam. I take in air in slow shallow breaths thinking maybe if air gets into my lungs, thinking if I relax a little all this pent-up angst will miraculously disappear. I absently study a thread coming loose on my jeans and begin to pull on it, going for Marla's fidget-fashion trick. I avoid looking at Sam at all costs.

"Are you okay?" He asks.

"I'm fine." The standard Tally party line. He shakes his head at me in disbelief. "We're over. We've been over for a long time now. Actually, two weeks after it first happened," I finally say.

"But why?"

I stare at Sam and hesitate to put it all into words, and yet he waits patiently while I try to get air all the way back into my lungs. "The LA Times had it right. He doesn't…" I start again. "He. Doesn't. Remember. Me. At all. He lost at least six years of time, maybe more. When he woke up from the coma, he didn't know who I was. He thought I was his nurse." I shake my head and try to smile. "Davis Presley, his dad? He wanted his only son to concentrate on baseball, and since Linc didn't remember me...well, Davis just thought it might be best to cut off all contact. In other words, I was in the way. I naively thought that Davis or someone would eventually tell Linc about me and Cara, but I suppose she just represents an unnecessary complication, to Linc's father, at least."

"It's not really up to his father. It's up to Linc."

"He doesn't remember...any of it. There are millions of dollars at stake as well as his career." I wince, remembering Kimberley Powers' exact words. "I just thought he would be told about us, and at least he would want to see Cara...I didn't know they would keep his past from him, or that the Giants would consider sending him down. I'm sure he's just trying to keep his head above water right now. Baseball is an intense sport. The schedule is brutal. And now he may have to pitch for the minor leagues. He's basically starting over," I say with an unhappy sigh. "And the LA thing royally pissed me off, so I had my lawyer draft up a no-contact agreement. I needed to protect Cara as much as myself. I didn't want his whoring around splashed all over the sports pages or ESPN to reach my daughter somehow. Or me." I laugh, but it doesn't quite work.

Sam looks sympathetic. He puts his left arm around me. "I'm sorry. I didn't know. How have you been coping with his not remembering you?"

"Not well, obviously." I frown and try to smile. "My parents have been great. My best friend Marla, you remember her, right? She keeps me in line."

"The knockout blonde? Yeah. She was there when you dropped in months ago. She's married to Charlie, right? And they picked you up that day with the Moscow thing."

"The Moscow Thing. That's a good way of putting it. Yes, they were there that day too. It's been kind of awkward. Charlie is Linc's first cousin. I've refused to be around the family very much because of all that went down after Linc's injury. His dad was solely focused on Linc returning to baseball, and Charlie's parents sided with him. As I said, I was an unnecessary encumbrance and so was Cara. And when Linc didn't remember either of us, well, that gave Davis Presley all the power he needed. There was a bit of character assassination with Linc's six million dollar signing bonus missing for a time, but I managed to work it all out. No big deal. I was just the fiancée, and I was clearly in the way of Linc's sole focus on returning to baseball at least as far as Davis was concerned. Family ties and all of that." I take a shuddering breath at all I've just revealed. "So, here we are."

"I think you should try to talk to him."

"Why?"

"To be *free* of him."

"*I am free of him.*"

"*No.* You're not."

"As free as I will ever be." I study Sam. He is bold and enlightened and a grown up. And I want to be all of that. "Love isn't everything, Sam Wilde; surely, we've both learned that much."

"You need to talk to him at least one more time."

"Why? You need guarantees, Mr. Wilde? I can't give you those. I'm broken, remember? Besides, now there's the six-month no-contact agreement in place. And I like it that way because I am *free* of him." I get this defiant look.

Sam looks skeptical. "He'll be in Fresno if the Giants send him down. You can find him there just by tracking the minor-league baseball schedule. You should go see him."

"He'll be in Fresno," I echo Sam. "Which may as well be a different country. I don't get there too often. In fact, I can easily say I've never been Fresno and will likely never go there."

"I know how to track him down."

"How? And what is it *exactly* that you do, besides tend a bar?" I ask with an exasperated sigh.

He gets this solemn look. "I can't tell you any of that *exactly*, but I can track him down for you. I've got some extraordinary skills in that area." He gets this funny look and starts to laugh at my confused expression. But then he looks a little uncertain and gets this guilty-as-charged look.

"A man of intrigue. Just what I need," I say softly.

"A man of intrigue doesn't begin to cover it." He gets this tight smile and I know he's not going to tell me anything more. "Time for bed. I'll take the sofa. We'll start up later today now that we've talked."

"What are we starting?"

"This." He kisses my forehead.

I regard him with a stony face laced with notable disappointment. "That's it? That's supposed to tide me over? Surely, you can do better than that, Sam Wilde."

"In time, my lady."

The Shakespeare thing is surprisingly sexy. Maybe I'm too tired to complain. He pulls me up from the sofa in one swift motion. Arm-in-arm, we walk up the stairs. My heart pounds and I begin to wonder if he's changed his mind about the no-sex-tonight thing. But no. He's pulling down the covers and beckoning me to climb inside. *Alone.*

"But I want you," I say, although my words come out a little slurred, more like, *I-wanch-yew.*

"I want you too," he says kissing my forehead once again. "Soon."

I laugh but then start to whine, telling him that Cara will be here later today. After that, I remind him that me and him must remain a separate thing from Cara.

He gets this quizzical look and reminds me that Cara already knows him. "Bonus," he says in this brazen way.

"We're a separate deal. For the time being. *Separate*, Sam. That's the way it has to be. So we won't have another chance to be alone like this for a while," I say in warning. "You should take a chance. On me. *With* me. You're not afraid of me, are you?"

Even so, he remains committed to the idea of leaving me alone in this bed. I resort to begging him to stay after I glimpse his ornate tattoos across his chest and upper arms when he adjusts his shirt collar and slips from my arms one last time. He is so different from Linc, and I am intrigued with this concept and the entire idea of Sam Wilde now.

Sam Wilde is a good idea.

"Please stay. I need you," I say.

And yet, after he's performed the knighted duties of checking the entire house for intruders, he prepares to leave me anyway insisting the sofa will be just fine after one final kiss on my forehead again. I label him a bad boy anyway for making me wait like this. I tell him this as he stands in my bedroom doorway.

"Goodnight, Tally," he says easily.

Too easily.

"Please stay," I say one more time as if I haven't said this fifteen times before in as many minutes.

"Soon, Tally," he says a little breathless. "Let's begin tomorrow; I mean, later today."

"Okay. Then," I finally say.

"Okay. Then."

And with that simple promise, he leaves me.

And I can't help but think, *they all do.*

PART 3

air & water

"There are all kinds of love in this world but never the same love twice."

-F. Scott Fitzgerald

CHAPTER TWENTY-ONE

missing you

LINC

"THIS WAS FOUR YEARS AGO. MORE than that, actually. She was seventeen," Kimberley says.

I'm staring at numerous photographs of Tally Landon similar to the one in my wallet I asked my dad about more than three months ago. The same girl who showed up in my hospital room the last night I was there. *Miss Vanilla and Cloves.* Just the thought of her amazing scent stirs up her image all over again. At least, I have that going for me. I can remember the recent past even if it's one I've royally fucked-up.

"Like I told you earlier, this is *Miss Cloves and Vanilla*," I say gloomily to Brad.

At least, the good doctor knows what that means even if Kimberley just looks at the two of us like it's some private joke she'd rather not be privy to. Instead, she shrugs and says, "moving on." It's obvious she's not in the mood for games. Kimberley is stressed out like I've never seen her before. "You rescued her from a car accident on the 101 where her twin sister Holly was killed. She didn't remember you then. Ironic, right? Then you two met at a party at Charlie's house months later. And things went from there."

"What do you mean things went from there?" I'm wary because Kimberley looks guilty about something and anxiously looks over at Brad. He just nods and doesn't say anything. He's already stated more than once, he's here as an observer only. This is Kimberley's show, as usual.

"She was seventeen, still at Paly high school, lover boy. She wouldn't turn eighteen for a few months, and you'd just gotten the offer with the Angels."

"She was at Paly? *Geez.* Did I *not know* this? And I was drafted by the Angels first *before* signing with the Giants?"

Kimberley gets this vexed look and starts to chew on her lower lip. She's nervous, but still refuses to tell me why. "Yes. Let's focus on the Tally part of this story, shall we? It's complicated. It gets more complicated. Maybe, that's enough for now."

Brad inclines his head at her. "Keep going."

She stalls for time and sips at her beer and casually looks around with a trained PR eye at the little cafe we've discovered in the town of Malibu. More than half the restaurant is filled with the rich and famous all trying to go incognito and remain unrecognized. I wear my baseball cap low over my face because the last thing we need is for someone to find out I'm here and ask me about baseball or the Giants or anything to do with the incident two weeks ago in LA with that blonde.

"There's millions on the line. If they get wind that you still can't throw a baseball, it's over." It's an ominous tone.

She sighs big.

"There's millions on the line. There's a song lyric in there somewhere. And show me that money because right now I don't have any of it," I say irritably.

"I'm already fielding calls left and right from the Giants to ESPN to the LA Times. Amy Ransom wants an exclusive, and I've promised her one if we can figure out what you should say. The Giants are going through your contract as we speak looking for any and all loopholes. Yes, you're on IR but if they can find a way to avoid that second year bonus, you can bet they will," she says. "They'll call it just business of course. I'm sorry I wish I could tell you some good news, but you touched Kryptonite, Superman, and right now we're a little powerless to fight them. Just know, the Giants' front office is not happy; they are worried on a multitude of fronts, including your on-the-job injury and the implications of all of that as well as the fact that they like their contract dollars to be well spent." She mimics me from earlier and takes a deep breath and holds it.

"Slow down, Kimmy," Brad says. "I thought we were going to focus on his past, not his contract."

She exhales slowly. "You're right," she says to him then looks over at me. "But that's why you pay your team the big bucks—me, your agent, and your lawyers; and we'll do what we can." She shoots me this fake smile.

"Just tell me what's really going to happen. Don't sugarcoat it for my benefit. Keeping me in the dark the past few months has done absolutely nothing for me. Perhaps, if someone had *bothered* to tell me about my relationship with Tally, including *Miss Cloves and Vanilla* herself, I wouldn't have screwed this all up so badly."

"Yo, bro, here to help. Calm down," Kimberley whispers but looks a little guilty because some of what I've said applies to her, and she knows it. "You are talking way too loud. This isn't for public consumption." She glares at Brad. "I told you this was a bad idea. We should have just stayed at the beach house. You are trouble, Stevenson." She points a finger at him, and he playfully bites it.

"Can we stay on track here?" I ask in frustration. Watching the two of them interact over the past several days has been its own special brand of torture. I'm in a damned-if-I-do-and-damned-if-I-don't position when it comes to women, seeing Kimberley and Brad together isn't helping me feel any better about my situation.

"Yes. Sorry." Kimberley says, patting my hand. "Look, you do need to prepare yourself, Linc. I think they'll be announcing that they're sending you down in the next week or two. There's too much money tied up in your contract and they want a ballplayer who can pitch. *Sorry.* That was bitchy. You know what I mean. Let's talk about Tally. What did you call her? *Miss Cloves and Vanilla?* Cute."

I nod, then vaguely her words register. "You think they'll send me down?"

She looks appropriately sympathetic. "They're tight on the forty-man roster for next season and they want to go back to the big dance. *You know this.* Let's just see what happens, okay? Let me worry about that should it come to that. We'll deal with it and the fallout and—"

"Linc, right now, all you need to do is focus on getting well by working with me on getting your memory back," Brad says interrupting his wife. He smiles an apology at her and she nods and bites her lower lip. "So. Let's talk about Tally. She's important. An important piece of the puzzle to your past."

"She told me she was the best one-night stand I'd ever had. That's about all she told me," I say quietly so we won't be overheard. "That was the last night in the hospital. You left, and she showed up. Davis wasn't too happy."

"I bet not." She shakes her head back and forth. "I guess you have to see it from her point of view at the time. Tally had a rough day if I'm putting this all together right. I don't know maybe that's enough for now." Kimberley looks around the restaurant looking nervous all over again.

"Keep going," Brad says encouragingly. "He needs to hear this in order to better understand how to cope with everything and everyone going forward. He's rested for a few weeks now. I'm here to help him sort it out as we go along," Brad says to her. "Keep going. I need to hear it too, so I know how to help him."

Kimberley still looks uneasy. She holds her breath for a moment and then lets it out. "You were twenty-two; she was seventeen. I was looking at it all with your best interests from a career perspective." She winces. "So, I told you to send her packing as soon as I found out you two had been together." She finger-quotes the word *together,* "And so you did."

"I did? Just like that?"

"Like I said, she was seventeen. You were twenty-two almost twenty-three. She was still in *high school* for God's sake. You'd just gotten the offer from the Angels—a lucrative contract and a signing bonus. It was big. She didn't fit into those plans and I told you that and so you broke it off with her. She was on her way to New York to become big time in the dance world. But the break-up was rough on her. You two had an intense relationship from the start. Anyone could see that."

Kimberley looks away and out the big picture window we're stationed in front of at this diner, suddenly taking an interest in the sidewalk life happening in this little beach town. She looks back and studies me. "What you didn't know at the time—what *we* didn't know at the time—is that Tally was pregnant. She had a baby girl at the end of January that following year." She pauses.

I struggle for breath but hold it together enough to nod and meet Kimberley's steady gaze head-on and realize she's serious. "She had a kid? And you think that kid is *mine*?"

"She *is* yours. She's three. She'll be four at the end of this month. Suck it up, buttercup; she's yours. We verified all of this about a year ago. I'll pull the file for you. I can't believe your dad kept all of this from you. I shouldn't be the one telling you all of this."

"I think your dad was just trying to protect you," Brad says. "That's what families do. Sometimes, they don't receive any guidance in the early stages of a patient with a head trauma. The medical team doesn't always pick up on all the family dynamics going on, especially when there are memory issues involved. There are a lot of moving parts for the patients as well as the families. I'm sure Davis was trying to protect you from all of this, Linc, and maybe Tally too. It happens. We can't change it." He gives Kimberley this stern look. "Just tell him, don't editorialize it so much, babe."

"I have a daughter. With Tally." Just saying those few words ignites fresh panic.

I have a kid, who is almost four years old. A daughter.
I don't even know what to do with a kid, let alone a girl.
I guess you buy them dolls and stuffed animals and dresses.
I have child with Tally.
Miss Cloves and Vanilla had a baby with me.

Kimberley grabs my hand, forcing me back to the present. "*Breathe*, Romeo. You're a father. It happens to the best of you boys," she says softly. "*Yes*. Tally had a child, *yours*, but she gave Cara up for adoption."

"Wait. *What*?"

"Yes, she gave the baby up to her dance teacher, Allaire Tremblay. It was basically a deal made with the devil, and I think Tally felt she really had no choice at that point. She was eighteen, confronted with life's hard choices, she made a difficult one." She nods slowly. "I've worked with a few ballerinas in my time. It's a hard life. It doesn't come with multi-million dollar contracts like yours, but those dancers work their asses off night and day to make it and then stay on top. She's an athlete just like you, and basically sacrificed everything for it, just like you've had to do. And, so she did too."

"*Cara*? After my mom?"

"Yeah, she named her Cara. I'm not sure that it was intentional— to name her after your mom—but she did."

"She must have been desperate," I say slowly, looking over at Brad who nods in agreement. "Pregnant at just eighteen and feeling like there was just no way out. And I dumped her for baseball."

"I think she was. She's been through a lot and has had to sacrifice pretty much everything. And she did most of it for you, even if it didn't always appear that way."

Kimberley looks away from me again. Same routine. She stares out the window at the passersby. "We haven't even talked about Moscow yet."

She turns to me, looking sadder, and then looks over at Brad. He's shaking his head side-to-side. "And I can't tell you about that. Not today."

"*Moscow?* What about Moscow?"

"*Not* today," they both say together.

I change tactics and make a note to myself to circle back to the topic of Moscow. "Allaire Tremblay the ballerina? Famous years ago, right?"

"Ten years ago. Yes. I knew Tremblay—not well, of course— no one did." Kimberley frowns. "I did a few events for the New York City Ballet with Sasha Belmont and Allaire spent some time there too. But Tremblay died in a car accident a year ago this coming March. Cara was with her in the car at the time. She was okay when they found her and eventually custody reverted back to Tally as Cara's birth mother once they located her. So, Tally left the NYC Ballet and took a position with the San Francisco Ballet and basically moved back to San Francisco with Cara to be near her family, and because of you." She takes in air and then sighs. "It hasn't been easy for the two of you. I'm leaving a ton of stuff out, but I think that's enough. For *today*."

Kimberley finishes her beer and then eyes mine. I slide it over to her and try to smile. My head begins to hurt. Brad had my doctors adjust my medication but the headaches are still too frequent for everyone's liking. I'm not sure I want to hear anymore but I say, "finish the story. There has to be more."

"It's not a story," Kimberley chides, "it's your *life*. It *was* your life. On some levels, I can see why your dad wanted to protect you from all of it."

She shakes her head slowly back and forth. "Because it has always been pretty complicated." She half-smiles and twists her wedding ring around. Brad grabs her hand and puts it to his lips.

Kimberley sighs and looks over at me. "From the outside, you guys appeared to be two star-crossed lovers—things never seemed to work out for long. But you called me last summer to let me know that you and Tally were getting married."

"I was getting *married* to Tally? When?"

"It was supposed to be after the playoffs and the World Series. That was the plan. But actually, you guys had plans to elope that following morning. *That Friday*. But then you got hit with the line drive in Thursday night's playoff game."

"I was getting married. We were eloping? Why didn't anybody tell me all of this?" I groan.

Now it all makes sense why Tally was so angry that night. Miss Cloves and Vanilla had every right to be mad at me and my dad.

Shit.

"Lot of agendas going on. It was touch and go for a while, big guy. We were focused on you making it through surgery, and no one could predict how much damage that line drive had done. Truly?

I think your dad was so scared of losing you that he took it out on Tally. Everyone was trying to cope. I'm sorry I didn't think through the situation more clearly at the time. I was scared of losing you, too. But I should have seen it for what it was…everyone was just so scared for you. I'm sorry. And yes, you loved her, Linc. You came to play for the Giants and turned down a bigger offer with the Angels to come home to San Francisco, mainly for Tally. And now? Now, everything is just gone. You don't remember any of it, and she's royally pissed off. Yes, she wants the six months of no-contact, but what we haven't told you yet is that she threatened to start legal proceedings against you because of that temper of yours," Kimberley says softly so she won't be overheard.

"Wait. What? A legal battle? She contacted a lawyer?"

"Well, your dad basically accused her of taking the six million and thought it was best to keep Tally and Cara away from you, so I think Tally thought the whole world was against her at that point, except for Marla and Charlie. Even I didn't act fast enough. But then this most-recent episode unfolded on the front of the sport pages with Trinna Danner and that really pissed her off. Believe me, I experienced her wrath first-hand. She's obviously intent on protecting Cara, and even though I told her not to, she contacted her lawyer about all of this. I'm sorry. I should have flown up there and talked to her, but by then it was already too late. We've agreed to a no-contact clause for the next six months. There's a little less than five months to go. We received a copy of the official document a few weeks ago. Brad wanted to give you some time before telling you about the rest of it." Kimberley holds up a FEDEX envelope and pulls out a single sheaf of paper.

"Why would she do this?" I ask after reading it. It's all legalese but the gist of it is all communication needs to go through Kimberley to Tally's lawyer.

"She's protecting Cara."

"Why does Cara need protecting, especially from me?"

"Cara was there for hours by herself in that car accident. We don't know what all she saw, but it can be surmised she most likely saw Tremblay die right in front of her, and she hasn't really been talking since then. The two of you have been taking Cara to a psychologist, trying to work through her issues. Fear of abandonment, lack of trust. That pretty much sums up Tally too, you know. And you, some of the time." She hesitates. "The threat of a restraining order if you don't comply with Tally's requests will essentially take you down if that happens. This is all related to your unpredictable temper and Tally's concern with all of that as it relates to Cara. We *do not* want a restraining order against you, Linc."

I'm speechless, done in by the veiled legal threats Kimberley's called out in the lawyer's letter and the bad mix of beer and too many painkillers that I quietly took before we started out on this little venture.

I cannot think straight.

I am fucked in so many ways right now.

I feel sorry for me.

Brad lasers in on me. "How many pills did you take, Linc? I thought we agreed you were going to cut back?"

"I have a headache worse than yesterday's. I thought we'd cut back tomorrow." I reward him with a I've-got-this-not-today look.

"You okay?" Kimberley asks gently.

"She hates me." Just saying the words practically cuts off my air supply. "What have I done to this girl that she hates me this much? Oh, I know. I don't remember her at all. I accused her of stealing; well, my father did. And then there's the whole screw-up in LA"

"There's a fine line between love and hate, Romeo."

"Is there? Have we *found* that line?"

Kimberley laughs. "It's not a stretch to say you the two of you have been here before. There's a lot more to your story—to the two of you. It's never been easy. Plenty of mistakes and false promises made on both sides." Kimberley frowns again and says, "I'm sorry seems inadequate."

"It *is*."

Her face twists up. "Just try to see it from her point of view for a moment. Imagine what it feels like to not only lose the guy you love because he doesn't remember you, but to be falsely accused by the guy's dad of embezzlement and then have your fiancé's supposed hook-up with some girl in LA plastered all over the sports pages of America with every reporter camped out on her doorstep asking how she feels about it. Obviously, none of these scenarios are sitting too well with Tally right now. And she has a child to think of."

"Obviously." I sigh deep. "My kid too, remember?"

"Yes, I remember." Kimberley reaches for my hand on the table and pats it gently. "It's complicated. It'll take some time to work things out with her, but it'll happen."

"Yeah, but is she worth it?"

"Sometimes you can be such an asshole," Kimberley says softly and then looks over at Brad again before going on. "You were going to marry her. You two had plans to elope just hours before you got hit by the line drive. You have a history. You two are pretty epic. Believe me. I've seen it. And you *gave* her your mom's diamond engagement ring; I think you thought she was *worth it* at some point."

"She has my mom's ring?" I groan feeling remorse for the LA thing for the millionth time. "I must have loved Tally if I gave her that ring."

"You did."

"But I definitely screwed it all up with her now because of LA and now a lawyer's involved. Great. Just great."

"I'm not convinced she's giving up. Yes, she's royally pissed off at you right now, but that will fade. She left the door open for six months from now."

"I'll be in the middle of baseball season, pitching for the Giants if I can get my arm back or the Fresno Grizzlies if I'm lucky. Six months from now may as well be a lifetime away. I've lost her already. I've lost my kid. Even if I don't remember either one of them."

"I could try to talk to her." Kimberley looks uncertain.

"No. Not right now. It would probably just set her off even more. Let's give her some time to cool off like Brad said. You responded for me with her lawyer a few weeks ago, right?"

Kimberley nods.

"So, I'll comply with not contacting her, while I try to figure out my next move."

"Your next move—*your only move, right now*—is to pitch a baseball faster than ninety miles an hour, so you don't end up as the ball boy fetching the bats for everyone else."

"Funny," I say airily.

"Sorry. Kidding. Sorry. That was harsh. You can do this. Brad's going to help you get your memory back, and I'm going to help you rehabilitate your good-guy image. It'll come together. Trust me. You're a great guy. Everyone who knows you knows that."

"Kimmy," Brad says looking at both of us. "His next move is to get well. Baseball will come to him when he's ready."

She frowns and grabs Brad's left hand. "You have to keep working with him. You have to. It's the only way he has any hope of winning back his life in baseball."

I sigh. "But the doctors say that—"

"*Forget* what the doctors say, Linc. No pun intended." She smiles a little and then gets this sobering look as she looks first at Brad and then me. "Let Brad help you. He's amazing. Look what he's done for me. He found this skeptical, promiscuous girl, who slept with half the guys in Manhattan, and made me believe in love again. Look how happy I am."

She smiles wide and then leans over and kisses Brad. It makes me smile a little and feel downright envious because I can tell she is genuinely happy, and it's almost painful to watch the two of them. "Get a room, you two."

Kimberley sighs and waves her hand around. "You know I wouldn't give you false hope if I didn't believe Brad can help you find your way back. To baseball. To Tally if that's what you want."

"I just want to remember all of it. I just want to be able to re-member *her.*"

"I know. Brad can help you do that if anyone can."

"I'll give it my best effort, Linc. I'm pretty good at this stuff," Brad says.

"Do you think I should send her some flowers or something? I feel like I need to do something."

"No-contact means no contact," Kimberley says looking uneasy. "Give it some time. Let's see how the next couple of weeks go and see where things are." She looks over at Brad. "So how did I do?"

"You did great," Brad says with an easy smile.

Kimberley grins at him, while I manage to grab the check before either one of them can. I go up to the counter and pay the bill. I smile at the waitress because, for some reason, I'm weirdly cheered at the fact that I at least now know how *Miss Cloves and Vanilla* fits into my life, and she has my ring and maybe Brad can actually help me get my memory back. The ring might be the only connection between us in the next six months, and I have to hope it's enough until I figure out what I'm going to do if my memory returns. Or if it doesn't, what then?

The facts are these: I have a kid, a former fiancée. Miss Cloves and Vanilla loved me at one point. Could she love me again?

Kimberley is already out the door and heading towards the car while talking to someone on her cell phone.

Brad watches her walk out. He smiles and waves at her and then turns to me.

"Send *Miss Cloves and Vanilla* some flowers. She's not going to initiate a court order over that, now is she?"

"No, probably not. Hey, thanks."

CHAPTER TWENTY-TWO

It only hurts when I'm breathing

TALLY

IT'S THE LAST DAY OF JANUARY, and my baby turns four today. She wanted the Disney *Frozen* theme, and we've gone all out. Elliott is dressed as Olaf and Cara plays Elsa trying to turn anything and everyone to ice with the little wand I gave her as soon as she woke up. Sam and Charlie worked all morning on the backyard stringing shimmery white and blue streamers along the gutters that fan out across the yard to a large party tent set up in the middle of the yard. There are white, blue, and pink balloons and matching streamers everywhere.

With a little help from the San Francisco Ballet, we've managed to transform the party tent into a winter enchanted ice castle using the props from the ballet for *Swan Lake*. Mikhail Rostov finally comes through and proves he's human.

Now, twelve children from Cara's preschool merrily dance through *Elsa's ice castle*, elated with our decoration efforts even if it's a little chilly for an outdoor birthday party in the middle of winter.

The music from the movie blasts all around and the kids sing the words to every song. Two spires out of four and half of a castle are all that is left of the cake that I actually made from scratch. "You baked and decorated a cake. Not just any cake, but a *castle cake*. Oh my God. See? Miracles happen all the time," Marla said when she first arrived early this morning to help me.

The party tables are strewn with empty cups and plates of half-eaten cake and melting cotton candy ice cream, which is colored blue that no one can explain. Marla and I start to gather up the kids' discarded plates while Sam and Charlie interact with some of the parents who linger longer even as the afternoon party begins to wind down by fetching drinks for people and keeping them generally entertained along with my parents' help.

"Does he have to look so much like Chris Hemsworth?" Marla asks as soon as she sees Sam disappear up the back steps and into my house. "*Thor's* a bit of a distraction."

"Careful now, Mrs. Masterson. He's Sam Wilde, bartender extraordinaire, and a good friend, but that is all there is to it."

She gets that knowing look. "Yeah, it's obvious you haven't slept with him yet. The PG-13 PDA is a dead giveaway, but it's been *weeks*, Tally. What *is* your problem? Seriously, you need to do him, or I will."

I stare at the back door Sam just disappeared through for an answer to that and decide to sidestep the issue entirely. "Funny. Such brave talk from a girl who hasn't been with anyone but Charlie Masterson, for what, five years running? More than that, actually, now that I do the math. Do tell, Marla. Why don't *you* sleep with Sam?" I mock and then laugh at her twisted-up face. I don't think she expected me to call her on it quite so openly.

"In a proverbial heartbeat I would," she says grinning wide. "Oh yes indeed. If I wasn't married," she adds with a little sigh.

"Well, give me some time I was almost married too, remember?"

I get a little mired down, gripped by these thoughts of Linc that have been troubling me since I woke up this morning. *Today of all days, I regret issuing the no-contact thing ultimatum. I wish he would remember me. I actually wish he was here.*

Guilt for my part in all of this begins to rain down on me. I avoid Marla's laser-like gaze because she can still detect what I'm feeling before I do. "Damn it, Marla. I wasn't going to think of him today. See what you've done. Why did you have to bring *him* up?" I glare at her.

"Yeah, like *that* wasn't going to happen since we're celebrating the birth of his child and yours today. Truly, it's an impossible wish and a little hard to avoid even for you." She hesitates and shakes her head a little. "But since you brought him up…he sent a present for Cara." I'm too surprised to respond. "He brought it to me, so I could see it first and ensure it was okay. It's this huge pink unicorn probably as big as Cara." She laughs and grins over at me. "It's perfect, really. I wrapped it, which was no small feat. It's in the car. He wanted me to ask you first—to see if it was okay if she opened it—and was told it was from him," she adds, wincing, obviously unsure as to how I would react.

"From him," I snort.

Cool Tally snorts. Great. Impressive.

"He's trying, Tally. He's working with Kimberley's husband, the psychiatrist? He's trying to get his memory back. He's here in San Fran, actually, and wanted to know if he could…."

"Don't." It takes a huge effort to keep it together, but I manage even as I angrily brush tears away with my coat sleeve. I avoid looking at Marla altogether for a few minutes. *And he's here in San Fran. No wonder I feel him all around me today.*

My throat closes up, and I wonder for the millionth time when I'm actually going to let him go. "No."

"I wasn't going to say anything, but you seem to be doing all right. You seem happy. *You baked a cake.* There's *Sam.* You're moving on," she says gently. "Cara's so happy, but maybe she needs to see him, deserves to see him and—"

"It's not that simple."

"Maybe it should be."

"I said, *don't*. I don't want to talk about this. Look, my heart was broken in October, okay? But then, he managed to shatter it all over again five weeks ago. *No.* He can't storm into my life whenever he feels like it."

I've caught the attention of a few of the preschool parents. I stalk away from her toward the side of the house. Of course, she follows me.

"Look, I get it," she says.

"No, you don't. Imagine Charlie is screwing around with someone else. How do you feel?" I whip my hand through the air. "Don't tell me you know how I feel. You don't know how I feel. I had everything. We had everything. Now, it's gone. I spend every morning waking up and spending a few seconds just reminding myself how to breathe again. How to *breathe*, Marla."

"So it's not about Cara's birthday and seeing her daddy. It's about *you*. I'm just pointing that out because that is my job as your bestie and confidante."

"You *suck*. You know that?"

"I have been told by a very reliable source, I happen to be married to, I am good at that too."

The idea of her on her knees before Charlie does the trick. I laugh. I run my hands through the ends of my hair and look over at Marla. "You know this makes it extremely complicated if he comes over here. Sam. Cara. Me. My parents. *Those* parents." I gesture toward the dwindling birthday crowd.

"They'll be gone soon. It's already past the two-hour limit. I'll tell Charlie to tell him he's on clean-up duty. Just let him give her the present in-person. It's a good idea. It's a start, and you know it."

"I don't know. She's doing better with the other kids at preschool now. *Obviously.* She's not acting out anymore and now they almost have this secret sign language thing worked out with her. She's better, Marla. I don't want to undo all of that. I don't know." I shrug feeling helpless. Then without thinking say, "but the teacher's been asking me about Linc and when he's coming home. Cara's been drawing pictures of all three of us. She's started drawing Sam as some kind of stick figure. He's really small in one corner of the picture and then she always has me in a hot pink tutu and then she's been drawing

Linc. She always puts him right in the middle next to me in all of her pictures as some kind of big superhero with a flowing cape, usually one she's colored hot pink as well."

"Always hard to resist a superhero in a hot pink cape," Marla says with a little knowing smile.

"Always hard to resist a superhero. Maybe that's my whole damn problem in life. The *superhero*." I frown trying to work this all out in my head.

"Maybe you just need to get over the memory thing and start over."

"Maybe you forgot about LA just a little over a month ago," I automatically unleash my never-ending fury on that on Marla. Within seconds, anger manages to burn all the way through me as I think of him with that blonde.

"He has more to say about that, but he told me he would only say it to you," Marla—the anointed foreign affairs' diplomat—says softy.

"Geez! How often have you been talking to him? And I thought we had established you were on *my side*?"

"I *am* on your side. I'm on both of your sides. I'm on the side of Linc and Tally and still holding out hope to be able to stand up for the two of you at your wedding someday. I'm here to serve."

"*Someday*? Don't hold your breath on that one. I haven't been," I lie. "And Sam? What do I do about Sam? Where does that leave him? With me?"

"I think you've already asked and answered that question for yourself. The Tally Landon I know would have jumped his bones by now. The fact that you haven't," she says with her special brand of wizardry, "tells me everything I need to know. You still love Linc. Of course, you do." I follow her gaze as she watches Cara and Elliott play with the other kids on the swing set. "He'll always be a part of your life because of Cara. And, Tally?" She glances sideways at me. "It's not just the idea of him or the memory of him that you loved; it's the guy himself, and he's still *here*." She bestows me with a generous smile. "Sam's been great at holding your hand, but Linc still holds your heart and everybody who knows you and loves you sees that."

"Well, I'm so glad you all can *see* that, but I can't. And remember, they say you can't go back."

"*Forget* what they say," Marla whispers. "Look, he's wallowing today in that great big ol' house all by himself wishing his life wasn't so screwed up, and that he could be with his daughter on her birthday. I think Charlie should call him and invite him down."

"There's the no-contact thing."

"When has a lawyer had the best idea for solving your problems? Get over it, Cinderella. Do it for Cara. Do it for the guy she remembers as Daddy—the superhero in that pink cape she keeps drawing. She's trying to tell you something in her own sweet little Cara way. She loves her daddy, and she wants to see him. She remembers him, and that should be enough. It's her *birthday*."

"Sometimes I really want to hate you when you play the guilt card like that."

"I don't have a card. I don't have any guilt. Do you?" She laughs and then asks, "have I ever consciously steered you wrong, Tally Landon? Like ever?"

"No." I hold my breath and then exhale slowly. "What about Sam, huh?"

The knight in shining armor is coming down the steps. He stops and looks around. We can see him, but he can't quite see us yet from where we stand on the side of the house. Marla watches him too.

"I'm pretty sure Thor can hold his own. But let's find out; shall we? That'll really liven up things around here."

Marla saunters off with a fresh purpose. I watch her in action still hidden from Sam's view as she goes up to Charlie and gestures toward Sam.

"You've been awesome, Sam." I hear her say loud enough for my benefit. "Thanks for all your help today. I know Tally appreciates it." She turns to Charlie. "Linc's going to be able to make it after all. Can you call and see when he'll be here, babe? Tell him he has clean-up duty."

She laughs at Charlie's astonished face, as he dives for his phone on the party table and makes the call.

"Prez? You're in. How long before you can get here?" Charlie says with a wide grin into his phone.

As I walk up to them, Charlie looks over at me and subtly nods his approval.

Suddenly, on edge at the idea of seeing Lincoln Presley again, I concentrate on Cara. She's excitedly pointing to her cake, indicating she wants another piece. I go into mommy mode, maintaining complete and utter focus on my child, and avoid looking at Sam altogether.

CHAPTER
TWENTY-THREE

come on get higher

I'M ON EDGE BATTLING THIS GENERAL foreboding in seeing Tally Landon again. I practice what to say on the drive over. It's not working.

Hi, I'm Lincoln Presley. I know I don't remember you at all, and I know I fucked up big time a month ago in LA, and the world knows you as my fiancée, and I called you baby the last time we saw each other, but will you forgive me? Can we at least be friends?"

Tally Landon aka *Miss Cloves and Vanilla* would probably like to slap me instead. I know everything about her now, and if I can't remember I can look it up.

Kimberley and Brad set me up with an iPad that contains photographs and profiles and time lines on just about everyone I've ever encountered in my life. This proves to be good and bad. I now know the history of Tally and me, but I still don't remember any of it. Kimberley warned me three weeks ago it wasn't pretty, not all of it anyway, and that has held true.

I stare at the *Sports Illustrated* cover. It's my favorite photograph of her of the ones I've seen so far. I'm lifting her up in the photograph like the actors Patrick Swayze and Jennifer Grey did in *Dirty Dancing*. Tally's looking directly at me and the photographer got the angle just right from below us to capture her breathtaking smile. It's a surreal moment in that movie, and it seems just as surreal for the two of us in this photograph.

I just wish I could remember it. I read the headline, *The Surreal Life of the Ballplayer & his Ballerina*. It's a play on words, and the interview was a bit of a hatchet job on Tally, but I can't stop looking at her photograph. I'm captivated by it. *Her.* I have a feeling every guy subscribed to *Sports Illustrated* feels the same way I do.

I glance through Kimberley's latest text. She sent it about ten minutes ago when I sent her the message that Tally had okay-ed me coming to Cara's birthday party.

"Focus on the birthday girl. A four-year-old child loves you unconditionally. "Daddy".

Moscow. Don't bring this up; not good. We still need to go over that one.

Okay. She's human; be sensitive to what she's feeling and where's she's coming from.

You're going to have to explain LA and I'll leave that up to you.

You are so SORRY. Bowing at her feet might be in order.

DNA results=not yours. Negative. Do with that 411 what you will.

You're lucky is all I'm going to say.

I don't want to talk about LA anymore.

You're a great guy. She remembers that.

No temper tantrums.

Avoid alcohol. Have some cake.

Stay a few hours at the most. Give her space and time to think.

Let her decide how things should go with you two in going forward.

And I KNOW about the flowers sent to 'Miss Cloves and Vanilla,' Elvis.
Brad approved. OK. Me too.
Good luck.
Call me later.
Call. Me. Later.
Is this the longest text, like ever?
xoxo Kimmy

Charlie meets me in the front yard as I'm getting out of my rental car. I need to buy a car. It's been a bizarre week on many fronts already. I plan on signing the papers to put the house on the market tomorrow before I leave for Fresno. And it's now official; I'm being sent down. *What else can happen to me in the space of forty-eight hours?*

Charlie grips my hand hard. "You okay?"

"Think so. How's the party?"

"It's a kids' party. We're low on booze." Charlie laughs. "But I'm on call anyway so who cares, right? So. You ready? Just know, Cara is crazy about Elsa in *Frozen* so that's what she's dressed up as. That's a Disney princess movie thing. Just pretend she can turn things to ice, and you'll be good. She'll love that. Elliott is Olaf. Okay, I realize you don't even know who the characters from the movie are, but in about five minutes you will. Welcome to parenthood, *again*."

I run my hands through my hair and sigh, overwhelmed by all he's just said. "I don't know. Maybe this isn't such a good idea."

"It's Cara's birthday, man. That's all that matters. She's going to be so happy you came. Trust me. It'll be fine." He goes over to his SUV, unlocks the back and reaches inside. Then, he places a huge pink box into my arms. "Here, Marla wanted me get this for you. It's the unicorn you bought for Cara. *Relax.* Just have some cake, watch her open her gift. And, Prez, I think if you just smile at Tally, she'll be fine. Her boyfriend's here anyway."

"*Boyfriend?*"

"Well, he'd like that role. His name is Sam. He's cool. Not as cool as you, but he's been helping Tally out. Obviously, Marla tells me way too much." He hesitates. "Tally's still getting those panic attacks, and Sam's been helping her through them. It's been a rough go."

"Tally gets panic attacks?"

I'm strangely cheered. I smile a little but then it fades as my mind lasers in on the word *boyfriend*.

"Sam, the boyfriend," I say irritably. "Great. Just great. Holding her hand and everything, huh?"

"Hey Prez," Charlie says with a huge sigh. "The whole LA thing is fresh in all of their minds so watch the attitude, okay? You're not exactly in their good graces again yet."

"Wait, her *parents* are here too?" I ask incredulous. "I didn't study up on them."

"Yeah. I thought I told you that. *Everybody's* here."

"I can't do this."

"You can and you will. I'm your wingman, remember? You've got this. You do. Come on. Let's go watch Cara open her present. That's what you came for."

CHAPTER
TWENTY-FOUR

forever and for always

TALLY

It's been twenty-two minutes since Charlie made his phone call. *I'm on edge. I can't breathe. I can't look at Sam.* All my defenses are down. Inside, I'm screaming, "the shields are down, Captain, prepare for an attack!" I'm definitely in a time warp, up in space. Or, I'm Sandra Bullock in *Gravity* and unable to find air of any kind, and I'm drifting fast away from George Clooney, which is never good. *I think I'm going to pass out.*

Marla's gone around and informed the *need-to-know* crowd that Linc is coming. *My parents. Tommy.*

Her parents.

Charlie's parents who I begrudgingly invited at the eleventh hour.

"Act normal. Remember, he doesn't remember you so don't ask him about the past. Just make small talk with him," she says to the gathering group. "Tell him who you are. Fill in the gaps if he asks, but only then. Got it?"

I'm not sure when she picked up her degree in psychology, but she is so together that I take solace in just watching her work the *need-to-know* crowd that now flock together like birds and tweet at the news.

Of course, I am a mess, an emotional wreck incapable of finding air of any kind. I lean against the kitchen counter, technically in hiding, and study the refrigerator manual flailing about trying to find a sense of calm and can only pray to miraculously mimic Marla's *cool-girl* persona. *It's not going well.*

"You okay?" Sam asks handing me a bottled water as he returns from outside. In the next, he's smoothing the worry lines that must appear on my forehead.

"Are *you* okay?"

"I asked first."

Sam half-smiles, tilts his head to one side, and looks at me intently.

"I'm not completely okay. This whole thing has gotten weird. Welcome to my complicated, fucking life." I frown at him. "I'm worried about Cara and what she's going to do when she sees him."

"She's a little girl, Tally. She's four. She's going to be elated and feel like her birthday party is complete because everybody she loves in the entire world is here. It's going to be okay, believe me."

He grabs my hand and holds it. Of course, he's taking my pulse again, but there are way too many people still around—now that word's gotten out that the famous baseball player is coming to Cara's party—to question why he is doing this and how he knows he should.

"Just breathe. You're going to be fine." He tucks a strand of my hair behind my ear and leans in close. "Trust me. It'll be okay."

"I thought all this would go so differently," I say slowly.

"Me too."

"How did you see it going?"

I laugh a little at his weird expression. He's looking a little bemused but there's this hint of disappointment on his face too.

"I had a date planned," he says with a nonchalant shrug.

"What *kind* of date?"

"A dinner and a movie kind of date. Dessert of some kind." He sighs looks away and then looks back. "The two of us. Maybe."

Sam Wilde looking unsure is a sight to behold. "Oh," I say with a nervous laugh, "I finally make it to the big dance, and the ex shows up. *Classic.*"

He's giving me this none-too-subtle look now and traces my lips. Then he trails his hand along my shoulder and down to my collar bone and then lingers near the neckline of my dress.

It's a white jersey dress that clings in all the right places that I bought for the special occasion, although it's been largely hidden under my white winter coat most of the time because we've been outside. Because it's *January. But in here? Boom!* I am the official ice queen as anointed by Cara earlier today. I don't usually go for white, but black seemed too somber for Cara's birthday, and for once I eschewed my favorite color for its exact opposite. *It's not a permanent rejection. Just today.*

Why am I going on about this?

Sam leans in and kisses the side of my face. *This is new.* He's been a forehead man for the past month. And sometimes the way he kisses my forehead is more than enough to drive me wild, although I do wonder when we're both going to be brave enough at the same time to get to the good part. I lift my head on the chance of discovering more with him, but he consciously steps back from me.

"Not today," he says softly. "You need to talk to him. That's our deal for moving forward with *us.* You have things to work out with him first. You need to get your footing. Find your path. Find your way."

"Thanks for the wisdom there, *Thor.* Very nice. Really sets the tone." He looks a little irritated with me now at the Thor reference. "I'm sure you've had *plenty* of girls call you that before."

"*Thor? Plenty.* Sure." He runs his hands through his hair and looks extremely unhappy all of a sudden. "I've got to go. *The Promissory Note* calls."

"I thought you had the night off?" I ask irritably.

"I *choose* what nights I have off. I've decided to work this one."

"That must be some boss you work for," I say airily.

"I work for myself."

"Wait a minute. Do you *own The Promissory Note?*"

"Yeah, I do." He studies my face. "You make a lot of assumptions, baby. Maybe you should start asking a few questions. Look around, Tally. You need to…" He sighs big. "Forget it. I've got to go." He pushes away from the counter and starts to leave.

"*Why* are you behaving like a two-year-old that didn't get his way all of a sudden?" I'm getting whiplash just watching him transform from seductive lover to tantrum boy. *Thor didn't get his way.*

"Because I didn't get my way. Okay? I had plans for me and you tonight, baby."

"Well, I'm sorry that didn't work out, but we talked about this. My life is beyond complicated. You're lucky I let you come to Cara's birthday party. You know I don't want her confused. *About us.* Whatever that is. And I'm *broken.* And you know that. On second thought, let's be clear: *Don't like me. Don't count on me.* I can't give you anything in return. And quit trying to *fix* me!"

"She doesn't like to be called *baby*," says a familiar voice I can't help but recognize. My heart does a full stop. "She *hates* that term, in fact. And I think the lady just told you to back off. I suggest you do so. She's wearing my engagement ring, which should tell you all you need to know about where she's at right now. I'm Lincoln Presley, by the way. Who might you be?" The baseball player extends his hand.

Sam ignores Lincoln Presley as well as his hand.

And, Elvis doesn't like that.

The baseball player clenches his fists together. All at once, I'm clairvoyant and get this uneasy feeling knowing he's about ready to punch Sam.

Meanwhile, my heart restarts and is now going about a hundred beats a minute, and I begin to gasp for air. *Perfect.*

Sam looks past Linc at me. "You okay?"

"Don't call me *baby*, like ever," I say to Sam, lean my arms against my thighs, and attempt to catch my breath. Of course, I am desperate to appear normal but that's failing fast.

"Breathe, Tally," they both say at the same time.

I glance up and see these two sizing each other up. *Perfect. Two gladiators going at it in my kitchen. Fight to the death! Bring it.*

Charlie steps in between them. "Hold up. Focus," says the sanest guy in the room to Linc. I give him a grateful smile.

Linc nods at Charlie and comes over to me and takes both of my hands in his. "Hi. Breathe," he says softly. "I get them too. Just focus on me. And breathe in and out. Easy. Look at me. Count backwards. Calm your mind."

Why did I leave his ring on?
Why didn't I take it off as soon as I knew he was coming?
Why can't I breathe?
Where the fuck is Marla?

And as if on cue on a stage, she's appears at the back door. "There you are," Marla says. "Cara, look who's here for your birthday. Wait. What's going on? Tal?"

"I'm fine," I say.

"You don't look or sound fine. You look like you're about ready to pass out," she says. "What's going on? Sam? Linc?"

Cara runs at Linc at full-speed. I think she's knocked the wind out of him.

"Daddy!"

I think she's knocked the wind out of all us.

Oh my God. Cara is talking.

"Where have you been?" She asks Linc as he kneels down and sweeps her up into his arms. She touches his face in awe seemingly trying to determine if he's real or imagined.

Shock filters through me as the remnants from the panic attack from minutes ago start to make me light-headed. Seeing Cara speak in full sentences for the first time overwhelms me too. Somehow, we're doing this kind of family hug thing with Cara. Linc and I kneel side-by-side hugging our beautiful little girl between us.

"You're *talking*, baby," I say. "Mommy's so glad," I whisper against Cara's cheek. "Mommy's so happy."

Cara touches my face and wipes away the tears streaming down my face as if she can magically staunch the flow with her fingers before they fall.

"Mommy, don't cry," she says sweetly.

"She wasn't talking before?" Linc asks, openly looking at me over Cara's head.

"No." The answer comes from both me and Sam.

Clearly, I'm out of my depth here and unsure of what to do next. Cara is finally talking and yet seeing Lincoln Presley again within the same expanse of time is too much for me to process.

"Who are you?" Linc asks Sam leaning back from Cara and me. He openly assesses Sam as he slowly stands up and reaches his full height towering a good three inches over my good friend *Thor*. If there wasn't so much tension building it would be funny. I press my lips together to keep from smiling and wipe my eyes with the back of my hand. "Who are you again? I didn't catch your name," Linc says to Sam, somewhat gentler this time.

"I'm Sam. I'm a friend of Tally's." He gets this defiant look, but then he's gazing over at me as if he's my sole protector.

Holy shit. This is not going to go well.

"Sam. Hi. I'm Lincoln Presley. Cara's dad. Tally's fiancé."

"*Ex*-fiancé."

"She's wearing my ring. I think I'm still her fiancé," Linc says easily. He smiles wide as if to say, *I've got this. Thanks for playing, but I win. Like always.*

Sam looks unsure of how to respond. I hide my left hand to avoid the implications of the conversation altogether and helplessly watch Linc as he disappears in the direction of the living room from whence he came. *Shakespeare anyone? We do Romeo and Juliet enough during the fall season that I am quite used to drama. But this? This is real life right here getting more surreal by the minute. Get your ticket, get in line, and watch this reality unfold.*

Linc returns carrying the biggest present of the day all wrapped up in bright pink wrapping paper with white and pink unicorns all over it and the biggest pink bow I have ever seen. Carla claps her hands with absolute joy and rewards him with the biggest smile ever.

Marla whispers, "It took the entire roll of wrapping paper."

"Thanks for helping out," I say to her with the wisp of a smile.

"You okay?"

"Not sure yet." I move to the farthest edge of the party and in an attempt to regroup while Sam takes the opposite corner. I've hidden my panic attacks from Cara. She works as a deterrent. I don't want her to ever feel like she can't count on her mother. I focus on breathing and watch in fascination how enchanted Cara becomes as she and Linc hastily unwrap the gift box. He pulls out this gigantic pink unicorn and hands it to her. It *is* almost as big as she is.

"Daddy, I love it," she says softly to Linc now. "Come play with me. *Please,* Daddy."

I can't look at Sam because what seemed so easy for us just a half-hour ago becomes immensely complicated by Cara's simple request of Linc. She still remembers Linc as her daddy, and she loves him unconditionally. *And where does that leave Sam and me?*

When I finally do look over at him, he's watching me intently and then the corners of his mouth curve up ever so slightly. We trade apologies for the past fifteen minutes of shared angst in that one exchange, although I am beginning to wonder when his complete understanding about my complicated life will finally end. Because it surely has to end. But right now? He looks surprisingly cool. The god is undeterred by today's surprising turn of events of Lincoln Presley's unplanned arrival and the generous gift of the pink unicorn essentially making our child's day. Sam gave her a doll. I would like to consider it a tie, but I know better. The doll sits in the box it came in.

Cara skips over to me and shoves the pink unicorn in my face. I get a good whiff of cloves and vanilla as if it's been intentionally spritzed with my favorite French perfume. I glance over at Linc and study him intently for a few seconds then focus back on Cara. "Mmm...This unicorn smells so good. Have you named her?" She nods. "Let me guess."

"Elsa," she says with a laugh before I can answer.

"Elsa is perfect."

My daughter is still talking. I thought maybe it would be a five-minute fleeting development, and she would regress for some inexplicable reason. We'd suffer yet another setback like so many others I've been a part of the past several months. But no. She smiles and laughs and claps her hands and keeps talking.

It's a miracle. And Linc was the catalyst.
That can't be denied.

She is so happy it makes me want to cry. Instead, I attempt to recover and look into the glassy black eyes of her now-prized pink unicorn and laugh. "Welcome to the family, Elsa." Cara kisses my cheek and the buries her little face in my neck. I kiss the top of my child's head. "Love you, Cara, so much. Happy Birthday, sweetie."

Overjoyed, Cara runs off toward Linc and I automatically seek him out. Our eyes connect and there is no one else but the two of us in the room for a good thirty seconds. He slowly smiles. And I return it.

I remember that look.

I'm in trouble here.

Linc whispers something to Cara and she nods at him and then he turns back to me. "Can I talk to you?"

"Tally, are you okay?" Sam asks from behind him at about the same time.

Linc turns back to Sam, even his stance says, *look, I'm in charge.* I hold my breath waiting for some kind of outburst from Linc, but he just clasps both hands to his sides like before even though he still looks like all he really wants to do is deck Sam. "Can I talk to you *alone?*" Linc looks solely at me as he says this.

"Marla, can you take Cara outside? I'll be out in a few minutes." I turn to Sam. "I just need to talk to him. Like you said." I smile sweetly while Sam impatiently nods. "You said we should talk. It's okay. I've got this."

"Yeah, okay, but I need to take off in about twenty minutes," Sam says tossing his notable displeasure at the turn of events into the fray. I've never seen him act like this before and it sets me off.

"Of course you do. You *own* the place, which you've failed to mention to me before today, but okay. Give me twenty minutes. You can take off then. My parents are still here. Marla and Charlie are still here. It'll be fine. I'm *fine.* Or, take off now if you need to. *I'm fine.*"

He's leaving me in my hour of need, and I am royally pissed. My look tells him this in a span of ten seconds.

Oh the things we do not say that our looks convey.

"And I almost believe you, *baby,*" Sam says as he lifts his chin and then smiles at me all benevolent.

Linc grunts from behind me; I'm pretty sure it's for the baby reference.

"We will have *that* chat later," I say to Sam rewarding him with a tight smile. "Give me some time."

"I will. And I have." He smiles wider and then he says, "Okay. Then."

"Okay. Then." I smile wide too, remembering the first time he said this to me. He leans in and kisses my forehead and the room of onlookers seems to stop and watch as all chatters ends for about thirty seconds. I step back from Sam and give him a thumbs up.

Then I turn to Linc, who looks stunned and possibly out of his depth for the first time I've ever seen, since I met him.

Yes, Elvis, this is what moving on looks like. How's it feel?

In the meantime, Marla distracts Cara from the tension that's begun to swirl up in the room again and leads my child by the hand toward the back door. In fact, my bestie manages to distract Sam too and leads him out of the back door with her other hand. *Comical. If only it wasn't such a real-time drama.*

"But I want to play with Daddy," Cara says to Marla.

"I know. And you will. Just give Mommy a few minutes to talk to Daddy. Come on, let's go find Elliott. Come on, Sam. Let's get you a drink. Charlie, let's get Sam a drink." Marla smiles at our favorite bartender restaurateur and gives me the *I've-got-this* maneuver with a wave of her hand. They all start to follow her outside.

I almost laugh.

Almost.

But then, Cara turns back looking uncertain at Linc. "I'll be there in a few minutes, Cara," he says gently.

She's immediately cheered by his promise and grins wide with complete adoration and waves at him.

If only all of his promises were that easy to make and keep.

And now it is just Linc and me.

"I wanted to talk about the LA thing," he says looking mighty nervous and apologetic at the same time. "Is there somewhere *private* we can talk?"

I lead him to the guest bedroom which is off the living room on the main floor. I don't use this room anymore. And now as I walk in, I remember the two very best reasons as to why.

Silk satin. Gathered French silk. Tulle. London. Catherine Deane. The bridal gown I never wore hangs on the open closet door right next to his fine-looking, tailor-made black Armani tuxedo. The red roses Elvis sent to one *Miss Cloves and Vanilla* rot upside down in the vase they came in. The pungent smell of the dead roses permeates the space. I'm instantly reminded of Holly's funeral. As a general rule, I hate flowers of any kind now and the Lincoln Presley of old would have remembered that.

The entire room resembles a shrine or a tomb. Other than a hasty placement and subsequent rearrangement of the roses on the far nightstand I haven't been in here, but everything else about this room captures and effectively enshrines our life together.

Damn. Why did I bring him in here?

He's closing the door and locking it behind us. "It's a private conversation. It's not my proudest moment then or now."

"No. I bet not," I say quietly.

Now, he looks around the room with interest. "I see you got the flowers." He gets this lazy smile for all of two seconds.

"Uh-huh."

Then, his smile disappears all together and he stops abruptly in the middle of the room as he spies the bride-and-groom gear that now dominates the space and the two of us.

"Oh," he says with heavy sigh as he runs his hands through his hair.

"Yeah," I say.

Silence.

The sadness in both of us comes out of nowhere as if its sole purpose is to entomb us right here.

CHAPTER
TWENTY-FIVE

heroes

LINC

S HE'S CLOSED OFF. I CAN SEE that. She plays with her hair which the breeze from the heat register directly overhead keeps undoing. She repeats this nervous cycle of tucking it behind her left ear but then the rush of air blows it back into her face. A stray piece lands in her mouth. Her lips part ever so slightly and then she sighs. I push my hands deep into my pockets to keep from reaching out to touch her face which I find completely mesmerizing. *She* is mesmerizing. I can't help but watch as she continues to play with her hair. I shift my stance. She is attractive from a distance, but up close like this she is beyond the description of beautiful. There are no words to describe her. *Ethereal?*

I've never thought of a girl as ethereal until I saw *Miss Cloves and Vanilla* in that hospital room, but it's just like before.

This whole scene seems ominous. My palms sweat, and I begin to rock back and forth on my feet to combat this disconcerting feeling of being this close to her while she studies me intently awaiting my apology.

I'm nervous.

Because of LA

Because it's Miss Cloves and Vanilla.

The girl I haven't stopped thinking about since that last night in the hospital.

Reconciling that girl to Tally Landon has been a challenge, but everything comes together in a span of a few seconds in just seeing her again.

Photographs don't do her justice at all.

It's not just her incredible face and eyes that captivate me. It's her amazing body and the way she moves about the room now. Even her height is perfect. She would most certainly fit perfectly in the middle of my chest just below my chin if I were to hold her.

What is going on with me?

If she gets any closer to me, she will probably hear my heart, which beats wildly, because she's having this mysterious effect on me and my general well-being. My mind clicks with an easy summation: she's perfect in every way. Somehow, she appears delicate but unreachable at the same time, and you find yourself just wanting to take care of her, to protect her in every way; and yet the airy defiance so easily discernible upon her beautiful face already tells you that is never going to happen. Her green eyes flash in the same way that lightning strikes, there one moment and gone the next. And yet, I glimpse this incredible sadness that is almost glacial in its permanence within their depths just before she turns away from me. *She takes my breath away, and I'm having trouble hiding that fact now.*

"So you wanted to talk about LA," she says firmly. "Well, let me just say right now that I *don't* want to talk about LA like ever." She's said this just like a valley girl would.

I press my lips together to keep from smiling because I'm pretty sure that would piss her off even more.

"But what does it matter what I think or feel or say or do? What the fuck ever. Say what you have to say. How is *dear Trinna,* by the way? *Trinna Danner.* How is she?"

I flinch because it is a little disconcerting that she knows the girl's name. Yet I barely remember anything about that girl and never think of her at all.

"I don't know how she is," I finally say. "I don't even remember what she looks like."

Bad move.

I regret these words as soon as they leave my mouth.

"*Baby*, you don't even remember *me*, and we were *epic,* so that's not exactly consoling," she says with a harsh laugh. "But I guess I'm old news. I'm sorry to hear that she's no longer your consolation prize. Do go on. Tell me what you have to say about LA that is going to make me feel all better inside and persuade me to hold onto all those fond memories of the two of us." She waves her arm through the air like a sword in battle and all I can do watch. "I've got places to be, people to see."

She sighs big and takes about three steps back from me. Now, she's practically at the door.

"*Sam.* Right? Places to be. People to *see. Sam. Right?*"

"Right." She gets defiant. "Don't worry I've remained loyal. To you. I'm all fucked up for some reason, and have been unable to let you go. Let's fix that right now." She slides my engagement ring off her left hand. "Hold out your hand."

I refuse and keep them clasped behind my back.

She stalks over to me. "Cute, Elvis. Really cute."

She grabs my left front jeans pocket and jams the ring down inside. Of course, that brings her right to me and my arms go around her, and I hold her there.

"Let me go," she says tightly.

"No."

"Not funny. Let me go." She starts to struggle and looks exceedingly unhappy and glares at me.

"No."

"I'll scream and then where you will be?" She rewards me with this sly smile.

"First of all, I don't think you will, and secondly; I can take *Thor*, anytime and anywhere." Now, I smile because holding her this way is its own reward, and the dig at her boyfriend gives me the upper hand for at least six seconds. "So calm the fuck down, *Princess*. And if you *promise* to listen to what all I have to say, I'll let you go."

She relaxes a little and looks up at me with these blazing green eyes of hers that practically shimmer.

"*Promise*," she says it like a swear word.

I let her go. She steps back and warily watches me.

I run my hands through my hair preparing for confession by taking a deep breath. "I'm sorry. I'm sorry I hurt you. It was stupid and thoughtless and even though *no one* had yet told me who you were to me at the time, I know I caused you a great deal of pain, and I would never intentionally do that. *Truly. I'm sorry.*"

She barely nods then waves her hand around as if to say, '*go on, peasant; explain yourself.*'

"Secondly, nothing actually happened on the hook-up front."

She starts pacing again and flails her arms about. How I ever mistook her for a nurse I don't know because it is so obvious she is a dancer. I bite my lip again because watching her dramatic movements is its own kind of funny and instantly becomes my preferred form of personal entertainment.

"Really, that's what you're going with here, Elvis. That's the best you can do? *Really*?"

"Hear me out," I say sobering a bit at what I have to tell her next. "Just *listen* to all I have to say. Just listen and know that nothing actually happened. The thing to know about Kimberley Powers is she is damn thorough and even when her clients fuck up, she is *on the case* so to speak. So here's the truth about all of that."

I close my eyes for a few seconds as the shame assails me as if I'm being dumped with tar from above. I open them and regard her intently. "I took too many painkillers that night. My headaches were getting worse. I'd had it up to here with the camp," I put my hand above my head, "and Beau Wilson and my dad. I was out of control that night. Add to that the alcohol I consumed; I was pretty much telling Amy Ransom, the LA Times reporter, my life story without a proper filter."

I stop and take a breath and kind of cringe knowing the next part will most likely set her off all over again. "And then the blonde… Trinna. Yes, she did take me home to her place. That did happen. I used the worst judgment possible. And yes, I got caught looking and acting like a complete jerk to you and everyone else on the front sports page across our great land. Like I said, I was on Percocet for the headaches, took too many of them that night, and between those and the booze, I couldn't get it up for that girl, which she unhappily informed me of the next morning. But yes, it's been confirmed she is a fan-girl of the worst kind in search of a ballplayer's golden ticket. We know this because the four condoms I collected per Kimberley's vital instructions for me to do so—two of which I found in the crazed fan-girl's freezer, two by the bed—and yet all four were somebody else's DNA, not mine. I didn't fuck her, but I obviously thought about it and must have wanted to, at some point, so you have every right to hate me, I suppose. And I guess you will, if you decide not to forgive me. Even so, I wanted to set the record straight and admit to everything I know as it relates to my amazing fuck-up in LA and state, for the record—*yours*—that I will never do anything like that again nor go out of my way to purposefully hurt you or Cara like that ever again. That's not who I am, and I think you know that. So, there you have it."

She starts to step forward and accidentally trips into my arms, and I catch her and manage to keep her upright.

"Let me go," she says weakly.

I move her bodily toward the bed and set her down on top of it and then step back from her and sort of bow like a knight would before his queen.

She gets this vague smile so vague I begin to think I've imagined it.

"One more thing," I say in the breach rapidly developing between us. "It's not that I don't *want* to remember you; it's that I *can't*. There's a difference, *Princess*."

She drops her head into her hands and won't even look at me now.

"Say something," I beg after two minutes of her silence.

At last, she looks up at me. Her eyes shimmer with unshed tears.

"I don't know what to say. I don't know where…to go from here."

"I know." I hang my head and refuse to look at her as I admit to one last complete and utter failure. "They're sending me down. I leave for Fresno early tomorrow. I have to find a place to live, buy a car, and secretly work out somewhere with one of Beau Wilson's guys on my pitching because, these days, I can't throw a baseball even if it appears my life depends on it, which it does. I've got four weeks to figure it out, or I lose everything—the contract, the signing bonuses, and the house I apparently just bought that I'm signing papers to put back on the market tomorrow. Yeah, I've fucked-up all around, haven't I?"

"I heard you might be sent down."

"You did? Who *told* you?"

"Sam thought that might happen," she says looking uneasy.

"Of course, he did. I'm sure he couldn't *wait* to tell you. Speculation at its finest."

"He's not like that. He's a good guy."

"Well he has you so of course he's a good guy," I say sounding grudgingly diplomatic.

This strange look fleets across her face. Her lips part like she has something more to say, but she stays silent.

And because I can't quite recover fast enough from all the atonement of confessions and hide the disappointment of being sent down, I turn away from her and go over and touch the silky dress running my hands along the fabric like I've wanted to do the last twenty minutes. Well, really, I've wanted to touch Tally Landon like this for the same amount of time, but I settle for the dress.

"This dress is amazing. Did you get to wear it? Did I get to see you try it on?" I say looking back and just watching her face. She looks conflicted. "I suppose it's a weird question, but I don't remember the past six years. None of it," I say as if that explains the reasoning for asking something so out of left field and decidedly personal.

She shakes her head. "No, I didn't wear it. I never wore it," she says in a low voice. Then she gets this little smirk. "I did almost set it on fire one night, but then I couldn't do it when it came right down to it. I still owe quite a bit of money on it as Visa will attest to, and I was afraid of accidentally setting the house on fire instead."

She laughs a little. "It was too cold to do it outside—to set it on fire, I mean—and really when it came down to it the last thing I needed was the fire department showing up. The paparazzi would have had a field day with that, now wouldn't they?"

We both know exactly when she was going to set the dress on fire.

We share this funny moment and then it turns awkward because I caused all of this.

"I'm sorry," I say looking over at her.

"I know. And I..." She bites her lower lip and shakes her head side-to-side, and then she looks at me intently. "And I forgive you because you've said nothing happened, and I believe you." Then, she smiles. It is both generous and moving. It is the magic of the sun's rays and the miracle of a rainbow after an unexpected rainstorm. *She could charge people to come and see it.*

I have to stay exactly where I'm at, concentrate on taking in air in any way still possible, and keep myself in check. It feels like I might lose it right in front of her because her benevolent smile makes me want to break down for some unfathomable reason. There is this overwhelming sense of loss that is trying to take me down from the other side. My head starts to pound. I wince at the sudden onslaught of pain.

"Are you okay?" She asks.

"I'm fine. Just a headache. They come on like a freight train sometimes. Brad has me on supplements of every kind and off of the Percocet completely now, but it appears chronic headaches are something I'm going to have to learn to live with from here on out. That and this raging thirst all the time."

She's looking at me strangely as if she has something to say about that, but all she says is "do you want some Tylenol?"

She makes Tylenol sound sexy. And my body reacts in kind.

"Sure if you have some. I ran out of the house without all that stuff. I was in a hurry to get here before you changed your mind." I dip my head. "Thank you for letting me come to see Cara. And you."

She nods. "I'm sorry about everything. *Too.*" She sighs and looks at me for a long time. "Thank you for the flowers. That was very thoughtful of you. No one knows about them though. Because that's easier, and I was still really pissed off at you. *Obviously.*"

She frowns. "Although I must confess I don't completely under-stand the *Miss Cloves and Vanilla* reference. You'll have to fill me in sometime." She laughs. "Okay. Let's get you some Tylenol."

She's almost at the door and unlocking it when I say, "Will you try it on sometime? For me."

She turns back with the ghost of a smile. 'Sometime, yes. For you."

"Okay. Then."

She looks taken aback by what I've just said. She sucks in her breath and seemingly holds it. "Okay. Then," she says but looks guilty at having said these two little words back to me as if they belong to someone else.

We enter the world now destined for chaos despite all the guests having left including Tally's parents. Tally dutifully hands me some Tylenol and a glass of water, but her attention is needed elsewhere.

We've been gone longer than a half-hour and in our absence, Elliott fell off the slide, and he's sporting a two-inch gash across his little knee that's bleeding profusely. Marla is now an official wreck while Charlie performs first aid on his son's knee at the kitchen sink.

Sam glowers in the farthest corner away from everyone holding my kid. Of course as soon as Cara sees me, she flies out of Sam's arms into mine. I know, deep down; this is how the battle is going to go with this guy. We will be vying for Tally and Cara's attention at every turn. I will always win on the Cara front, but I have serious doubts about the Tally front. *Miss Cloves and Vanilla seems pretty tough to convince let alone tame.* And I'm out of practice and still not completely in her good graces already because of the LA thing.

After some kind of order returns, Tally walks over to Sam, ex-tends her hand to him, and he pulls her into his lap. Fascinated by their heady exchange, I can't help but watch them interact with each other now. I'm looking for all the telltale signs that they are sleeping together. So far, the jury is out on that one. Charlie will have to fill me in later.

Then, Cara pushes on my face demanding my attention. "Daddy, Elliott hurt his knee. *Bad.*"

"I know, but he's going to be okay. Charlie is a great doctor." I carry her over to Elliott where she begins to stroke his hand and sweetly tells him he's going to be okay. Tired out from the true confessions in the guest bedroom with my former fiancée just minutes ago, I make myself useful by putting my arm around Marla, hugging her tight, while she holds onto Elliott's little hand, and Charlie does the gory clean-up and assessment. Elliott is still crying, but Cara and I try to help him out by cleaning up his face with a wet cloth just to distract him. "Hey buddy. It's going to be okay. Don't cry, Elliott."

Tally continues to talk to Sam in a low voice so none of us can hear what she's saying to him. Sam's looking decidedly unhappy but he's nodding.

"It's going to need stitches," Charlie says to me and Marla. "Looks like we're going to Daddy's work, big guy," Charlie says gently to his son. In a daze, Marla nods while her lips tremble. I move to help them pack up all their stuff.

All the while, Tally still talks to Sam but soon enough she's walking him over to the front door. There are brief good-byes for him among the group except for me. But let's face it; we're not ever going to be friends and neither one of us wants to start down that unproductive path in the first place. We share an interest in the same exquisite prize and only one of us is going to win her. Instead, we nod at each other. Sam says his good-byes to Cara and wishes her happy birthday one more time. And then, he's gone, and Tally's shutting and locking the front door.

Next, she goes over to Marla and hugs her tight and tells her everything is going to be okay. Marla laughs for probably the first time in the past half-hour at something Tally whispers to her, and then they're joking aloud about role reversals.

It's half past five and just beginning to get dark outside. I help Marla and Charlie load up their SUV as well as the wounded Elliott. After saying quick good-byes, they leave for the ER.

It is suddenly down to the three of us—me, Tally, and Cara. There's an awkward silence forming like smoke slowly builds up in a closed

room, and you finally start to notice. For something to do, searching for some reason to remain here as the uninvited guest, I start picking up the party trash bags someone left behind in the kitchen and take them outside.

Taking out the trash.

See?

Look how useful I am, Miss Cloves and Vanilla.

I'm just coming through the back door when I hear Tally trying to convince Cara it's a good time to take a bath.

"Only if Daddy stays." Cara gets this defiant stance and crosses her little arms and looks expectantly at us both.

"If he wants to stay, that's fine," Tally says without looking at me.

"I'll stay."

There is only one girl squealing with true joy over that announcement, the other stands perfectly still and stays absolutely silent.

Giving Cara a bath is an experience. A wet one. She gets more water outside the tub than is in it.

She plays all these games with these imaginary friends made from bubbles. Tally drops a colored tablet in the water, and it turns pink. Then later, she drops a blue tablet in which turns the bath water purple. Each tablet drop produces fresh fun for Cara. She squeals and splashes and laughs with every color change.

This kid makes you believe in magic. She tells me in great detail all about the movie *Frozen.*

"You should be Kristoff because he's the guy, but how does that work?" She laughs. "Because he likes Ana. And Mommy is the queen, and so you'll be the king, but neither of you will die," Cara says thoughtfully. "Okay, Daddy?"

"Okay. I'll be the king, and Mommy will be queen and neither of us will die." I look up at Tally but she's turned away from me.

We spend the rest of bath time talking about colors and reviewing her day and the birthday party while Tally stands to one side with her arms crossed with her mouth half-open looking utterly amazed.

"What?" I finally ask.

"She's *talking*. It's a…miracle really." She laughs a little and then brushes at her face and quickly walks away muttering she forgot Cara's pajamas.

A half-hour later, Cara is changed into her new Elsa nightie and crawling into her big-girl bed. I stroke her long dark hair as it fans out on her pillow. "Sleep well. Daddy has to go to Fresno for baseball. It's a long way from here. But we'll talk soon if it's okay with Mommy. Don't worry, Cara. I'm right here." I touch her little chest and feel her heartbeat.

Cara nods. Slowly, her eyes close and within sixty seconds, she's breathing evenly and appears to be asleep already.

"Is she…okay?" I turn to Tally with alarm. "Does she always fall asleep this fast?"

"It's like a switch with two modes—on and off. But let's face it; she's had quite a day." She gets this slight smile and then heads for the open door.

I slowly follow her into the hallway and down the stairs.

Now what?

CHAPTER
TWENTY-SIX

paper doll

LINC

NERVOUS, AS WE CONFRONT AN UNFAMILIAR scene for one of us—*me*— we take to the opposing leather chairs and sit directly across from each other like we're conducting an interview. *Maybe we are.* She gets this anxious face again but refuses to say why when I ask.

"She really wasn't talking before this?" I'm amazed at all our little girl has said to me today.

"Not really. We worked out this sign language thing, and she would use the word, '*Mommy*,' every once in a while. '*Daddy*' when she wanted to know about where you were." She sighs.

"We've been going to the counseling sessions. She—the counselor—couldn't figure it out either, but she did say Cara would talk when she was ready. I guess she was ready…after she saw you. Thank you." Tally shakes her head and goes silent.

Then she moves to undo her hair which she's worn up since I arrived running her fingers through it all the way to ends. I push myself back further in the chair and hold my breath and just watch. She gets self-conscious and colors a bit under my unintended scrutiny, and eventually stops.

"She's incredible," I say as an opening line.

Cara is our safe topic. Our safe word. I secretly smile at that thought and Tally responds with a smile of her own. *If she only knew what I was thinking about.*

"She is."

"Look, I don't want to make things more difficult with you and Sam."

I'm such a nice guy and apparently out to convince her of this on all levels.

Why don't I just serve Miss Cloves and Vanilla up on a silver spun mattress for Sam's personal pleasure?

Stop trying so hard, bro.

"You're not," she says softly.

"Okay. Then." She flinches again. "What's up with you and those two little words? You did that before," I say.

"Sam says *okay then*. Like *all the time*. You're freaking me out."

"Sam *owns* the words *okay* and *then*?"

"Kind of." She smiles ever so slightly.

"Well, shit I don't know what to say to that."

"You swear a lot more now," she says softly.

"I do? I'm sorry. I don't know why I swear so much. I guess I'm pissed off. About many things."

"I like it. I swear a lot more now too. Out of earshot of the little one most of the time of course, but I wouldn't be surprised if *fuck* isn't her favorite word some day."

"Fuck is everyone's favorite word."

"You think so. *Everyone's*?" She teases.

"It's mine."

"It's mine too, Elvis."

So. Where do we go from here, Tally Landon, *Miss Cloves and Vanilla?*"

"The card with the flowers," she says. "*Miss Cloves and Vanilla.* So. You nicknamed me. Why? And how did you come up with that title?"

"You already took Elvis." I shrug. "*Miss Cloves and Vanilla* is how I remember you from the hospital. It's stayed with me. The memory of you and how you smelled that night like cloves and vanilla stays with me. It's my favorite scent now. You ruined me."

"My smell stays with you? I *ruined you*...for what?"

"Your smell keeps me going all the time. I'm in a clutch game or at practice and it's full count? Your cloves and vanilla scent calms me down. I spray it on the front of my uniform and rub my right hand across like this." I demonstrate by rubbing my chest and she watches me in fascination like a starstruck teenager watches a rock star play his bass guitar. "I went to three different stores before I found the exact scent. Expensive. French perfume. *Chamade* by Guerlain."

She nods looking fascinated or charmed by me at least for a few seconds. "I got it in Paris when I was there a few years ago. I love it."

"I do too. So yes, you *ruined* me. For anyone else."

She's smiling but then it slowly disappears like a countdown does as it goes from ten to zero. "What are you doing to me, Elvis?" She asks, looking troubled.

"I'm not trying to *do* anything to you. I'm sitting on your sofa and talking to you like it's a first date or something."

"I don't date. I don't think we ever dated. Not really," she says, twisting her hair.

"That's too bad. I'm a good dater. At least, I think I was. *Dater.* Is that even a word? Dinner, a movie, ice cream. I would do it all with you."

"Disneyland, pancakes, bubble baths?" She asks playfully.

"As to imply an *overnight date* of some kind at Disneyland complete with bubble baths at night and pancakes in the morning? We can do that too, but only on our third or fourth date. First base. Second base. Third base. Home. I've always been partial to baseball in all aspects of my life." I laugh and at last so does she.

But then, she stops and looks uncertain again. "What are you doing to me, Elvis?" She asks again slower this time.

"I'm not sure." I hesitate. "*How* am I doing?" I reach in my back pocket and pull out my wallet and take out the note. It's a dry cleaners receipt from almost five years ago. She'd written: "*Thank you, Elvis*" on the back of it in this fine script handwriting. "Can you tell me *why* you wrote this note to me and what you were *thanking* me for? It's your handwriting. You wrote it; I checked your message board in the kitchen earlier. What you were thanking me for?"

She takes the note from me and stares at it for a long time.

"Such a sleuth," she finally says with a resigned sigh and gets this solemn expression.

Our friendly banter is now over.

"I was in a dark place. My sister had just died in a car accident on Valentine's Day. Marla wanted me to go to Charlie's party Memorial Day weekend. He invited her. Two years of heartbreak over that guy and she comes running as soon as he called. Anyway, of course, I didn't want to go, but I was her wingman so I was there, drinking the punch, intent on getting thoroughly wasted, and somewhat desperate to feel something with somebody again. My goal was to get lost, lose my tragic story, and be someone else for the night. And you were there. We hit it off—you and I. We danced. And let's face it; I am a hot young thing on the dance floor. You were definitely my conquest for the evening. I had you at hello." She laughs at her clever movie reference.

"God, I wish I'd been there," I tease, and she laughs harder.

It's like a little miracle to see her this way. Relaxed and carefree.

"You invited me back to the guest house, showed me all your trophies, all your ribbons. I told you I was twenty. I was seventeen and still in high school. *I lied.*"

She looks apologetic for a few seconds and then shrugs. "I told you my name was Holly. That I had birth control covered." She winces. "Which I thought I did." She shakes her head and laughs. "Hook, line, and sinker, Elvis. You would have done anything I asked."

"I'm sure that's true."

"You told me you went to Stanford, played baseball. And that baseball was your only focus. You were very honest about that right from the start." She nods and glances away for a moment and then looks back more intense than ever. "I don't know, in some ways, you seemed as lost as I was. Maybe that was the attraction. And yet, in others, you had it all together in ways I'd never been able to achieve. We shared the same fears—falling, failing, losing. The baseball player and the ballerina. A good match. Fire and water. Oil and water. Water and air. *Something.*"

She looks uncertain for a few minutes, shakes her head side-to-side, and seems a bit lost in the memories. Then, she smiles.

God, that smile.

"You cooked for me—some sautéed chicken dish that was utterly mind-blowing. I hadn't eaten in a couple of days, and it's like you knew. It was as if you could see all the way to my soul and didn't want to look away. You saw me, dark as I was, and you saw something good. In me. Something worth saving. And I could breathe again, which I really hadn't done since Valentine's Day, since Holly died. It was weird that first night. Make no mistake. I liked sex and I used guys. I'm in; I'm out. Everybody wins. So I was busy trying to get to the good part, you know—*doing the deed*—but there you were cooking for me, feeding me, taking care of me. So I wrote the thank you note in gratitude, to you, for giving me a respite for a few hours from the pain I carry. I left it on your pillow planning on never seeing you again. And the rest is history. Our history. Solely my history now I guess."

She's bared her whole soul to me, and I am at a loss as to what to do or say. As she was talking, these memories began to flash through my mind. Her words give life to pictures that still make absolutely no sense to me. I shake my head to try to clear the jumbled-up images from my mind and then the pain comes down on me like a hatchet has just sliced through my skull. I close my eyes, which makes it worse, so I open them again and just look at her struggling to find the right words.

"Say something," she says softly. "It's a good story. It's *epic*. I told you all the good parts. Do you want me to cover the sex scene in detail? *That* was epic too."

"Tally." It comes out like a plea or a cry for help and suddenly she looks uneasy. In a foolish and desperate attempt to help her out and get back from the emotional ledge I'm precariously too close to, I go for levity. *"Doing the deed?* Do people still say that?" I try to laugh but it doesn't quite work with the pain lashing at my head.

But Tally isn't laughing. She's staring at me, looking completely undone by what I've just said. "Don't do that," she says flatly.

"Do what?"

"Say shit like that, like you *remember.* You said that exact same thing that night. At Charlie's party, later, but before we did the deed. You were teasing me about saying *do the deed.* That night."

"I was teasing you?"

"You were. You said almost the exact same thing. God! Don't do this to me, Linc." She gasps for air. "I have triggers and you're pulling them. Don't do this to me. Stop it. Right now."

She looks wounded in all kinds of ways. Three words—*do the deed*—cause her to practically fall apart right in front of me. She's delivered this soul-lancing speech ever so calmly like she's on stage easily honing an already perfect performance, but she's losing it over my teasing her about *doing the deed.*

"Okay, I won't say it again. I'm sorry."

"Doesn't matter," she says getting up and turning away from me. "I think you should go."

"You cannot blame me for the things I do not know. Look… it hasn't been a walk in the park for me either. I just want some answers about my life. About *us. Tally.*"

Her agitation returns. She paces the room, kind of strutting the length between the living room and adjoining dining room. *It's sexy as hell.* And all I can do is watch her move. I can no longer concentrate on anything else because I'm instantly captivated by her. Caught up in her presence. She moves through space as if she owns the atoms themselves, and they split upon her command.

She is fusion. Nuclear. Cold.

Yet, she is so graceful and purposeful it makes me want to follow her wherever she goes. It's not just a mental thing it's more like a mind meld. *I get her.* I think she knows I get her, but I would bet that neither one of us can explain the why.

And then there's the physical attraction. That's a given. But there's so much more to it than that. It's everything about her from the melodic sound her voice makes that seems to have worked its way into my brain like the lyrics to a song. It's the way her eyes metamorphose into different shades of green depending solely upon her mood in that given moment and being lucky enough to be the one who lives to see it.

She is living color, and I've been in a black-and-white world for far too long without her.

Powerful stuff. It surrounds me. I've felt it since I first arrived. The forcefield of her. The magnetism of her. The power she wields over me. I'm alive again because of her, like a dying plant that finally gets some water. *I've got it bad for this girl.*

Reality dawns.

The light comes through the darkness and shines on me.

She's my water.

I open my mouth to tell her, to share this profound revelation with her, but no words come out. *Instead, I'm breathing fast. Too fast. I can't get any air. I try again inhaling again and again. I need air.*

It's been a while since the last one, but it feels exactly the same. *I'm suffocating. Or, drowning.*

"Tally." Her name rushes out of me taking all the air I have with it.

She's made her way to the farthest side of the dining room—away from me. Now she turns, glares at me, but then witnesses my personal battle. "Are you? Linc, are you okay?" She rushes over. "Okay. Look at me. Keep your eyes on me. Just breathe. In and out. See? You're going to be fine. It's going to be fine. I'm right here. Everything is going to be okay."

My head still pounds and seems to have been synchronized with my fast beating heart. It's a long while before I slowly start to drift down back into the atmosphere like a parachuter in mid-flight with a chute that mercifully opens.

And yet it swiftly changes to a hard landing. I'm drenched in my own sweat but shiver with cold. Tally's stroking my clammy face and is busy telling me I'm going to be okay. It appears; I'm breathing. The room begins to look normal.

Miss Cloves and Vanilla sits perched on the arm of my chair and pressing a damp cloth to my forehead. Her white dress shimmies up her thighs as she leans in closer to me. I get a good view of the top of her breasts which causes me to get an immediate hard-on. Now I sweat for a different reason. I'm too close, too turned on, when I'm clearly supposed to be the patient to her nurse. I turn my head away from hers because her laser-like green eyes are too upfront and center in my personal space. I cannot handle seeing her disappointment in discovering yet another of my failures.

Lincoln Presley panics. I'm a freak show. For free.

"What's with the panic attacks?" She asks gently after a few shared moments of silence.

I turn my head and look at her, smartly feeling my designated loser status. "Yeah, came along with the headaches and the memory loss. It's a package deal; you have to be super fucked-up to get awarded all three."

"Are you seeing someone about them?" She grabs my wrist and takes my pulse. I stare at her fingers. The left one where my ring should be. It's still in my jean's pocket, and I can feel it there grinding into me like the point of a dull knife.

"I see Brad. I'll tell Brad. I forgot my medication. I'm off my schedule. That's why."

She looks worried. "I'll tell Brad. Where's your phone?" She reaches into my right pocket without waiting for me to answer. "Password?"

"8-2-5-5-9." Please don't let her figure out what *that* means.

She stares at the screen. "Kimberley's sending you frantic texts. Mostly, *call me*. All caps." She gets this bemused look and starts reading aloud. "Okay. She's human; be sensitive to what she's feeling and where's she's coming from. You're going to have to explain LA and I'll leave that up to you. You are so SORRY. Bowing at her feet might be in order." She steps back from me with my phone still in her hand and tilts her head to one side. "Hmmm…you didn't bow. I don't recall any bowing." She sighs dramatically and then she's typing a text.

"What are you going to say?" I reach out in an attempt to get my phone from her. She holds it up in the air off to one side and then moves further away but not before I catch a glimpse of a wicked smile.

She reads it out-loud.

> "Elvis had a panic attack. No meds with him. What should I do? This is Tally, BTW."
> There's a little zing sound fifteen seconds later.
> Tally reads it to me. "Hey it's Brad. Has he eaten?"

She looks at me with a raised eyebrow. "Have you eaten?"

I have landed into ten-year-old boy land and she is my mother all of a sudden. I shake my head side-to-side because there are no words for this surreal scene.

She texts Brad back:

> "No. I'll feed him. I've got this. He's fine now. Thx Brad."

She moves off toward the kitchen. "Food. Damn. The endless forage for food. Do you like birthday cake? Though probably not really considered a food group, huh? Let me see what I can find. You stay there."

"I'm not going anywhere." I cover my head with my arm to try and stem the pain, wishing for painkillers, wishing Tally was a narcotic that I could swallow down and have live inside of me forever.

CHAPTER TWENTY-SEVEN

in repair

LINC

I wake up to Tally pushing at my right arm. "You fell asleep. You still look like you're in a lot of pain. I brought you something to eat." She hands me a plate with four mini sliders on them. All warmed up. I've already wolfed down three when she says, "Sam brought them from the restaurant for the party."

Now, the last one is harder to chew let alone swallow. God damn Sam. "Thanks."

"You don't have to sound so glum about it. They're sliders. They're so good. He brings me food like this all the time. It's a mission of his getting me to eat. I'm his mission, but I'm not sleeping with him yet. You can still try to win me back." She gets this little smirk.

"I think I hate you."

"Hate is the best defense, Elvis. Good job." She pats my right knee and moves away from me altogether.

I set the empty plate down. "What the fuck are you doing to me? Are you *friend-zoning* me?"

"Yes. Yes. Yes, I am. It's the best way. Let's-be-friends. Let us be friends." She grabs a pill bottle. "Brad sent another text while you were sleeping. He wanted to know how you were doing. He wants you to call him first thing tomorrow morning. He said you could have three more Tylenol." She counts them out and hands me a fresh glass of water. "Here you go."

I drink down the pills with the water and manage not to choke even though she watches me the entire time making me self-conscious.

Then, she starts pulling at the neckline of her white dress, which causes me to say, "you're really beautiful. It's not a pick-up line. The way you move…you're so graceful…just like a dancer. I don't know how I ever thought you were a nurse. Although you're being a pretty good nurse right now."

"*Friends*, Elvis." She draws an imaginary line between us. "Come on. Let's-be-friends. It'll be fun. Let's *really* confuse the paparazzi by just being *famous friends*. 'Cause, I'm a pretty famous dancer, you know." She laughs. "SFB…San Francisco Ballet is up and coming. It's not New York but it will do. For now," she says softly. "And there's always the Bolshoi this summer with Sasha. She wants me to come see her. Bring Cara. For the summer."

"Who's Sasha?"

"This really gets confusing, doesn't it? All these people you don't remember. Sasha was my director at New York City Ballet. She's one of the reasons I came back to San Francisco. Then, she married Michael. He's a doctor, and now they're in Moscow."

"Nobody will tell me about Moscow. Have you ever been?"

She looks uneasy again. "We don't talk about Moscow. That's actually when I first met Sam…after Moscow. We don't talk—"

"About Moscow," I finish the sentence for her.

Silence.

A long one.

"We should probably talk about Moscow," she says with a heavy sigh. "Everything kind of leads to Moscow. Eventually."

"Only if you want to. We don't have to."

She slides into the chair opposite mine and twists up her hair and holds it on top of her head with one hand. "The Giants got you for a song because of Moscow. The Angels left you high and dry after you got arrested."

"Wait *what*? I got *arrested*? I'm a bad-ass?"

"Not a bad-ass, Elvis, a hometown hero, actually." She nods as if giving herself permission to proceed. "You were in Moscow with the Angels for an exhibition game with Nika. Not a fan of hers by the way. I was in Moscow as part of NYC Ballet's exchange program dancing with the Bolshoi Ballet. I'd had some trouble before with crazed fans in Paris. Little things. Someone broke into my hotel room. Another followed me home. Moscow was different, vaguely worse for some reason in my mind." She sighs. "But I was determined to overcome my fears and not let them rule my life anymore. I was actually the bad-ass, Elvis." She smiles but then it fades just as fast. "So. I was walking, *alone*, back to the hotel after a luncheon thing with the other dancers when I passed this guy on the street. It was just like those movies you see. A questionable part of town. A girl walking alone. Too far from her hotel. All of those indelible facts ran through my mind in those few split seconds before this guy turned around, grabbed me, and pulled me into this alleyway. Nicholai Balanchine." She winces upon saying his name. "He attacked me at knife-point, and things went from there."

These haunted shadows flit across her features. She lets go of her hair and stares off into space for a long twenty seconds.

"Tally, we don't have to talk about Moscow," I say feeling uneasy. "We *don't*. Kimberley said *not* to bring it up. She told me she'd tell me about all of it someday. We *don't* have to do this."

"No. It's okay. I've got this. I should be the one to tell you. All of it." She takes a deep breath and studies me. "I got away from him. *Somehow*. I pushed him hard enough and he landed on some rebar, which lanced straight through him, pinned him down like a butterfly. He wasn't dead. Not then. And I was terrified, injured, bleeding profusely. I just wanted to get away, get to my hotel, assess the damage of what he'd done to me, so I made my way to the street. And there you were. The first car I stopped was a taxi and you were the passenger. Moscow, this huge city, and you were there. Cosmic, right? You took me to the hospital. You saved my life. You and Dr. Michael Markov. Actually, Sasha met Michael because of me. Love. You find it in such strange places sometimes." She smiles for a few seconds. "Anyway, emergency surgery. Drugs. Never enough. Pain. Yes, lots of pain. And many lies told by me to better cope with the scene unfolding in front of me."

She gets up from the chair and crosses her arms and stares out the window. "You told me you were marrying Nika, and that I couldn't have any more children, possibly in the same sentence, at least it felt that way." She gets this sad twisted smile. "I kind of lost it after that. So, I left. *You*. Moscow. But then, Balanchine died and I hadn't given them a statement, and you didn't have an alibi for that alley scene, and the Moscow Police didn't care. You were arrested. They threatened you with these trumped-up murder charges and the Los Angeles Angels baseball team was none too happy about all the negative press involving their superstar pitcher."

She looks at me intently. "I didn't know you were in trouble because of me. Ten days after your arrest, Marla and Charlie tracked me down here in San Fran. I returned to Moscow, gave a statement, and they finally released you, and me, I guess, for seven hundred thousand convincing reasons. A hundred of mine; six hundred grand of my ex's, Rob Thorn. At the time, Rob led me to believe that he had paid the ransom for your release. I felt I owed him, so I went back to him. Yet, it turned out that you reimbursed him. So, technically, I still owe you six hundred grand. Damn. I'm in some serious debt as it is," she teases softly. "How am I going to pay you back? I'll figure it out; I promise." She frowns and gets this brittle smile. "I guess your father wasn't completely wrong about your money as it relates to me. So, yeah, we don't talk about Moscow, like ever."

"You don't owe me anything."

I sit here in total shock at her story. What she went through sounds like a horror movie and yet she attempts to smile, to laugh it off.

"So. You can't have any more children. I'm so sorry," I say gently.

She looks taken aback. "That's all you got out of my little story about Moscow?" She looks unsure as how to handle my sympathy. "No," she finally says in a low voice. "They still say it's unlikely I can get pregnant again. One ovary—yada, yada, yada. Scar tissue. Impossible odds. Shall I go on about the girl stuff?" She smiles again but it doesn't diminish the grief reflected in her eyes.

"I'm so sorry." I grab her hand and squeeze it tight trying to relieve her of some of the pain. "At least, we have Cara. And she's more than enough." I smile.

"Stop this." She jumps out of her chair in one swirling motion and begins pacing. "Stop this," she says again. "*Please.*" She practically moans the word.

"Stop what?"

"This *thing* you're doing…saying things like that. You wanted a *son.* I couldn't give you one. It's important to you. Quit acting like it doesn't matter. It *matters* to you!"

"I wanted a son? Tally, *every guy* wants a son. But we have Cara so it *doesn't matter.* Wait. Did I…did I make you feel bad because you couldn't have any more kids? That we couldn't have a son?"

She stares at me as a single tear rolls down her face. "Yes. Not intentionally or cruelly, but *yes*, you did. It tore me up when you admitted this to Pastor Dan."

"Who's Pastor Dan?"

"It doesn't matter. It doesn't matter anymore. Quit doing this to me. Stop saying things like that as if you remember me at all. You're confusing me." She looks stricken and I begin to hear her wheezing. But in the next ten seconds, she's at the front door undoing the locks as fast as she can. She wrenches the door, and points toward my car parked at the curb. "Please. Just go."

Now *this* is a turning point.

"Tally," I say gently as I slowly walk over to her. "We can't change the past but we can embrace the present. We can start over." I stand in the open doorway and look at her intently. "We can figure this out between us."

"No. We can't. Stop it," she says irritably. "You need to go, Linc. *Now.*"

"What if I don't want to?" I ask.

"It's not about what you want. It's about what *I* want. And right now, I want you to go home to your big ol' house in the land of Sea Cliff, get a good night's rest, pack your bags, move to Fresno and not confuse me anymore. I have *Sam*. And Cara. And this thing with you is all too much." She takes a shaky breath.

We stand there for a few minutes and share our misery.

"What time do you leave for Fresno?" She asks.

"I've got to buy a car, sign some IR release forms with the Giants, finish things up with the house, call Kimberley and Brad." I sigh. "I'll be on the road by noon, if I'm lucky. What are the odds?"

"May the odds be forever in your favor." *The Hunger Games* reference should serve as levity but neither one of us laughs. She tries again. "You need to go. You're leaving for Fresno. You have baseball. You have to focus on that. You know it; I know it." Now, she gets this impenetrable stony look on her face. "Now is not the time for us...I have *Sam*."

Sam has become her secret weapon in the last six minutes. Every time she says his name I flinch.

"I don't like Sam," I say irritably.

"You don't *get* to like Sam or *not* like Sam. That's my business. *My affair*." She catches her lower lip between her teeth seeming to regret what she's just said to me. But then, she stands up straighter and starts her little speech all over again. "You can't afford to lose your *focus*. It's like you said, you lose baseball; you lose everything and I'm not going to be the one who causes you to do that."

She's right of course. What can I offer her? I'm playing baseball practically every damn day until September beginning now. I'll be in Fresno and up and down the West Coast with the Grizzlies all summer. *If I'm lucky*. If I don't somehow blow it all together. *Fresno*. I may as well be in Texas or New York or Toronto. *When would I see her? What can I give her?* And if I lose baseball because I can't throw a fast ball or a slider, well, I lose everything. *I wash out*.

"Okay," I say, feeling the ebb of another panic attack coming on. "But how do you want to work this? With Cara. With us."

"Stop it. Stop it. Stop it." She leans against the open door and closes her eyes. I step closer to her and they flutter open. "Go. Now."

"Tally." I run my hands through my hair in frustration because

I can already feel her pulling away even though she's standing right in front of me.

"I'll call you." She gets this sly half-smile.

"No, you won't."

"I'll call you. Now go, Lincoln Presley," she says with a heavy sigh. "You need to go right the fuck now."

The defiant queen has returned and I already know she's not going to back down.

And somehow I know if I push her too far, it will be the end of us.

And so I leave.

I sit in the rental car for a long time. Long enough to watch her turn off all the lights inside the house. Long enough to watch the early morning fog roll in and turn the dark night into a grey dawn silently marking the first day of February.

At last, I recover.

Defeated, I start the car and drive away.

Within blocks of leaving, I'm thirsty again.

And all I know for certain is that it's going to be a long season. *Without water.*

PART 4

the truth about

air & water

"If I know what love is, it is because of you."
-Hermann Hesse

CHAPTER TWENTY-EIGHT

ride

TALLY

Y OU KNOW WHAT THEY SAY, DON'T YOU?

Everything comes together.

You know what I'm going to say, don't you?
Everything comes together and then it falls apart.
But who's right? You ask.
I am.

February, March, April lands us into May. Sam stays around. Sam helps me rent out the studio apartment downstairs for a screaming deal to an enthusiastic college student who loves kids and will nanny on the side which leads me to Andrea Lynn Dawson. *Andy* is a god-send. My little girl loves her. Andy has no problem playing with Cara for hours. The two take walks and go to the park and play dress-up and when I'm not at the dance studio, I join in on all the fun. My mom and I can breathe a little easier because Andy takes some of the pressure off of us in helping take care of Cara. Andy can be here when I can't be. We are one big happy family sliding into the middle of May quite nicely.

Sam's been busy with *The Promissory Note* and other secret career-minded things he doesn't talk about, and we are still taking it slow, which inexplicably works for me. However, taking it slow is something I think he plans to remedy this weekend. He tells me he has a getaway planned, but he won't tell me what it is or where. I've been told to pack lingerie.

It's black.

I've worked out a doable routine with Linc. He calls on Tuesdays and Thursdays at four in the afternoon just after Andy returns from picking up Cara from preschool on her way home from her own class and before I head off to late rehearsals.

Linc calls. I answer. And we do our thing that goes like this:

Hello.

How are you?

I'm fine. Good.

Here's Cara.

Talk soon.

Bye.

Twelve words give or take are exchanged with each of the past twenty-nine phone calls done twice a week since early February, and I'm good with that. *Surprisingly.*

I don't think Linc feels the same, but I am trying to figure it all out, and he still doesn't remember me, and so I've recently begun to believe that I can move on with my life now. I believe I can. That's probably my second mistake. The first one is believing that everything has finally come together. I've apparently already forgotten what I know to be true—it all falls apart in a lot less time than it takes to put it all together. *Don't believe me? Just watch.*

It's Wednesday. It's Linc's day off. The only day off of two he has this month.

Just a bit of trivia.

Things I know but do not say aloud.

I also know it's Wednesday because I have tonight off too. It's my only free day to pack for the big trip with Sam this weekend. Because I am finally going to whore it out with Sam this weekend. Or, die trying. One of those two things is likely going to happen.

I have decided that only way to move on is to move on with somebody else. Am I the *last* one to figure this out? Maybe I've watched *Silver Linings Playbook* one too many times. It always makes me cry at the end, but maybe it's the moving on part that has been making me sad. I am in a surreal place because I know Sam wants more, and I know I'm still not ready, but I'm determined to move on. *To do something.*

And so I pack and unpack the black lingerie, six times and counting. I leave it out of the bag this last round, deciding this isn't going to work, and that I need to call Sam and call it off. I need to be honest about whatever this is between us and let him know I'm not ready. *I'm not ready.* Maybe that's all I need to say. I'm not ready.

But what if I'm not ready precisely because the thing is I haven't been moving on? The thing about moving on is you need to take some sort of action. You actually need to *move on* to *move on*.

I sit on the bed contemplating my life and debating the packing of the lingerie and wondering what Linc is doing on his only day off this month.

Andy is downstairs with Cara. They're watching *Frozen* again. I smile because I can vaguely hear the two of them singing Cara's favorite song, *Human*. They both belt it out just like Christina Perri does.

The doorbell rings. It's only nine in the morning too early for my afternoon rehearsal and even Cara's preschool. Andy doesn't have classes on Wednesdays.

These are all the things I know to be true.

It takes a few seconds to recognize Marla's frantic voice. "Is she *here?*"

"Yeah, she's upstairs. Is something wrong?" Andy asks.

I don't hear Marla's answer I just hear Elliott's cherub laugh and watch from the top of the stairs as Marla adroitly hands her son off to Andy.

"We'll be upstairs," Marla says to my nanny. I grip the railing and closely examine the stricken look on Marla's face. She takes the steps two at a time, and as soon as she reaches me and says, "let's talk."

She heads to the master bedroom without waiting for my response. I follow more slowly filled with instant dread.

Somebody died or somebody's going to.

She grips a newspaper under one arm. "Have you talked to *him*?"

Linc.

I swallow hard. "No, it's Wednesday." *Like that explains everything.* "It's early. What are you doing here so early?"

"Tally."

My name becomes a four syllable word and I am underwater all at once straining to hear my best friend's words because this rushing sound comes out of nowhere and clamps down on my entire existence at a soul level.

"I haven't talked to him yet," Marla is saying. "God, as soon as I saw it…well, I was standing in the check-out line, I bought all the copies they had and then headed here."

"Saw what?"

She's pale, shaking her head back and forth. "I know it looks bad but he *told* you *nothing happened*."

"LA," I say as the air rushes out of me.

It is clear. I hate that town.

Marla comes over and puts both arms around me. Our foreheads mash together. "Yeah. If it's true, it's bad. And I wanted to be…with you because I know what it will mean to you," she whispers.

She starts crying.

I step back and just stare at her. Marla doesn't cry. *It's bad.*

"Show me." I'm calm as if I'm ordering up the daily special in Manhattan at our favorite diner. Maybe I am. Maybe I've transported myself back to five years ago when it was just me and Marla against the world. She holds my hand the same way she did then as she unrolls the tabloid.

The headline reads: **Trinna's Pregnant! Lincoln Presley's baby? The son he really wants.**

Nice. The photo says it all as if the headline hasn't covered it enough already. It depicts a slightly pregnant Trinna blissfully smiling and looking straight into the camera. She holds a Starbucks cup in one hand and her already bulging tummy with the other wearing these little yoga pants and matching top. They've photo-shopped a smiling Linc in the photograph right next to her—I recognize this one from another tabloid last season—and yet; my stomach spins up.

Even so, I miraculously manage to keep it together.

It's like I've finally made it to the grown up section on the game board of Life.

But now what?

"Maybe it's not true. Look, he's photo-shopped in," I say a little too brightly. "Kimberley warned me about this kind of stuff a long time ago. It's probably nothing."

Marla stares at me like I've lost my mind. *Well, there's that.*

"She *gave* an interview. She's quoted in the article. She *named* him, Tally. She said something about genetic testing being done as soon as the baby is born and that Linc has already agreed to do it."

Now THAT gets my attention.

I secretly implode on the inside, while Marla stands only inches away from my face and stares me down obviously getting ready for my expected meltdown.

Wait for it.

"Okay," I say at last on one long gasp for air. I turn and head downstairs to find my cell phone. Marla follows.

I'm still calm, still keeping it together.

This is a miracle. God and Marla and my beloved sister Holly can stand as my witnesses.

Marla is enough of an emotional wreck for both of us. She's *still* crying.

The kids glance over at her and look a little taken aback when they are normally riveted to the best part of *Frozen*—when Elsa runs away and turns everything to ice in her wake. *Everyone* loves this part.

I
am
Elsa
today.

I pause from my mission to take a few precious moments to watch this scene because *it is crucial* to get it exactly right.

"*What* are you doing?" Marla asks wiping her face with the back of her hand.

"Just looking at how it's done. It's important to know exactly how to turn your world to ice, stone, or fire and brimstone. One of those. Unleash the power. Watch out." I actually laugh a little and Marla eventually does too. *Oh good, we're both going to make it to the other side together.* I grab her hand and dance around with her. She's looking at me like I'm crazy, but the kids are happy and Andy is smiling wide trying to take it all in and understand what has happened to Tally Landon.

Everyone wants to know. Don't they?

"How do they know Linc wants a son?" Marla asks after our few minutes of levity ends. "I mean," she pauses, "who would have told them such a thing?"

And we're back to the matter at hand just like that.

"I don't know. It's not public knowledge. Maybe they're guessing. But it doesn't matter; it's true. He does." I frown.

"But he *told* you he didn't want one even at Cara's birthday party." Marla's eyes fill with fresh tears.

Clearly, she is taking this outwardly worse than I am.

And *clearly*, I've told Marla way too much about my last conversation with Lincoln Presley.

My heart is frozen, and the freezing is branching out like a spider web to the rest of me. The pain is real and definite, but it is still far away, but I know it's coming for me.

But the clarity I feel? Is fucking fantastic.

"He *told* you he didn't care. He told you *nothing happened*," she says shaking her head.

"Yep. Maybe he lied. The old Linc cared. He wanted a son. He told Pastor Dan that a long time ago. Maybe he remembers. Doesn't matter." I wave my hand dismissively about and grab my phone from the kitchen counter and note the number of missed calls. *Six in all. One from Sam. Five from Kimberley. Zero from Linc.* "He should have called me and told me about this himself. I don't appreciate being blindsided like this." I silence the cell and slip it into the pocket of my jeans and nod with sudden decision. "Marla, I need you take Cara for a few days."

She's following me back up the stairs and looks confused about my request. "*Where* are you going?"

"I'm *going* to go figure this out."

"*Where* are you going to go to figure it out?"

"Fresno. Mikhail was looking for someone to go over there and check things out for a possible fall program. So, I'll go. But you need to watch Cara. I don't want to burden Andy with this, since I don't know how long I'm going to be gone exactly."

"Why wouldn't you know that? What are you going to do *exactly*? Why are you already packed?" She looks around the bedroom and sees my open bag and continues to follow me around the house asking more and more questions which I ignore while I feverishly shove more stuff in the overnight bag. *Now*, I grab the black lingerie I unpacked earlier because I'm going to need that after all. She watches me do this without comment. Her lips clamp together forming a thin pretty red-lipped line on her beautiful face. I think she's afraid to say anything to me now. Speechless, she follows me into the guest bedroom where I grab the bride and groom gear and zip it up into a large black garment bag.

"*Why* are you taking your wedding dress and his tuxedo with you? *Tally.* Now, I'm really getting worried. What are you going to do? *For real?*"

I turn to her probably perfectly mimicking dear Elsa at the ice castle. "I'm going to ask him for the truth, and he's going to tell me. Don't worry so much. I've got this. Can you drive me to the bus station?"

"You're taking the *bus*? Can't you fly?"

"Not today. Today I need time to think, to prepare. The bus is *perfect.*" I award her a miraculous smile, and Marla looks stunned.

Yeah, me too, girlfriend.

Me too.

We leave a bewildered Andy behind. She promises to clean the house and do the laundry. This generous offer almost causes me break down and cry—such a wealth of love and friendship right in my midst: *Cara. Sam. Marla. Charlie. Mom. Dad. Tommy. Andy.* I don't need anyone else.

Why didn't I realize this sooner?

Why did I waste so much time and energy on this hopeless love for Lincoln Presley?

Why?

We load up the kids in her SUV along with Cara's overnight bag which Andy amazingly keeps packed for my baby now. I try not to dwell on the failure-as-a-mom stuff too much because I am over-burdened as it is and not sure how long this calm-as-fuck state I'm rocking will hold out. Marla is awaiting my expected meltdown like a hawk looking for its next meal.

"Stop by *The Promissory Note*. I need to talk to Sam."

"What are you going to do about him?" Marla sighs.

She looks conflicted.

Tell me about it.

"Cut him loose," I say quietly. "I'm not ready. It's not fair. I've got to solve this thing with Linc and I've hardly been fair to Sam. I'm all fu…s-c-r-e-w-e-d up." I glance back at the kids in the back loaded in their car seats and smile wide at them. Marla pulls up along the restaurant's front curb. I study the sign, *The Promissory Note* for a few seconds. "Five minutes," I say getting out of the car.

She nods and gives me her best I'm-in-this-with-you-no-matter-what-you-do look.

Yeah, I'm in this alone other than with Marla.

The idea of cutting Sam loose makes me sad but I can't deny my visceral reaction to hearing Lincoln Presley's latest news and I have to deal with that first. I walk through the doors in search of him. He's at the bar stacking liquor bottles which he must have just un-packed from a recent delivery. He looks surprised to see me and then this notable disappointment crosses his face. I hear him sigh.

"Hi," I say.

"Hi," he says, shaking his head side-to-side at seeing me this early in the morning. "I'm assuming this isn't a social call to tell me how much you're looking forward to the weekend," he says dryly. "Geez, I knew it was coming, but I didn't expect it until Friday." He gets this crooked smile and then frowns at me. "Don't do this, Tally," he whispers.

"I'm not ready." I hang my head and wipe away a tear because it is really crazy to be letting go of a such a great guy like Sam. "It's not fair to you. I'm broken and you can't fix me. Not right now. I have to do this on my own."

"What happened that made you draw this conclusion," he asks studying me intently.

"A few things. My inability to pack lingerie for this weekend." I try to laugh and he smiles. "Some unfinished business with Linc." I wince as the image of happy pregnant Trinna flits through my head causing me fresh pain. "I can't do this to you or *with you*, right now. It's definitely not fair to you and there are things…I need to do for myself." He sets down the liquor bottle he's been holding since I got here and comes around the bar and puts his arms around me.

"We'll be friends. We've *been* friends," he says into my hair. His chin fitting perfectly on the top of my head. His breath stirs my hair.

I pull back a little and look up at his sad face. "It's not enough and you know that. It's too one-sided, and I can't take anything else from you. I can't. I need to be free in order to give something back to you, and right now I can't do that. I haven't been doing that. I'm not free of him."

He closes his eyes and nods. He said this a long time ago.

Deep down, I think he knows I'm right in what I'm saying. "As I said," my voice wavers on the words, "I have some unfinished business with Linc, and you might not like all that entails." My eyes sting. Sam nods and gently kisses my forehead. I close my eyes, and wish time would go back to two hours ago when I was packing for an experience with Sam that held the potential of our future.

"Are you sure you're okay?"

"Have I *ever* been okay?" I ask.

Sam pulls back and studies my face. "You are a lot more together than you ever give yourself credit for," he says softly.

What am I doing? Why am I giving this superhero up?

"Thank you for being you and allowing me to be me." I pull him to me and kiss him. He pulls me in tight and kisses me thoroughly back. There's a hint of sadness and inevitability in it all though that we both seem to feel. It really does feel like good-bye. "Thank you," I whisper.

"I'm here for you, Tally. Do what you have to do but know that you can always come back to me. I'll still be here."

"Like a promissory note. Thank you for always being here for me. You are more than I deserve. Thank you." I kiss him again and then step back because there is a huge part of me that would rather stay and do inventory with Sam and find a future with him and I need to leave like right now.

He nods and then looks a little wistful. "Call me if you need me, okay?"

"Okay. Then." I walk out before I can change my mind. The vacillation back and forth of breaking things off with him has already been more difficult than I ever thought it would be. But you can't stay with someone because it's easier. And I finally have to ask myself, if Linc got his memory back tomorrow and our history was cobbled back together, despite the Trinna thing, would I still be with Sam? Probably not. And we're back to me and my sudden urge to be free of Lincoln Presley and how to make that happen to have any chance a future with anyone else, including Sam.

Marla give me the hawkish look all over again as I slide back into the passenger seat. I don't say anything as she starts the car and heads toward the bus station. "So?" She asks after few minutes. "What did *we* do?"

"*We* cut him loose." I wipe at my face and look out the car window as she maneuvers onto the freeway. Now she looks as completely undone as I suddenly feel. *Granted, it's been quite a morning already.* "Tell me it's the right thing to do. *Go.*"

"Okay. Then," she says, rewarding me one of her fake-it-until-you-make-it smiles even as her words echo mine to Sam and cut me to the core. "You're doing the right thing for you. Today. Now, you're clear to do anything you want. There's that. We do what we have to do. We don't do what is easiest anymore now, do we?"

"Not often enough." I half-smile because she's right. Sam was easier—in a good way—but how fair is that? Cutting him loose doesn't feel great. In fact, it feels downright insane because I'm on my own all at once. *Completely alone.* I've got nothing but my best friend and the kids in the backseat of this car in this particular moment. *Yay, team!*

"Geez, Tally," she says shaking her head as the decision of what I've done cuts in on both of us. "When are you going to catch a break?"

"I don't know. Maybe I just have to make my own from now on."

"What does that mean?" Marla asks looking anxious.

"Not sure yet. All I know for sure is I've got to come up with a plan. Thus, a bus ride to Fresno." I shake my head and try to smile. The implications of it all start to weigh me down. *Linc. Babies. Trinna. Me. Sam. When did it all go so wrong? Why is it all so impossible? Where do I go from here?* I nod at Marla and tell her I can't do more than that take a bus ride and think it all through.

On the way to the bus station, I call Mikhail and finalize the details about going to Fresno for SFB. My boss is too surprised that I'm willing to schlep it to Fresno for SFB to question my motives, and I'm too stunned by his rare gratitude to fully explain. I'm taking one for the team, and Mikhail Rostov is pleased. The world is righted for a few hours more at least for one of us.

I manage to keep it together as I kiss my kid good-bye after purchasing a Greyhound one-way bus ticket from San Fran to Fresno. I decide that should be a title of a movie—*San Fran to Fresno*. Now *that* would be epic. The bus ride is estimated to be about five hours according to Julian, the ticket guy, because of a few stops along the way scheduled to provide the extra fun, and we just make it in time for me to get in line the before the bus is loading and due to take off because that is the kind of luck I'm having today. *With Greyhound.*

Ten missed calls from Kimberley now.

Call me. Call me. Call me. The tone of her voice starts out casual but by the tenth message it sounds mildly desperate. 'Hey, Tally! Call me back 'kay?"

But we know what she's calling me about. And still nothing from Lincoln Presley himself.

As the miles pass, service becomes intermittent. I've tried to call Linc a few times, but it goes straight to voicemail, and I don't leave a message. I'm secretly relieved because actually talking to him seems impossible right now. And as we descend into the central part of the San Joaquin Valley, I decide an ambush—*I mean, surprise*—of him is best.

He did it to me. Why not return the favor?

Engulfed in anguish over calling it off with Sam and this blazing fury at Linc that seems to take me over, I stare out the window at the passing countryside but register absolutely nothing. I'm encircled in some strange bubble; it protects as well as centers me. I remain suspended within it in this ever calm state. Nothing can touch me. Nothing can reach me. It's as if I can see all of my fears lining up on the other side—failing, losing, falling—they're all there waiting for me, but nothing can get through this bubble. *Yet.*

I'm reminded of the train ride Katniss takes that first time to the Capitol in *The Hunger Games*. Same kind of deal I suppose, only it's happening to me in real life.

I wish I had a bow and arrow like hers though.

That would come in handy because you never know what you're going to require in Fresno.

These outrageous thoughts makes me laugh and Rose, the little old lady, sitting next to me thinks for about ten seconds it's a way to break the ice and have a conversation with this semi-famous ballerina after all. She recognized me right away and proudly told me she has season tickets to the San Francisco Ballet, but I was unable to do more than thank her for her patronage—I think I actually said that, 'thank you for your patronage.' *Mikhail would be so pleased with me.* Beyond signing an autograph on her checkbook cover, we haven't spoken since then. It remains unlikely we will, and I know my face tells her this again now.

But still, it surprises me, when she pats my right hand and says, "it's going to be okay, dear. *It is.* The world can be a hellish place and full of disappointment but there's always a silver lining. Tomorrow is another day."

So she reads the tabloids, too.

Does everyone?

The coined phrases slay me too. Tomorrow's silver lining, my ass. But all I say is, "it's Wednesday. It's his only day off. It *has* to be today." She pats my hand once more, and then I have to look out the window because I can't handle the sympathy I detect in her warm brown eyes for the crazy bus passenger she's ended up sitting next to.

I check out.

I don't get as much clear thinking done as I thought I would, but I've got a plan. I typed up a plan. *Tally's Epic Plan.* Because if Lincoln Presley thinks he's going to break my heart for a third time; he's mistaken. Payback is a bitch, and he's about to find out why. First, I'm going to wear the dress like he wanted. Then, I'm going to do the deed with him like I wanted. And then I'm going to break his heart and leave him because that's what everybody wants to see. But first we're going to perform for the LA Times and a few others. I've already called Candy Baxstrom and told her to be ready.

Yeah, I've got everything. A wedding dress made of French silk and Tulle by Catherine Deane. His Armani tux. I'm all set. I just haven't quite decided when the show will begin. I fish his engagement ring out of my pocket and look at it for a few seconds. He left it on the steps before he drove away in the early morning hours on the first of February.

He left a note, too. "Thank you, Tally. I want you to keep this for now. Let's see where things go."

I'll show him where things go.

I slip the ring back in my pocket and continue to study *Tally's Epic Plan.*

CHAPTER TWENTY-NINE

dare you to move

LINC

FRESNO IS DUSTY BUT DOABLE. JUST like I anticipated, nobody expects me to know their name and there is profound relief in not having to meet everyone's expectations on that front. My dad is mostly satisfied with my pitching. He declares the season long, and it's early, so he returned to LA to close up his house a week ago. He's still hell-bent on moving to San Fran, despite the upheaval of my life over the past seven months. He remains surprisingly optimistic that the Giants will return me to the line-up before summer ends, and he wants to be settled in San Fran for that. I have my doubts about returning to the majors, but I've kept those to myself. No sense getting my dad all riled up about my confidence level in throwing a baseball in the strike zone. He remains steadfast and entirely focused on that aspect of my life far too much already.

"Hey, Presley. We're headed to O'Riley's. You coming?" Doug Hillman taps the dirt from his ball shoes and then places them on the bleachers nearby. He's already changed out of his uniform into his evening attire—Polo shirt, jeans, and black dress shoes.

Ferragamos. I have the exact same pair in my locker.

He looks up from what he's doing when I don't respond.

"It's not a date or anything," he says with a hesitant laugh. "It's just what we minor-league players do. We play ball together. We drink together. In other words, we *socialize* with the other players and try to find the fun in Fresno. Your dad's gone, right? So, now that the close examination of how fast you're pitching or not has come to a close with his departure, maybe you can afford to let loose a little with us mere mortals who still play ball because it's fun and might eventually lead to something else down the road."

His words sting as intended. The underlying resentment for my dad and for me and my lofty baseball career follows me to Fresno. Nobody likes the guy who appears to have everything. I don't like that guy either. But I'm not that guy—even if this ballplayer doesn't see that.

Anger rushes me. *If I had just left five minutes earlier. If I hadn't hung out to take a few extra practice swings with the bat.* Because in the minor leagues, sometimes pitchers handle a bat as much as a baseball as part of the lineup. *And I am rusty or washed out. One of those.*

I suck air in order to get my temper under control and shake my head. "No, I can't make it today. I've got to get some more time in throwing."

"You can overdo the throwing thing. You know that, right?"

"Yeah, but my trainer—"

"We've all heard what your trainer says, what your coaches say, what your dad says, what the infamous Beau Wilson says, and what your hot publicist Kimberley something or other, says. Hell, the only one we haven't heard from about you is your supposed fiancée Tally Landon. What does *she* say?"

Do I want to get a drink with this guy or deck him?

"Hillman, back off."

He raises his hands at my warning and takes a few steps back. "No foul, Presley. It's just a drink, man. Forget it." He turns and heads towards his car in the team parking lot.

"Where again?" I call out after him.

He turns back, shading his eyes. "O'Riley's."

I nod slowly. "Okay, I'll be there."

O'Riley's is the epitome of Fresno. It's a joint off of Main Street with fine film encircling the place like fairy dust, complete with Budweiser beer as the only on-tap offering and free overfilled baskets of peanuts where the establishment's patrons are encouraged to drop empty shells onto the floor. There's a black-and-white tiled dance floor at one end that looks like it has been around for a few decades, while the tall bar tables and stools front the bar bookending what remains of the space. It's only half past seven on a Wednesday night, so the place hasn't gotten all that crowded yet. This 411 is according to Hillman. "The place rocks when the band starts up," he says.

Right now, the four tables nearest the bar are filled with Fresno Grizzlies ball players. Hot and thirsty and ready for whatever O'Riley's has to offer. I'm surprised to see so many ballplayers here since today is only one of two days we all have off this month. Maybe they're like me—maintaining an all-out focus on baseball because anything else serves as an unnecessary distraction. Or, they're just really bored and there's really nothing else going on in this town.

Brandy, our waitress, sets down a fresh round. She has already been propositioned twice since she started serving us. Both times she's rolled her eyes, set down our drinks, and retreated before one of the guys could get too familiar with any of her assets. We've all noticed them, of course, and some have talked about them at length among themselves; however, it turns out that Hillman is a nice guy like me, so we take care of the tab and protect Brandy the blond beauty from the more lascivious among us. She seems to have already figured out Kevin Steinway and Seven Tall—his actual name, a name his mother was convinced from birth that would afford him the ability to hit his way to fame with baseball, or so he tells us, over and over.

The bad-boy behavior causes Brandy to make a wide berth. She's started avoiding that end of the table all together. So now we hand Seven and Kevin their beers whenever Brandy approaches asking us to pass them down in order to help her out.

A few beers in, I'm feeling fine and feeling no pain for once even if it is still there. Properly soaked in alcohol and the camaraderie that comes with the territory in hanging out with ballplayers, I begin to relax. My star trajectory didn't have me in the minor-league system too long, as if I remember any more of it other than what Kimberley has told me. Even so, like everything else I've had to adapt to over the past several months, I've begun to acclimate to my current surroundings. Like I told Kimberley and Brad on a call a few days ago, I'm still considered new around here and there's this welcome relief in not being expected to know everybody's name. Here, it's okay if I don't remember. In Fresno, I'm just like everybody else. *Sort of.*

"So what's the deal with Tally Landon?" Hillman asks again. We've both been watching with interest as the band began to file in to a few cheers and whistles with the bass and piano players immediately starting to tune up their gear.

I take a swig of the third beer Brandy has just set down in front of me before answering. "There's no *deal* with Tally Landon."

I've put her out of my mind as much as possible since being sent down. My focus needed to be on baseball to save my illustrious career from sinking any further. It was the one thing my dad and I agree upon—that all three of us ended up agreeing on. So I've spent the past three months training myself not to think of Tally Landon hardly at all. I call at a regularly scheduled time, four in the afternoon, on Tuesdays and Thursdays, and talk to Cara. Tally always answers, says a little hello, and hands the phone to little Cara. A thirty-second conversation with Tally is not enough to go on, certainly not enough to build a relationship on; and after basically asking me to leave the last night I saw her, it would appear that ship has sailed.

And now? The LA thing has come back around to haunt me in a new and ugly way that Kimberley and my lawyers are busy trying to resolve for me. I'm not looking forward to having *that* conversation with Tally. I already know what it will mean. She won't believe me. She won't ever trust me again, and we will be essentially over, like it appears, we already are. I've begun to question what really happened that night in LA, but as much as I wrack my brain to remember what all went down with Trinna, I can't even conjure up a memory of her face let alone remember what we did together. I fucked up doesn't really cover it anymore and admitting this to Tally is something I've been avoiding for as long as possible.

I check my iPhone for messages from Kimberley and discover it's dead. That's what happens when you don't plug it in the night before and you spend your only day off at the practice field and in the film room which pretty much sums up my day as well as my life right now.

Despite the additional workouts and training, it's been a slow go getting my arm and my confidence in pitching back to what it once was. At this point, it is pure desperation and a vague sense of seeing what I used to be—based solely on the film I've seen—that keeps me in the hunt at all. I'm almost there. That's what they tell me anyway. Trainers, coaches, my father—anyone who gives a shit about my career and diligently watches the way I throw a baseball.

Now, it's the middle of May. One could hazard a guess I'm pissed off. And one would be right. At this point, I no longer want to know any more about my past because I still don't remember it or Tally, and I've grown tired of trying because she doesn't seem to care. So. Why I don't remember her at all remains one of life's biggest mysteries. As it stands, Tally has absolutely nothing to do with me throwing a baseball and since baseball is apparently all I have left, except for two little phone calls with Cara each week, and since the LA thing continues to haunt me, I've come to realize I'm seriously fucked and that's just the way it's going to be.

Hillman is still going on about Tally. I drink down the rest of my beer and nod at him.

"She's pretty famous, just like you," Hillman says with a wide smile. "What's that like? To date somebody almost as famous as you? Hard to enjoy the everyday normal part of life I bet. You two probably can't even go to Costco together without getting mobbed by fans." He laughs. "But the *Sports Illustrated* article didn't seem to hurt her very much even though Baxstrom did perform a little character assassination on Tally. So what's a dancer like? She's got to be all kinds of epic."

"All kinds." I frown. "*Sports Illustrated* was off the mark. I don't know why Candy had it in for her like that. But we're not together anymore." I throw him a we-broke-up-I-don't-talk-about-it look hoping he'll move on because just saying her name causes my head to hurt. Yet, Hillman seems to be gearing up to ask me far too many personal questions about Tally Landon that I won't be able to answer. *Not good.*

"*Sports Illustrated*. Yeah, the cover was amazing. Let me see if I can find it." He pulls out his iPhone, does a search, and ultimately holds up in triumph the photograph of Tally and me. "This one. This is my favorite. Not of you but of Tally."

"Wow," I say to amuse Hillman more than anything else. There we are on the cover doing the famous *Dirty Dancing* move. Tally's in this filmy white dress number and I'm wearing a Giants uniform. *Good times. Wish I could remember them. Or do I wish I could just forget her?* I kind of flinch at seeing her face again. It's taken a lot of willpower not to start back up on the painkillers again because I *know* that would help put Tally Landon completely out of my mind.

"She's so beautiful. She doesn't even look real, does she?" He sighs. I don't even have to answer him. "Too bad the piece ran right before your Giants tanked in the playoffs. Karma...she's a bitch." Hillman gets this easy-going smirk.

"Karma. Yes." I shake my head at him and try to smile but between being reminded of Tally again and the whole the LA debacle rising from the ashes all over again I start to get worked up. *I've got to tell Tally. Warn her this is coming back around.* Kimberley's probably tried to call me a dozen times today about that.

As Brandy swings by our table, I ask her for an iPhone connection of some kind she tells me she can take care of it and promises to charge it for me. Hillman's going on about the Giants spectacular rise and early fall in the series. I quietly admit to him that there's a small part of me that doesn't feel that bad about the Giants tanking in the playoffs. "I'm not exactly enamored with the Giants for sending me down in the first place."

"No shit, bro. That sucked. And you *know* they did it to save a buck or two somewhere else," he says quietly so we won't be overheard.

Ballplayers are a funny breed. We stick together for the playing of the game, but when it comes to contracts and trades, a player is all on his own.

We stick together until we fall apart.

The thought leads me right back to the LA and Trinna Danner, who appears to be ready to sue me for paternity of her unborn child. *Let the dick hunt begin.*

I numbly nod at Hillman. He is rather likable because he is perfectly capable of carrying on a conversation by himself and he obviously hasn't screwed up as much in baseball and his personal life as I have. I figure the only way to get him to put his iPhone away so I'm not feeling the familiar pang in seeing Tally's photograph is to move on to an entirely different topic.

"Yeah. It's a great photograph of her," I say. "But I was dealing with the fallout of the line drive shortly after that. And like I said, we broke up."

"Right. So was Tally part of the fallout of that? Why would you break up with her? It doesn't make any sense. I mean, she's gorgeous and you're not bad-looking. You two seem to match up pretty well."

"I don't know. I wasn't thinking straight." My memory loss isn't front-page news anymore, but it's still out there filtering through the organization after the comments I made to the LA Times reporter. I start to feel uneasy. Hillman's looking at me like he has a lot more questions he wants answers to.

"Obviously." He looks away toward the front entrance then taps the table vying for my attention some two minutes later. "Looks like you'll be thinking straight soon enough. Damn! She's even better looking in person than on SI's cover. Jesus! Why don't you want her around again? *That* makes *no sense* whatsoever."

"It's never been a question of not wanting her," I mutter turning to look in the direction Hillman is still staring at with his mouth open.

Sure enough, Tally Landon is making her way over. She still has the graceful walk of a dancer who invariably reaches for my soul at just seeing her again. She moves without seeming to, as if guided by magical guide wires; she glides more than she moves. Meanwhile, the air seems to part like ocean waves would respond should a goddess be passing through. Our table is the farthest from the entrance, nearest the stage. Her eyes stay on me while every baseball player within her realm is keen on proving his existence to her. Her lips part as she gets this faint smile and I actually know when she takes her next breath. It's intense all around me as every guy in the room watches Tally Landon arrive on scene.

I'm rewarded her queen's smile and reminded of Elsa in *Frozen* for some inexplicable reason. I think I've watched that movie about a dozen times now because Cara is so obsessed with it, and I wanted to impress my kid in knowing the storyline when we get to talk on the phone. And let's face it; there isn't much else to do in Fresno so that movie is now a part of my repertoire these days.

"Jim Frazier said you were here," she says about halfway toward her destination. *Our table. Me.*

Jim Frazier. Jim Frazier? Oh yeah, the third baseman.

"Where's your cell phone? I've been calling it." She's asking questions like we just saw each other two hours earlier instead of almost three months ago.

"Oh, Brandy has it. The waitress? I ran out of battery a day or two ago. She's plugged it in for me."

"Oh I bet she did," Tally says with a backhanded wave. "That explains it." Her eyes gleam this Incredible Hulk green. It's kind of thrilling and disturbing at the same time. "Can I talk to you? Later then?"

Miss Cloves and Vanilla wants to talk to me.

I am reborn.

"Sure. We can talk." All I can do is nod and then grin like a fool. *Which I am.* And yet, thoughts about LA, and what is transpiring there, wipe it off my face ten seconds later.

"We should talk," I say with a hint of despair. *I have to tell her.*

Her lips curve upward but she's got this glacial glare thing going and this unmistakable bewitching air is all about her.

"Yes," is all she says.

CHAPTER
THIRTY

slow dancing in a burning room

LINC

SHE INTRODUCES HERSELF ALL AROUND THE table and shakes hands with a now speechless Doug Hillman and rewards him with her winner-takes-all smile. "For later," she says to Hillman handing him a black garment bag which he dutifully goes off to hang up on a hook near the bar. She studies me for a long moment before averting her gaze and proceeds to slide onto the bar stool Doug's retrieved for her, while I just continue to stare at her with my mouth half-open for the next ten seconds. She laughs at something Hillman says and then looks at him with renewed interest. I finally close my mouth, shake my head side-to-side, and wish to start the scene over. "So, what are we drinking?" She asks.

He holds up his beer glass. Tally wrinkles her nose at him. "No. Something stronger. Tequila, I think. Patron, actually. Mmm…."

Considering she looks like she hasn't had food in a week I'm surprised she wants something as strong as tequila which I proceed to tell her. She gives me this killer look. I shut up.

Meanwhile, Doug flags down Brandy and places Tally's order for two shots of Patron with orange slices in lieu of limes like she's specified. With *Miss Cloves and Vanilla's* drink order out of the way, she turns to Doug giving him her undivided attention.

So what position do you *play,* Doug?"

"I play first base."

"First base. *Nice.* I like first base. And how's your season going for you so far?"

"Not too shabby. Hitting two seventy at bat and mid three-hundreds for on base."

"Very good. A hot bat. How long have you been with the Grizzlies?"

"Second season. We can't all be Presley and serve half a season before getting called up to the majors."

She glances over at me as if she's forgotten I am here and then again, centers her attention on Hillman again. "Nothing wrong with the minor leagues," she says softly. "At least you can still shop at Costco without getting mobbed."

"*That's* what I was telling Presley. All that fame makes it tough. Right, Tally? You two probably can't go anywhere together without being hit up for autographs and photos."

She gets this bemused look. "Something like that. So how old are you? A year older than me; I'm guessing twenty-three? I'm sure your time will come soon enough. Hitting two-seventy and three-fifty for on-base is going to get someone's attention. Just watch out for those line drives toward first, right?"

"Right." Hillman laughs but looks uneasy by the suddenly serious look on Tally's face. "Good guess. Yes, I'm twenty-three. First base is good. Stats are there; I can't complain. I used to pitch but that was a long time ago," Hillman says nodding in my general direction.

Tally looks over at me. "Pitching is as much of a mental game as a physical one." She turns in her chair leaning toward Hillman.

"So how he's doing? Better, I hope, because he sure has had to sacrifice everything to get *here*." She waves her arms around the bar and laughs at her supposed innocuous dig at Fresno. Hillman looks at me and gets a little smile.

"He's coming along."

"That's good. That's good." Tally gets a little smile too.

I nod as a way to enter the conversation and prove my existence to her. I haven't actually paid all that much attention to Hillman's play at first base. I've been too focused on my own stuff. *How is that possible?* Maybe because I have five people around me at any given time, even here in the minor-leagues. *Perhaps I've just been too self-centered.*

"Centered on self," I say aloud.

Tally's head whips around and she looks at me intently. "*What did you say?*"

"I've been too centered on self, lately," I say unable to meet her eyes. As LA manages to assail me once again. *I need to talk to her about LA soon. Now.*

"No kidding," Tally says dangerously soft.

I look over at Hillman. "I didn't know you used to pitch. You're good at first base though. Awesome stats, too, by the way."

"Yours aren't too shabby, bro." Hillman turns to Tally. "He's hitting two-sixty, and his on-base percentage is improving. He's over three hundred. He's getting worked out—or is that *worked over*—pretty well. And, it's tough to concentrate on anyone or anything else with an entire entourage all around you," he says more to me and then grins wide as if to help me out. He slides his chair back and gets this curious look. "I'm going for another round. Tally, can I get you anything? It looks like Brandy has her hands full."

The three of us look up and over at the waitress all the way across the bar from us. She carries a tray full of empty drink glasses and none of Tally's drink order.

Why can't I be the cool guy here? But no, I'm too busy admitting to a long list of character flaws so she'll be sure to never really like me again. *And then, there's the LA thing.* I need to call Kimberley for the update about that some time tonight. *Please God, let Kimberley fix it or make it go away. I still need to tell Tally.*

Meanwhile, in less than a minute, Hillman steps in again offering to play the white knight by offering to place Tally's food order for a hamburger with the bartender and get her the coveted Patron shot with the orange slice from the bar. For some reason, I'm reminded of Sam Wilde, hovering over her and taking care of everything. Twenty-nine hellos from Tally in the past three and half months haven't exactly tided me over and now Hillman appears to be moving into the open slot *Thor* may have vacated, since he's obviously not here with her.

We both watch Hillman saunter off with Tally's food and drink order as if he's been knighted by the queen. He has a wide smile and a new swagger. He stops and talks to Brandy and mouths the words, "put it on our tab."

So, I'm paying.

Perhaps, in all kinds of ways I don't know about yet.

With I'm-a-jerk status now established, I look over at Tally. "I'm sorry I should have asked if you wanted something."

"I don't know, Prez, have you ever actually asked me what I wanted?" She catches her lower lip between her teeth and shakes her head and then she sighs. "Not a problem. Doug took care of it."

"Yeah, well Doug would like to take care of just about everything for you right now, I'm afraid."

"Are you *jealous*, Elvis?" Tally asks and then laughs a little but she seems off and yet I'm captivated by her sounds already.

"Don't call me Elvis," I say trying to gain some ground in some way around her since I can feel myself falling straight down into her abyss.

"I always call you Elvis. It's my thing. Don't deny me my thing. Not tonight. I'm running the show tonight." Her eyes get this dark green, and she winces a little as if she's remembering something sad and then it's gone. She's smiling again.

I'd like to think it's for me but then Hillman returns with her tequila shot at the exact same moment. He sets it down in front of her and tells her he ordered it just the way she likes it pointing to the dish of orange slices he's put right next to her.

"How do you know what I like, *Mr. First Baseman?*" Tally teases.

She's flirting with him right in front of me.

Now, I'm pissed and wounded.

Hillman looks at me in a you-good-with-this? kind of way and then grins at her. "Presley told me."

"*That,* I find hard to believe. He doesn't know what I like. His best friends call him *Prez,* by the way."

She leans forward and considers the tequila shot looking at it like it's her new favorite toy. She holds it up to the light and swiftly drinks it down, and then she's biting into the orange slice. The entire ball club appears to be watching Tally do her tequila shot and that orange slice.

"Mmm...Patron very nice. Smooth. Perfect," she says only to Hillman, who looks like a Kindergärtner getting a gold star for exceptional spelling with his first word.

She glances over at me. "I think we should definitely talk, but I am absolutely starving so I'll eat and then maybe later we can...*catch up.*" She gets this weird-ass grin.

"Sure. Maybe later sounds good."

What am I? A twelve-year-old with my first girl crush all over again? I've already been through this once with her. I know I won't survive this time.

Talk to her? Forget talking to her. No more talking to Tally.

Except about the LA thing. Except once I talk to her about the LA thing she won't talk to me ever again.

So, fuck talking altogether.

Brandy *brandishes* Tally's hamburger as well as a knife and fork and a unopened bottle of French's mustard. I'm curious about all this extra utensil power and the condiment choice Tally's got going. But all I can do is watch in wonder as she slathers the mustard all around and then proceeds to cut the hamburger in half, then quarters it, and then slices it up into eight equal parts. It's not a hamburger anymore. It's a cut-up mess on her plate. She forks a bite.

It's erotic just watching her chew and swallow. And she seems to know this. She smiles at me.

"You're supposed to eat that whole, you know," I say with a shake of my head trying to clear this hypnotic effect she's having on me in the space of fifteen minutes. "Pick them up and eat them one bite at a time."

"Is that so? Well, you'll have to teach me sometime."

Our table for four contains no less than four other ballplayers now besides me, Hillman, and Tally. They are all crowded around to watch the San Francisco Ballet's star ballerina eat her food. I've never witnessed anything quite like this. One minute she's chatting away with Hillman as well as the others at the table asking all kinds of questions about playing baseball; and in the next, she's teasing them about their secret aspirations to play for the Yankees. "Come on, everyone wants to play for the Yankees except *Prez* here, of course." She looks distinctly vicious for a couple of seconds, and then she smiles.

I'm a goner with that particular smile and shocked into answering. Nobody knows that I secretly hate the Yankees, although Tally seems to. I give her a questioning what-are-you-doing-to-me? look. "Overrated," I say to the overly interested group of ballplayers. "Not a fan of New York."

"Me neither," she says softly.

Then, Hillman asks her why, even while she's remains singularly focused upon me. "I left the chaos of New York to come home and be with family. I needed a simpler life. An easier pace. Sort of." She laughs again. "SFB keeps me on my *toes*. Ha ha."

"So you're off for the summer, right?" Hillman asks beating me to the question I didn't think to ask.

"Not exactly. Paris is a possibility. Moscow." She lifts her chin in defiance with that one. "Fresno," she says smiling. "I'm here on business so to speak checking out the facilities for my director, Mikhail Rostov. We're looking at the expansion program for SFB, which may include this little oasis for the fall line-up. I told him I would check it out to see if the venue works for our *Swan Lake* performance. Stage. Lighting. Accommodations. At the Saroyan Theater. I'm to meet with them tomorrow for Mikhail. We've been here before. There are a few special requests for the accommodations we need for a bigger production like that."

"Nice," Hillman says.

"Fresno isn't exactly San Francisco," I say, finally managing to work my way into the conversation that's been whipsawing back and forth between Tally and Hillman for the past five minutes.

"No, it's not, but it could lead to something. You never know."

A loaded answer to a stacked question, I guess.

I'm not sure how to respond. The band starts to play so I don't get to.

"So Tally," Hillman says with an easy grin. "You seeing anyone?"

"Yes," she says although her smile seems off again. "Sam. His name is Sam. I was…sort of seeing Sam." I look up and over at her use of past tense. She turns her attention back to her food and ignores my probing stare altogether.

"Was? And *sort of* means no sex," Hillman says with an easy laugh, looks at me, and then slaps my shoulder. "You're good, bro. You're in." He smiles wide and winks at Tally and then saunters off with her latest request for tequila shots for the entire table after announcing his intentions of getting Brandy's phone number before the night is over.

"Sam. Sort of seeing Sam. *Was?*" I ask, forgoing any attempt to play it cool.

"Sam. I was sort of seeing Sam. I guess that's another reason I'm here." She gets this grim expression and looks away.

"Another reason. What's the first again?"

She looks a little unnerved now. "I thought we were going to talk about this *later?*"

"Right. Eat your food then."

She proceeds to eat a quarter of the burger over the next ten minutes. Food seems to be a religious experience with Tally and, on some level, I realize I already know this.

She glances up and catches me watching her intently, her lips part as if she has more to say but then slowly shakes her head and tells me she's not hungry anymore and slides her unfinished burger over to me.

"Did you eat?" She asks. I shake my head. "You finish it then," she says quietly. "I'm going for another shot since Hillman's taking so long. And I need to make a phone call."

"I thought one drink was your limit."

She gets this wounded look.

"Don't fuck with me, Prez. Not here. Fresno is neutral territory. Don't pretend to know anything about me when you clearly don't."

Her words are like a slap in the face, but I can't take my eyes off of her as I watch her walk away.

Hillman returns and follows my gaze. "Man, you've got it bad for her. You might not remember why you two broke up and what you had with her once, but your soul surely does. If you don't ask her to dance, I will."

"Hands off," I say quietly.

"That's what I thought."

CHAPTER
THIRTY-ONE

free fallin'

LINC

I T'S ANOTHER FIFTEEN MINUTES BEFORE TALLY reappears, and she looks a little unsettled. She bestows me with stony silence at first. When I ask her what's wrong she says, "later" through clenched teeth. "We can talk later."

Hillman leans in, interrupting the moment. I can't decide if that's good or bad. "So Tally. You have to show us the *Dirty Dancing* move. *You have to.* This place would go wild. It would be the best thing to happen to Fresno in years." Hillman laughs.

The Dirty Dancing move. I don't remember the move, of course, and this quiet panic assails me.

Now I'm really in trouble.

Hillman looks expectantly at me and then Tally, who definitely looks intrigued as if it's the best idea of the night.

So far.

"I can teach you again, *baby. Remember,* I do most of the *work,*" she says getting this slow wicked smile. "In fact, let's give them a good show. I brought you something. You know, to make it authentic. Doug, where's my garment bag?"

She stares at me for a long moment while Hillman races off for the mysterious bag. Then, she's busy downing another shot and sucking an orange instead of a lime again, and still insisting to the entire table that this is how it's done. Half the ballplayers are following her lead shooting Patron and sucking on orange slices now.

"They're going to think you know it," she says to me alone. Then she grabs the bag from Hillman upon his return. "So *man up*, and let's do this."

"I don't remember it," I say getting a sixth sense that I'm being played although some part of me knows it's already a little too late to back out. "I'm not going to do it. I could drop you. You could fall then where would you be? No. No way."

"Yes. Yes way. Don't be *afraid.* Don't be afraid of *falling.* Oh, but you *are afraid* of falling, failing, and losing; aren't you? I *forgot. I* forgot. How funny, I *forgot.*" She's baiting me good but then she sets her sights on Hillman. "I can show you how to do it, *Mr. First Baseman.* What you need to do. You should try. You want to impress Brandy, right? This will do that."

She unzips the garment bag and out comes her wedding dress. In the next ten seconds, she's effectively pulling it on over her clothes and performing some kind of magic trick—like with a costume change—shimmying out of her black jeans and T-shirt and even takes off her bra like the dancer did in *Flashdance.*

Classic. She has the undivided attention of the entire bar. There are long whistles, loud shouts, and heavy-duty table pounding happening now. She looks at me thoughtfully. I'm speechless of course, but in the back of mind things are beginning to come together. "You said you wanted to see me in it. So here you go, Prez. You're seeing me in it. Now, let's show them the move. Your tux is right there. I'll wait. For you."

She grabs Hillman's hand and leads him across the dance floor away from our table. Hillman's bravado recedes within a few steps. "I don't know, Tally. What if I drop you? Let's see Prez do it first."

He looks uncertain over at me.

I'm shaking my head side-to-side but feeling no pain as I dutifully change into the tux as Tally commanded in hopes of receiving redemption of some kind, although a distinct part of me already knows it's too late for that. I shuck the jeans, and the polo shirt even smoother than Tally did and do this all right in the middle of the bar, which causes a mini uproar. Brandy averts her eyes but everybody else gets a good look at the Calvin's while I climb into the tuxedo pants and zip them up. Two of the guys help me out with the cuff links on the tuxedo shirt. Another helps me with the jacket.

Two minutes in, I'm good to go.

I can feel Tally's stare at me from a long way off. She's nodding, and the weird gleam in her eyes is back while Doug Hillman gets the honors in doing up all the pearl buttons on the back of Tally's dress. "Just do some of them, Doug, I need to get out of this thing, pronto." I hear her say to him.

Pronto? What the hell does that mean?

"Prez, you about ready?" Doug asks looking guilty for bringing up the idea of the move in the first place.

The crowd grows restless. We've stolen the show and now they want one.

I know Doug was trying to set this up in my favor, but since I don't remember the *Dirty Dancing* move, and I could drop her just as easily too, anger streaks through me serving as an adrenaline rush. I decide to try one more time to talk Tally out of this. Doug can live with the disappointment and so can the crowd.

"I'm not sure I remember how to do this," I say running my hands through my hair as I walk over to the Hillman Landon duo. "So, let's *not* do this."

This admission apparently pisses Tally off. "Just give the crowd what they want, Prez. Everybody wants to see us do the move."

Hillman's looking more anxious but clears out the dancers who still linger on the dance floor telling them to make way for Tally and Linc's dance move. A few other ballplayers hurriedly sweep the peanut shells from the floor. Another is talking to the band about Tally's song choice.

They are all at her command.

"What the hell?" I ask Tally as I stand between her and Hillman.

"Come on. They want to see it. You can do this. Get over *yourself*," Tally says irritably. "I can tell you what to do since you've obviously *forgotten*." She turns to Hillman. "So, Doug, I'll tell you how it works. You can watch Linc do it first and then you can. Okay? If you want. So, it's kind of a run-up. Linc will stand over there about thirty feet away kind of in an upright catcher's stance." She demonstrates. "Maybe more like first base, huh?" She smiles at Doug. "He'll keep his arms out in front of him like this and he'll catch me as I run up to him. Then, he lifts me straight up overhead." She looks at me finally. "Arms straight up, Prez. *I* do the rest."

"Fuck, Tally," I say under my breath.

"Maybe later," she says with a wicked smile. "I do the work here, Elvis." A shadow crosses her features. "Just catch me, okay?" I start to walk away taking my position across the bar from them when she says, "Oh, don't over-rotate, Prez."

"Great."

The band cooperates by putting on the song Tally requested. It's John Mayer's version of *Free Fallin'. Surprising.* Yet, half the bar is already singing the words to the song.

A few people have their smartphones out ready to snap a photograph. Tally bites her lip when she sees this, but then shakes her head side-to-side and starts to laugh.

Then, Brandy is running up to me with my cell phone.

"You got a call. It's Kimberley. She *insisted* I find you."

She holds it to my ear while I keep my arms outstretched and watch for Tally and whatever signal I'm supposed to be looking for. To my surprise, it *is* Kimberley.

"Kimmy, kind of busy here."

"She knows about Trinna!! She called me ten minutes ago. Candy Baxstrom has a crew there. So does Amy Ransom. What is *she* doing? The Star ran the story this morning with Trinna's photo. TMZ's running the story tonight. Prez!! *Tally knows*!!"

At that moment, Tally raises her finger at me. *The middle one.*

Oh yeah. I'm so dead.

"Christ, Kimmy. I've got to call you back."

Without a word, a sympathetic Brandy slips my phone into pocket of my tuxedo jacket, and everything around me transcends to slow motion. I watch Tally take a deep breath, tilt her head to one side apparently detecting a rhythm of some kind from Mayer's soulful song, and then she move towards me.

Graceful. Hypnotic. Erotic. I am lost. The lyrics play through my head at half-speed. *She's a good girl. Loves her momma. Elvis. Jesus. She's a good girl. America too.* Tally's dress sways with every twist and turn, and the bar is captivated as am I. She waits for the chorus, and then she's running full-speed at me on the words, *and I'm free, free falling.* I thrust my hands out which miraculously catch and span her small waist as she flies at me, and then I'm lifting her up on her momentum alone. She's high overhead seemingly ascending with the euphoric rise from the crowd.

The place goes wild because somehow she's timed it perfectly to the crescendo of Mayer's song—something I didn't even notice because my ears have been humming for the past three minutes. Everything centers around Tally—the world stops on its axis—as we all take flight and watch only her in absolute amazement. The dress flows out behind her. Perfect legs. Pointed toes.

She is mastery itself. Toned. Muscular. The only athlete in the room at the moment and owning all of us. She makes it all look easy as she holds the pose for all to admire while I feel her sinewy muscles contract and gather strength within my upraised arms and hands.

There are no words worthy enough to describe her. Her arms span out like the most graceful bird in the sky, and her hands do this mesmerizing ballet thing like she's holding a diamond between her fingers.

Ultimately, she mimics the end of the move—sexy and sultry— as she slides down the front of my tuxedo shirt to Mayer's chorus. The words *free falling* get stuck in my head and repeat themselves another ten times.

She has this twisted smile on her face—a mix of devastation and unexpected elation. It appears like she's unable to fully control either one.

We have stolen the show at O'Riley's and probably the move as well.

Doug waves us off, laughing, and telling us he won't even try to compete with me. Tally hides her face in my chest for few seconds and then she smiles in triumph as the camera flashes go off again.

"And that's how it is done, Prez. I hope you had fun," she says in warning.

I semi-carry her back to our table where she turns down at least twenty offers to *do it again.*

"Sounds like that's the last fun I'm going to have," I say bleakly. "Are we going to talk about it? I know you *know.* Kimberley called me seconds before the big move." I look up for some reason. "Oh shit. Candy Baxstrom *is* here. And Amy Ransom? You *called everyone?*"

"Yep. I called them all. Everybody gets to record the epic moment between us." Hillman lingers about. "Once is enough," she says to him sweetly. "I'll work with you on the moves sometime, so you can try it with Brandy when it's not so crowded." Hillman is perfectly happy with this compromise. "Twice with me would be pushing it actually," she says breathlessly to the ballplayers still lining up at our table hoping to change her mind about *doing it again.* But I begin to think her comment is directed solely at me and has nothing to do with the move we just did.

I still hold onto her hand. She looks down and sees this and quickly pulls it away.

"I was going to tell you," I say. "I just didn't...know how."

"Yeah. That's a tough call, Prez. Well, at least we fed the sports and entertainment news channels what they wanted to see, right? They got the money shot. The two of us together. One. Last. Time."

She looks at me with such intention that I think my heart stops beating for a few seconds. "Nicely done, Prez. Your fame status in the Star continues to soar. Of course, it will be on the Internet within thirty seconds so no surprise there. You better call Kimberley back; she'll be demanding to know what the hell is going on."

If there was a smile on her face, it is now gone.

"I called Kimberley about fifteen minutes ago to let her know what was about to go down."

"What? Why Tally? Why would you do this?" I ask.

"I was helping you out, but now I'm done." She turns to Hillman. "Hey, come with me a second. I need your help getting out of this thing."

An uneasy Doug shakes his head side-to-side at Tally. In fact, all the ballplayers take a hard line, and nobody will help Tally out of her dress.

"Fine. I've got this." She pulls at the back of her dress and rips it from the back top to bottom. Some twenty-five pearl buttons scatter to the floor like marbles falling from a jar suspended overhead. *"Perfect,"* she says as she grabs her jeans and shirt that someone has nicely stacked for her.

About that time, Brandy delivers her another shot and tells her it's from Candy Baxstrom. Tally looks up and over at the reporter who sits at the bar looking almost stunned by what just took place as I am. Tally gives her the parade wave and drinks the shot down sans orange slice.

We have hit a new level, but I'm not sure if it's up, or if it's down.

Then, she stalks off with her clothes, announcing to her newest fans—the entire Grizzlies ball club—she's going to change.

And I just stare after her without saying anything.

My next mistake.

There will be others.

CHAPTER THIRTY-TWO

your body is a wonderland

LINC

"SHE'S IN THERE. SHE TOLD ME to tell you she's fine, and she will be out when she is good and ready," Brandy says to me and then looks anxiously at Hillman as if he can miraculously fix any of this.

It's been more than a half-hour since Tally disappeared.

The entire bar misses her.

"Is she crying?" I ask softly.

"I'm not supposed to say." The blonde nods yes.

"Geez," I say. "All right I'm going in." I've just gotten the words out of my mouth when Tally appears before us in the doorway.

She lists to one side, but she's looking extremely hot in this sexy, Neo-goth look. Her eyes are a little red—the only dead giveaway that she's been crying at all or done one too many tequila shots.

Brandy looks taken aback at Tally's fast recovery. "Are you sure you're feeling okay?" She asks.

Tally nods at Brandy and doesn't say anything. She looks at me. She's dressed all in black. Jeans. A black T-shirt. Shoes that are so high they could be used as a weapon. There's a black ribbon in her hair that seems to serve some special purpose. All I can do is stare at her with my mouth open.

She was beautiful before in the white dress but now all-black ensemble, and the fierce look in her eyes takes her to a whole new level. One part of me is busy saying, 'go for it', but there's this other part lecturing me. *Stop. Take a good look at her. What do you see?* That part seems to know the wrong move with Tally will fuck this up but good if I haven't already.

"Can we talk?" I ask like a prayer.

"Oh yes," she says throwing her head back with this harsh laugh. Then she stops and zeroes in on my face. "But our darkest hour approaches. Mine anyway," she says. The torment in her eyes is unmistakable. I look down in search of words and discover she carrying the wedding dress over one arm. She follows my gaze. "French silk. Tulle. Catherine Deane's design all the way from London," she recites and then smiles like she holds the last secret in the world. "Come on, Prez. I've got one more thing to show you, but we have to go outside for this one. And then we'll *talk*. You and I will *finally talk*."

She actually smiles. It's wide and beautiful and benevolent. I'm riveted by it. Still staring. Still stunned when I realize she's already walked off down the hallway. I've never seen anyone move so fast. She's about thirty feet ahead of us before I realize she's dead serious about going outside.

O'Riley's front doors fly open and she slips past the people coming into the bar while she is clearly headed out.

Meanwhile, a cool breeze assails the three of us—Hillman, Brandy, and me—as we hit the street just outside the club in search of Tally. We round the corner of the building preparing to fan out and start looking for her when all three of us seem to spot her at the same time. She stands at the far end of the parking lot about a hundred feet away from us.

Her dress glows all white. She holds it out in front of her and seems to admire one last time. Then she throws it up in the air and we all watch it billow out like a full sail suddenly let go into the wind and watch it float down and land on a top of a pile of trash stacked into a nice tidy pile like a bonfire all ready to go.

It's only then I notice the bottle in her hand. She uncorks it and soon she's pouring it all over the dress and trash pile. "Who sold her the bottle?" I ask.

"She ordered it when she first came in and said to put it on your tab," Brandy says. "That you like scotch and it had to be scotch."

I know this scene. She told me this one.

I break out in a dead run toward Tally. "No. No. Tally. No. Don't do it. Don't!" My feeble attempt to save the dress evaporates when I'm only about halfway across the parking lot. Powerless all at once, I watch as the dress catches fire with the lighter Tally holds to it.

It's about that time, I register the pavement's uneven, and in the next second I fall hard to the concrete.

It's not a baseball field. That's my first thought.

My head throbs with fresh pain. That's my second.

I'm fucked. That's my third.

The hiss of burning silk and paper has me turning my head in time to watch the entire trash pile catch fire as orange and blue flames rage upward and obliterate the fine material of Tally's dress. It only takes about sixty seconds to watch it turn to all flame. Tally steps back and dazedly watches the fire get bigger. Even my precarious side view of her face shows it looking grim and tragic. I can feel her pain all the way over here. It feels like our whole past together was just ignited and went up in those flames right along with the dress. I moan, roll over onto my back, and look up at the black sky filled with stars in a moment of wonder laced with pure dread.

What the hell just happened?

Then, Tally comes into view. "Are you okay?" She asks, leaning down on both thighs, trying to catch her breath. Somehow, I take solace that she must have run all the way over to me. *There's that.*

"Running to save me?" Of course, I'm immediately feeling sorry for myself. My words come out all wrong. My head really hurts now, worse than ever the entire night. All at once, I'm impatient with the constant headaches that plague me, the memory loss, the LA thing, being sent down, this mess that is my life and in the next three seconds I take it all out on her. "Why the *fuck* did you do that?"

"Why the *fuck* do you care?"

I run my hand across the left side of my face checking for damage. My hand comes away sticky and wet. "Perfect."

"You're bleeding. It's bad." She impatiently extends her hand and helps me up from the ground.

Hillman and Brandy come running over to us. "I think the dress is a total loss," Doug says sadly as he points to the still glowing orange fire about fifty feet away. "Prez, you're bleeding all over the place."

"Thanks for the 411," I say feeling a little queasy.

Tally searches the left side of my head for the gash, squinting in the semi-darkness as her fingers trace my face. "It's pretty bad. Come on. Let's get you to your car."

Hillman helps me out as I lean on his shoulder as the four of us make our way over to my truck. My whole body aches along with my head on my head as the blood streams down my face.

I lean against the driver's door while Hillman takes over assessing the damage to my skull. Brandy races back into the bar and returns sixty seconds later with a med kit. Tally wipes my face with some dance tights of hers she found in her bag. The fawning by all three of them becomes a bit too much and my temper has me lashing out yet again. "Everybody just back off. Doug knows what to do. Hillman, there's QuikClot in my workout bag."

Tally looks like I've just struck her and moves back about three feet away from me. Brandy goes over to console her, putting her arm around her, and saying something neither Hillman nor I can hear.

Meanwhile, Doug retrieves the stuff from my workout bag like I told him to and acts as the newly anointed medical chief by me. He presses the white packet to the side of my head to stop the bleeding and then applies three butterfly bandages in quick succession to the gash to essentially close it.

Cuts. Nicks. Bruises. Baseball players get them all the time. We know what to do. QuikClot, the cure-all, along with band-aids.

"You'll live," he says to me quietly. "If you want to. She's beyond pissed."

"You *think*?" I mutter.

"You need to talk to her, Prez. She needs to hear it from you. The truth about LA," he says quietly. I nod.

Then Hillman turns to Tally who still stands to one side looking wounded in all kinds of ways while the first baseman's been performed his medical techniques on me. "Tally, you got this? You're not going to kill our boy here, are you?" He looks sympathetic and smiles at her. "You know girls like the one in LA make shit like that up all the time about ballplayers like us. It takes a strong woman—a very special one—to ignore it and know what's real and what's not."

Tally lasers in on Doug for a few precious seconds. It appears Hillman gets to learn firsthand that if looks could kill we'd both be dead right now. "Well, it takes a strong man—*a very special one*—to be loyal and resist all of that shit in the first place, Doug. And our boy, *Prez*, here, may not have done that this last time around. Nevertheless, we are surely going to talk about all of that like right the fuck now. So, thank you. *Brandy. Doug.* I've got this."

Hillman won't let it go. I can't decide if he's seizing an opportunity because of Brandy or trying to save my ass. "Maybe we'll see you two tomorrow morning. Breakfast? We've got a game tomorrow night, Prez." Hillman's looks questioningly at Tally for a response.

It takes her a good two minutes to give him one. Tally looks a little undone. "Surely, there's a decent place for breakfast around here," she finally says. "It's Fresno after all."

She rewards them with her best stage smile, but I'm not sure he completely understands how royally pissed off she still is at me, but somehow I know.

"There's Lily's Diner. They make great pancakes," Brandy says, now helpful about a half an hour too late. "If you're serious…about not killing him and if Linc's still with us in the morning." Brandy laughs easing the tension for all of us.

"Oh, we'll be there." Tally looks intently at me after she says this. "I think I made my point."

"I think you did," Hillman says gently. "You can always buy another dress, Tally. I'm sure he's going to ask you again before the night is over."

Tally and I both stare up at the black sky overhead and note the stars are too far away to help us out. It appears we're both unable to acknowledge Hillman's last words as a dire prediction or even as a possible promise.

Brandy laughs nervously again and quietly chides Hillman for getting in the middle of our fight. Then starts to grab his hand and gestures toward the bar. "They need to talk. We don't know their history."

"Damn straight," Tally says under her breath to the three of us.

The blood starts running down my face again despite Hillman's stellar bandage job. As a last ditch effort to help me out he hands me another QuikClot and tells me to keep it on there for a few minutes more. There's another camera flash from behind us near the fire at the far edge of the parking lot that's now smoldering but still going with a few persistent flames.

The four of us decide that now is a good time to part ways. Brandy and Doug head back inside still holding hands and make it all look easy being together. A couple without baggage and simple promises. I like you. You like me.

Easy for them.

Apparently impossible for us.

"I wish it was that easy," Tally says aloud as she too watches the two of them walk off together. Then, she's staring at my truck. "You drive a truck." This is apparently bad news to the girl who's been leaning up against it this entire time. I unlock the cab and slide sideways in the driver's seat and patiently wait while watching Tally contemplate her next move. She has this vexed look as if she's been foiled on some level. "You drive a truck," she says again shaking her head.

"It's transportation. It was cheap. It holds my gear." I wave toward the truck bed where my workout bag sits. She raises an eyebrow and just looks at me without saying anything more. I sigh, secretly upset that she doesn't seem to appreciate the coolness factor of my truck on any level. "It's *Fresno*, not San Fran."

"But it's a truck."

"But it's black. I got a good deal on it and look at those wheels. *Chrome.*" I gesture toward them as if chrome explains everything, but she just shakes her head and sort of grunts as she turns me facing forward in the drivers' seat and then proceeds to climb over me. It would be fair to say that I'm milking the latest head injury and attempting to save my ego at this point, hoping to score sympathy points with her in any way I can, so she doesn't actually kill me. "It's not that bad. It's actually beautiful. It's reliable."

"Reliability is so important," Tally says flatly.

We are no longer talking about my truck.

"Where are your keys?" She asks.

"You are not driving. You did like four shots that I was able to count. You were swaying earlier. *I'm driving.*"

"You're still bleeding. We should probably take you to the ER." She looks annoyed and shoots me this angry glare as if a trip to the ER seriously messes with all of her plans.

"I'll live."

"Probably."

"Don't sound so disappointed."

"Don't fuck with me, Prez."

I sigh big and wince as I run my hands through my hair and discover it slicked with blood. She searches around and finds the box of baby wipes and cleans my hands with one.

"You know you call me Elvis when you're not mad and Prez when you are. Do you know that?"

"No, I don't," she says haughtily. "What does it *matter*? After tonight, I won't be calling you *anything*." She tosses the baby wipes aside when she's finished. Then, she looks at me intently for a few precious moments. "You ready for this?"

"Ready for what exactly?"

"The next part of the plan."

"Okay. Sure. What's the next part of the plan? We've heard Mayer's fantastic rendition of *Free Fallin'*. Nice song choice, by the way. We've done the big move. TMZ as well as *Sports Illustrated* and the *LA Times* got their stories. We've fed the paparazzi photographs for at least the next couple of days. I landed on my face, put a gash in my head because what I really needed was another head injury. And last but not least, almost as spectacular as the big move, you set your dress on fire. What's next, *Miss Cloves and Vanilla*? What could you possibly want to do next?"

"This," she says gravely.

Her lips claim mine.

We slide sideways together onto the bench seat of the truck. I manage to reach over and slam the driver's door shut and lock it only because on some sane level I know cameras and reporters still lurk all around us.

In the next short stint, the two of us lose our minds together. She's stroking me in all the right ways and there is too much alcohol consumed and too much shared passion, remembered or not, between the two of us to stop things from progressing in any other way. My mind flashes to LA and I actually believe that's what Tally is trying to teach me here. It happens just like this, just this fast. Mistakes. Past transgressions that can't be reclaimed or redeemed. Redemption sucks. Atonement eludes. Sex is good and bad and everything in between. A fire we can't always control nor want to.

It's a few minutes before I realize she's miraculously shimmied out of her jeans and unzipped my tuxedo pants seemingly at the same time. There is no *are-you-sure?* kind of talk between us. She lowers herself on my ready shaft, and I'm lost in the feeling of these first moments of being inside of her while she expertly slides up and down in a renewed quest for madness and ownership of my very soul. Her eyes close, and she is making all kinds of sounds that make me hot and want to give in and lose control with her.

She gets this triumphant smile as we come together battling too much angst and pent-up emotion for each other over the past several months to even attempt to try and control it or slow it down. I kiss her hard. She likes it. She kisses me back the same way and bites my lip drawing more blood from me. And I'm coming inside of her in search of elusive equilibrium within minutes. And it's another breathless five more before we come up for air at the exact same time.

Her eyes gleam again. Her lips are partially swollen from our somewhat crazed passion. *Lovemaking. What would you call it?*

"Now that was a fast fuck," she says blazingly calm. It's as if she's taken a sharp blade and plunged it directly into my heart.

"This next time we'll go slower because I want you to *remember* all of it, Prez." She sounds ominous the way she says this and looks completely ruthless.

Then it dawns on me as to what her plan has been all along. "You're going to break my heart, aren't you?"

"That's the plan."

She doesn't smile or say anything else. No. She starts it up between us all over again, and I'm too captivated by her and too invested in her already to stop any of this from happening again. We ignore the intrusion of cameras and flashes and reporters. There's only a small part of my mind that even acknowledges what those headlines will read tomorrow. I don't care, and I already know Tally doesn't. She's going to go all out. And if she's going to flame out, it's going to be in her own spectacular way.

Miss Cloves and Vanilla is clearly running this show and I am just the front man.

It's another half-hour before I start up the truck and drive home in this completely sobered state in ultimately realizing I may not survive the night after all. My heart seems to have already stopped beating. She's going to leave me or kill me, and it will feel the same either way. My spirit is already suffering in her expert hands. Sex with her has already taken me under. I am a drowning man. Our coming together seems to exact some sort of toll that will need to be paid again and again, and it appears; she remains unsatisfied with my brand of payment.

I'm too late.

"I'm sorry." I look over at her in quiet desperation as we cruise through peaceful streets of Fresno around midnight toward home.

"Not nearly sorry enough."

The sharp edge of her despair reaches for me like an ice pick pressed hard into my side. I gulp for air, wipe the blood from my face with the back of my hand, so I can see to drive while she leans away from me as far she can get. She presses her face against the window and looks out into the dark night at the nothingness we both seem to be experiencing at the same time.

"You know what they say about air and water when it comes to fire, don't you?" She asks.

Now, I'm curious. She hasn't spoken for the last ten minutes of the drive. "What?"

"Too much air blows out the fire. Too much water destroys it."

I nod trying to determine what she's really comparing us to. "The idea would be to keep the flame going, right. For years?" She nods. "Like a relationship. Like a marriage." She cringes at the word *marriage. Noted.* "So you need the air—to stay constant—to fan the flames of the fire, and you know, grasshopper," I smile at her and catch sight of the corners of her mouth turning slightly upward in response to the endearment, "a hot enough fire will burn water, so you have to be careful with the water too."

"*That* I do know," she says softly. "So that's the truth about air and water." She sighs deep.

"Which *is?*"

"It's hard to maintain the balance to keep the fire going. You have to fan the flames without putting it out with too much water. But too little water will burn the fire right up. Too much fire. Too much destruction. We're out of control."

"You're talking in circles," I say.

"No. That's us," she says with certainty.

"Maybe there's more than one way to keep the fire going, but like you said there's got to be a balance between air and water."

"Maybe," she says gently patting my hand where it rests on the steering wheel. She gets this sympathetic face.

I gather she's trying to let me down easy.

"But maybe it's just too hard. Maybe it's just too impossible. Maybe the thing is you can't control the fiery passion well enough to achieve a balance." She tilts her looking at me intently. "You're my air; I'm your water, but the fire between us is impossible to control or maintain. The flame is either burning too hot extinguishing us both or burning out altogether. Maybe that is the only truth about air and water. About you and me."

"But there's got to be a way to balance it," I say desperate to make her understand. "Maybe the truth about *us* is simply you and me and our amazing ability to *play* with fire."

"Is this fun for you?" She asks quietly as she moves her hand away from mine. "We're like a circus act without a safety net. Step right up, folks. Watch Linc and Tally play with fire and spin out of control. It's not pretty, but you won't be able to turn away. Your satisfaction is *practically* guaranteed."

"Now you're mixing metaphors," I say with a hesitant laugh. But she doesn't laugh.

"Maybe all it ever was…was a metaphor. A metaphor of us," she says.

I'm losing her.

The realization arrives in all its fiery glory.

Just for me.

"You're breaking my heart, *Miss Cloves and Vanilla*."

"Yes," she says without smiling and gets this haunted look. "As I said, that's part of the plan."

She turns away from me again and looks out the dark window but after a few minutes she reaches up with the back of her hand and wipes at her eyes.

CHAPTER THIRTY-THREE

dark horse

TALLY

KIMBERLEY CALLS HIM. IT'S THREE IN the morning in New York, and she still calls.

"There's hardly any battery left," Linc warns us both as he sets the iPhone on speaker and places it up on the truck's dashboard. Apparently, we are both privileged to hear Kimberley Powers' giant words of wisdom. I still lean with my face pressed against Linc's window counting the street lights in an attempt to find some sort of solace or sanity, perhaps both.

"First, you two do the *Dirty Dancing* move in wedding attire and as if that wasn't memorable enough. But *then*, you set the dress on fire fifteen minutes later, Tally." She sighs.

"TMZ is running the footage on their website as we speak. The Giants are calling. Your Grizzlies' coach is calling me." She uses a few choice swear words that are hard to make out. "And Tally? Mikhail Rostov even managed to find a phone; he wanted to make sure you were okay. I lied and said you were and that is was all in fun and possibly just one tiny misunderstanding."

"There is no tiny misunderstanding about Trinna Danner or what must have happened in LA and someone is *lying. And it isn't me*," I say into the dead silence. I do not look at Linc. I just hear him draw an unsteady breath and hold it.

There's a rustling sound on her end. "Hey, Tally." A sympathetic Dr. Bradley Stevenson gets on the line, sighing big, which causes me to smile a little at least. "Are you okay?"

"Sure. I'm fine. Thanks for asking, Brad."

"The dress." He sighs again. "The dress is replaceable although if one of you had been injured that wouldn't have been good. But you're telling me you're okay, right?"

"I'm doing okay, but Linc fell trying to stop me with the dress thing. He's got a pretty big gash on his head, but his buddy Doug fixed him up. But now, he's bleeding again. I'll put fresh bandages on it when we get home. *If* we ever get home." I signal my impatience with Linc by glaring at him.

"Linc, are you okay?" Brad asks.

"Yeah, I'm fine." He glares back at me apparently unhappy that I mentioned his fall and his head gash and Trinna Danner in the last two minutes.

Well yeah, what-the-fuck-ever.

"I suppose they got pictures of all of that too," Kimberley says in despair. Her general well-being seems to deteriorate with each pass. For some reason, I find this incredibly funny and start to laugh. Linc tries to shush me putting his fingers over my mouth which just spurs me on.

"There may have been some extracurricular activity inside his truck in terms of *doing the deed* that the media may have seen and also photographed."

I flip Linc off to match his finger play.

"I'm resigning both of you as clients," Kimberley says wearily.

"I'm *not* your client," I say airily. Tequila continues to dominate my thought process or lack thereof.

"Oh, but you are," she says quietly. "Who do you think pays me to watch over you? San Francisco Ballet that's who. What do you think I spend that retainer money on when I can't be there twenty-four seven with you? Sam Wilde is a friend of mine, Tally," she says with a heavy sigh.

"What?" The air rushes out of me. "You know Sam?" *She knows Sam. What all does she know? And why didn't Sam tell me?*

"Yes, we go back a ways," Kimberley says sounding less sure of herself.

"Kimberley, leave Sam out of it. That's Tally's business. And he doesn't belong in this conversation," Linc says irritably.

"Sam is as much a part of this conversation as the two of you are," she says.

"Geez, Kimmy, you are messing with her life way too much," Linc says with a groan. "As much as mine!"

"Really? You've got your life so under control, right now, Linc?" She asks. "This is why I'm fielding calls for you left and right! *Both of you* are spinning out of control. We only have the upper hand with how the world views you when we have the power, but you two are just *giving* it away. I told you I would handle the LA thing. I told you to tell Tally, but you decided to wait and now it is blowing up in your face as well as hers. You both need to listen to me good and well and often. *I had this.* You both just made it into something bigger than it was in the first place. The *Dirty Dancing* move might have been epic. The wedding clothes, too. But then you literally destroy the perfect moment with the big move by setting your dress on fire and having make-up sex, so *it all looks staged*. I really can't believe this. This reckless behavior. What I don't get is *why*. You *love* each other. Start acting like it."

"That wasn't make-up sex," I say into the warring silence that follows. "That was *good-bye sex*. There's a *difference*." I can feel Linc's mortal wound all the way over here some four feet away from him.

"Oh, Tally. Please stop. Both of you need to quit hurting each other this way. Talk to each other like Brad has told you more than once! And let me do what I can to fix this. For the record, Sam is a friend of mine. Sometimes he works for me. He has for a long time. Three years, maybe four years, on and off, on the down low. He does data analysis and security detail for some of my clients and —"

"*I* was his security detail?" I ask feeling mortally wounded myself.

"No. No. No. I called him in early January and he mentioned you—told me he knew you as a friend and would keep an eye on you. He wasn't *technically* working for me. Frankly, I think he got in over his head and naively thought he could handle you, Tally; and yet…" She sighs. "He called me last night fairly distraught telling me you'd broken things off with him. And then called back again when he saw what TMZ was running."

I moan out-loud. Of course I didn't allow my plan and the tirade that followed to message my psyche as to what all of this would do to Sam.

"Tally? I warned him a long time ago that you and Linc were pretty epic," Kimberley says. "I think he'll survive. It's probably the timing of your hook-up with Linc that upset him the most but—"

"Can we just stop talking about Sam? *Please*?" Although I go on to talk about Sam. "I cut him loose earlier today because I had things to take care of. It wasn't fair to him. I haven't been fair to him. I needed to be free of Linc before we could move forward. Before *I* could move on." Linc is looking at me but I just stare straight ahead. "Get away from you. Be *free* of you." I finally look over at him. "That's what this is. That's *all* this is. To be *free* of you." I slice at the air with my hand and Linc flinches.

"How dare you mess with my life this way, Kimberley," I say irritably summoning up the last vestiges of anger anywhere I can find it.

"Why? Because you were doing so well on your own? No panic attacks, huh, Tally? You're in debt to the max paying for a wedding that never happened. Who do you think hired Andy? Go ahead and ask yourself how the perfect nanny falls into your lap like that? Sam took care of it. I encouraged him to help you out and didn't worry about it too much because normally Sam knows how to handle things doesn't get emotionally involved with any of my clients. Do I think he came close to the line as it relates to you? *Yes*. *But* I made it clear to him how things were with the two of you weeks ago and I warned him you needed time to work things out with Linc without his interference." She sighs. "Because, Tally, you do still love Linc and Sam must see that too. And for the record, Linc did not know about Sam. Trust me on that one."

"Quit defending Linc. He can defend himself. But none of this excuses what happened in LA and what he did with Trinna Danner," I say harshly and hear the guy sitting next to me suck in air as fast as the couple on the other end of the line.

"LA is hard to explain or escape," Kimberley says sounding a little shaken. "I'll handle it. Miss Trinna Danner will have a lot to answer for when a lawsuit lands on her doorstep for all of these false accusations; and it will; trust me. I can make her life a living hell and I will."

"Kimmy, *chill*," Brad says. "Tally, take a breath. Take a moment. Think this through. Going nuclear is not a strategy; it is an end-game. All I ask is that you just listen to what Linc has to say about the night in LA, just *listen*. You two can work this out if you still care about each other. If that's what you both want. Just trust that Linc has told you the truth, what he knows to be true. And know, that is all that matters."

"That's so easy for you to say, Brad. The Lincoln Presley I know would never have done this to me. *Never*."

Linc sucks in more air beside me. It is quite possible he's having a panic attack, and it could be said that I have crossed the line over into new territory and reached a new set of lows. *Gone nuclear* as Brad just said. *An end-game. Yes. That's what this is. That's what I want.*

I can't really look at Linc right now. My mind tumbles with thoughts of Sam. The phone calls. The talks. Lending his shoulder to cry on. A good friend. *Without the benefits.* We'd fallen into a safe routine with all of that. He was safe. And now that I'm cut loose look at all I've done to Linc and to me and to Sam in a matter of hours. Just reliving the disastrous deeds of this evening cuts me to shreds. "I think I'm going to be sick," I say to Linc. "Stop the car."

"It's a truck," Linc says mildly, but then he gets a good look at my anxious face. "Kimberley. Brad. We're going to have to call you back."

He ends the call with Kimberley in mid-sentence, pulls over to the side of the road, leans over, and flips open my door. I slide down the seat to the ground without tripping and race towards the grassy field I can see up ahead gasping for air and trying to make it as far away from Lincoln Presley as humanly possible because I am absolutely fucking done with all of this. *Done. Done. Done.*

I'm in a field because we're in Fresno on the edge of town, and they have farmland here as well as orange groves and orchards instead of manicured lawns and concrete sidewalks like San Fran. Alamo Square. Sea Cliff. Still too drunk to stand properly, I fall to my knees and vomit up the tequila and parts of the hamburger meal from earlier. Within seconds, Linc holds my hair, but I hit that too along with his right hand.

It's a long while before I'm through with this part. Linc eventually undoes his cuff links, takes off his white tuxedo shirt, and starts to clean my face with it despite my protests.

We are way past wicked.

We have passed up malicious and perhaps even evil.

We are in the midsts of Neverland with nothing of good in sight.

Rock bottom.

The darkest hour has arrived.

For me.

"Thanks," I say in small voice.

"Better?" Linc asks pulling me back along with him towards the truck. "I've got a bottled water in here somewhere, behind the seat I think." He hands me one. I gargle, spit some of it out and then drink the rest of it down. He unwraps a stick of gum and hands it to me and then grabs a fresh baby wipe from the back and starts cleaning the goo that landed in my hair and on his hands.

"Memorable. Not part of the plan." I have difficulty meeting his eyes.

He nods and says offhand, "hey, thanks for not throwing up in the truck. Very thoughtful and much appreciated."

It makes me laugh. "Sure. You're welcome." I turn away embarrassed by tonight's latest event and feeling like a loser on too many levels to comprehend. I cut Sam loose and now he knows all the sordid details and the untold depths of my fucked-up-ness. I'm without a safety net of any kind to save me from the charms of one Lincoln Presley. And the night is not yet over. *Clearly.*

Linc calls Kimberley back. He launches into a five-minute lecture about her messing in his affairs and mine. He shoots me a *we're-in-this-together-comrade* look but I just vaguely nod. "You have to let us handle this on our own. If she lets me live, I'll call you tomorrow. I know. She knows that too. Marla has Cara. I've already talked to them." He hangs up the phone and stares straight ahead out the windshield.

"*When* did you talk to Marla?"

"Charlie called while you were in the restroom changing at O'Riley's." He frowns. "Getting ready for the next part of your epic plan." He hesitates. "So are you going to tell me what the plan is?" Before I can answer, he's saying, "here we are. This is where I live."

I look up at the dark house and can't quite hide my smile. "I know. A taxi dropped me off here hours ago with my stuff—waited for me, actually—but I left most of it on your front porch. Except for the dress and the tux."

"The dress," he cringes upon saying those two little words. "Wait. Your stuff is here? No hotel?"

"I didn't think it through; a hotel was not part of the plan."

He sighs looking frustrated. "So what's the *plan*, Tally? Just *tell me*, so I can be properly prepared."

"On the bus on the way down, I typed up the list on my iPhone. *Tally's Epic Plan.*" On edge now, I still manage to hand him my phone displaying the list.

1. *Go to Fresno.*
2. *Find him.*
3. *Bring Garment bag.*
4. *Do The Move.*
5. *Call Amy LA Times*
6. *Call Baxstrom.*
7. *Call Kimberley.*
8. *Do the deed fast.*
9. *Do the deed slow.*
10. *Write a note.*
11. *Leave him.*

He reads it aloud. Then he doesn't say anything more.

Instead, he gets out of the truck and comes around to my side and opens the door for me. His head is bleeding again. It takes all my willpower not to reach up and help him out when he starts swiping at it with a baby wipe. But then he's picking me up and putting me over his right shoulder taking me completely by surprise.

"Put me down."

"I know that's not in the plan," he says gravely. "You've got to stick to the plan, Tally. We're on number nine then. Prepare yourself. You've got to keep it together until you finish what you've started. That's how a plan works."

He's not smiling when I get a glimpse of his face, not at all.

CHAPTER THIRTY-FOUR

white horse

TALLY

"Y OU REALLY NEED STITCHES." I PRESS a fresh QuikClot packet to his head and dab at the wound hoping it will stop bleeding with each pass. He winces, and I hold myself back from tracing his jaw line and kissing him again because we are far too close in proximity to each other in his small guest bathroom.

Yes. It would appear, we are too far into the game—the list, the plan—this insanity.

His hair is wet from the shower, and he smells so good. Standing between his legs and playing doctor to his head wound is messing with me.

My mind and my plan.

"Okay," he says squinting up at me in the bright bathroom light, while I still firmly hold the packet to his head. "Let's say I *do* need stitches. That's three hours in the ER for them to figure out that I *need stitches, maybe a tetanus shot.* The media will surely find us there because—*let's face it*—news was a little slow in Fresno until you showed up." He laughs. "So, now that would make it four in the morning which means no sleep at all because we basically spent the majority of the night in the ER. *Waiting. Getting stitches. A tetanus shot. Dodging the press.* And more importantly and the worst news of all, there's no chance to finish number nine before you say with remarkable certainty *I've got to go, Elvis.*" I frown at the way he's looking at me. "So. We don't get to finish your list. You leave. I'm screwed out of number nine which I'm really looking forward to, by the way," he says softly, "all because I need four little stitches for a superficial head wound. *No.* That's all I'm saying. Just *no* to the ER and getting stitches."

"You're just saying *no*? That was quite a speech leading up to a simple *no*, Superman." He laughs again.

"Kimberley calls me that."

"Not tonight. I don't think she called you *or thought you were* Superman, tonight. And I am certainly not Wonder Woman in her eyes tonight either."

"Not tonight."

"I can't decide if she likes me or hates me," I say on a sigh.

"She *loves* you," he says with confidence. "She never did any of this stuff before for any of my *other* girlfriends that I can *remember*." He grins at my unhappy look. "*Kidding.* Not that many girlfriends that I know of."

He frowns and looks a little uneasy as we both seem to drift toward thoughts of LA and Trinna Danner *again.* "Just know, she's very protective of those she cares about. Kimberley Powers is brilliant. Controlling. Powerful. She was engaged to my brother and then when Elliott died... Well, we've been close ever since. Sure she handles my PR stuff, usually there's not so much to handle. She's a tough talker, and appears to gloss over other people's feelings half the time, but she has good intentions and big heart. She's like a sister to me. And she loves you, Tally. She loves me. Brad."

He gets this delectable smile and I have to fight off the desire to kiss him. "I'm glad she has Brad. She's really happy these days—the most I've seen her since Elliott..." His smile fades. "But Kimmy knows pain, just like you and I do. Okay, that's enough with the feels. Please focus on fixing my head. I don't want to spend the night in the ER and miss out on all the fun associated with the ninth item on your epic list." His mouth curves up. "We deserve to give each other a proper number nine, don't you think, *Miss Cloves and Vanilla?*"

"You are way too optimistic—laced with far too many lofty expectations—about number nine." I laugh nervously and then lean over to examine his head wound again and avoid looking at him altogether.

Instead, I announce the good news: the blood has stopped oozing from his head.

"Okay, you're going to have to be patient and let me do this and trust that it's going to work. Cara hit her head on the edge of the swing and Sam did this same kind of thing a few months ago so we didn't have to traumatize her with a visit to the ER." I steal a look at him. He's frowning over the mention of Sam. "Anyway what you do is knot the hair, tie it actually from each side, pulling the edges of the wound together." I bite my lip at the intense look he's giving me. "And there's always the option of a little Super Glue if that doesn't work."

"*Anything* to preserve the...what did you say?" He grins. "The *lofty expectations* as it relates to number nine."

I'm a little taken aback by the provocative look on his face. My hand starts to shake. "Let me see if I can do this."

"You can."

"How do you know?"

"Because I'm sure of you," he says simply.

After that unexpected praise and the way he's gazing at me, I can no longer look at him. To break the spell he's trying to cast on me, I grab a comb and carefully part his hair around the wound. "Good thing you need a haircut. It's long enough. I think this will work."

"Then, do it." He gets this wicked smile. "So we can do something else that is *guaranteed* to be a lot more fun."

"*Guaranteed?* But is there a return policy?"

"Not exactly, but I can almost guarantee your satisfaction. A little trust?"

"*Trust* you?" I shake my head side-to-side.

The revelations with LA come back to me full-force where I envision Trinna Danner's pregnant form and glowing smile. Pregnant. Linc's baby? We don't have those answers yet and won't for some time, and trust is nowhere to be found in any of that.

There's a plan. Stay with it.

My smile slips from my face.

Linc looks up at me and doesn't say anymore because somehow I think he knows what I'm thinking.

Instead, he closes his eyes and leans into me a little more.

"Just do it, Tally. I can take it. I've developed a high level for pain."

"Me too," I say simply.

He's playing John Mayer's album, *Where The Light Is. Naturally.* Because what we need around here is more seductive innuendos between us. There are never enough of those. He pours me a glass of wine, assures me I'll like it as he touches my hand in passing, and then continues to move around his kitchen as the confident gourmet chef I know him to be. He insists we eat, that we need the nourishment for what lies up ahead.

Who's running this show?

I watch him intently looking for signs that this is all prearranged, a set-up of some sort. And yet, it's the little things about him now that zing through my psyche like little arrows lancing my memory each time.

It's the ease with which he is just being with me. His patience. His kindness. The way he gestures with his hands. The way he pours my wine first and waits until I taste it before he pours himself a glass. The way he talks while he cooks. He always used to do that. The way he stops and gets this look of contemplation before he answers my questions—simple or more complex—he takes his time in answering, like he always did.

It's all the same. Lincoln Presley is the same, but still different somehow. *Dare I say, better?* That thought alone does something to me.

I'm the one who's free falling here.

We eat in silence side-by-side at the bar and the déjà vu returns. "You like it?"

"Yes."

It's the same. It's the same dish he made me the first night we were together almost five years ago—sautéed chicken with this touch of rosemary and garlic. The herbs, the seasonings, the memory of him assails my senses and leaves me breathless and undone.

He's the same but different.

How is that possible?

How does that work exactly?

Where do we go from here?

How can I possibly leave him?

"Tally? Are you okay?"

I look over at him and smile a little because one side of his hair goes every which way like a little boy's untrained cowlick because of my doctoral skills. "I'm fine."

"And you're lying."

I sigh and wilt under his steady gaze. "What are you doing to me, Elvis?"

"So. I'm *not* in trouble," he says with a wide smile. "Good, it's working."

"What's working?"

"This."

He lifts my chin up and kisses me. First gentle then more insistent. Five minutes. We've torn each other clothes off and now go at it on his living-room rug. Faster, smoother, better than before. His fingers move along my inner thighs and his breath and the distinct touch of his tongue soon follow this magical trail as I willfully part my legs for him. Soon, I'm crying out his name as his amazing body urges mine to respond to his miraculous touch. I'm more than ready for him when he gently lowers himself inside of me. With our eyes wide open we gaze at each other and brazenly acknowledge what it feels to connect in this way. I rise up to take more of him inside, and he whispers my name as he moves deeper.

We are together and we are changed because of it. I can sense it and when I look into his eyes I know he feels it too.

Who's running this show? Where's the plan now, Tally?

I lay on top of him. Naked. Our sweat runs together but the slightest of movement between us causes me to start to slide off of him which we both find extremely funny for some unknowable reason that only carnal knowledge permits.

"Tally." The way he's said my name causes me to raise my head from his chest where I've been listening to his thundering heartbeat since we first finished.

"Yes, Mr. Presley." He winces at my formality, but then he gets this dazed smile and traces my lips, which have been all over his body in the last half hour, and leans in closer and kisses me again.

"It's important. Don't ruin it," he says breathless when he finishes his latest exploration of my mouth.

He watches me closely again. I can't help but smile at his suddenly serious expression. "Okay, I won't ruin it. *Go.*"

"I love you."

"Elvis," I say helplessly. He puts his fingers to my lips.

"*Listen.* I love you. You need to know that and *hear* it. I think I fell in love with you that last night in the hospital when you swung by my room all pissed off with my dad and me in being unbelieved and wrongly accused about my money. *You owned me then.* Or maybe it was even sooner—when I woke up and you were the first person I saw—of course this was before I threw the water pitcher at the wall and demanded to know who you were. And yet I think my heart knew, has always known since the first time I saw you." He nods while I just stare at him feeling completely undone. "All I know for sure, right this very second, is that I love you, and I will always love you. I should have told you sooner—that day at Cara's birthday party—when I realized….you are my water. I love you, Tally. And I need you in my life."

"Why are you doing this to me, Elvis? Not part of the plan. Don't love me. Don't *say* you love me. *New rule.*"

I move to get away from him, but he grips my arms from both sides and keeps me in place. In the next, he's switched positions and I'm pinned beneath him because he's definitely moving faster than I am now.

I'm seized by recognizable panic even while he's kissing my face and my throat. I gasp for air. "Don't. Love. Me."

"I'm going to make you want to stay. With me. That's my plan," he says into my neck then trailing his lips down to my breasts where he swirls his tongue and lightly blows air on them which causes the entire conversation to come to a full stop. Now, I'm breathing fast for a whole new set of reasons.

I open my eyes and recenter myself gaining a little equilibrium noticing the last traces of alcohol have finally burned off in my system.

Gratitude.

It's dark. We're lying together, intertwined actually, on the living room floor. A naked, sleeping Lincoln Presley imprisons me with his arms and legs effectively holding me in place, and I have to wonder if this is a part of his plan—the one he spoke of a few hours before. I squint and make out the time as half past four on the mantel clock.

The sudden urge to pee won't leave me, so I cautiously lift one of Linc's arms and with the stealthiest of moves, I escape his captive grip. He murmurs in his sleep as I get up, which freezes me into place for another sixty seconds. It's comical; I stand over him completely naked, and he's missing the whole thing. When he begins to make recognizable sleep sounds again, I gingerly walk down his hallway in search of the restroom.

After doing more ladylike things than I've done all night, I stare at myself in the mirror. Let's face it I have been out of control for the past ten hours, give or take.

I need to call Sam and at least apologize. I should call Marla and check in on Cara. My parents. Mikhail. I still need to check out the Saroyan Theater for SFB while I'm here.

It's all good to have a meltdown in Fresno and make the head-lines in sports America and on TMZ and all the rest, but I still need to keep my job.

There are no promises here. There is Trinna Danner. There still needs to be a conversation about all of that. There is the possibility of a paternity suit. There is my broken heart which is still broken.

I am still broken.

Some things change. Some things are different. Not enough things stay the same.

There is nuclear. There is fire. Air and water. There is us. *There is no us.*

There are the lies and lines and things—horrific things—and a forgotten past between us. It's not a lot to go on.

This huge chasm of deception and dysfunction that lies between us.

A good name for a book. A movie. Our life. I mean, *my life.*

My list. This show. My show. The plan.

Where is the plan, Tally?

Stick to the plan.

Let the self-talk begin.

I thought it had?

The best thing I can do is leave. Pack up my stuff, call a cab, stop by the convention center downtown, check the stage, amenities, dressing rooms, get to Greyhound, buy a ticket to San Fran, get in line, climb those bus stairs, grab a seat, see Rose again, and return home.

How can I leave *him?*

I try again. *Leave. Now. Tally.*

Nothing.

The girl in the mirror is still smiling. Some weird-ass grin is on her face that will not leave.

The truth is I *breathe* with him. He is my *air. Raison d'etre.*

Why don't I tell him? Because there's a plan and we—*I*—need to stay with the plan. *I need to stay with the plan.*

Falling in love with him again is *not a part of the plan.*

Falling in love with him again is *not a plan.*

Stop this while you can.

Save yourself.

Save your sanity.

Get it together.

Go home. To Cara. To Mom and Dad. Tommy. Marla. Charlie. Elliott.

Sam?

I could go home to Sam.

I could feel safe with Sam.

We could be sane. Together. Sam and me.

Sam, me, and Cara.

Sam hates me now.

Go home.

Tally.

Tally.

Tally.

What are you doing?

What do you think is going to happen here?

You've got to stick to the plan. He will hurt you. You will hurt him. You *know* this.

You need to go. You need to leave like the plan says you will.

Leave Tally.

Just go.

Stop this while you still can.

Get it together.

A shower is in order for lots of reasons.

I stand under the water and make it as hot as I can stand it in an attempt to clear my head. And yet the more I try to put him out of mind the more persistent Linc's face appears in it. I cannot escape these salacious thoughts of him and how he makes me feel but that's not good because we are out of control. *Out of control.* I lean against the shower wall beginning to ponder how this will end. The urge to cry is powerful and begins to overtake me. My breath comes too fast and I gasp for air. *Why is this happening to me? How can I stop this? How can I stop?*

And then he's here.

"I missed you. I thought you'd left." He looks worried knowing leaving is part of the plan. *My plan.*

"No. I've decided to stay and see your game tonight."

Wait.

What?

What did I just say?

He gets this very satisfied smile.

Relief.

We both feel it.

Relief. It's like a hit of pure oxygen to our brains.

Instant relief. Floaty.

Don't be floaty, Tally.

Stop this.

"I'll stay one more night and then I'm *outta* here." *Such brave talk for a girl whose heart is racing at more than a hundred beats a minute.*

"You're going to want to stay. We haven't even done the deed *slow* yet, that will *really* win you over."

I have no reply to his little speech or this air of confidence he exudes like a superhero.

I've got nothing.

No comeback of any kind.

I'm in deep trouble here, and he knows it. It's the way he's looking at me as he steps in the shower and the water runs over both of us.

"Plans change," he says with a laugh. "They always do. And the best way to handle a change in plans is to *adapt*, Princess."

CHAPTER
THIRTY-FIVE

suspicious minds

TALLY

"Bacon," Sam said once. "You put it in a pan on medium heat, and it cooks. Whisk the eggs and scramble them up with a little butter in the pan. Done. Timing the toast with the eggs? Tricky, but doable." Lucky I remember what all Sam Wilde said and taught me, and it works. I spent many a morning cooking breakfast with Sam. He'd come over before heading to work at *The Promissory Note. How many? Some thirty times over the last four months. Maybe more? More than I ever have with Lincoln Presley.* This last thought has me pausing in midair with the spatula.

"You're cooking," Linc says looking at me in surprise.

"I cook." *Turn over the eggs. Don't look at him.*

"Sam taught me," I say softly.

"Sam. I'm sorry about Sam. The break-up thing." Linc gets this twisted face. It's not quite a frown, not quite a smile.

Twisty. He's twisted up.

"No, you're *not*," I say trying to sound annoyed with him but failing. I grin instead because he is too.

"No. I'm not."

We look at each other. Three hours of sleep has partially restored us.

"What can I do to help you?" He asks. "I called Hillman and told him Lily's Diner wasn't going to work out for us today and that we'll see him at the game. He's stoked you're coming. So, how can I help you?"

All I can do is nod because I'm thinking about the plan and Trinna Danner all of a sudden. "The toast? You could butter the toast. Then, we're all set."

"Butter, Tally? You *are* going all out today."

"Funny. Just be glad I can cook a little. Don't get real lofty expectations in the cooking department, okay?"

"I'm good. You're mighty fine in all the others."

He sets the table and the whole domestic action scene gets a little too surreal.

He looks dangerous. To me. To my very well-being. He's wearing his Fresno Grizzlies jersey. It's black with a big yellow "F" with bear claws across the logo on the front. He's also got on these black athletic shorts that cling to his hips just so. He's barefoot. He's shaved. He's showered.

Fresh. Hot.

Stop it.

"So what's the plan?" He asks looking all innocent like I haven't just checked him out thoroughly, and he didn't notice.

"I have to go meet with the people at the Saroyan Theater at ten. I could use a ride. You can drop me off. That would be great."

"Or, you could borrow my truck. I don't need to be at the field until four-thirty if you don't mind hanging around early even though the game doesn't start until seven. I'm pitching." He smiles wide. "I'm glad you're staying."

I concentrate on my eggs pushing them around the plate. "I don't drive actually. I haven't for years."

"Like at all?" He asks surprised.

"In San Fran, that is not that hard to carry out. BART, the metro." I lift my head in defiance and stare at him. "New York it was even easier…I don't drive."

It's like confession. You just say it. I said it to Sam and he got it.

Why is this so hard for this version of Lincoln Presley to understand?

There are *versions* of Lincoln Presley.

Think about that.

"I could teach you. I mean if you wanted to—"

"It's not a question of *learning*. It's a matter of I don't drive anymore; okay?" I shake my head. "You and Sam. *Stop teaching* me things. Just accept me for who I am. Just drop me off. You never stayed anyway. Just drop me off. Okay?"

"Okay. Okay. I never stayed? To watch you rehearse? Dance?"

"No." The air rushes out of me again at the curious look he's giving me and I rush to fill the vacuum. "It was complicated. Our life together. It was new. A few months at the most since we got back together? I'd just moved back from New York with Cara. We'd just gotten engaged. It was all new. To us. There was always a baseball game or a practice. Cara would need to be picked up from preschool, daycare…*things*. I've solved some of that with Andy. She's our nanny. Sam hired her for me…"

"Sam," Linc says looking decidedly unhappy. "He took care of everything for you, didn't he? Better than I did?"

"It was different. He was *there*. You were always…*gone*. I don't know. We *won't* know, will we? It was baseball season. It's *still* baseball season. You play for the next twenty days, right?" He nods slowly getting this stricken look as if he's finally figured out the punchline just as much as I suddenly have. "We've never been together in the off-season. Weird, right?"

"The whole thing about us is tragic."

"Tragic?" I shake my head side-to-side. "A *guy* using the word *tragic*? You wound me. Or, you've ruined me. One of those. We were *epic*. Trust me on this, Elvis." I try to laugh but it doesn't work.

Fun time is over.

He looks at me intently and goes for the charm. "Well now. Now we're even. You ruined me, too, *Princess*, for anyone else…about seven months ago." He gets this serious face. "Five years and three months and one day ago." He holds up his iPad and slides it over. It's a time line. He points to Valentine's Day more than five years ago. The caption reads: Valentine's Day - Met Tally for the first time. Car accident.

"The best and worst day of my life rolled into one." After another two minutes under his intense scrutiny, I stand up, pick up my plate, and start to clear the table.

"You've barely eaten anything."

"Don't."

"Don't what?" He asks.

"Don't try and *rule* me, sire. I've got this. This is still *my plan*. Back off," I say irritably. "Food is my issue. I deal with it in my own way. You got that?"

"Somehow I doubt you're going to call me Elvis right now," he says slowly. "Or do the deed with number nine slow like you've planned and promised."

"No."

I stare at him feeling sudden waves of unhappiness wash over me. He takes the plate out of my hand and scrapes the food into the trash. And right then, I decide to bring up the topic we've managed to avoid for the last thirteen hours.

"Trinna Danner. I want to know about that night…start to finish. So you think about that, Prez. I'll be in the living room waiting for the truth from you about that one." I slice my hand through the air and stalk from the room leaving him staring down into the trash bin. He's probably looking for the answers in there.

Suffered enough?
I don't think so.

What am I doing?
  What am I doing?
  The plan.
  The plan.
  The plan will save me.

I start moving through the house stuffing my castoff clothing and things into my carry-on bag. *Make-up. Hair brush. Jeans. Shoes. Pick it up. Pack it up. Let's go.*

Once that's done, I grab my iPhone and text Marla as I go.

Text: "Hey, how's Cara this AM? Avoid the news. I'm okay. Don't ask."

Fifteen seconds later.

Marla: "You sure know how to rock a dress AND set it on fire. E-P-I-C."

Me: "Something like that."

Marla: "What's the plan?"

With a grim face, I send Marla the plan.

It only takes twenty seconds for her response. "I assume you're looking for a pen."

Me: "Yep."

Marla: "You okay?"

Me: "Think so. Favor? Book a flight for me from Fresno to San Fran this afternoon. Pick me up at SFO?"

Marla: "Demanding. Sure you're okay???"

Me: "Never better. I'm free of him."

Marla: "How is that possible?"

Me: "Nuclear version. Trinna Danner. He forgot one or two. In the bed. You dig?"

Marla: "Ah. Not cool. United. 55 min. Check-in at 1 for 2PM flight."

Me: "You're a travel agent & psychic in one. Perfect. Call you when I land. xoxo"

Marla: "Sure you're okay?"

Me: "I've got this. Trust me."

And just like that, the plan becomes clear again. I call Yellow Cab, grateful they have these in Fresno and ask them to send a driver to pick me up in the next half-hour after checking Linc's mail for the address.

Me to Sam: "I'm sorry. About everything. I never deserved you & now deserve you even less."

Sam: "Are you free of him?"

Me: "Almost???"

Sam: "Come home."

Linc walks in looking troubled. The Trinna Danners of the world can rock it just like that. *Been there. Served in that role once too. I can't blame her. I don't hate her. Our motives might have been different, but the results are the same.*

Clarity. Fucking clarified. I am.

I don't even let him start.

I start.

I finish.

"It occurred to me early this morning," I say slowly.

Breathe. Prepare. Get it out. Get it right.

"Something about what you said before on Cara's birthday… about Trinna. Two near the bed. Two in the freezer." I look at him long and hard. "You forgot the one in the bed, didn't you?" He's nodding even as his face goes white. "Say something. Explain yourself, Prez. *Try*."

I sink down slowly to the stairs and then lean back even as the step's edges cut into my back and look up at him. *Not a superhero in sight right now.*

You guess.

You guess right and you inadvertently rock your world when you just meant to rock someone else's.

"You're right. I forgot about the bed." He runs his hands through his hair. "I didn't check inside the bed because she was there still sleeping. I didn't check. It doesn't matter, does it?"

I shake my head side-to-side real slow. "Tell me all of it. *Now*."

"I was ordering shots. Patron with orange slices. I guess I know who taught me that one. But I didn't remember you, did I?" He smiles a little but it disappears when he see my impassive face. "I was feeling no pain. I took twice the dosage of Percocet. My head was raging, but it felt like everything was finally coming together in slow motion and I thought I was in control."

"You *were*," I say deathly quiet. He jolts back a little as if I've just touched him with a Taser.

"At the bar, Amy Ransom the LA Times reporter? She was asking questions about baseball, and Trinna was asking me questions about what I liked. Food. Drink. Clothes. Movies. Sex."

He hangs his head and won't look at me.

"She was fun and I wanted fun. I was pissed off. Camp wasn't going well. Kimberley was gone. I had no one. I was washing out. I panicked; no, I fucked up," he says in a toneless voice. "We stopped and bought condoms. She insisted. I told her my brand. Then she took me to her place because I was in no shape to drive. She opened some wine. I remember dancing in her living room with her. I think I even called her Tally a couple of times. But how would I know that? I didn't remember you."

I cover my face with my hands because looking up at his contorted face while he's confessing all of this suddenly becomes too painful to watch.

I hear him sigh big, and I look at him through my fingers.

"I didn't know about you, Tally. Please listen to me about that. I remember stumbling to her room, and then the trouble began. I couldn't get it up and no matter what she did, it didn't work. But there were condoms, more than one, and I forgot to check the bed, and it's possible that she's pregnant with me from a condom I forgot to grab from the bed because I'm stupid, and I don't deserve you and—"

"*When. Did. You. Know. This?*" Each word is long and loud and cuts a wide swath through both of us as I say them. Simple sounding words that zing across space and destroys the universe. *Ours.*

"A few weeks ago. Kimberley kept asking me. 'Could you have forgotten anything? Is it possible that it's yours?' And that's when I remembered I didn't check the bed because she was in it. So that's why I agreed to the paternity test after the baby's born in the middle of September."

"You lied to me essentially. You didn't tell me all of it before."

"Yes," he says as I stand and turn up toward the stairs. "Where are you going?" I hear the panic in his voice and the wheezing begin.

"Just checking around for my stuff. I've got a meeting in less an hour. I've got to go."

"Tally. Don't leave me. I'm begging you. We can work this out."

Keep going. Up the stairs. Don't look at him. I pass up the guest room. *Head to the master.*

We haven't been in here. We slept in the guest room. *Me in the covers. Him on top. Sam and I used to do this. Sam. Good. Linc. Bad.*

I go to the night stand and pull out the first slip of paper I find. *Perfect.* It's another receipt. A dry cleaners one again. *Classic.* I write: *Thank you, Elvis* and twist up the receipt and feed it through the loop of his mother's ring and toss it onto his bed.

He can find it when he cries into his pillow later tonight.

I just make it to the doorway before he comes into the room.

"Tally. Don't leave me." Linc looks completely undone.

"We're a metaphor. A circus act, just like I said before." I move past him and start down the hallway and then turn and face him. "I don't want this. I don't want to go outside and fight the press while they try and get another salacious story about us while we attempt to get to your car—truck, what-the-fuck-ever. I wanted a simple life. I wanted simple. I wanted that. I wanted us. I wanted to trust you and love you and be with you forever. I wanted a little wedding at Half Moon Bay with Pastor Dan and a dozen of our friends and family. I wanted a life with you. But now it's all gone and we can't get it back, Linc. No matter what we try. I'll resent you because you can't remember. And you'll resent me because I can't give you a son."

I take a necessary breath and blow it out. "I gave up pretty much everything for you. And it's not that you're not without your own set list of sacrifices. *You wanted a son.* You admitted this to Pastor Dan Reeve months ago. *Before.* And you *told* somebody you wanted a son recently. *Trinna. Amy. Candy.* You told *somebody* you wanted a son and they reported it in their little story. *Okay. Then.* Maybe you'll get one. Be happy. You're forever free of the damaged goods—*that is me*—because I can't give you what you so desperately want. We'll work out the details with Cara through Marla or my lawyer or my nanny—*my people.*"

He grabs my arm.

I stop a second and take a shaky breath. "Don't. Touch. Me."

He lets me go and looks completely broken. "Don't do this to us. I'm begging you. I love you. I told you, Tally. I *love* you."

It's nuclear.
Finish it.
Geez, once you start you can't even begin to pull back the levers even if you have second thoughts or thirds.

"So you said. Well, you have a strange way of showing it." I try to smile and then it's gone. "And I don't feel the same way about you anymore. We're done here. I'm out."

I take the stairs two at a time heading down. I grab my bag, purse, and phone. I'm out the door and a good twenty feet ahead of him even as I can literally feel him stumble after me. Predictably, the press is there but so is Yellow Cab and while Linc is stopped by various reporters with their cameras and questions, the crowd parts for me and allows me to pass.

I'm not the story. Trinna Danner is. And Lincoln Presley. And their precious baby expected to be born in September. I'm just the barren bitch that got in the way of all of that. I'm the girl who burned a two thousand dollar wedding dress because she'd been scorned, and she's nuclear and apparently very pissed off and still owes $28,000 and change on her Visa card.

Ninety seconds.

I leave him.

The cab speeds off in the direction of the Saroyan Theater. *Classic.* *I'll be on time.*

"Wait for me," I say to the driver when we arrive and hand him two twenty-dollar bills to ensure he does.

And that is how it's done.
That's how you leave them.
And that's the end of *Tally's Epic Plan.*
From here on out, there is no plan.

CHAPTER
THIRTY-SIX

stop this train

LINC

PLANS BACKFIRE. PLANS CHANGE. CLARITY GETS clarified. Fucking clarified. Tally's wrath fuels me. My goals get simpler, and I become laser focused. I have to get back to San Francisco. I pitched a perfect game the night she left me and an almost perfect game on the next outing. Then in outings three, four, five, six, and seven I come close again. My stats soar and now the Giants just look like imbeciles for keeping me here. The fans galvanize. The sports reporters start to talk, start to write, and start to print: *when is Lincoln Presley coming back to the line-up?* Talk of my return becomes the common editorial theme among all the sports pages and ESPN and I am clarified as well as justified.

Clarified.
Justified.
I am both.

We're in Sacramento for a four-day tournament, and it's the second day. Eight weeks less two to the day Tally left me; the call comes in from the Giants. I know it as soon as I see Coach Reynolds of Grizzlies fame comes out toward me on the pitcher's mound during warm-ups. All the players seem to stop what they're doing and watch the two of us—Coach and me.

Hillman's on first. He yells, "Hoo-yah!" And fist-pumps the air even before Coach Reynolds utters a single word to me.

"Well, Prez, the brass finally took notice. You're up. They want you pitching in Miami at the end of next week after the All Stars game. Congratulations. Way to hang in there even with all the bullshit that's been thrown your way."

Those headlines include: The Giants taking their sweet ass time in calling me up and Trinna Danner being sued for falsifying medical records. She's not pregnant. Never was. Tally may have set a nuclear fire between her and me, but Kimberley ensured Trinna Danner suffered her own. So much so that Ms. Danner has left LA and returned to her parent's home in Georgia and given up acting and issuing false paternity claims altogether. I didn't even catch a southern accent in her speech, but then I don't remember a lot about Trinna Danner other than how she attempted to ruin my life and get to my money. Those headlines have gone far and wide, thanks to Kimberley.

However, *Miss Cloves and Vanilla* remains very pissed off at me. Our communique consists of confirming plans around my visits with Cara. It's a nightmare with the schedule, but I make it happen. I use Tally's continual indifference with me as motivation toward my one and only goal—my return home.

I nod at Coach. "Thanks for helping me get there. Like I've said many a time, you just got to be the one who remains standing." I force a smile.

Baseball is just a means to an end. A means back to Tally. I already know that *Miss Cloves and Vanilla* is only in town a few more days. On Thursday, she leaves for Moscow to see her friend Sasha and check out the Bolshoi Ballet. I know this because of Charlie not because Tally bothered to tell me. I also know she's leaving Cara with her parents because I don't think she wants to be the one to ask me if she can take our kid out of the country. I think she knows I will say *no*, so she doesn't ask me. So my plan has come together just in time. *I'm going home.*

Clarified.

We all are.

Coach Reynolds nods and quints at me before he spits onto the ground. "Just don't let 'em push you around so much, Prez. You've got the arm; you've got the head for it. You'll be at the All Stars game next year. Enjoy your time off and then just avoid the line drives, okay?"

"Right." I shake his hand. He grins wide. I spy a speck of tobacco on his front tooth that I wouldn't dare mention to him. "Thank you for the opportunity to play. It's been an honor to work with you guys."

"Yeah, well, you're easy to coach. A regular guy. You're grounded and that's what will take you far in this game. Keep it simple. Wife. Kids. Home." He looks at me. "I hope everything works out for you and her. She's still the talk of O'Riley's." He smiles wide. I'm shocked. I wasn't aware he was there. He laughs to himself, turns, and saunters off.

I raise my cap to the team while they all start whooping and hollering when I yell out, "I'm out of here!"

Hillman runs over and shakes my hand and clasps my shoulder. "Go get her, Prez. She can't stay pissed off at you forever. Just be back in Fresno in November for the big wedding with Brandy. Geez! Why did I have to fall in love with a hometown girl who will never want to leave town?" He asks with a groan and then laughs as he starts running back toward first base.

"Hillman," I say.

He turns.

"Thanks for being a good friend."

He smiles.

"We'll always be friends. San Fran isn't that far away. Go pack your gear. Don't make me cry. Shit, you're probably flying out in two hours back to Fresno, and then you still have a five-hour drive after you pack up. But you're buying me a beer next time I'm up in the City."

"Deal," I say.

"And there's always November." He salutes.

"November. Off season. Looking forward to it." I salute him back.

CHAPTER
THIRTY-SEVEN

who am I to say

TALLY

Plans backfire. Plans change. Life gets clarified. Fucking clarified. My wrath for Lincoln Presley continues to fuel me. My goals in life get simpler. I become more laser focused. There's Cara and ballet and Marla. I leave for Moscow in two days to see Sasha and to check out what the Bolshoi Ballet might have to offer me. Cara is staying with my parents while I'm in Russia. It's been a few months since the nuclear war with Linc, and I am still here.

Living? *Sort of.*
Breathing? *Sort of.*
Clarified? *Most definitely.*
"You know what your problem is?" Marla asks sweetly.

She's three months pregnant. Thus, all the crying of a few months before has finally been explained.

I'm driving her to her gyno appointment with Dr. Eldon. Yes, we're best friends so of course, we go to the same gynecologist.

I'm driving.

Did you catch that, too? It's our deal. I have to give up my hangups—the triggers, and she doesn't get to talk about Lincoln Presley like ever. It's a fair trade. I'm driving her Escalade. She's happy. I'm happy, *mostly,* although this boat of a car is a scary monster to drive even as we cruise down the 101 without mishap toward Dr. Eldon's Palo Alto satellite office.

"I have problems?" I ask with a laugh. "No, I don't. I am *clarified.*"

This is my new thing. *Clarification.* I think I mention it in every other time we talk. Clarification is my answer to everything these days. Marla hates it. She hates it that I'm clarified. She doesn't like the new Tally that is somewhat hell-bent on life improvements of all kinds that may entail destruction give or take. I call it righting my life. Marla calls it destruction. Reconstruction. One of those. A lot of dismantling is going on. I'm getting ready to lease out Tremblay's house. Cara and I are moving in with my parents to save money. Pay off the Visa bill. Pay off the damn dress. *Stuff.* I'm half-packed for that adventure which will happen at the end of the month depending upon what happens with the possibility of a Bolshoi Ballet job offer. Marla thinks everything about Moscow and the Bolshoi is a terrible idea but she won't say exactly why.

"Do you ever think about what could have been?"

I glance over at her momentarily losing my happy face. "What the…hell, Marla? That is so like *mentioning him.* What are you doing? I'm *driving.* We have a *deal.*"

"I know but I was just thinking about all of it, and it makes me… sad."

"Don't be sad. Don't talk about *him.* Geez, *I'm driving.* We have a deal. Don't ruin it. You're ruining me."

The words are out before I can take them back. I catch my lower lip between my teeth and taste the blood in my mouth two seconds later.

"Don't talk about him. No *side references* either. I'm going to pull over if you continue down this path. We don't *talk* about him *ever.*"

"He called Charlie earlier. He's getting sent up. He'll be in Miami with the Giants at the end of next week after the All Stars game. He's coming home. I thought you'd want to know so you could be prepared. You know, so you know." She grins wide.

"You're *talking* about him," I scold as pull into Dr. Eldon's wide parking lot. I carefully park in space far enough away from all the other parked cars and then turn to her. "Don't do that."

"Tally," she says wagging her finger in my face, "you're too stubborn. You've got to let it all go. Trinna Danner has been exposed for the whoring slut she was, and he's coming home. For you. Prepare yourself."

"He hates me now." My voice trembles. "He loves Cara, but he hates me."

Marla's looking at me intently as if she's going to find a secret way into my head for a cosmic mind meld of some sort. "Stop it. You're being ridiculous. He loves you. He will always love you." She gets this secret smile. "Big day," she says.

I'm grateful she's changed the subject. "Big day." Smiling again, I squeeze her hand. "I'm so happy for you." She's having an ultrasound and hopefully Dr. Eldon will be able to tell if it's a boy or girl.

"Thanks for coming." She gets this wistful look. "If Charlie were doing any other stint for his rotation other than the ER…I'm glad you're here with me, Tal."

"Nowhere else I'd rather be. You've always been here for me. I'm here for you. That's how we do it."

She grabs my hand. "Let's go do this. Maybe Dr. Eldon is ahead of schedule today because I'm absolutely starving."

"Yeah, me too. Must eat soon." She stares at me. "What?"

"I don't know," she says looking at me closely. "You're *never* hungry."

"Yes, I am."

"No, you're not."

I laugh. "Okay. It's a fluke. Just be glad 'cause I'm *paying* today. Lucky you."

Marla's having a girl. She is so excited that she is practically sliding off the exam table unable to remain still. I'm here holding Marla's hand providing her with awesome moral support. We both screamed at Dr. Eldon's news that the baby is a girl.

Dr. Eldon announces she is ahead of schedule and gives me a curious look as she finishes up her charting about Marla and her baby girl. "You missed your six-month check-in, Tally."

"Oh, did I? I've been slammed with work and all. I guess I forgot to call for the appointment."

Marla slides off the table. I let go of her hand. We exchange a knowing look. I am as thrilled as she is that she's having a girl.

"All right. Well, since you're here let's get your lab work done," Dr. Eldon says, "and then we'll schedule you for a regular exam in a month or so." She gives me the there-will-be-no-arguing-with-me-today look.

"Okay."

I'm not exactly thrilled with being cornered about the labs because it involves drawing blood, and she's going to bust me again about eating, not eating, although lately I've been better about all of that. So whatever. I follow her out and Dr. Eldon's nurse, Stacey, guides me to another room to draw blood and other fun stuff inside of twenty minutes.

We are back in the doctor's front office, and all is right with the world as Dr. Eldon calls out, "Congratulations, Marla. I'll see you in a month, just like Tally." She smiles at us both and then proceeds to say, "I'll call you with the lab results in a couple of days, Tally."

"Okay sounds good." Then I turn back. "Oh, I do leave for Moscow in a couple of days, this Thursday, actually."

Marla rolls her eyes again demonstrating she's not exactly enamored about me making a return trip to Moscow.

"Moscow? Really? The Bolshoi?" Dr. Eldon asks. I nod and smile wide. She returns it. "Okay. Well, I'll have the lab put a rush on it. Are you sure you're caught up on all of your shots to travel?"

I frown. "I should be. I guess I'd better check all that out before I set off for Russia and fly on out of here; huh?" I laugh.

Marla's looking at me strangely. "What?" I ask.

"What's up with your flightiness today?"

"I didn't eat?" I say thinking. "Oh yes, I did. A tuna sandwich. For breakfast."

"That sounds disgusting."

"Not to me. It was fabulous. I even toasted the bread. Who knew?"

"Still sounds disgusting."

"You're pregnant. Certain foods sound disgusting to *you*," I say.

We're back in Marla's Escalade in under an hour which she points out to me as I pull out of the parking lot and she rewards me with one of those sly smiles of hers because she's still has me driving. "You're doing great, Tal. You really are."

"Yep." I signal for a left turn and gun the engine so we escape the oncoming traffic still stopped down at the next light.

"So where are we at with Sam?"

"What is this? Break all of Tally's rules day? We are *nowhere* with Sam. We don't talk about Sam either, remember? He…I don't know…he's busy with secret stuff he can't tell me about, and frankly, I'm beginning to find it annoying. Plus, every time he looks at me, I know he's thinking of the somewhat compromising positions I took with Linc in the baseball player's truck that night." I glance away for a second to gain some control. "Every time. I guess Elvis ruined that too. He ruined me. Damn. He ruined me," I say softly wiping at my eyes and then I laugh and shake my head.

"I *did not* bring him up."

"I know. I did."

"Okay then. I just want to be clear. I understand the rules and I only break them *consciously*." Marla looks at me intently.

"You are so weird sometimes," I say with a laugh.

"And you are downright giddy. And you are *never* giddy," she says getting this all-knowing face.

"I'm not." Then, I smile wide again.

In solidarity, we order virgin Pink Lady daiquiris to celebrate Marla's girl news while I order a hamburger, and Marla orders a salad.

We've been at the restaurant about half an hour when she looks over at me and her mouth drops open. We've been talking about

Moscow; the latest, dirty going-ons at SFB; Mikhail Rostov who I've grudgingly have begun to admire; the fall schedule; Marla and Charlie's continual talk about moving closer to me; Cara's preschool; Elliott's acceptance of the new baby when she arrives; and Marla's due date, which is the middle of November, and how that's going to affect Thanksgiving. *Stuff.*

Marla's staring at my plate. "You ate the whole burger."

I look down. My plate is empty. I swipe up the remaining crumbs with my finger and suck it. "I did. Yum."

She gets this look—the stunned one that metamorphoses into her particular brand of wizardry. She gasps and holds her breath and then she bursts out laughing. This happens in all of twenty seconds.

"What is your problem? And can I just say I really hate that we have given up the word," I lean forward and whisper, "*fuck.*"

She leans forward. "I know me too. However, if Cara and Elliott were saying it, we both know where they got it from and Charlie busted me for it. So there you go."

"I know," I lament this major parental error of my own making. "I know. I just *miss* it so much." We grin at each other.

It ends up being only forty-five minute drive home to Alamo Square as we've miraculously timed it so we missed much of the traffic. Andy has been watching both kids. The three of them are playing outside in the kiddie pool I bought for Cara the week before when the heat got to be too much around the fourth of July. They look to be having a glorious time.

Marla and I stand arm-in-arm at the back door watching them for a few minutes.

"Don't let them know we're back quite yet. I still need a little longer break from it all," Marla says.

"You okay?" I eye her more closely. "You're good, right? It's a *girl.* You're doing great. Dr. Eldon says everything is fine."

"I know. But you just don't know. I mean I know everything looks great, but you worry about everything. Every little thing. *Fuck,*" she whispers.

We laugh.

I'm still laughing when my cell rings and *Elvis* comes up on screen. "It's Linc," I say in surprise. "I mean I know we talked about him earlier but this is weird, right?"

"Answer it."

Why is this suddenly like prosecuting a federal case in my mind?
Answer the phone, Tally.

He probably just wants to see Cara. Make plans to see Cara. He has been seeing Cara sporadically.

We make the most convoluted plans to ensure that happens.

He talks to Andy all the time—making those plans. They meet up in the strangest places wherever the team happens to playing while on the road that has him near enough San Francisco.

Why shouldn't he talk to me?
I'm the mom after all.
Answer the phone.

"Hello." *I'm three-years-old again taking my first phone call from Grandma.*

"Tally. Hi. It's Linc. I'm just about there. I'm a little early. Andy said it was fine."

"Aaaannnnnddddyyyyyy said *what* was fine?"

"Yeah, I talked to her about two hours ago? I'm driving up from Fresno. I should be there in about fifteen minutes. Just wanted to swing by and pick up Cara. She's spending the night at my house and we're going to the zoo tomorrow. I've got about nine days off before the trip to Miami when they'll work me into the rotation. I want to fit in as much time with her as I can."

"Of course. Right. Okay. Your house? I thought you sold that place? I'm sorry; I just got home so this is all news to me, but that sounds fine." I flash Marla a thumb's-up sign. "Marla's having a girl by the way. It's okay to tell you because she already told Charlie. We're stoked."

"Awesome! Girls are the best. I'm not selling the house. I've just stayed focused on getting back here."

"Right. Oh and congratulations on making it all the way back to the majors. Marla told me? Quite a feat. The Giants are lucky to have you; it's high time they made good on that with you."

"Yes, it is. Thanks."

"You deserve it. *Really.*"

"Well, thanks. That means a lot especially coming from you."

He is giddy if a guy can actually be described as giddy.

I am giddy back to him, which is like a fucking miracle.

The home line is ringing I frantically gesture to Marla to answer it and hear her say, "Dr. Eldon. Yeah, she's on her cell with Linc. Yes. He's coming home. Made it back to the majors. Well no, not exactly."

"Tally? Are you there?" Linc asks gently.

"Oh I'm sorry, yes, Marla is answering the home line. Dr. Eldon's calling and I'm spacing out. *Again.*" I laugh a little as if that will make up for it. "Wow. Okay. You're on your way. That's great. We'll see you in a few. I'll get Cara's overnight stuff packed up. She's going to be thrilled to see you."

"Hey, Tally?"

"Yes?"

He sighs deep. "The nuclear war is over by the way. There's been a peace treaty signed, sealed, and about to be delivered. I'm not sure you heard me say that just now, but it's true." He laughs.

I'm enchanted with his sound and it momentarily stops my brain from functioning. "Uh…A peace treaty? I did not hear you say that. No. Are there terms I should know about?"

"Yes. I'll go over them with you when I see you."

"Funny. Okay then," I say with the weirdest laugh ever. It's a cross between a monkey and a human girl. Marla's waving her arms all over the place gesturing that I need to come and talk to Dr. Eldon like right the fuck now. In fact, she's mouthing those very words to me. "Linc, I've got to go. Marla is freaking out about something."

"All right. I'll see you soon," Linc says.

"Okay. Then," I say ending the call. I stare at the phone a few seconds wondering what the terms are for this peace treaty but then Marla is practically ripping the land-line phone cord out of the wall to reach me with it.

"What is going on with you, girlfriend? He just declared the nuclear war is over and there's a peace treaty, and he's going to go over the terms with me. What does that *even* mean?" I ask while the biggest smile ever recorded attacks my face.

"You need to take this call like right the fuck now." Marla gets this crazed look.

"Language," I say with a laugh and grab the receiver. "Hi. It's Tally here, Dr. Eldon. What's going on?"

"Tally. Oh, I'm so glad you're there." She sounds out of breath like she's half laughing or half crying.

"Dr. Eldon, is everything okay?"

"I'm supposed to be a professional about all of this but I just can't help it. I'm just so happy for you."

She's giddy too. What is going on with everyone, today?

"What's going on, Dr. Eldon?"

"Your test results are back. Tally...are you sitting down? Go sit down."

I walk over to the kitchen dinette and slide on in on the bench side. "Now, I am," I say impatiently. "There, I'm sitting. What's up, Dr. Eldon? You're freaking me out."

I hear her sigh big. "Okay, I decided to run a complete work-up on all your blood work, including hCG levels—"

"Okay," I grin at Marla assuring her I'm fine. "Whatever hCG levels are. Fine. Are they good?"

"Yes, Tally. They're good. They're *high*. They're high because you're pregnant."

"What did you just say?" I ask.

"Tally, you're pregnant. Of course, I didn't think to do the physical exam today which would tell us so much more, but I did have the lab run the levels and they confirmed it *twice* for me. I don't know why I'm getting so emotional about all of this," she says. "I'm just so happy for you. Gosh, can you tell me when your last period was or even the last time you had sexual intercourse?"

Doctors say sexual intercourse like the rest of us say, *Wonder Bread*. It's funny and weird. It causes me to laugh and it takes a few seconds to recover.

"Um. That would have been about two months ago. May 14th? Is this really happening? I thought you said that I couldn't get...that this wouldn't happen."

My heart begins to race. I grip the table. Marla slides in across from me and grabs my hand and squeezes it tight.

"I know. I didn't want to get your hopes up. It's just so devastating to go through all the steps and not get pregnant. The thing is I'm not ready to call this a high-risk pregnancy, but we need to be on top of this and take all the necessary precautions until I've done an ultrasound. You carried Cara to full-term less two weeks. But I'm not really keen on your dancing past twelve weeks if that, for one. Obviously, you have a few weeks before you need to let your director know, but not much more than that."

"A few weeks?" I ask faintly.

"Well, based on paper calculations with the date of May 14th, I'd say you're about nine weeks. We need to do the ultrasound to get the exact due date, but right now I'd put it around mid-February."

"Like Valentine's Day?"

"Around that. Plus or minus a few days."

Marla is dancing around the kitchen.

I think I want to smack her.

"And there's absolutely no way I can give you authorization to go to Moscow knowing you're pregnant until I've done an ultrasound. Frankly, I'm not crazy about you traveling out of the country right now. But look, I'm actually going to be at the Alamo Square office, and I put you down for nine tomorrow morning. Can you make it? That way we can just confirm everything looks good and we can both stop worrying."

Words. Need some words here.

Words would be good about now.

"Tally?" Dr. Eldon says.

"Sorry. I'm…just…I'm beyond stunned. Sure. I guess… Tomorrow. I'll make it work. Thank you for fitting me. So, we'll know more tomorrow."

"Well, we know quite enough today. You're pregnant. Around nine weeks. Congratulations. I know how much you wanted this."

"Yes. For some time. That's all we wanted. Now?" I take a shaky breath. "I don't know. It's overwhelming to say the least."

"It's early," she consoles. "Just go about your normal routine. No alcohol. Watch the shellfish. Exercise is fine. So is sex. The usual stuff you've been doing. I'll go over it all tomorrow. It's all good. We'll do an ultrasound, an exam, and get the due date nailed down and then we can go from there. Maybe we can even talk about the trip to Moscow. I know we're cutting it close with your travel plans, but we'll know more tomorrow. It's just amazing news and I'm so happy for you. Congratulations."

"Right. Okay. Thank you so much…I think. Thanks for calling me and everything." I hang up the phone and stare over at Marla who is happy crying and just waiting. "Oh. My. God."

"You're pregnant," she says without hesitation. "I put it together at the restaurant but I didn't want to freak you out. This is beyond amazing."

Marla's already tapping away on her iPhone. Dr. Eldon might be able to wait until tomorrow for an official due date but my bestie won't be waiting.

"What do you mean you figured it out at the restaurant?"

"The tuna sandwich for breakfast? The hamburger you finished at lunch? Ring a bell? It should. You ate the weirdest stuff when you were pregnant with Cara. Plus, the way you look all blissed out is the biggest clue of all," Marla says sounding like Velma on Scooby-Doo putting all the clues together and solving the case. She holds up her phone in triumph. "February 16th. You're like nine weeks already. The first trimester is almost over, baby."

"No way," I say gasping for air.

"Yes way. Come on." She grabs my hand pulls me up. "We'll run our own tests. Just to convince you."

Marla and I race up the stairs because she knows I have pregnancy tests here and in our minds this all needs to be confirmed by First Response. We like theirs the best because the label is easy to read and it's two minutes faster than the next leading brand. Marla watches me from the bathroom doorway. We have thrown protocol out the window and I'm shaking from head to toe and trying to pee on a stick while she looks on with this wide smile. My hand is now soaked with urine and I don't even care. I hold it over the sink and we lean over it together as the plus sign comes up in the test window in a matter of sixty seconds.

"Oh my God. This cannot not be happening," I say to the mirror and my best friend.

"Double negative," we say together.

"Oh but it is and the timing is epic, as in, ever," Marla says looking blissed out herself.

I place the stick on the sink and tear into another test box. I have like twenty of them because there was a time I was obsessed with getting pregnant and Linc was all too willing help me out. I'm peeing on stick and my hand again. It's harder this time because the adrenaline has kicked in at full-warp speed, and I can barely concentrate.

And if that isn't enough I hear a distinct guy's voice calling from downstairs. I descend quickly to Linda Blair exorcist mode. "Do not tell him. Go get him outside. I'll pack up Cara's clothes. Are you *listening* to me?"

I'm possessed. I'm yelling at Marla and watching the stick turn with a plus sign all over again. I set that test down on the sink next to the first one.

"This is insane." I call out to Marla as I grab the soap and wash my hands.

I've managed to go all over my yoga pants, so on top of everything else, now I'm stepping into the shower for a quick rinse. Thirty seconds later wrapping a towel myself and thirty seconds after that I'm racing through my dresser drawers looking for underwear of any kind and jumping into those, then pulling on a T-shirt and jamming my legs into a pair of black jeans only to discover they are tight as I zip them up, which is completely ridiculous but explains just about everything surreal about this day.

Suddenly, out of breath, I sink to the floor and tell myself not to cry, and this is how Marla finds me—in the middle of the master bedroom floor in tight jeans that still kind of fit and a black T-shirt that is actually turned inside out, plus I'm not wearing a bra of any kind.

"Let's start over," she says eying my outfit with notable fashion sense disapproval.

"They're tight. Already. How is that even possible?" I ask bewildered and losing control all at once.

"It's might be possible. I started showing early and you're tiny. It's happening."

I look at her with a raised eyebrow.

"He's outside pushing Cara on a swing and checking out the kiddie pool. I told him you were on a call with Mikhail."

"That's good. That's good. Good job."

"Tally, I've bought you about six minutes of time to pack up Cara's things and get yourself dressed in something else or at least turn the T-shirt right side out before he's going to wonder what the hell is going on."

"How does he look?"

She grins. "He looks like he just got sent up from the Grizzlies to the Giants, which would make anyone's day, but I'm pretty sure your news will send him over the moon."

"No moon." I still sit on the floor.

Marla comes over and sits down directly across from me. We grab each other hands like yogis do.

"You have to tell him. It's his baby. Don't even try to deny it with me. I can't even believe I'm hearing this. You have been wallowing around here for *months.*" I hold up two fingers. She ignores me. "Turning your life upside down for the silliest of reasons all in the name of some weird-ass insanity you call *clarified* and the rest of us just label *plain crazy*. So, all you're going to do is forgive the man and get on with it."

"It's not that simple." I shake my head side-to-side

"Oh yes. Oh yes, it is. And if you don't tell him, *I will.* I've had it. I won't allow this. I heard all about your nuclear behavior in Fresno from over two months ago. I saw it all on TMZ and then it just got worse from there. You *cannot* do this to him. Or yourself. You just can't."

"Pick a *side*, Marla."

"I just did." She gets up somewhat awkwardly, glares back at me which I return full force, and just stalks off.

I'm slow to get up because the jeans are tight. *Like uncomfortably tight. Like too tight. Shit.*

I hold onto the doorway and fight off being dizzy and grope the walls as I make my way down the hallway toward Marla's retreating back. "Marla, you cannot interfere in my life this way. You cannot! It's not fair. I won't allow it."

She whirls around.

"No! Too many times I've stood by you and watched as you allowed all the best opportunities pass you by. Grow up, Tally. No one gets a free pass. No one! Yes, you've had it rough. It's been downright tragic at times, but even Holly would side with me on this. She would. Gah! The voice of reason has always been Holly. Are you listening to her? Can you hear her? She's screaming at you right now. Tell him. Tell him. Tell him. Do you hear her? Because I sure as hell can."

Four pairs of eyes watch us from the landing below. Two pairs are this amazing grey-blue. Andy is open-mouthed holding a subdued Elliott who has probably never seen his mother have a meltdown of any kind because the girl exhibits angelic traits about ninety-nine percent of the time.

"Momma, are you okay? Look. *Daddy's* here," Cara says grabbing Linc's hand who swiftly pulls her up into his arms.

"I'm fine." I reward them all with my best stage smile and remain standing at the top of the stairs.

Marla descends the stairs like a beauty queen holding onto the banister and immediately takes Elliott from Andy without uttering a single word to anyone, although she does exchange a sympathetic look with Linc. Plus, I swear I see her roll her eyes. Andy makes an excuse to go to her studio downstairs, and I give her a little wave and a reassuring nod when she shoots me this is-everything-okay-with-you look.

It's all going well from the standpoint that I too descend the stairs, just like Marla did a few minutes ago, until I again realize my shirt is on inside out and also backwards.

Ten seconds later, my baby girl is pointing this out. "Momma, your shirt's on wrong. You look funny." Cara laughs. I avoid Linc's grey-blue gaze all together.

"Yeah, Mommy got dressed in a hurry. And I forgot to pack your stuff for the overnight with Daddy, too."

"I'll do it," Linc says.

My eyes automatically go up and over to him and get caught in the tracking-device gaze he's got going with me.

"Okay. It's just for the night. Right? Her laundry is folded on her bed. There's a few things for her on mine if you need them. That would be great. Thanks for helping me out."

"You're welcome." He gets this sexy I've-been-sent-up-by-the-Giants smile and the scent of his cologne has this dizzying effect on me. He still carries Cara as he goes to climb the stairs. "Hi," he says softly as he passes by me.

"Hi," I say back while telling myself to breathe.

Then, I seek out Marla, who is having trouble coming back down from her own temper tantrum from minutes before. She stands to one side holding her head in one hand and Elliott with the other.

I go over to her and put my arms around her and Elliott. "I'm sorry. I suck. I love you."

She lifts her head up and looks at me. "That about covers it." Her lips twitch, and she presses together so she won't smile. "I do love you even when you're a B-I-T-C-H."

"Especially then, I imagine." We go for the full-court-press-frontal after that.

"I'm sorry I yelled."

"I'm sorry I caused you to yell," I say.

We're squishing Elliott, who kind of pushes at my boobs, which are sore, which is completely insane and ridiculous. I pull away and cross my arms over them and yelp a belated response.

"Nine months or more of delicious cleavage. Are we the lucky girls or what?" Marla asks.

"Stop it." I smile anyway, then start to laugh and find I can't really stop. We collapse to the living-room rug laughing until the tears start to roll down our faces. Elliott snuggles in between us. And this is how Linc and Cara find us five minutes later.

"Tally, can I talk to you alone?" Linc asks.

It's a simple enough request. Déjà vu sets in right away at his words. I sit up at once and look up at him.

He looks good. Too good. Tan. Tall. Perfect. He's got on a black Polo shirt with the Grizzlies logo. *A rebel to the end.* It makes him even more attractive.

"I need to talk to you. *Alone. Now.*" He extends his hand and pulls me up from the floor to a stand.

"Oh. Okay. Sure. Peace treaty terms. Got it." I half-smile at him but he just studies me even more intently and isn't actually smiling.

Uh-oh. What now?

What more could possibly happen to me today?

I mean, really.

I completely ignore the implications of the scene that Marla and I just had in front of everyone.

"We'll wait. We'll watch Cara," Marla says softly from behind me.

I turn to her, confused and on edge. "What? This will just take a second and—"

"In fact, you know what? Andy and I are going to take the kids to dinner. We'll swing back in a couple of hours or so. That way, you two can talk." She gets this wicked smile as I pull her up from the floor just like Linc did for me. Then she goes right over to Linc and hugs him. "Congrats again, Linc. On returning to the Giants' lineup, I mean. Charlie is stoked. We all are."

"Thanks, that means a lot," he says to her. "Congrats to you. A girl. Awesome."

"I know, right? Thanks!" She laughs. "Anyway, Tally and I are going shopping for baby clothes within the week for sure now." Marla steals a look at me and turns so Linc doesn't see her face and mouths, "tell him."

I give her the I've-got-this-signal with a lift of my finger. It takes a lot of willpower not to just flip her off which would better convey my exact thoughts, but we've got the children around, so I refrain. *Somehow.*

It takes all of five minutes for the four of them to clear out. I actually think Andy was stationed at the basement door awaiting orders; it was that fast.

And now, I'm alone with Lincoln Presley.

"So you wanted to…talk to me?" I look up at him and swallow hard suddenly nervous.

In fact, I feel like I could almost throw up which is weird.

And then? The power of suggestion takes over, and I'm racing past him in search of the downstairs restroom.

Déjà vu pays a visit. Or is that karma? One of those.

CHAPTER THIRTY-EIGHT

adore you

TALLY

E'S HOLDING MY HAIR BACK. AGAIN. Déjà vu. Karma pay-back is in full force. The vomiting incident involving Patron was worse, although I still manage to hit my hair and his hand with this one. He's busy wetting a towel and dabbing at my hair and face. I take the towel from him and avoid the incredible urge to cry, but it's close. Dr. Eldon's news hasn't quite settled in on me completely yet; so instead, I say, "I. Am. Going. To. Go. Change."

He follows me up the stairs. "I'll run you a bath."

I turn as I hear him stop at the guest room and stare at him questioning his motives but simply nod and manage to say, "okay."

The test sticks. My bathroom.

My heart races as fast as my body moves. I sweep them into a drawer, strip off my dirty clothes, and grab a towel from the rack and wrap it around me just as he appears in the doorway.

"You okay?" He asks. "Must have been something you ate." He gets this twisted-up face where he's kind of smiling and yet his eyes are now this blazing blue like he's mad about something, but he just watches me warily and doesn't say anything.

"Must have been." I'm having trouble reconciling the scene. There's a role reversal of sorts going on. He's a little pissed, and I'm a little blissed. The incongruence makes me want to laugh, but somehow I'm guessing he won't appreciate that right now. I slip past him. "You're running water in the guest bath?"

"Yeah."

"The tub's overflowing."

Sure enough water's streaming down the hallway just like before all those months ago. I catch my lip between my teeth, both remembering and feeling the loss of the past, but then I just laugh and he's staring at me intently for a few seconds before he actually turns and sees the water is indeed coming down the hallway toward us.

"Fuck," he says it just like before but this time he grabs my hand and we walk past the mess together. "Be careful. Don't slip," he says sounding impatient.

We reach the guest bath, and he shuts off the faucet and starts throwing towels everywhere. Just like before. I'm fascinated in watching him move about the small space. He's lit candles. The air smells like lavender. I pull the towel around me tighter reminiscing about the past scene that went just like this, calculating the differences, and feeling the nostalgia for it all—for us—all around me.

"Tally? You can get in. I'll make you some tea. Do you think you can eat something? Maybe some toast?"

"Tea and toast would be great." I look at him completely blown away by his generosity but acutely aware of his indifference.

He seems a little far away.

Subdued.

Something.

It's not the same. He's not the same. I'm not the same.

Of course, it makes me want to cry because the emotional pendulum—given Dr. Eldon's news less than an hour ago—starts to move in on me. I watch Linc retreat from the bathroom, lean my head up against the tub, and try to relax a few minutes.

On some level, I prepare myself for things to get weird. And we're short on time like always. Marla and Andy will be back soon enough with the kids. And we haven't even said anything of significance to each other as of yet. Nothing meaningful anyway.

The bath grows cold. It's been ten minutes since Linc left and I'm bored. The thing is I don't want to spend time with myself. Alone, I can feel myself start to splinter and all kinds of thoughts intrude upon my psyche. I have basically three weeks before I have to tell Mikhail and give up dancing which means no fall line-up for Tally. No Swan Lake. No Nutcracker at Christmastime. I can probably return by March which would mean only missing four weeks or so of rehearsals for the spring performances but still, it will be a long while before I'll dance again. Bolshoi. Out. SFB? In. Most likely if I continue to stay in Mikhail Rostov's good graces, but how will that work if I'm not dancing?

"Oh God."

"Get out of your head." Linc stands over me saying this.

He proffers tea and toast. He sets the cup of hot tea and the plate of toast on the widest edge of the bathtub. "You okay? Everything all right?"

I start to form the words *I'm fine*. I may actually breathe them but then I stop.

This cat and mouse game is too taxing, and I'm tired of playing it. With him. Without him. I need to know where we stand and I need to know like right the fuck now. He sits on the edge of the tub and trails his hand through the water. *I swear he's baiting me. I swear it's working.* "I have something to tell you." My voice trembles as do my hands. *Really.* I need a little help, a little faith, and my hands betray me along with my voice. *Great.*

"I have something to tell you too," he says. "You first." He smiles ever so slightly.

I stall by drinking the tea, then taking a bite of the toast, and pronounce it good. "Fit for a queen," I say with a little laugh.

What am I doing? Flirting? Why?

"So Marla and I gave up the word *fuck* because Cara may have started saying it one day."

I wince because this is seriously bad stuff but really I'm just trying to soften him up for the more sobering news I have to tell him, of course.

"Cara's swearing?"

Now he smiles.

"She doesn't *know* she's swearing. It's just a word she picked up. It's not like she knows why we say it. In any case, I've had to give it up, and it's been a bit of hardship, and I was wondering...if perhaps... we could try it slow. Note the absence of the word. And see how it loses some of its sexiness and forcefulness with that edict alone? But I was wondering if you were good with slow and if, in fact, you are good for slow, then we best get on with it because they're due back in forty-five minutes and my throwing up episode puts us seriously behind."

He looks a little pissed. I'm getting a little anxious at how thunderous he looks, actually.

"Why would I do that? I'm not good with slow or *good for it*. I've got an early day with Cara tomorrow. I think I'll leave you to your tea and toast and just wait for Cara downstairs. Do you *mind*?"

"Do I mind?"

Tears rush my eyes. I make a show of taking a hand and wiping my face so water mixes with the tears and have to hope he won't notice. "Nooooooooooooooooo. I guess not. Okay."

Now his gaze is more intense and I kind of laugh in an attempt to get it together.

"How long are you going to keep this up?" He asks gently.

"Keep what up?" I ask nervously. He's confusing me. He's got this bemused look on his face.

"You gave up the word fuck. You proposition me with the idea of a slow F-U-C-K telling me we best get on with it because Marla and Andy and the kids will be back soon. Why don't you say what you really mean, for once, Tally? Just say it. Or should I say it? Should I tell you that about an hour ago your daughter and I were in your bedroom getting clothes that you directed us to pack up, but then

Cara had to go potty and she disappears into this very bathroom for a few minutes and when she returns she's holding up two pregnancy test sticks in her chubby little hands and asking me, "what are these for, Daddy?" And I was just wondering, frankly, wondering is not a strong enough description." He runs his hands through his hair and sighs. "I was just *wondering* if you were going to ever *fucking tell me* that you're pregnant because I'm pretty sure those aren't Marla's test sticks since that question has been asked and answered for Mrs. Masterson. Or is this between you and *Sam*? Because *I*, for one, would like to know what the fuck is going on!"

"*Language,* Prez."

"Great and now you're mad. *Perfect.* You know what? I can't concentrate when you're all wet and naked in the bathtub pretending we're just platonic friends. And don't think I don't recognize the *friend-zone* with you. So if you don't mind, I'd like you to get dressed and then come talk to me. I'll be here another five minutes and then I'm out. Tell Cara I'll pick her up for the zoo tomorrow morning. Have her ready by nine."

He leaves.

He just leaves.

I spend a few more minutes in the bath, and it finally dawns on me that the water is really cold. I gingerly get out of the tub, towel myself off, and grab my bathrobe from the back of the door.

"You blew it," I say to the girl in the mirror. "Nice job." The girl in the mirror cries and ruins the makeup on her face as fast as it's being applied. She combs her hair. She gives up on the rest of it and walks into the bedroom.

The place is lit up with candles flickering shadows across everything. *And Linc is here.*

"I think I'm done," I say with a nervous laugh taking a special interest in the candles all around, "with the bath."

I turn in a complete circle in wonder and look over at him.

"Really?" Linc asks.

"Really."

"So. So far, the biggest news you have to share with me is that you and Marla have a pact going and can no longer use the word *fuck* because our kid is picking up on that."

I nod. "Elliott too. Charlie busted Marla for it. What kind of parents are we? Of course, Marla is perfect otherwise, but I am... hopeless." My hand goes up watering my face again as the tears betray me by coming down faster.

"How long are you going to keep this up?" He asks again like before.

"I think I'm done."

"Okay. Then. Tally, why don't you tell me what it is you *really* have to tell me that is causing you to cry as if I'm not going to notice that at all."

"Okay."

Six minutes go by.

The candle light flickers and casts shadows across his face. I get caught up in the nuance of all of that. Finally, I steel myself with a fresh cleansing breath while he just patiently waits for me to speak. "Well. Okay. Then," I say uncertain but force a smile.

The corners of his mouth turn up ever so slightly at this.

"The thing is...I...*we* are pregnant. Nine weeks. I just found out two hours ago. I have to stop dancing in three weeks. I'm due to leave for Russia the day after tomorrow. I have an appointment with Dr. Eldon tomorrow morning at nine which blows the zoo plans if you want to go with me."

He gets this joyous look and a wide smile. It is particularly distracting. I stop and take in air readying myself for the next part.

"Go on," he says like a prompt.

"And I was wondering if you wanted to spend the rest of your life with me, as more than a friend, despite my ill-timed ability to get pregnant whenever we have clandestine sex it seems. I was hoping that you could possibly overlook my sometimes beyond cruel tendencies that could be classified as downright crazy behavior toward you these last few months as well as some past transgressions of this nature that you may not remember. I sincerely hope you just know and accept my intentions are somewhat good and might even be considered somewhat pure. It is fair to say that my fury and hurt over Trinna Danner was real enough, bordered nuclear. But I want you to know that I've forgiven you, and I sincerely hope you'll forgive me too for my part."

He's stopped smiling. He has this dazed look. He's taken to the chair that sits near the window and stares out it.

I swallow hard. "I guess what I'm trying to say—and not very well—is I've come to the conclusion that it's actually possible, if we both really try hard and perhaps at the same time, we can find the balance to the fire between us. Restore it in fact. To before. To the big move moment," I smile at him, "when I knew that I loved you—fell in love with you all over again—to this one when I know I love you no matter what you remember or what you'd really like to forget. In any case, to *now*, I love you, Elvis. And I'll be your water and you can be my air, and we'll just figure it all out as we go along into forever because we're together. If you want."

He holds his head between his hands and is no longer even looking at me. "Elvis?"

He looks up at me with this little smile. "How do you want to do this? Either I strip down and get naked with you back in the bathtub like before. Or, we continue this discussion here in this bed. It's your call."

"My *call*. Did you say like *before*? Do you remember before?" I whisper.

"Some of it. It comes back like parts of a scene from an old movie." He nods slowly. "Yeah, you were upset one night about pretty much everything and I gave you a bath and then I joined you." He gets this uncertain smile.

"Yeah." I lick my lips and search his face. "And you remember?"

"I think I do." Then he frowns. "I don't want you to take me back thinking it's all coming back. Only bits and pieces have returned. I'm still getting headaches. I still don't remember everything." He sighs. "But I still…love you.""

"Elvis," I say softly crawling across the middle of the bed. "Come here." He gets up, strips off his shirt and kicks off his shoes and jeans. Commando has the power. *Holy shit.*

I get on my knees to meet him. We are willing bodies comprised of arms and legs. He kisses me and then we both move in on each other as the fire between us combines to make a bigger flame. No hesitation on my part and none on his. I settle down on his shaft because I'm most definitely ready for him as he is for me.

We take it slow, which is its own particular brand of eroticism because I've missed him, and I know he's missed me, and it takes so much discipline to come at each other slowly and not rush into the good part that will take us both over the edge. The connection between us has a memory, and it comes to life with every touch and trailing kiss of his, and I give it back to him in kind.

Love. This is love. What else could it be?

"Let's not talk anymore," I say nipping his neck with my teeth and laughing. "No more talking."

"Got it. No more talking," he says moving even closer in on me. "Nice. We're finally getting to number nine with *Tally's Epic Plan*. It's like Christmas in July." He sighs big and plants kisses along my shoulder and laughs.

"I thought this was the peace treaty you were telling me about? These are the terms, right?" I ask with a laugh.

"It's that too."

"I accept," I say airily.

"I thought you might."

We make the most of our time in exploring number nine despite the implications of the fearsome foursome's return. I tell Linc that Marla will figure it out and give us some extra time. She's resourceful that way, my bestie.

As we finish, I settle in on his chest and listen to his heartbeat as it beats so steady against my cheek.

"Tally," he whispers after a few minutes. "Was it always like this? *Before?*"

I lift my head and look up at his face. He looks a little anxious, a little unsure, which is funny considering we just did the deed at an epic number nine level.

"Every time is more amazing than the last. No need to look back, Elvis." I crawl all the way up onto his chest and settle in on him as his arms come around me. "There's no need to look back. This is *us* moving forward. That's all we need."

"Okay. Then," he says simply.

"Okay. Then."

CHAPTER
THIRTY-NINE

you're still the one

TALLY

DID YOU KNOW YOU ONLY NEED five people to get married? Pastor Dan, the groom, the bride, Charlie and Marla. We have extras though. My parents. Marla's parents. Charlie's parents. Tommy and Cara and Elliott and Andy. And Davis. And Kimberley and Brad. Did you know if you request a wedding date on Thursday instead of Saturday for the little church in Half Moon Bay that Pastor Dan Reeve can fit you right in? And that a dress off the rack fits and flows just fine and if your future-father-in-law buys it and brings it to surprise you—it is its own special kind of atonement. Did you know that flowers sold and bought at a roadside stand smell wonderful and tied with a white satin ribbon look amazing and perfect?

And finally, did you know cupcakes are everyone's favorite dessert and you can stack them as high as you want? At least, my mom can. Of course, the best thing about cupcakes is you can steal a few (*four*) before the ceremony to appease the two hungry children whimpering in their little flower girl and ring bearer outfits that they are starving almost as much as the bride and the matron of honor. Marla and I are carefully peeling the wrapper from the last one and sharing the last bites when Charlie walks in. Never mind no guy is supposed to see the bride before the big *I do* part. He looks a little shaken and I have one of those heart stopping moments, but then bravely look at him with a raised eyebrow and a it's-my-wedding-day-bridal look before asking, "Charlie, what's up?"

Marla is already berating him for barging in on us. She takes her matron of honor duties very seriously.

"He wants to talk to you now, before the ceremony, before things get started."

"Why?" I ask suddenly afraid of what Linc could possibly have to say that can't wait until after.

"He wouldn't say. He's got a bad headache, and a shot of whiskey didn't help him out." Charlie grins but looks a little worried which causes me to worry. "He insisted I come find you. He said he has something to say, Tally, and he needs to say it *before*. That's all he would tell me."

"Is he okay?"

"He's acting kind of weird and he insists on talking to you first. I left him talking to Brad to come find you. They just got here from the airport. We're almost ready but he said to go find you. So here I am."

"Fine. Fine. I'm sure it's nothing." I force a brave smile and reassure the small bridal group, the cherubs, Marla and my mom as much as myself. "Groom nerves. I'm sure that's all it is. Let me go talk to him." I pull up the front of my dress and gather up the train from behind and race down the other end of the hallway.

Ten seconds later, I burst into the dressing room designated for the groom and his groomsmen only to find Linc standing all alone at the far window quietly gazing out of it. His arm is over his head like he's staving off pain.

I'll give him pain.

"This better be good, Elvis. *Seriously.* Charlie looks like he's about to attend a funeral instead of standing up for you at this wedding. You've freaked him out. Just so you know we're due to walk down the aisle in fifteen minutes. There's got to be a very good reason why you had to see me—*the bride*—before the ceremony and mess with the whole voodoo hoodoo superstitions associated with *that*. So, let's hear it. What could you possibly have to say to me that couldn't wait?"

Full stop.

"Oh. *Hi,* Brad. I didn't see you."

"Hey, Tally. I was checking on the groom here. He's good to go, but he wanted to talk to you first." Brad gets this easy reassuring smile.

I haven't spent a great deal of time around Kimberley's husband, but he helped me out during the whole LA thing, so I am partial to his brand of charm. I smile back at this smooth-talking blond giant whom Kimberley has married and try to make up for bursting into the room like *Bridezilla* by flashing him my biggest star smile—the one I reserve for Cinderella or Giselle performances to really wow the crowd.

Brad laughs a little and then the good doctor turns to Linc, clasps the groom by the shoulders and leans in to say something I'm apparently not to supposed to hear.

"All right," Brad says. "We'll see you two downstairs in a few minutes."

Linc nods at him and then turns to me as Brad slips out and the door clicks behind him.

"What's up, Elvis?" I say softly.

"Tally."

His utterance of my name causes my heart to beat faster. Then, he turns more fully toward me looking a little pale. My breath rushes out of my lungs in one big swoosh. "Don't. Do. This. To. Me."

"Tally, I should have remembered you."

He looks unsteady as he takes my hand and gently pulls me to him. I grab his arms for balance and then step back to take a good look at his face which looks beyond tormented.

"I don't want to make you do something you don't want to do," he says gently.

"I want this." My throat constricts, and I can't say more. I take another step back from him and bend over, so the tears rushing my face won't ruin Marla's stellar make-up job. "Please just tell me this extraordinary reason you have for giving me a panic attack, today of all days."

I breathe through my nose in an attempt to stave it off. It's been a while.

Since that time with Sam?

Sam. Shit.

And now, Linc. Oh God.

He's going to break my heart. Again.

I probably deserve it after the nuclear behavior in Fresno.

"Don't do this to me, Elvis. Not today." I straighten, slipping past him and go to the window furthest away from him and stare out at the church lawn so green and perfect and the Pacific beyond that is so blue and vast and epic. *Like us.*

Linc comes up behind me. "Tally. You're so beautiful. I don't deserve you."

I turn from the window and then step into his arms. "Thank you? Why are you freaking out like this? Today of all days?" I reach up and trace his face. "It's okay that you don't remember before. It *is*. I've told you this at least a dozen times since Tuesday. At the *zoo*."

I actually smile up at him, remembering our time at the zoo, after the ultrasound when we learned everything was okay with this baby, and my official due date is February 16th, and I was kissing him in front of the lion exhibit well really just about everywhere in that zoo.

The past forty-eight hours have been amazing. And now we're at Half Moon Bay with this whirlwind of a wedding that appears to be all kinds of grand because of its poignant simplicity and the arduous path we have taken just to get here.

A brilliant plan has come together, and we leave for Florida next week. I've promised him that we would attend all his games all summer. We'll be in the stands cheering him on, watching him play. Cara and I are going to be there because that's what ballplayers' families do. We are a ballplayer's family as of two days ago when he slipped a ring on my finger—a different one that is brilliant and new. Like us. A symbol of us starting over, starting again. All of that.

Linc touches my face and traces my lips. "It's not okay. That's the thing. I love you, but I should remember you. Tally, you're my water," he says slowly. "I should remember that much."

"I think you do. Like Brad told you, more of it seems to be coming back, more every day. Maybe it's mixed up with new memories as much as the past, but it's fine. It's fine with me, Linc."

"So why did you really leave me in Fresno? Why didn't you stay?"

I step out of his arms again. My heart races. We're at the pinnacle and suddenly I realize it really could go either way.

Why did I leave?

I know why.

He doesn't.

"Our love was *epic*. I couldn't really breathe properly without you." I look out the window again and begin counting the whitecaps of the ocean to steady myself. "And then you got hurt. Then you didn't remember. I wasn't strong enough to remember for both of us. I had to think of Cara. You were different. You didn't love me anymore, and I didn't want to force you into a life you no longer knew to want."

"That explains it all before Fresno. But what happened there?"

I turn back to him visibly pleading with him to understand. "I went a little crazy. I felt like I was a consolation prize more than ever for you. I couldn't get past Trinna Danner and what she could give you that I couldn't. I was angry at you, but mostly angry at myself for being so cruel and there was Sam. He was my go-to guy; I thought I could move on so I came home to start things over with Sam."

I shake my head side-to-side. "But you were there—in my mind—all the time. I couldn't shake your image, and after a while I realized I didn't want to. I began to solely focus on work making Mikhail happy, and simply ensuring Cara was happy, and I think I grew stronger. Strong enough to face my fears. *You. Love. Loss.* Somewhere along the way, I changed."

I smile up at him and trace his face. "I finally realized that I couldn't control love anymore than I could control the weather. Of course, for a while, I thought I could outrun it, outrun *you*. Thus, the plans for Moscow and toying with the idea of the Bolshoi Ballet and working with Sasha again." I tilt my head and really look at him.

"But I already knew it was all so temporary. I couldn't leave the country forever. I couldn't leave *you*. Forever." I nod, but the rest of the words won't come for a few minutes. Finally, I say, "I thought I wanted a simple life, but what I now realize is that life, simple or not, is with you. I need a life...with you. It has always been you. I need you, Linc. I need you in my life for always. We are two parts of a bigger whole when we're together. Maybe that doesn't make any sense to you right now. Maybe you only partially love me as much as you used to. But after Fresno, after finally telling Sam *no*, I got clarity. I know, *me, clarified*."

I shake my head and smile and grab his hand and put it to my lips. "What we have is so rare, and it's so much bigger than the two of us, and yet; it takes both of us to make it work. And it's not about this baby. Or Cara. It's like Pastor Dan said, "it's about the two of us." The thing is, Elvis, you are my air, and I'm your water and that's the way it's been since the beginning, since we first met. And it's not about anyone else. It's about us. It's always been about us, and I don't want to lose that. And, *you*?" I pause and slowly smile. "You wouldn't want to lose that either, Linc. Trust me."

"That's what I thought." He nods slowly. "And I *do* trust you."

There has been too much truth telling in the last ten minutes, and I can't take much more.

"So what's going on? Why did you need to talk to me before the ceremony?"

"I just wanted to make sure this is what you wanted."

I nod, and he sighs big.

"I was in love with a girl who didn't appear to love me back. You, Tally. That day you left me in Fresno. I knew it then, but I was too angry with you for leaving me, and I buried my feelings for you deep because I thought you had Sam, and I didn't want to interfere if you'd truly found someone else. But we had Cara, and I thought I would start there. I also knew the only way to have the life I wanted was to fully concentrate on baseball, so I could return to the Giants, so I could come home and work things out with you. To be with you. It's always been you. All summer long all I've been thinking about is you. You kept me going. You brought me here. You brought me back. I just wanted you to know my heart realized it has always been you, even if my head hadn't caught up to that fact, until—"

"Are we going to do this thing or what?" Charlie asks clearing his throat as he bursts through the door with Marla following closely behind him. Their hands are linked.

"You're timing is like amazingly bad, bro," Linc says in exasperation.

Charlie doesn't miss a beat. "Well, Pastor Dan is wondering what's up and the kids are going a little crazy. I'm not sure how much longer Tally's mom is going to be able to hold them off from eating every last one of those cupcakes. And frankly, I think we've all waited for this moment long enough."

"True that," say Marla with a giggle. She links her arm with her husband's.

"So are we doing this thing or what?" Charlie asks.

"It's up to Tally," Linc says looking at me with this secret smile.

I'm confused, trying to remember all of what Linc said to me in the last five minutes before the best man and matron of honor so artfully interrupted.

I nod anyway as if we'd just agreed on the grocery list. Then, I slowly smile. "Let's do this. I wrote some killer vows, and I so want to say them to you in front of everyone, Elvis."

"Yeah," he says with a sexy smile. "Me too, *Miss Cloves and Vanilla.* Me too."

Cara is restless. She's waving around her bouquet of flowers like it's one of her Barbie dolls, while Elliott joins in the fun doing the same with the small silk pillow that the rings are tied to with a little white ribbon.

Borrowed. The ring pillow is borrowed from Marla's wedding.

I've got these things covered. Marla is busy trying to keep both Cara and Elliott in line, but the flower girl and ring bearer have had enough. Then the clouds part and the sun's rays stream through the stained-glass windows behind Pastor Dan's head just when he's getting to the good part—the exchange of vows. I decide it's a sign that even God thinks the two of us getting married is a good idea.

Linc winks at me, squeezes my hands, and tells me everything is going to be okay like he always does. Pastor Dan directs him to go first with his vows like tradition dictates through all of time.

Linc smile wides as he slowly unfolds a piece of paper that looks a little worn to have just been written up yesterday. He holds up the weathered page and allows the breeze coming through the window to take it as if he's performing some sort of magic trick for us all.

"I know these by heart," he says, smiling at the scattering of family behind us, and then he looks at me so intently that I forget to breathe.

And the word *epic* comes to mind. Surely we've used the word a bit too often in the last half hour. Not believing that he can possibly have his lines for me memorized I smile somewhat encouraging. "Go ahead. Tell me you love me," I say after a few seconds when I see him hesitate. Everyone laughs.

"Tally, we met under the most extraordinary of circumstances. Your sister's life tragically ends, and our love for each other is fated with a single look on that Valentine's Day. It's been more than five years since that day. Five years, three months, sixteen days, two hours, and ten minutes since that first look in your eyes quenched the thirst in my heart. I love you. I'll love you forever in sickness and in health until death us do part, I'll be there for you. You're my water, Tally, you always have been. And I'll remember the day we first met forever and treasure you always for saving me, and I just thought I should be honest with you as we stand up in front of our families and friends and promise to love each other for all eternity that I remember all of it. The truth is I've fallen in love with you twice now, and each time is even more epic than the last. So just say yes, *Miss Cloves and Vanilla*," he says with this little secret smile.

Movement, words of any kind would destroy the moment and possibly me.

So I just stand there and breathe his air and take it all in.

Then all of his words begin to register with me. "You remember? Don't you?" I ask him quietly. "That's what you were trying to tell me before. You remember me. Don't you, Elvis?"

I brush back tears, but they keep on falling.

Linc nods and I know by the look in his eyes that all the versions of Lincoln Presley are here for me today. "You're impossible to forget. Forever."

He smiles.

My mother cries in the distance to my left. And soon, more crying can be heard from everyone else directly behind us.

Cara pulls at the folds of my gown asking if I'm okay. Linc is looking more certain by the minute, smiling wide, and assures Cara that everything is fine.

I have so much I want to say. I memorized my lines but now I can't think of a single one. A breeze from the open window to my left stirs my hair and veil. It brings me back and I smile as I find my voice and remember my vows for this man.

"Valentine's Day will forever be marked as sad because of Holly. You should all know that."

I turn toward Marla. She nods at me.

Then I turn looking at the small group surrounding us.

"I lose my twin and receive the gift that is Lincoln Presley for rest of my life with a single glance. But Holly's still here, you know. Watching all of us and laughing in her own special way. And she loves Linc. She loves that he makes me laugh…and cry…and feel. She loves that he tells me everything is going to be okay pretty much daily like she used to do, even if I only believe him half the time. She loves his patience, and his steadfast kindness that he shows to everyone but especially to me. She likes that he makes me meals and forces me to eat even when I tell him I already have because Holly knows the truth about me and so does Linc. He always has."

I turn to face my groom.

"Lincoln Presley, you are the very air I breathe. You give me the best of life and sustain hope and tether to me so closely that I never feel lost. You shield me from pain and heartbreak…when you can, and hold me up even when you are far away in heart, mind, and soul. You have given me love and life and Cara and more of yourself in the past five years than I deserve, although I've made up for much of that in this past one, as we all know, waiting for you."

I laugh a little but then it fades away.

"I've been waiting for you to remember. Although, deep down, in my heart, where Holly lives on, she told me to wait to just wait. Her words live on in the breeze where she whispers assurances so clearly. "He'll find you again," she said. "Just wait." And so I have. And here you are. And so I stand here before our family and friends truly grateful for having found you in the first place and again now and loving you the way that I do. You're my air, and I'll be your water every day of the week and twice on Sunday."

I hold his gaze and he smiles wide. "I say, yes. Let's grow old together, Elvis. So? Just say, *yes*."

"Yes," he says sweetly.

the end

ABOUT THE AUTHOR

K ATHERINE OWEN IS THE BESTSELLING AUTHOR of *This Much Is True, When I See You, Seeing Julia, Not To Us* as well as *The Truth About Air & Water*. Owen lives near Seattle with her husband and son and daughter, where she is working on her next novel.

ACKNOWLEDGMENTS

THANK YOU TO ALL THE READERS and bloggers—fans of my work. It is because of you that this second novel about Linc and Tally was even written. Your encouragement and enthusiasm about This Much Is True led to the continuing story line (or, is that saga?) for Linc and Tally. I hope you enjoyed this additional look at their epic love story. Thank you all so much!

I should stop here. Stop here, KO. You'll just get yourself into trouble if you go on and on…Huh…the thing is I always imagined myself as Meryl Streep at the Oscars on stage one day and getting to the microphone, mostly glad I didn't fall on the stairs, although Jennifer Lawrence *owns* that role, and it makes you love her even more. *I digress.*

Anyway as Meryl, I would say, "I thank no one. I owe this epic moment all to myself. Thank you. Good night. Tip your waitress. Run along. Nothing to see here." And then I would flip off all the one-star reviewers and all those agents who sent me rejection notes, especially those who asked for the full copy of my manuscript and never contacted me again. Gah! It would be in such bad form and awesome for a few seconds anyway.

But then you know what? You want to thank those people too because despite their thoughtless even sometime vicious selves, they do spur you on. *I digress again.*

But truly? There are those people who actually matter, who do the little things that add up to the epic (there's that word again… I may have to retire it from my vocabulary along with the f-word

375

after this novel) that make you feel whole again and encourage you when you are ready to GIVE IT ALL UP. Those people need to be thanked, and so I do.

This is an incomplete list and if I didn't mention you specifically by name, please don't hate me. There will be other books and this will end up being a living document that I update as some of you can attest to. Please let me know if I didn't put your name down here and you feel it should be here.

Onward.

I start with Jamie Stokes who did this fantastic Pinterest page of *This Much Is True.* She still adds to it from time to time and *I get inspired by her page of This Much Is True. Now that's an impact on a writer* who has written a little love story. Treasure her! *Thank you, Jamie. The link is: http://www.pinterest.com/jamieestokes/this-much-is-true-the-truth-about-air-water/.*

I go next to the *big three super fans.* These are the ladies who periodically check in with me to ensure I'm still *writing* and haven't gone off *the deep end* as it were.

They are: Chelcie Dacon Holguin, Anne Morillo, and Kim Standridge Boykin.

Dear Chelcie who has helped me so much with *The Truth About Air & Water* serving as a beta reader and soundboard when it came to the awesome *cov-uh.* And just so you know, when Chelcie told me she loved *The Truth About Air & Water* it was a gift. That's all I needed to hear. When the super fan is happy, so am I. *Thank you, Chelcie, for your awesomeness.*

Dear Anne, who champions *This Much Is True* for me all the time. If a fellow reader or blogger is asking who their favorite author is, Anne is adding my name to that list. Anne also served as a beta reader for *The Truth About Air & Water* and helped me tremendously with the little typos and forgotten words. Every time I edit the MS they come back in a like a little weed and Anne caught many of them. *So helpful. Amazing. Thank you, Anne.*

Dear Kim, periodically sends me a message asking me how I am coming along with the next book. Kim, who is traditionally published, is so encouraging and I feed off of her legitimacy and her generosity because she champions little ol' me. *Thank you, Kim!*

Kim wrote one of the first reviews of *This Much Is True*:

"NOBODY holds the human heart in their hands, deconstructs it, and puts it back together like Katherine Owen. Reading This Much is True was a privilege. THANK YOU!" -Kim Standridge Boykin

Wow. I'm still moved when I read that one.

Thank you, Chelcie, Anne, and Kim. Treasure you all so much!!!

So. There are the critics who push you to try harder or betray you in real life, and you learn from that too. There are friends and family and followers and each one gives you a little *something something* you can take away. I thank you all for that. The good and the bad and the in-between. It all helped. These are not in order. *Just sayin'.*

Onward to thank: Melissa, Scott, Darla, Steve, Michael, Lauren (help-with-the-cover girl), Blake, Mom, Dad, Dave, Stacey, Colleen, Karen, Christopher, Melanie, Nina, Jennifer, Gail, Heidi, Dina, Cheryl, Angie, Faith, Kristine, Carol, Karen, Jennifer, Michelle, Jaimie, Janell, Naomi, Orly, Laurel, Beth, Sarah, Sandra, Tiphanie, Brittany, Patty, Sandy, Kelly, Marianne, Victoria, Karen, Nora, Debbie, Sherri, Shellie, Nancy, Hikitia, Mo Mabie (author and blogger extraordinaire), StacyHgg Reads, Mare Slitsread Thomas, Happily Ever Ebooks, Laura, Way Too Hot Books, Purple, Daisy Calloway, Kimberly Faye Reads, Giselle at Xpresso Book Tours, SBookLover Reviews, Lit Junkie at Lit Jungle Book blog, Over-Reader Anonymous blog, Debbie D. At Bookish Reviews, Deb at Books and Gibberish blog. And last but certainly not least, Michele with one *l*, Jen, and DCB for teaching me in real life what matters and what doesn't. Oh so many things I've learned along the way and yes there are so many I've learned from, *still learning.*

Oh, and Gabriella. She can't read; she's a Himalayan cat, but seriously she's been here every flipping day while I wrote this one. And let's face it; cats are cool. They get you when no one else does.

I know I've missed someone. I'm sorry. There is a more comprehensive list of all that encouraged me with *This Much Is True* at my website: http://www.katherineowen.net should you be inclined to check it out. I hope this attempt at a list demonstrates how much I cherish you all and please understand that your support and critiques and love and enthusiasm for *This Much Is True* encouraged me to write and ultimately finish *The Truth About Air & Water*.

Writing is not an easy journey, but I so appreciate the readers that enjoy my work. YOU make it all worthwhile.

So.

Thank you for reading my work.

Katherine Owen

Writer | Dark angsty love stuff

A NOTE
FROM *KO*

LIFE IS UNBELIEVABLY SHORT AND YOUR book list is probably pretty long, so thank you for spending your time reading *The Truth About Air & Water*.

If you share your thoughts about the book by leaving a review, please know how much I appreciate your time and effort. *Thank you.*

I love hearing from readers! You can reach out to me at my website for more information about my novels, find the social media contacts for me as well as a sign-up link for new releases newsletter.

Lastly, if you're curious about the chapter titles those are tied to the play list of songs I put together on my blog from Spotify. Music plays an important role in working with the storyline. Just click over to: http://www.katherineowen.net for more information.

Thank you for reading my work!

—*Katherine Owen*

www.ingramcontent.com/pod-product-compliance
Lightning Source LLC
Chambersburg PA
CBHW050503110726
47899CB00005B/1305